THE HOUSE ON THE HILL

The House on the Hill

JUDITH KELMAN

BCA

LONDON · NEW YORK · SYDNEY · TORONTO

This edition published 1992
by BCA by arrangement with
OCTOPUS BOOKS LTD

Copyright © Judith Kelman

CN 1768

Printed and bound by
Clays Ltd, St Ives plc

For my evil twin

1

The beige pickup was approaching the Waldorf-Astoria.

Pressed in the shadows of a rock maple, Abigail Eakins watched as the truck bumped over a frost heave in the dirt access road, trundled across the covered bridge, and stopped at the gate in the Waldorf's split-rail fence.

The driver, a burly man in a baseball cap, stepped out. Abigail didn't recognize him, but he was clad in the local uniform: jeans, plaid flannel shirt, and a dun-coloured goose-down vest. His boots were caked with the annual spring bounty of prime Vermont mud.

After a beat, the man passed through the gate and walked towards the house. His stride was tentative, and he stopped completely a few feet from the hedgerow fronting the weathered colonial. There, his image was trapped and splintered by the broad bay-window in the Waldorf's living room.

The man's lips moved, but any sounds he made were swallowed by the wind. Seconds later, he pulled two crumpled wads of paper from his vest pocket, tossed them on the ground, and lumbered back to the truck. The engine caught, and the pickup spat a wake of pebbles as it set off down the road.

The Waldorf went bristling still, and a soupy darkness leaked from inside. Rumour had it that the ramshackle dump was haunted or worse, but Abigail refused to be intimidated. From what she'd seen, the abandoned house served mostly as a hangout for the older kids and a dump site for slovenly locals like the man in the truck. Anyway, she had weighed her meagre options, and the Waldorf seemed her best chance for escape.

Abigail waited to be sure the pickup was gone for good. It was crucial that she slip into the deserted house undetected.

Then, no one would be able to find her and try to make her go back to the inn.

She would never set foot in that place again. Not after what had happened. Her cheeks flamed at the memory, and she felt the sting of impending tears.

If only Mom hadn't married Charlie Brill and forced her to move to this stupid cow-town in the first place. If only they were still living in Manhattan where Abigail had her school and her friends and her gymnastics team and her normal life.

With a stab of fury, she thought of all the fairy tales Mom had told her about the glories of Vermont and how wonderful everything was going to be once they came to live at the Brills' family inn.

Abigail had believed the phony promises. After Mom and Charlie's wedding four months ago, she'd done her absolute best to fit in and feel part of things. For a while, she'd even thought the situation had possibilities

Most of the new family had been nice enough at first, especially Grandmother Brill, who liked to be called 'Mim', and Cousin Stephanie, who was popular and gorgeous and not the least bit stuck-up.

Abigail had enjoyed Mim's patient lessons in gardening, gourmet cooking, and flower-arranging. Everything had the potential to be transformed: radishes to roses, roses to radishes. All it took was the will, Mim said. You were never stuck with the way things were unless you chose to be.

Which Abigail definitely did not. She had decided to make the heady leap from radish to rose herself. Stephanie, who was fast approaching sixteen, had coached her on the fine points of eye makeup and hairdos. For hours, Steph had perched beside Abigail at the vanity mirror and showed her how to highlight her watery blue eyes with a slim line of brown pencil and a lick of mascara. With deft fingers, Stephanie had shaped the hopeless cider spill of Abigail's hair into a sleek French braid. Then Steph had demonstrated how the younger girl could position her hips and shoulders to make the most of her figure.

Abigail treasured such information though, at eleven,

her figure was largely theoretical. Her naked form in the mirror was a juice can with chopstick limbs. Her boobs were bug bites, which would have been discouraging if not for Stephanie's admission that she too had started at Abigail's age with mosquito bumps and a wish. Having Steph for an imaginary big sister had made Abigail almost glad about the move to Vermont.

But then it had started.

Little things at first. Sly threats. Teasing. Tiny seeds of planted fear that sprouted and spread until she was hopelessly trapped in the brambles.

Then came the sessions. He'd waited until she was powerless to do anything but co-operate. If she told, he'd threatened to claim the whole thing had been her idea. He said he'd be able to prove it by showing the secret pictures he'd taken where she was laughing, obviously enjoying herself. Abigail knew it had been the shame that made her giggle, the shame and the awful nervous fear. But who'd take her word over his majesty's? No one would believe her.

No one except Daddy.

Even with all his travelling, Daddy had to have gotten some of her letters by now. Abigail imagined he was already on the way. She could almost hear his booming laughter and the melody of his Dixie-dipped accent. 'That you, Abby Gail? You've grown a mile, girl, I swear it. Come on over here and give us a hug.'

Soon. Any minute, he would drive up in his shiny black Lincoln with his elbow propped on the open window and his straight chestnut hair blowing in the breeze.

From the Waldorf, she'd be able to keep an eye on the inn and watch for his arrival. Daddy would take her far away from the strangers and the sick jokes and the poison secrets that thickened the air until she could barely breathe.

Clutching her gym bag, Abigail peered up the road. The pickup was long gone. No cars were coming. No sounds pierced the persistent warble of the wind. From the edge of the road, she peered back over her shoulder at the inn. As expected, the parlour, living room, and library were deserted. At this hour, everyone on the staff was back in the kitchen or in one of the three dining rooms preparing for the first dinner patrons at six-thirty. Even in mud season when most of the guest rooms were empty, the Brills' four-star continental restaurant was booked solid every night. This was her best chance to slip away unnoticed.

The child drew a breath and dashed across the road. She ran with the fleet easiness of a trained gymnast, her moves sure and light-footed. On the opposite side, she ducked beneath a ragged line of wild shadbush and raced in a nimble crouch up the meandering dirt path towards the covered bridge. As she went, her red nylon windbreaker rustled like dried leaves.

The run was no challenge, but she was burdened by sadness and desperation. By the time she crossed the bridge, her heart was stuttering and her breath came in shallow stabs. Perspiration streaked her face, and her T-shirt was pasted to her back. Slowing to a walk, she crossed to the Waldorf's fence and stooped to slip between the splintery rails. But she was stopped by a sudden shock of pain.

With the glare of the descending sun, she had not noticed the mesh of green wire nailed to the fence posts. Now, she'd caught her head on it. Whimpering, she recoiled.

Less than a week ago, she'd tagged along while Mom took pictures of the Waldorf for a tourist brochure. She was positive there hadn't been any wire between the rails then.

So who'd put it there? And why?

No time to worry about that now. Tossing her gym bag over the top, she deftly vaulted the fence and dropped into the yard. It was only a short distance to the house. She'd slip in through the kitchen window, and they'd never be able to find her.

Almost there.

But now she stopped. Uneasily, she shaded her eyes with cupped fingers and stared at the empty building. Something was different. Something was wrong.

At once, she noticed several obvious changes. The snarled tufts of wild grass around the porch had been mowed level,

4

and the shadowy trail of ivy had been cleared from the stairs.

But it was more than that.

Instinct urged her to get away. Eyes fixed on the house, she groped for the fence behind her. There was something very wrong here. She'd find another place to wait for Daddy. She'd think of something.

Turning for an instant, she threw her gym bag out of the yard and stepped back to gain momentum for the vault. Her heart was squirming like a hooked fish. Once she was over the fence, she'd be safe.

But before she could move, a hot presence materialised behind her. In a breath, she was trapped by hands. Dozens of iron python hands assailed her from all directions at once. She was caught, paralysed. She tried to scream, but steel fingers had coiled around her neck and started squeezing.

Odd feeling. Her head expanded like a pumped balloon. Her mind went fuzzy, and the terror receded in the gentle rippling of a spent tide. This could not be happening. It was too weird. Impossible.

Maybe she was dreaming.

Yes, that had to be it. This was all a dark, ugly dream. Soon, she'd wake up in her bed at the inn, lace canopy arching overhead, limp and exhausted from a night full of imaginary escape attempts and invented menace. The wooden fence had gone liquid. The rails undulated on the wind like twin lengths of enchanted rope.

Abigail yielded to a dreamy numbness. The hands holding her were Daddy's hands, strong and comforting. Forcing her eyes open, she searched overhead for Daddy's sea-green eyes and ruddy face.

But all she could see was the sky shivering out of focus. Then the sun went black as death.

2 She could feel his blind eyes watching.

Driving her jeep through the gate in the split-rail fence, Quinn Gallagher spotted the figure at the living-room window. He stood still and unblinking, his breath fogging the glass.

Quinn looked away and shook off the same shudder of revulsion she felt when her little brother, Brendon, commandeered her to go to the reptile section at the Pet Center in downtown Rutland. Bren found snakes intriguing. Quinn had tried to catch the boy's enthusiasm, but she couldn't see past the slimy ugliness. Anyway, she decided, she had to deal with more than her fair share of reptiles on the job.

When she eyed the window again, the lurking figure had abandoned his sightless vigil. Through the mullioned glass, she watched as he crossed to the far wall, turned, and slowly retraced his steps towards the window. He was shadowed by his seeing-eye dog, a huge German Shepherd with a triangular grey bib and eyes the colour of fog.

For several minutes, Quinn sat in the jeep observing the latest addition to her caseload of ex-prisoners on parole. She was hoping to get some sense of the monster beyond the dry contents of his corrections file. Given that they were going to be keeping company for the next couple of years, Quinn wanted to know what made him tick and the precise location of his fuse.

His name was Eldon Weir. He was also known as Weird Ellie and Professor Pain. A dozen years ago, Weir had committed one of the most brutal mutilation murders in national memory.

Quinn remembered the flurry of sensationalist press coverage and public hysteria that had preceded Weir's capture. Afterwards, the professor had faded quickly from public consciousness, displaced by fresher threats and outrages. Most people had dismissed the terrifying spectre of Weir with a sense of relief and the false assumption that this monster had been put out of circulation for good.

First thing this morning, when her boss, Jake Holland, had handed her the assignment and Weir's records, Quinn had been horrified to learn that the case against Weird Ellie had collapsed on a technicality. The kidnapping, rape and murder charges against Weir had been thrown out during a preliminary hearing. The best the state had been able to nail him for was a separate pending charge of aggravated assault, which carried a maximum twelve-year sentence. Countless arms had been twisted and markers called to keep the embarrassing mess as quiet as possible. But nothing could be done about the reality.

Weir had a craggy face and the hulking body of a bear. Through the glass, Quinn glimpsed his grim expression: mouth a dry, ugly seam like a crack in the sidewalk, dead eyes narrowed to menacing slits.

Not pretty.

Quinn reminded herself she was not here to accompany Prince Charming to the ball. All she had to do was baby-sit the beast for the duration of his parole.

Stepping out of the jeep, Quinn eyed the property. Only minor, essential alterations had been made to the grounds and exterior of the long-vacant house. The fieldstone walk had been repaired and levelled, the weed-choked yard mowed flat. Several broken window panes had been replaced and a fat worm of weatherstripping sealed the gap around the front door. The broken-down fence had been reinforced with green-metal mesh to discourage stray animals and children.

Should anyone manage to slip through, she knew there were four closed-circuit cameras hidden in the surrounding shrubbery to flash the image back to central headquarters in Burlington, a hundred miles away. They would then alert local authorities.

Aside from those necessary modifications, the refurbishing had been restricted to the inside. Local officials had been instructed to respond to any questions with a statement that the absentee owner had decided to renovate the place and rent it. By keeping Weir's arrival as quiet as possible, the authorities were hoping he'd fade into the landscape as just another artsy eccentric. No one wanted the kind of panic and uproar that would likely ensue if the good citizens of Dove's Landing discovered the true identity of their newest neighbour.

There was a decent chance that the professor's presence could be kept under wraps. Rural Vermont was home to plenty of reclusive 'artists' like Eldon Weir. True, none of the others was a world-class sadist of Weird Ellie's renown. But many preserved their anonymity for reasons that would not make their mothers proud.

A nearly invisible row of slim stakes connected by string marked the twenty-foot tolerance limit of Weir's specially-designed monitoring device. Most offenders on electronic surveillance were allowed to roam one hundred and seventy-five feet from the computer link while in residence. And most were allowed out of monitoring range altogether to attend jobs in the community and run their own errands. But Weir was, by anyone's definition, a special case.

Quinn stopped three feet short of the staked boundary. At that distance, she was beyond the professor's physical reach. Weir could not step outside the monitored area without setting off an alarm at headquarters that would be relayed at once to patrol units in the area.

Warily, she watched the house. Parole officers were strictly prohibited from carrying weapons. With vigilance as her only defence, Quinn was highly motivated to pay attention.

From inside, she heard the dog barking furiously and pawing at the wood. Weird Ellie was not so eager to acknowledge her presence. He continued his restless pacing, pausing once on each circuit to train his vacant gaze out of the window.

'Mr Weir. It's Officer Gallagher from Parole,' Quinn called. 'Open the door. I need to talk to you.'

Several long moments later, Weir materialised in the doorway, shadowed by the dog. He wore a flowing black shirt, pleated black trousers, and a defiant smirk. His long, dark hair was gathered at the nape by a leather thong, and a ruby stud earring winked from his left lobe. Riveted around his right wrist was the black plastic bracelet by which he was electronically bound to the central Telsol computer in Burlington.

'I'll be your prime contact person from the department,' Quinn said. 'I'll be stopping by on scheduled and unannounced visits and to deliver your supplies. For now, I just wanted to get acquainted and be sure you understand the specific conditions of your parole.'

'Oh, I'd *love* to get acquainted,' Weir hissed. 'Come closer. Let me feel your face.'

His voice was a piercing, wicked rasp. Quinn tensed, but kept her tone level. 'No alcohol, drugs or weapons. No unauthorised visitors. You can and will receive calls from my office and random calls from the central computer, but your phone has been modified so you can't dial out.'

'You won't let me touch you? I suppose I'll have to read your voice, then.' His brow creased in concentration. 'Nice voice. Sexy. Says you're well built. Long legs. Three days of legs ending in a tight, little butt. Am I right, officer? Is it *high* and *tight*?'

He was dust. White noise. But even as she resolved not to hear him, she unconsciously squared her shoulders and raked her fingers through her froth of flaming red hair.

'The computer will also monitor your movements in the house through a constant, inaudible signal from your wristlet. You are limited to the interior rooms, the front porch, rear steps, and the yard up to the staked boundary, which your guide dog is trained to respect. If you violate the twenty-foot limit, you'll be subject to immediate rearrest and return to prison. Got that?'

'Oh, that voice. Simply *wonderful*. Do me a big favour, will you, officer? Say a dirty word for me.' He pressed his lower lip to his teeth and closed his eyes. 'Any one will do.'

Hot colour infused her cheeks. 'I decide how much and what kind of food you get, Mr Weir. How much and what kind of supplies. Keep up the crap, and it's all sardines. And I don't mean boneless.'

He sighed. 'I was just trying to be friendly.'

'. . . If you should need medical attention or experience any other emergency, you can violate your boundary and trip the alarm. If you're incapable of stepping over the line, you can summon help by pulling the plug on your phone link or knocking the receiver off the hook or breaking the band on your wristlet. Any of those moves will get you plenty of attention pronto. Understood?'

'Might I ask a question?'

'What?'

Is your skin velvety?' He stepped out of the doorway and walked towards her with outstretched arms. 'Is it smooooth?'

Her freckles were smouldering, and her temper was shooting sparks. He came within an inch of the staked boundary and sniffed. 'You needn't be afraid,' he crooned. 'I've been completely rehabilitated. I understand now what moved me to do those terrible things and how to avoid such temptations in the future. I'm harmless, really, officer. Gentle as a lamb.'

Rabid lamb, Quinn thought. 'You're going to set off the alarm, Mr Weir. Don't move.'

'Come inside then, why don't you? I'll make you a cup of tea. Show you around. I'm told it's a lovely place.'

Which it was. Through the bay-window Quinn had a clear view of the contemporary white leather furnishings and large modern lithographs in the living room. Beyond, the dining room was done in soft peach tones. There was a marble table on a sculpted chrome base and a ring of tiger maple chairs.

In this case, crime might not have paid, but it certainly picked up expenses.

Everything, including the seeing-eye dog, had been arranged and funded by the president of the Langdon Industries in Georgia Center. While on a supervised work-release detail from the state's correctional facility in St

Albans, a chemical accident at one of Langdon's plants had cost Eldon Weir his sight.

The disability had precipitated his parole. None of the state's six prisons was equipped to meet the needs of a blind inmate. Given that Weir's sentence was due to run out in under two years, it had not been deemed cost effective to adapt a unit for him. Quinn doubted that anyone in the prison system had been all that sorry to see him go.

The phone rang, but the professor made no move to answer.

'That must be a check-in from central, Mr Weir. You'd better get it.'

'But you told me not to move.'

'Get the phone'.

Trailed by the dog, Weir sauntered to the instrument in the hall and lifted the receiver. Quinn knew the drill, and Weir followed it without hesitation. He answered the prerecorded questions required for voice verification. Then he reported the time and date as they appeared on a small braille clock beside the phone, and he responded to the request for an item of personal information that changed with every call. In this instance, it was his mother's maiden name: Koswick.

On signal, he plugged the raised portion of his wristlet into the matching depression in the rectangular black box attached to the phone. There was a beep, confirming that the voice respondent was equipped with the proper bracelet.

Weir's moves were surprisingly adept given his blindness and the fact that he'd been on home release for less than twenty-four hours. The man was a quick student. Then, no one had ever questioned his intelligence. The open issue was his species.

At the tender age of twelve, he had mutilated and murdered a classmate named Jennifer Buckram in his home town of Douglaston, New York.

A neighbour's child, who'd seen him forcing the Buckram girl into a wooded area behind the school, had eventually led investigators to Weir. He was convicted and sentenced to the ten-year maximum allowable term at the Harlem

Valley Youth Correctional facility in upstate New York. As the law dictated, his juvenile record was sealed on his release.

Over the next three years, Weir drifted from Connecticut to upstate New York and finally to Bennington, Vermont. In each town, he took a variety of night-school classes and worked part time as a short-order chef.

A few months after Weir settled in Bennington, a local child was reported missing. Her corpse was discovered a week later in a skip behind the supermarket. The condition of the body had stunned authorities. They'd withheld graphic details in deference to the victim's family and public sensibilities, but enough had leaked to brand Weir as a beast without equal.

During the investigation, a member of the Bennington police force had spotted Weir working at a local diner. The officer had grown up near Weir's childhood home in Queens. He remembered the Buckram murder and did some simple addition. The Bennington child resembled the Buckram girl, and there were several other compelling similarities between the two cases. A rapid arrest and indictment followed.

The case had generated tremendous press and a public outcry for Weir's scalp. But during a preliminary hearing, Weir's defence counsel, Lane Heckerling, had petitioned that all charges be dropped. Heckerling claimed that the arrest had been made with prejudice. He asserted that there had been no reasonable grounds for the arresting officer to suspect Weir of the crime.

Richmond Brown, the presiding judge, concurred. The search and Weir's statements following his arrest were ruled inadmissable. According to Judge Brown, anyone could have mutilated the Bennington child in a pattern deliberately resembling Jennifer Buckram's injuries. In fact, the initial press reports detailing the grisly nature of the Buckram murder had inspired several copycat crimes that remained unsolved.

Quinn had read the whole sad story in the court records appended to Weir's file. 'Defendant did not carve his initials or write his name on the victim,' the judge had said. 'Lacking that kind of definitive evidence, I believe the arrest was made precipitously, without probable cause, and in violation of defendant's constitutional right to the pre-sumption of innocence.'

Lacking sufficient evidence to make a case, the district attorney was forced to drop the murder charges.

Weir would have walked altogether, but a computer check at the time of his arrest uncovered a separate pending warrant for aggravated assault. Shortly after moving to Vermont, the professor had tried to settle a neighbourly dispute over a parking space with the aid of a fireplace poker.

The prosecution had nailed Weir for the maximum term allowable for a C felony: twelve years.

In situations like this, it struck Quinn that justice was more dumb than blind.

Weir hung up and returned to the door. 'Do you enjoy watching me, officer? Listening in on my conversations? Does it make you all moist and tingly?'

'We can do this the hard or easy way, Weir. Up to you.'

He looked stricken, then contrite. 'Forgive me. You're right. I'm thoroughly ashamed of myself.'

'I bet.'

'No, it's true. I'm really a decent fellow. Completely reformed. According to one of my therapists, the insolence stems from a defensive desire to resist intimacy. It's a reflex. Quite harmless, I assure you.'

'Frankly, Mr Weir, I'm not interested in what you are, for real or otherwise. You follow the rules, and everything will be just dandy.'

Weir tapped a finger on his craggy cheek. His empty gaze was an x-ray, his mouth drawn in a bow of contempt. 'But you must admit your curiosity, Ms Gallagher. You would like to know how I think, what has led me in the past to commit certain . . . acts.'

'The rules, Mr Weir. That's all I care about.'

A dry chuckle issued from his thin-lipped mouth. 'You needn't bother to pretend, officer. I can read your thoughts.'

'Then you know the only thing on my mind is making sure you understand your restrictions and follow them.'

Weir frowned in mock dismay. 'So you're sceptical. But it's true, documented. I am possessed of second sight. Telepathy and prescience combined. I see what is and what is to be. Allow me to demonstrate.' Weir went silent, his hollow stare trained on the sinking sun. When he finally spoke, his voice was a soft, seductive chant.

'. . . I see grief, Ms Gallagher. You've suffered a terrible loss. Something quite sudden. Tragic. An accident?' He hesitated, tensed.

'Yes, I can see it now. Oh God, it's terrible. Blood everywhere, broken glass, flames. And oh, the victims! The woman is trapped, burned beyond recognition. She's dead, but the man is still hanging on, begging. "Help me," he moans. "Save her, please! Someone, anyone!"

'Wait. He's coughing now. There's a sick rattle in his chest. He tries to speak, but the cough consumes him. Wretched, bloody cough. Death rattle. He's clutching his throat. Can't breathe. Help! Oh, no! He's . . .' Weir shuddered and went limp in a grotesque parody.

Quinn suppressed a chill. Her mother and father had been killed three years earlier in a car accident. Fiery head-on collision. Both had been pronounced dead at the scene. She fought for control, struggling to push away the horrific images Weir had conjured up.

Weir straightened. 'I see a child as well. Hurt, but not in the accident. Emotional wounds, perhaps? Yes, there are definite psychic scars.'

He lifted his chin and squinted. 'There. It's clearer now. The boy is redheaded. Slim, freckled. But not your son. Your brother, is it? Wait. That's odd. A dark aura envelops the child. Do you have some kind of difficulty with him, officer? Has he stood in the way of your happiness?'

'That's enough,' Quinn snapped. 'I have no time for this nonsense.'

'Certainly. I can appreciate your sensitivity on the subject. After all, to have both parents killed like that. And then to discover that your father . . .'

'Are you telling me that you miss prison, Mr Weir? Do I hear you correctly?'

His expression brimmed with phony remorse. 'You're absolutely right, Ms Gallagher. It is most unkind of me to bring up such distressing memories. The important thing is that you've managed to get on with your life despite the burden. Hasn't been easy, has it? Attractive young single girl like you having to take on the care of your little brother. To think of all you've given up: a job you loved, a lover. And the boy does have his problems, doesn't he? Clumsiness, dyslexia. Enuresis.'

He ticked his tongue. 'His bedwetting is such a dreadful nuisance, isn't it, officer? You know you can cure him with a simple regimen of electric shock. I'd be glad to tell you exactly how much juice you'll need to convince the lad to stop pissing his bed. Won't be pleasant for him, but you might find it amusing. You simply attach two leads to a standard nine-volt battery and connect the opposite ends to his little penis. Then you . . .'

Quinn's teeth ached from clenching them. 'I said enough!'

Weir threw up his hands.

'But I thought you wanted to get acquainted.'

Hold your temper, Quinn. Weir isn't the first impulsive, moral moron you've had to handle. Let him get to you, he wins.

'That's not necessary. I know you more than well enough already, Weir. I've seen dozens like you. Hundreds.'

'There is no one like me. I am unique in the universe. Singular.'

'Amazing. That's exactly what they all say,' Quinn sneered. She turned on her heel and walked away.

Back at the jeep, she paused to survey the bucolic stretches of farmland, the pristine country inn down the hill, the row of sleepy shops on Main Street, the isolated homes dotting the distant landscape. No shortage of potential victims if Weir found a way to slip his bonds.

Unthinkable.

Jake Holland had described the professor's monitoring system as foolproof. Given the stakes, Quinn hoped no one

15

was overestimating the technology or underestimating Weird Ellie Weir.

If anything went wrong, Quinn knew the blame would somehow be laid at her doorstep. Electronic circuitry did not make a satisfying scapegoat. Neither did flawed security design. Reasonable or not, it would be her name, her neck, her life kicked back in that gruesome hole. She'd struggled too hard, too long to ever let that happen again.

She got in and revved the engine. From the corner of her eye, she saw the heavy drapes in the living room drawing together. Weir stood framed in the centre of the window, staring out, until the panels formed a seamless whole and he disappeared.

3 The inn at Dove's Landing had been owned and operated by the Brill family for six generations. The first owners, Irish immigrants, had offered the place as a haven for runaway slaves bound for Canada via the underground railroad.

Once a sprawling dairy farm, the property had undergone a gradual metamorphosis over the decades to a gracious resort hotel and gourmet restaurant. The central guest rooms, all formerly outbuildings on the farm, were named to reflect past incarnations: Sugar Mill, Cider House, Potting Shed One and Two, the Smithy and so on.

The separate structures had been strung together by catwalks and interior corridors. They now bordered three sides of a stone courtyard flanked by formal gardens and centred on the pool. The fourth arm of the square was the original farmhouse, which currently housed the inn's offices, restaurant, common rooms, kitchen, and wine cellar.

Beyond the core quadrangle was a scatter of private guest cottages, the family homes, the tennis court and lake, the greenhouse, and several small buildings given over to storage and other seasonal functions.

Nora seated the town's mayor at his regular banquette in the corner of the restaurant's glass-walled garden room and glanced past the row of guest rooms at her daughter's first-floor window. The lights were on, but there was no sign of Abigail sprawled as she usually was on the canopy bed or performing her forbidden handstands in front of the antique mirror.

The signal light flashed on the phone at the antique maple reservation desk. Nora answered and booked a party of twelve for an anniversary dinner on the second Saturday in June. She made the necessary notes about the requested table in the sun room and the hazelnut torte to be inscribed,

'Happy Tenth, Sally and Ken'. Hanging up, her thoughts veered uneasily back to Abigail.

It was almost nine-thirty. Ordinarily, the child would have drifted in two or three times by now to complain to Nora about homework or Cousin Hugh's incessant teasing or some imaginary threat.

Nora had never imagined that moving to Vermont would be so difficult for her daughter. Always resilient, Abby had dealt philosophically with the divorce though she still adored her father well beyond the bounds of reason and would probably never comprehend Nora's reasons for cutting him loose.

The child had also adapted well to their shaky financial situation after the split. As a freelance photojournalist, Nora had earned respect and honours. But assignments and commission cheques were sporadic, the deadly down-side of self-employment. Raymond had proven predictably unpredictable about child support, as he was in all things. By establishing a sideline in commercial work, Nora had managed to cover the essentials and keep Abby in her private school, but she'd had to staunch the flow of easy privileges most of her daughter's classmates enjoyed.

The little girl had accepted the tighter limits with equanimity. So Nora had foolishly expected that Abby would adjust as well to her remarriage and the move. Charlie Brill was warm and open and engaging. He'd loved Abigail from the beginning and courted her with nearly the same generosity and enthusiasm he'd shown Nora. And his family had gone out of their way to draw the child in and make her feel welcome.

After all the don'ts and dangers of New York City, Nora had thought that Vermont would prove a welcome change. In Dove's Landing, Abigail would never have to sidestep zonked junkies or sleeping street-people on her way to school. She wouldn't be accosted by strident panhandlers or hallucinating psychotics. No stray sniper bullets or maniac-of-the-week or combat zones to avoid. In this sleepy little town the worst threat of violence was the mythical sport of cow tipping.

18

But nothing was working out as Nora had hoped. Since the move, Abigail had grown steadily more sullen and withdrawn. She cried at the slightest affront and had developed a maddening tic in her right eye. Her school work had deteriorated, and aside from Charlie's niece, Stephanie, she'd shown little interest in making new friends.

No one had any answers - not Charlie, not the local pediatrician or the child psychologist Nora had consulted, not even Charlie's mother, Mim, who was unfailingly pragmatic and wise. Nora's own mother, consulted frequently by phone in Fort Lauderdale, insisted the antidote was time. But how much time? And how much misery would they all have to endure during the wait?

Sometimes, Nora wished she could simply run away and leave all the problems and questions and nagging recriminations behind. She'd pack nothing but the essentials: fantasies, dreams, a life neatly abridged and edited of all its mistakes. Might be a juvenile solution, but it was tempting nonetheless.

Arms slipped around her waist and Nora gasped, nearly knocking over the phone. She turned and warmed at the sight of Charlie. She loved his dimpled chin and soulful brown eyes. Even his imperfections struck her as endearing: the crooked pitch of his mouth when he was trying to look serious, the way his chestnut hair was thinning at the temples, the incipient love handles he was forever trying to combat with a dubious regimen of sit-ups, good intentions, and chocolate mousse cake.

Raymond was a strapping peacock of a man. A legend in his own mind. Full of himself and other things. She could imagine herself growing old with Charlie. With Ray, she might have grown old, but it would have been way sooner than necessary.

'Have I told you tonight how beautiful you are?' Charlie murmured, nuzzling her ear.

'Can't remember. Better say it again.'

'Most beautiful woman in the world. You make me crazy,

you know that? I keep wanting to ravage you on the dessert cart. What do you think?'

'I think it could get pretty messy. Anyhow, you know the rule against fraternising with the help, Mr Brill.'

He frowned. 'I'm sorry you had to fill in again. What's my dear sister's problem this time?'

'Headache, I think.'

'Pain in the butt is more like it.'

'It's okay. I don't mind.'

Nora didn't let the smile fade until he was out of sight. Ordinarily, she was glad to help out, though her sister-in-law, Victoria, was a shameless manipulator who had elevated laziness to an art form. Charlie's sister had separated from her husband and disassociated herself from her kids, which freed her to focus on the one true love of her life: herself.

The woman's days were a dizzy whirl of manicures, massages, ladies' lunches and shopping sprees. Understandably, she was left with little energy for such petty irritations as work and sought refuge in a variety of trendy ailments: carpal tunnel syndrome, cluster headaches, Epstein-Barr virus, Chronic Fatigue Syndrome. Everyone recognised the real problem as an allergy to gainful employment, but so far it had proven incurable.

Still, Nora didn't mind making what she saw as a reasonable contribution at the inn. To sustain the business through seasonal slow periods, most of the Brills did outside work. Charlie was an architect, Mim an interior designer. Even Victoria's kids, Hugh and Stephanie, did odd jobs to earn spending money. Unlike her sister-in-law, Nora had never been afraid of work. In addition, she'd caught the Brill family's love of the inn.

Looking around now, she took in the tables draped in floor-length ivory cloths, the fan-folded napkins and antique-silver appointments. Each table was graced by a long-stemmed crimson rose in a crystal vase. They set off the subtle floral motif on the wall covering and the tiny floral trellis inset at the border of the carpeting. Tasteful, lovely surroundings. And the job was never dull.

Without intending to eavesdrop, she'd catch loaded gestures and intriguing snatches of conversation as she made her obligatory table rounds to see that everyone was satisfied and getting properly stuffed.

Tonight, the pair at table three was playing a hazardous game of advanced footsie. At booth seven in the main room, a couple was locked in heated debate about a proposed visit from his father, who was either a latter-day Solomon or a senile slob, depending on where you sat. A foursome in the garden room were into their third round of double martinis and some heavy cross-court flirting. Nora made a mental note to have the bartender cut them off and call a cab to make sure they got home safely. Probably two cabs would be safer still, though she wouldn't have made a book on who'd wind up riding where or with whom.

Usually, the hours flew, and she was finished before she'd even had a chance to consider getting restless, weary, or bored. But tonight, she was anxious to break away and have a talk with her daughter.

Earlier, Abigail had seemed more troubled than ever. After school, she'd raced through the inn and gone directly to her room. Nora had caught a quick glimpse of her and hadn't enjoyed the view. The little girl looked taut and brittle, ready to snap.

When Nora went to their cabin to see what was wrong, the door to Abby's room was locked and so was the child. In a voice trembling with forced control, Abigail had told her to go away, that she wanted to be left alone.

After several minutes of useless wheedling, Nora had decided to heed her mother's advice and give it time. She'd gone to her makeshift darkroom in the old maple sugaring shed behind the barn and worked on the proofs for the new Vermont Tourist Bureau brochure. With all her 'filling in' as hostess for Victoria, Nora's own work was forever running behind schedule.

When she had finished developing the five-roll set, it was past six. By then, she knew that Maisie, Mim's house-keeper, would be feeding the children their dinner with

Charlie's father in the older Brills' gracious Georgian home beyond the lake.

'Poppa', as everyone called Charlie's dad, suffered from Alzheimer's Disease. The old man had memory lapses and spells of agitation, but at times he could be his old self as well: charming and disarming. For most of each day, Mim insisted that his world be kept ordered and controlled. But she was convinced that the children, in measured doses, had a therapeutic effect.

The kids seemed to benefit as well. Apparently Poppa could still pluck an endless supply of engrossing stories from his colourful past.

Nora had decided to go to the house and wait for Abigail to finish eating. Afterwards they could talk. But before she made it halfway down the stone path, Mim had corralled her to cover once again for the 'ailing' Victoria.

Now Nora eyed the grandfather clock near the reception desk. A quarter to ten, and still no sign of Abigail. Hopefully, she could break away before the child fell asleep.

In a week, the little girl would be out of school for spring vacation. Nora and Charlie had decided to take her back to New York for a visit. They'd planned to keep it a surprise, but that afternoon Nora had decided to tell her about it. Perhaps news of the trip would lift Abigail's spirits. Nora couldn't bear to see her little girl so miserable.

Mim drifted in to greet the regulars. Elegant as always, she wore a graceful French-blue chiffon dress with matching low silk pumps. Her silver hair was moulded in a chignon and she carried herself with a proud, confident air. Despite the daunting demands of her husband's illness, Mim never appeared defeated and she never complained. Her only concession had been to spend more time looking after Poppa and less at the inn. Her soft grey eyes settled on Nora.

'What's wrong, dear?'
'Nothing. Just thinking.'
Mim's gaze was an x-ray. 'Abigail?'
'What else?'

'Go up and see to her. Poppa's sleeping. I'll be glad to take over here for a while.'

'You sure?'

'Positive. Go on. Give her a hug for me.'

Nora went out through the candlelit lounge where several parties were sipping after-dinner drinks at the broad copper bar manned by Jory Albert, an aspiring young ski bum from New Zealand. In the antique-strewn parlour, several guests were sipping demi-tasses on the ring of chintz-covered sofas in front of a blazing fire. Their flushed faces were reflected in the polished copper hearth and the collection of copper vessels suspended from the stone face of the fireplace. A lilting piece by Vivaldi drifted over the sound system.

She was stalled at the courtyard door by Reuben Huff, the inn's caretaker. Huff was rail-thin, sallow to the precipitous brink of jaundice, and stoop-shouldered. He had a nasty habit of crowding too close when he talked. Nora found herself retreating from the stale-tobacco stench on his breath and the sour heat of his body.

'You want me to see to those stairs in Tack Room Two?' he said. 'Real shaky.'

'You'll have to check with Charlie or Mrs Brill, Reuben.'

'Yeah, well those stairs are a real menace. Someone's gonna fall and break his neck one of these days. So I could fix them myself, or I could call that guy from Wilmington I've been using to help me with the equipment shed. Important thing is no one gets hurt.'

'I understand. Charlie's in the office. Why don't you go ask him and see what he wants you to do?'

Nora was anxious to get past him, but Huff had planted himself squarely in the centre of the doorway. 'Excuse me, Reuben.'

'Going to see Abigail?'

'I said, excuse me.'

He shifted half an inch to the left. Disgusted, she edged past him, holding her breath. Out in the courtyard, she paused in the bracing, pine-scented air. Her short, sandy hair was tousled by the pungent breeze. Better. She was halfway across the yard when she realised that the door hadn't yet closed behind her.

Turning, she caught Huff staring in her direction 'What is it, Reuben?'

Huff was always skulking around. Over the years, Mim and Poppa had staffed the inn with a number of curious strays like him. Most of them had turned out to be dedicated and loyal. And to be fair, Huff couldn't be faulted for his reliability or job performance. But for some nameless reason, Nora didn't like or trust the man.

He shrugged, his eyes on her insolently. 'Don't think you'll find Abigail at the house, that's all.'

'Why not?'

'Just don't.' The door eased shut behind him and he loped down the rear corridor.

Nora dismissed the irritating creep from her mind. Right now, she didn't want to think about anything but Abigail. She passed through an archway in the string of guest rooms and trudged over the spongy lawn to their cabin.

Abigail's room was upstairs. Nora knocked and listened to the silence as she waited for the child's response. Nothing.

She rapped again and jiggled the knob. The door was locked. No answer when she called. Of course, if Abby were asleep, nothing short of a bomb would wake her. Funny for her to lock the door, but not worth an issue. Nora would have left it alone and waited to see Abby in the morning, but, troubled by Reuben Huff's strange remark, she went next door to Victoria's place to talk to Stephanie.

Victoria answered her knock. The woman had made one of her miraculous recoveries. Looked stunning. Liz Taylor without the weight problem though, in fairness, Victoria had some mighty weighty problems of her own. Nora started to explain that she was concerned about Abby and wanted to see if Steph might know what was bothering the child. With studied disinterest, Victoria waved her upstairs. Or maybe she was drying her nails.

Passing Hugh's room, Nora heard the angry bass of the stereo. Next door, Stephanie was on the phone. As Nora knocked, she heard the light trill of the girl's voice punctuated by giggles.

'Come in.'

Charlie's niece had inherited her mother's good looks and striking colouring: near-black hair, pale complexion, opalescent eyes, fine features. But Steph was even-tempered and displayed none of Victoria's stifling self-love. Nora had never met the girl's father, but he was reputed to be a world-class jackass. So Stephanie had to be the result of some fortunate genetic misfire, like mating two onions and somehow winding up with a bottle of perfume.

With a hand over the receiver, the teenager reported that she hadn't seen Abigail all day. Abby had not shown up for dinner, but no one had thought anything of it. They'd all assumed she'd decided to eat in the inn's kitchen as she sometimes did.

Nora tried questioning Hugh. She got nothing for her trouble but a grunt and a sneer. Both were standard for the sullen seventeen-year-old whose looks were a cruel parody of his sister's: the features harder and less symmetrical, the colouring pushed past striking to unpleasantly extreme.

Hugh was a difficult kid. Angry and defiant. His communications were limited to the adolescent anarchist standards: blasting music, walls scarred with hate posters, a screw-you wardrobe comprised mostly of torn things and studded black leather. Mim and Poppa were the only people he treated with anything resembling respect, and even with them the resemblance was shaky.

Determined to see for herself that Abby was all right, Nora headed back to the office to get the master key. She entered the inn through the front door to avoid Reuben Huff in case he was still on the prowl. When she passed the dining room, Mim cast a meaningful look at her. Nora managed a plastic smile.

The office was empty. Through the adjacent kitchen wall, Nora heard Charlie talking to the chef. Sounded like one of their typical conversations – Charlie's gentle reason pitted against Chef Villet's uncanny imitation of a tropical storm.

Villet was a temperamental genius. Or so he ardently believed.

Nora took the master key from the board beside the phone and quickly retraced her steps to the house. She kept telling herself it was foolish to be so anxious, but her gut was like a fist and her head throbbed.

Fumbling with Abigail's lock, she clung to a picture of the little girl inside, asleep and oblivious. Nora anticipated the same wonderful sense of furious relief she'd had the time Abigail had failed to come home after school. An hour and twenty anxious calls later, she'd discovered that the child had gone to play at a friend's house and simply forgotten to phone.

It took a couple of tries before Nora was able to slide the key into the slot correctly and work the cranky brass mechanism. The door opened with a mewling sound.

The room was empty.

Nora tried to deflect her mounting panic. Maybe Abby was only hiding, playing a game. She took a desperate look around. The canopy bed was smooth, the blue down comforter in place, the pillows still tucked in their ruffled shams. At the windows, the dotted swiss curtains were in the scrupulous alignment that meant they hadn't been touched since Greta from the inn's housekeeping staff stopped by to do her daily straightening. On the sill were several porcelain pots with clusters of fresh flowers from Mim's greenhouse: zinnias and dahlias in lavender and rose shades that complemented the room's apricot-and-white colour scheme. In the centre of the dresser was Abby's prized music box, a gift from her father for her last birthday. It was a pink confection complete with wind-up ballerina in a tiny tulle skirt. Nora flipped the top and heard the tinkling strains of 'Stardust'. *The me-lo-dy, haunts my memory . . .*'

She turned her gaze to the maple desk. It was littered with text books. The gym bag Abigail used to transport them in was gone. *Stay calm*. There had to be a simple, reasonable explanation.

She checked Abigail's bathroom and the rest of the first

floor. Downstairs, she hurried through the rooms and then went back to make a methodical inspection of closets, cabinets, pockets behind drapes, anywhere the child might think to hide.

Finding nothing, she went back to Abby's room. Searching the dresser drawers, Nora discovered that several of the child's other prize possessions were missing: her new red windbreaker, her striped team leotard from gymnastics. Gone too were her precious address book and the personalised stationery Raymond had sent her for Christmas.

Nora raced to the window. Maybe she could spot the child somewhere near the inn. But there was no sign of her. Nothing broke the desolate expanse of deep flannel sky rimmed by clouds and craggy black mountains.

She shivered with a sudden chill. This wasn't like Abigail. She had to find her little girl before things spun further out of control.

But where should she begin? Her mind raced through dozens of possibilities: friends, relatives, all the places an eleven-year-old child might think to look for her father. Nora couldn't bear the thought of her little girl wandering cold and alone in the vast Vermont night.

Then it struck her. Abby might have been gone for hours already. Maybe she'd already found her way to safety. *Calm Down. Abby's probably safe and snug somewhere. You're just over-reacting*.

Nora's phone book and the class list from Abigail's school were in the desk in the makeshift studio behind the barn. She was hurrying out to make the calls when she spotted the note.

4

Abigail struggled to come awake, but something was holding her under like teasing hands in the pool. Her mind was foggy, limbs slack as wet towels. A pulsating strap of pain bound her throat.

From overhead came a persistent thumping sound, deep and dull like an ache in a bone. A phone rang, and there was the subway rumble of a voice. Then the thumping began again. Steady dead-ball thumping moved nearer by degrees and then backed slowly away towards the dim edge of her hearing.

That was all.

She couldn't smell anything but the cloying scent of her own fear. Couldn't feel anything but the seeping cold. The darkness was a thick, unbreachable wall.

Aching to make sense of her predicament, Abigail decided it had to be the blackest possible night. Black images on an ebony ground, all cancelled to silly non-existence like polar bears in the snow. It had to be something as simple and innocent as that. Mom was forever saying she shouldn't surrender to her runaway imagination. Abigail imagined herself lying on a blackboard floor, swaddled by air the colour of squid's ink. The notion edged back the terror, though only a tiny way.

When she tried to extend her palms, she was stalled by a cold, slimy surface less than a foot above her face.

With the tip of a trembling finger, she traced the obstruction as it curved down and behind her and rose again to meet itself at the starting point. Squirming, she discovered the same chill dampness beneath her back and buttocks. Stretching down with a pointed toe, she was only able to move a few inches before she struck a solid mass below. The rubber toe of her sneaker bumped with a hollow

28

ring and bounced away. Same thing overhead. Inches above her was a frigid, clammy wall.

She was enclosed.

Trapped.

Buried alive like the shrouded vampire in the horror movie she'd snuck in to watch with Cousin Stephanie late last Friday night. Abigail pictured herself fleshless, her face wasted to gaping eye sockets and a grotesque lipless grin. Terrified, she gasped for breath and pushed frantically against the metal sides.

She felt the stab of a rising scream. But she swallowed hard and bit her lip to keep any sound from escaping. She would not give him the satisfaction.

It had to be him.

He'd grabbed her and stuffed her in this tube thing to scare her to death. One of his stupid, sick jokes. No one else was perverted enough to think of anything so crazy.

She remembered the first warped trick he'd pulled.

That time, he'd locked her in her room, made fat stomping noises so she'd think he'd gone downstairs, and then set a smoky fire in a trash can in the hall. Abigail had been sure she was going to burn to death. She'd imagined her skin ablaze like paper, hair sizzling to a stinking hill of ash.

He'd even nailed her window shut from the outside, so she could not lean out and attract attention. She'd pounded on the door until her knuckles were raw and screamed herself hoarse. But nobody came.

The creep had known no one would be close enough to hear her in the locked room. A sunny midday in late winter, and the guests were all out skiing or snowmobiling or shopping at the discount stores in nearby Manchester. He'd planned it for a time when he knew everyone in the family would be busy elsewhere.

An hour later, when he finally unlocked the door, he'd laughed his dumb head off at the sight of her. Abigail's eyes had been puffed to twice their normal size, and she couldn't stem the sobs that kept pulsing up from her gut.

That was funny to him.

Sicko creep.

As soon as her mother got back from her photo shoot that day, Abigail had started downstairs intending to tell everything. But the big idiot had followed her, taunting. She wouldn't dare say anything, he'd jeered. If she did, he'd show the pictures and explain how she'd begged him to have the sessions. Everyone would think she was sick and disgusting. She'd go mute and die before she'd have the nerve to risk that.

Abigail had tried to ignore him. But he was right there behind her, shadowing her steps. Breathing in her ears. Mocking her in mean silence. When she tried to speak to Mom, witch fingers started plucking at the corner of Abigail's eye, driving her nuts. And the words caught in her throat like a bone.

So he'd kept it up. More sessions, more warped jokes.

Once, he put a dead rat in her bed. Abigail still shuddered at the memory of that stiff, bloody thing. Lying down unawares, she'd felt the stab of its rigid claws and whiskered muzzle through her thin flannel nightshirt. The shock had iced her bones and made her heart flap against her ribs like the frantic wings of a trapped bird.

Another time, he'd had one of the session pictures enlarged and mocked up to resemble the front page of the *Dove's Landing Daily*. It seemed so real, Abigail had hidden in the potting shed for half a day, paralysed by humiliation.

All that was funny to him. Hilarious.

But now, she knew better. This time, she'd wait it out and not give him a damned thing to laugh about. Sooner or later, he'd get bored and release her from this cold, slimy place.

If only Mom and the rest of them knew what a vicious nut case he was. Abigail wanted him punished. Put away in a cage full of dead rats and stinking smoke bombs and phony newspapers so embarrassing he'd want to shrivel up and die.

But he was the prince. Centre of the universe. Untouchable. Everyone was afraid of him. Tiptoed around him like he was some kind of a God.

Tears stung her throat, but she breathed through her

nose until the pain blunted. He didn't matter anymore. Not to her anyway. There would be no more sessions, no more filthy jokes.

Soon, she'd be out of his reach, safe with Daddy. Then the ugly creep would never be able to find her or hurt her again. All she had to do was keep quiet until he got bored and let her out.

The thumping was moving nearer again. Closer still. Overhead, a door opened and the sound shifted.

Abigail could feel the difference. He was coming downstairs.

5 When her beeper sounded, Quinn was practising baseball with her brother on the field behind the Post Road Elementary School.

Glove aloft, the boy charged after a high pop. Squinting against the sunset glare, Brendon hesitated, feinted to the left, and then lurched forward in a jerky dance. His face was taut with concentration, tongue boring in his cheek.

Quinn's breath caught. She worked his moves with her mind. *Go, Bren. You can snag it, kiddo!*

But, as usual, he'd miscalculated. The ball whizzed past his upturned glove and hit the sodden ground with a disheartening thud.

Without a mumble or a missed beat, the boy knelt, scooped up the ball, and hurled it back to Quinn. Mouth set, he punched the pocket of his mitt and dipped his chin. Ready to try again.

Quinn nodded in response. Kid was a trooper. Never gave up or acted whipped. No small feat given how much he'd been through and how hard most things came to him.

At nine, Brendon was constructed like a cheap toy, all loose joints and limp gangly parts that refused to operate in smooth concert. Still, sports were his passion, and he was not the type to settle for a spectator seat. For the past two spring seasons, he'd spent weeks practising before tryouts. Each time he had failed to win a place on the local summer league softball team. Undaunted, this year he was fiercely determined to cash in his scorekeeper's pencil for a fielder's mitt.

Quinn suspected he was setting himself up for yet another disappointment. And the kid had not suffered from a shortage of those. But she refrained from registering her unsolicited opinion. Her brother was a feisty kid. Strong. Which was fortunate, given the circumstances.

32

After their parents' death three years earlier, Quinn had been appointed Bren's guardian. Wanting to minimise the disruption in his life, she'd moved from Boston to Vermont to take over the family house and what precious little remained of the family. Her intentions had been excellent, but she had to admit her qualifications were marginal at best.

Quinn loved her little brother, but she lacked any particular talent or affinity for kids. Years earlier, she'd taken it for granted that she was not destined or designed for maternity. But fate, with its highly questionable sense of humour, had dealt her a six-year-old boy.

At first, the situation had seemed hopelessly bleak. Quinn was forever stepping on the child's sensitivities. Saying and doing exactly the opposite of what Bren needed, and he'd needed plenty.

Problem was, Quinn had been in pretty grim shape herself, barely able to meet her own overwhelming emotional demands. But somehow they'd managed to get through the worst of it and started taking tentative baby steps towards the future. Ever since, they'd been muddling through together, Bren instructing her in the parenting essentials as they went along.

She pressed the receive button to still the beeper's incessant chirping. The number that flashed on the digital display was her boss's private line at headquarters.

Quinn left Bren dribbling grounders around the infield and dialled Jake Holland's line from the gas-station pay phone across the street. He picked up before she heard a ring.

Apologising for the intrusion, Jake said he had to see her on an urgent matter as soon as possible. Despite Quinn's curious prodding, he declined to state the reason on the phone. Something in his tone told her she was in no danger of suffering any pleasant surprises.

She dropped Brendon at a neighbour's and made the ten-minute drive to headquarters in seven.

The southwest regional offices of Vermont's Department of Probation and Parole were housed in a nondescript beige building on Grove Street in downtown Rutland. Quinn parked her jeep in the rear lot beside Holland's Buick wagon and picked her way through the gathering shadows to the building's ramped side entrance.

Through the empty reception area, she spotted Holland on the phone in his office. Old Jake blended perfectly with the decor: neutrals and tweeds. His space was cluttered with family photos and fishing paraphernalia: lures, reels, trophies. In the centre of the wall hung his prized stuffed sailfish from Antigua, which had been broken in a fall, hastily repaired, and now looked like something by Picasso.

From the honeyed tones, Quinn knew that Jake was talking to his wife, Marilyn. Married twenty-five years, the Hollands were still insufferably close and happy together. Worse, their mission was to see everyone else similarly paired and conjoined at the hip.

Quinn, whose parents had been close friends of the Hollands, was a prime target of their misguided matchmaking efforts. She'd suffered through interminable evenings with hypochondriacs, egomaniacs, shower-aversives, and more than one ambulatory cadaver before she firmly declared herself a dating-game player emeritus.

But Marilyn and Jake continued to plague her with their appalling notion of suitable partners. What they lacked in taste, which was plenty, they more than made up for in ambush ingenuity. Their 'perfect men' crept into Quinn's life like vermin: unexpected, unwelcome, and often resistant to extermination attempts.

The latest débâcle had been the chubby orthodontist from Middlebury who'd suggested on first meeting at a Holland dinner party that he'd be willing to repair Brendon's overbite at a substantial discount in exchange for free and regular access to certain of Quinn's body parts. Quinn had ached to inflict physical harm on the creep, but not wanting to mar the festive atmosphere, she'd settled for a nice, civilised, verbal assault on his manhood instead.

Jake motioned for her to sit while he finished cooing with his wife. 'Yes, honey. Me too you. See you soon.' Hanging up, his face went from googly to grim.

'So, how'd it go with Weir?'

'Not bad for a first date. No kiss good night, though.'

Holland didn't look well. His chocolate eyes were dull, and worry lines etched his forehead. A circle of freckled scalp gleamed through his sparse crop of wheat-coloured hair.

'I have to be honest with you, Quinn. If I'd seen a choice, I would never have put you on this case. It doesn't please me to have you anywhere near that maniac.'

'It's okay. I've had plenty of experience with obnoxious men. I'll handle him.'

'I'm sure you will, which is why you got elected. With Perone's back on the fritz and Kraus on leave with his new baby, it was you, Lisa, or Eleanor. Between us, you're the only one with the guts and instincts to stay on top of that character. But I still can't say I'm comfortable with the situation.'

'It'll be fine, Jake. I can take care of myself.'

'You've got one terrific attitude, my friend. That's what I always say to Marilyn, "Bless Quinn. Whatever comes up, she's ready, willing, and able to take it on." '

Quinn was getting one of those nasty inklings. 'So what's come up?'

'I'm afraid you're not going to like it. But it's out of my hands.'

'What?'

'The FBI wants to include Weir in a study of violent criminals. They tried to get to him before his parole, but it couldn't be arranged in time. So one of their agents is coming to the area for a while to review Weir's file and conduct an interview. Naturally, we'll have to co-operate.'

She bristled. 'You mean *I'll* have to co-operate.'

'I'm afraid so. You don't say no to the Feds.'

Quinn shook her head. 'The timing is terrible, Jake. Last thing I need is for Weir to feel any more important than he already does. Can't you at least put them off until I've gotten the beast paper-trained?'

Holland ignored the question and read from a letter topped by an official government seal. 'The agent's name is

Bernie Levitsky. He's based in the Behavioural Sciences Unit in Quantico, but he's been working for the past few weeks on a BSU case out of the New York office. He's made arrangements to fly into Rutland through Albany first thing tomorrow morning. I'd like you to meet his plane. Help him settle in.'

'Swell, so now I'm the Welcome Wagon.'

Jake kept his tone conciliatory. 'This may turn out to be a blessing in disguise. A couple of us went to hear this guy Levitsky speak at a conference last year. Happens he's among the country's foremost experts in the psychology of violent crime. Bet he'll be able to help you get a handle on Weir. No one understands characters like Weird Ellie better than the people from Behavioural Sciences.'

'This Levitsky person wouldn't happen to be single, would he?'

'Now how would I know a thing like that?'

'Come on, Jake.'

'All right. Bernie Levitsky happens to be bright, good-looking and unmarried, but that has nothing whatever to do with his coming here.'

'You bet it doesn't. I've told you, I'm perfectly happy the way I am. Last thing I need in my life is some shrink with a Rambo fixation. So please call off this Levitsky character and tell Marilyn to cancel the lingerie shower and take back the matron-of-honour dress.'

'I told you, Quinn. This is strictly business. We have to co-operate with the Feds, plain and simple.'

Quinn could read Jake's sincerity. Reluctantly, she holstered her tongue. 'All right. I'll behave.'

Holland perked up like a watered plant. 'Great, I knew I could count on you.'

'You can always count on me, Jake. Especially when I have no choice.'

Holland lifted the receiver and started dialling before she was out of the office. Probably missed his precious sweet-cakes already. Hadn't spoken to her in three or four minutes, after all. Quinn couldn't help but smile. The Hollands were probably the result of some Hallmark experiment gone haywire. The happy couple from Hell. Amazing that Jake was such a competent administrator with all those little hearts and flowers swarming in his skull.

Not that he was always right.

This Levitsky person, for example. Quinn couldn't imagine how he could be anything but a waste of her time. She already had more information on Eldon Weir than she could ever need or want. Way more.

The sky was glum. Rain threatened. Maybe even a late snow from the chill, fulsome droop of the clouds. Quinn hurried to her car, anxious to escape the piercing wind.

Halfway there, she realised the flaw in Jake's reasoning. This Levitsky person might know about violent crime, but the world's foremost expert on a vicious beast like Eldon Weir was bound to be the man himself.

6 The child had vanished.

Not a sign of her anywhere on the inn's rambling property. Nora had exhausted her list of calls and got nowhere. Not one of the friends or relatives she reached had heard from Abigail in the past week or two. No one had the vaguest idea that the little girl had been planning to run away or where she might have gone. Even Jeanine, Abigail's longstanding best friend and confidante from Manhattan, had been shocked at the news.

'She didn't say a thing to me, Mrs Brill. Honest.'

'Thanks, Jeanine. You'll call right away if you hear from her?'

'Sure. Hope she's okay.'

Nora had not been able to reach Raymond, but one of the several messages she'd left was bound to catch up with him eventually. She'd tried his apartment in Atlanta and his parents' home in Charleston. As an 'entrepreneur', forever dabbling in new ventures, Ray travelled incessantly and maintained no permanent office. But in case there was ever a crisis with Abigail, he'd left a list of emergency 'business' numbers where Nora might be able to locate him in a half dozen cities. Sounded like the same breathless woman who answered at each place she called.

One thing about Raymond. He'd always been all business.

Nora thought he should know about their daughter's disappearance, though she doubted he could be of any particular help. He would have called immediately if Abigail had contacted him. The man was capable of plenty, but he could never be so cruel as to let Nora suffer needless worry if their daughter was safe in his care. Both of them loved the little girl, wanted nothing more than to see her well and happy. On that much, if little else, they'd always agreed.

38

While Nora was making her calls, Charlie had contacted all the area hospitals. No reports so far of any injured children matching Abigail's description. Mim had gotten in touch with the state police who'd agreed to alert patrol units. Even Queen Victoria had rallied to the cause, phoning the inn's staff at home to ask whether they might have seen or heard something useful. Of course, she dialled with a pencil eraser. Nothing so minor as a missing child was going to make that woman risk injury to her manicure.

Ironically, Victoria was able to reach everyone but Reuben Huff. No answer at his apartment. Nora felt a pang of anxiety. How had the caretaker known that Abigail wasn't in her room? Maybe Reuben had seen her leave. Better yet, maybe Abigail had mentioned something to Huff about where she was planning to go.

Charlie went to the office to check the personnel files. Maybe he had some other way to contact the caretaker, he assured her, giving her a gentle hug.

Nora pulled Abigail's note from the pocket of her black slacks and tried to read something new into the poignant message: *'I can't take this anymore. I hate it here. I'm going far away.'* The familiar round handwriting was blurred by multiple erasures as if the child had agonised over every word. The message tugged at Nora's heart. Why hadn't she done something sooner?

Charlie returned from the office. 'There was a number in Reuben's file for his landlady, a woman named Bollard,' he said. 'She wasn't thrilled to get a call at this hour. But once I explained the circumstances, she agreed to take a ride over to Huff's building and try to track him down. Said he sometimes stays up most of the night playing cards with a couple of his neighbours. Should hear from her in about half an hour one way or the other.'

Nothing left to do but wait.

They sprawled on the ring of chintz sofas in the living room and settled in a taut silence. No sounds but the crisp ticking of the grandfather clock and the arthritic crackle of the old farmhouse frame.

The clock chimed five.

By six, the inn's star chef and the rest of the breakfast staff would begin returning for the morning shift. Somehow, they'd all have to put up a reasonable show of normality for the guests. Go through the motions.

Nora kept eyeing the front door. Any minute, Abigail could show up and the agony would be over. She stared until her eyes ached.

'Anyone for coffee?' Charlie said.

He went to the kitchen to put up a fresh pot. Mim left to check on Poppa. Victoria yawned and excused herself to take a shower. Hugh had lost interest early on and retreated to his room for some solitary seething. Stephanie had dozed off in the office where she'd gone to put together missing person flyers to post around town.

Alone, Nora tried to think of what more she could do. Nothing was worse than this impotent waiting. Crossing to the reception desk, she dialled Raymond's place in Atlanta again and listened to the desolate ringing until his taped drawl climbed on the line. 'You've reached Ray Eakins . . .' No point she could see in leaving another message, so she hung up.

Back in the living room, she settled on the sofa and wrapped herself in one of Mim's crocheted afghans. With her eyes closed, she tried to picture where Abigail might be. By degrees, a grainy image formed. She saw the child poised on the balance beam in her striped team leotard. Abigail was prancing and flipping to a lilting classical tune. Landing on a breath. Silken pony tail bobbling. Movements fountain smooth.

The music darkened and built to a crescendo. Threads of tension cinched the crowd and drew them to the child's spotlit form. The hush deepened as she hopped, turned, and hesitated in preparation for a daring, double flip dismount.

An instant's pause, and she springs skyward. Clutches knees to chest and starts to spin. She's twirling, catapulting in a dizzy blur. Too late, she tries to pull out. The downward force has consumed her. She's plummeting in a wild looping rush towards the ground. A gash opens in the earth beneath her and she plunges through. Spirals towards black obliv-

*ion. The darkness swallows her whole. Nothing left but the
cold, metal echo of her screams.*

'Stop, Abigail. No!'

'Nora.'

Charlie's voice shocked her awake. He stooped and
wrapped her in the protective sling of his arms.

'Nightmare?'

'This whole damned thing is a nightmare.'

'Don't worry. We'll find her.'

He sat behind her on the sofa and started kneading the
knots of tension from her neck. His fingers worked across
her shoulders and down the rusted pipe of her spine.
Charlie's touch could turn stone to putty. Thick, sure hands
infused with gentle warmth. Nora rotated her head and
revelled in the easy feeling.

'That better?'

'Thanks, much.'

She leaned back against him, and her eyes drifted shut.
She was melting, sinking under a wave of exhaustion.

She was nearly asleep again when she caught the sound
of an approaching car. Too early yet for the staff to start
arriving. Maybe it was someone bringing Abigail home.

Nora hurried to the window and spotted a maroon sedan
bumping down the hill towards the inn. Her breath caught
as the car slowed and turned into the driveway.

Still too dark outside to make out the passengers. Seemed
forever until the driver's door opened and a tall, fiftyish
woman with a bob of salted brown hair stepped out. She
cinched her blue wrap-coat tighter around her waist and
ducked her head against the wind as she strode towards the
front entrance. Nora's heart sank.

No sign of anyone with her.

Nora opened the door before the woman had a chance to
knock. The stranger stepped inside and proffered a knobby
hand.

'You Mrs Brill? Mr Brill? I'm Priscilla Bollard. I went
over to the Mayfair Arms to check on Reuben Huff like your
husband asked, and, well, it's so terrible, I thought I'd
better stop by and give you the news in person.'

Nora couldn't find a voice. Charlie came up beside her. 'Is Reuben . . . dead?'

'Dead? Hell, no. But he will be if I get my hands on him. He's gone is what he is. Took off like a thief in the night. Left me holding the bag for three months arrears and a fat phone bill to boot, the sonavabitch.'

'That's weird,' Charlie said. 'Reuben's been with us for almost ten years. I can't imagine him doing a thing like that.'

'Oh God,' Nora said. 'He's taken her. He's got Abigail!'

Charlie caught her by the shoulders. 'Easy, honey. I'm sure it's just a coincidence. Reuben would never . . .'

'That's how he knew she wasn't in her room, Charlie. Don't you see? He's got her. We have to call the police. We have to stop him.'

'Shh, okay. Okay. I'll call.'

Too small to support its own department, Dove's Landing was under the jurisdiction of the state police out of the West Brattleboro barracks. Charlie dialled the number and explained the latest development. He hung up and reported that they'd promised to dispatch a unit right away to get details.

As she shed her coat, Mrs Bollard made a slow, squinting survey of the room. 'Love those orientals,' she said. 'And all those old copper pots and those crystal doodads. Just fabulous. Worth a fat fortune, right? If I was you, I'd watch the likes of Reuben Huff around all these nice things. Man's not to be trusted. That's for sure.'

She draped her coat on a mahogany stand. She was wearing a flowered housecoat and pink leather mules. 'You trust him, you'll be sorry as I am. Like to wring his scrawny neck,' she declared. 'Like to pull him apart like a wishbone. Know exactly what I'd wish for too.'

Charlie shut her up with coffee and a blueberry muffin. Less than five minutes later, a state police car drove up with flashing lights and a wailing siren. Nora recognised the two troopers, a Mutt-and-Jeff pair named Herb Merriman and Armand DeSoto. Less than a month ago, the same duo had come to the inn to talk to her nephew Hugh about a break-in and unauthorised keg party at the abandoned house up the hill. Hugh was the sort of kid people thought of right away when the subject was trouble.

DeSoto, short, stout and voluble with a pencil moustache, started firing questions about Abigail's disappearance and Reuben Huff. He wanted to know everything about the caretaker: habits, haunts, identifying information.

Nora couldn't bear the glut of words. Something had to be done immediately. Every minute they stood around talking, Huff could be taking Abigail further away.

Near six o'clock now, and the staff was beginning to appear. There was the sound of approaching cars on the side road, voices, footsteps, the light squeak of the storm door at the rear kitchen entrance.

Charlie showed the slow-moving Trooper Merriman into the kitchen, so he could interview the new arrivals. Over six and a half feet tall, Merriman had to duck to avoid bumping his flat-topped head on the door arches. DeSoto stayed in the living room to finish up with Nora and Mrs Bollard.

'Never knew the guy was such a slob,' the landlady was saying. 'Place of his looked like hell. Take me a week of scrubbing and spraying to get rid of the mouldy smell. May have to replace the carpet altogether, and it was like new when he took the lease. Beats me how anyone could live that way. Like a pig.'

The woman went on and on. Nora could see that the trooper was running out of patience. He eyed his watch and drifted across the room.

'Makes me sick, honestly,' Mrs Bollard droned on. 'Man must've been raised in a barn. Guess no one ever taught him about soap and water. Plenty he needs to learn.'

DeSoto paused at the window. His eyes narrowed and he held up a hand to still Mrs Bollard's tirade. 'Huff has a brown Chevy, you said?'

'A Nova,' Nora said.

'Like that one?'

The two women rushed over to join him. The car pulling

into the drive was Reuben's. A moment later, Huff himself emerged and unlatched the trunk. Hauling out his battered tool kit, he scratched behind his ear and started walking towards the inn.

7 Brendon Gallagher was not a morning person.
Three times, Quinn had nudged him awake and watched until he began emerging from his blanket cocoon. But as soon as her back was turned, he'd turtled back under the covers and nodded off again.

Finally, she lifted a mock microphone to her lips: 'Now on deck for the Rutland Raiders is Brendon "the Brute" Gallagher. This guy's been on a streak, folks. Batting eleven hundred out of a possible ten. Dazzling them in the outfield. Leading the league in HRs, RBIs, and L-A-Z-Y-S. He's stepping up to the plate now. And the crowd is going wild!' She dropped her voice to a grunt. 'Galla-gurr, Galla-gurr, he's our man. If he don't get up soon, I'll kick him in the can.'

A puff of paprika hair materialised. It was followed by a scrunched set of blue eyes, a cup-hook nose peppered with freckles, and a mischievous grin packed with beaver teeth.

'Do the batter-up part,' he said. 'Don't forget when it's a full count and the frenzied crowd leaps to its feet.'

'No frenzied crowd until you're out of that bed, mister.'

He stretched out his pale, boneless arms and yawned. His pyjama top hiked up, exposing sheet-white skin over a xylophone of ribs. He was about to toss off the blankets when his face changed.

'See you downstairs, okay?'

'No batter up?' Quinn said. Then, realising the problem, she hitched her thumb and headed for the door. 'Cheerios or what?'

'What.'

'With or without fruit?'

'Without.'

'Fine. You've got five minutes.'

'Go then. How'm I supposed to get ready with you hanging around bugging me?'

Shutting the door, she heard him pad out of bed. There was a ruffling sound as he pulled off the wet sheets.

Quinn ached for the kid. He viewed every damp sheet as a personal failure. Worse, he refused to risk a public slip, so he turned down all invitations to sleepovers, campouts, and slumber parties. For his birthday, an elderly aunt had offered to fund two weeks at a baseball camp this coming summer. Bren was dying to go, but Quinn knew he wouldn't unless lightning struck and there was no more need for furtively stripped beds and sneaked trips to the washer.

She poured his cereal and juice and a cup of coffee for herself. A few minutes later, he slogged into the kitchen with his shirt tail dangling like a dog's tongue and his sneaker laces trailing on the floor. His hair was wet on the sides, a tangle of worms in back. There was a road of tracks on the top from a single swipe of a comb.

'Incredibly handsome,' Quinn said, taming the mess with her fingers. 'How are the girls going to keep their mind on their studies with you around, Brendon Gallagher?'

'Girls make me gag,' he said.

'Well, that will change, my sweet. Someday, women will make you gag instead.'

She dropped him at his friend Marc Dannon's house. At the door, the two stringbeans exchanged high fives, stuffed their hands in their pockets, and headed for the Dannons' backyard and whatever mayhem they could invent to occupy them until the school bus came.

Special Agent Levitsky's flight was due in at ten after eight. At a quarter to, Quinn made the right turn off Route 103 onto the Rutland Airport road. She followed the dips and turns in the rutted pavement past a scatter of modest houses including one that always made her cringe. It was painted a glaring robin's egg blue and sported a giant satellite dish. Beyond was a nursery fronted by buxom granite statues. And then came a string of rambling farms. One was the Pleasant View rabbitry from which she had once purchased, during what must have been a full moon, a bunny for Brendon.

The fragile little fur-ball had grown seemingly overnight

into a brooding enormous beast who ate massively and excreted precise replicas of Civil War cannon balls. After his first hutch-cleaning detail, Brendon had wisely suggested that they donate the creature to the children's zoo where he would be free to cavort with his fellow attack rabbits.

Quinn arrived at the airport entrance ten minutes early. With a glance at her watch and another at the pea-green terminal, she turned and drove into the Rutland Cemetery across the street.

Many of the gravestones were over a hundred years old. Age had thinned and darkened them in streaks, so the place had the charred, forbidding look of a torched tenement. A ribbon of muddy road meandered through the centre, and she traced it by habit to the second quadrant of Section C.

Quinn parked beside the granite bench at the end of a double row of stones and walked to the twin markers at the heads of her parents' graves. The earth was puffed like two loaves of risen dough and capped by a sorry mat of brambled grass. She knelt and plucked a clump of dandelions from the soil between the hillocks.

'Hey, you guys,' she said in a constricted whisper. 'How's it going?'

Eyeing the swollen ground, she asked her silent questions. *What should I do about Bren's tryout? Is it worth trying to bribe the coach to get the kid a spot on the team? Should I push him to go to the baseball camp Aunt Fritz has offered to pay for? And what do you think about letting Daniel come up from Boston for a visit?*

Since settling in Rutland, Quinn had avoided seeing her old flame. The sparks were mostly out, but there was still an outside risk she could get singed again. In Boston, she and Daniel had been suspiciously happy together for almost a year. And before Quinn made the move to Vermont, a long-distance romance had sounded manageable. But Daniel had soon balked at the inconvenience. He'd started peeling away before she'd been in Rutland a month.

Given Quinn's weakened state after her parents' death and the horror that followed, Daniel's defection had laid her out for the long count. Then, as soon as she'd finally recovered and flushed him nearly out of her system, he'd started phoning again, For her own sake, Quinn would have liked to declare him a permanent wrong number, but Bren was crazy about the guy and kept asking for him.

Or was the boy simply starved for male companionship?

Nothing was clear. Nothing simple or natural about this parenting business. Quinn's mother had often said that all you could do was your best. But where did that leave a little kid if your best was sorely lacking? Quinn had always been one to trust the fates, take chances. But it was a whole different story when the fates and risks were applied to a child she'd been entrusted to protect.

Quinn folded her arms against the ache of loneliness and the morning chill. Crouched low in the polished steel sky, the sun shot dazzling spikes of frozen glare. Knowing it was time to go, she touched her fingers to her lips and pressed them to the ground.

As she exited the cemetery gate, she spotted a small plane honing in on the airport. Moments later, it swooped in a graceful arc towards the tarmac. Quinn pulled in and braked the jeep in front of the terminal building.

Valley Air made two runs a day between Albany and Rutland. The trip took thirty-five minutes and the courage to fly in an anchovy tin with wings. Quinn preferred her aircraft considerably larger and at a comforting distance. She was of the mind that if people had been intended to fly, the good Lord would not have invented phobias. She watched as a half dozen dazed-looking passengers straggled through the terminal. Her man was last out.

Holland had described Bernie Levitsky as tall, thirtyish and dark. Jake had failed to mention the curly mop of dark hair, the oversized hazel eyes, or that uneasy-in-a-suit look that gave the FBI man the irresistible appeal of a kid playing dress-up.

She rolled down the window.

'Mr Levitsky? I'm Quinn Gallagher from Jake Holland's office.'

He eyed her quizzically, frowned, and approached the

48

jeep. He had the lanky lope of an adolescent. 'The guy couldn't make it?'

'What guy?'

'The parole officer in charge of Eldon Weir.'

'I'm the guy. Why don't we stop somewhere for coffee, and you can tell me how you'd like to proceed?'

Levitsky rolled his eyes as he slid onto the seat beside her. 'Holland's got to be kidding.'

'About what?'

'You. This. You can't be the one assigned to Weir?'

'Well, I am. And I can assure you Mr Holland made the assignment in all seriousness.'

'Well then, Mr Holland's elevator isn't running to the top floor. It's nuts to put a woman on Weir, and your boss should know it.'

'Oh really? And why is that?'

'Because the professor has this funny thing about females. Likes to turn them into steaks and chops.'

Quinn bristled. She'd had enough of proving herself to arrogant men with baseless opinions. More than enough.

'Well, I don't intend to give him the opportunity.'

She turned off 103 and headed in search of an open diner. Her temper climbed with the altitude.

'Being a woman does not make me stupid, soft, or vulnerable, Mr Levitsky. This might come as a shock to you. But I rarely even swoon.'

Levitsky shook his head. 'I don't care if you're steel-plated and descended from piranhas. Weir gets his hands on you, he'll treat you like a frog in high school Biology. Nothing personal, it's just what he does for amusement. His notion of fun. So you keep him away from females. It's simple common sense.'

'Simple maybe, but I don't happen to agree that your sense is all that common. Jake Holland put me on this case because he's convinced I'm the person in the department who can best handle Weir.' She did not mention the part about there being no men available. Smart people did not pass doilied trays of ammunition to the other side.

'Make an interesting epitaph.'

Quinn glowered. 'My understanding is that I am required to co-operate with you, Mr Levitsky. I don't think that includes putting up with your insults.'

He blew a breath. 'I don't mean to insult you. It's just crazy for you to be handed an assignment like this. Wait. You just passed an open breakfast place, back there.'

She veered onto the shoulder and whipped the car around in a screaming pirouette.

'Your boss made a mistake,' Levitsky said impassively. 'Obviously, he doesn't realise what he's dealing with here. So do yourself a favour and set him straight. Or, if you'd rather, I will.'

Big mouth, pompous, nosy, know-it-all. Quinn was fuming. No one was going to tell her she was too weak or vulnerable or incapable to do her job. Never again.

She slammed her way out of the jeep and into the Snowdrift Cafe. Levitsky followed at her heels like a pesky dog. They claimed opposite sides of a booth and dug in behind their menus.

The waitress, a lanky brunette with vulture nails, came to take their order. Levitsky asked for oatmeal and hot tea. Quinn requested her usual: a jelly doughnut and a cherry Coke.

They waited in taut silence for the food. Avoiding eye contact with the G-jerk, Quinn studied the paper placemat. It was a map illustrating Vermont's cheddar cheese industry. Schematic cheese wheels and parts of cheese wheels and cheese slivers in various colours represented the proportional output of mild, sharp, and extra sharp in Vermont's several distinct cheddar cheese regions. Fascinating.

She looked up and sneered at him as the waitress delivered their orders.

'This is not a contest, Ms Gallagher.'

'Who said it was?' She'd never met a lizard with big, soulful eyes before.

'You did,' he said. 'With or without words, you make yourself loud and clear. If you're out to prove something, that's your privilege. But this isn't the right time or situation.'

'I'm not trying to prove anything. I don't have to.'

He shrugged. 'Why argue? It's obvious.'

'All that's obvious is that you're the type who sticks his head up his butt and thinks he's seeing daylight.'

He stared at her as if she were mounted on a slide. 'You want to look like a daredevil, but really you're just more afraid of looking afraid than you are of taking dumb chances.'

'Nonsense.'

'And you're full of anger. But most of it's directed at yourself. You won't give yourself a break, because you're convinced you don't deserve one. Still inside that porcupine skin, you're a softie: loving, sentimental. Bet you're the type that cries at touching commercials.'

First Weir, now this idiot. Epidemic of mindreading among the jackass population. 'And exactly how did you arrive at all those brilliant conclusions, Mr Levitsky?'

'I get my information the hard way: study, observation, logical analysis from all angles. The fake daredevil bit is apparent from the way you order. You get a jelly doughnut, which is the nutritional equivalent of a suicide mission. But then you scrape off the sugar and leave the jelly on the plate. The anger is clear from the way you grit your teeth and shred your napkin. The softie part . . .'

'Eat your oatmeal, Levitsky. You keep letting your lips flap like that you're liable to hurt yourself. Not that I care.'

'Are you always this obnoxious?'

'Only when inspired. And you? Are you always this intrusive and overbearing?'

'Never. I'm a wonderful guy. A goddamned prince. What is it with you anyway? All I did was take an interest in your safety. Is that so terrible?'

'I beg to differ, Agent Levitsky. What you did was make uninformed comments about something that's entirely none of your business. A difficult assignment has never sent me screaming for shelter, and this one is no exception. I have no interest in playing Chicken Little to your neurotic Mother Hen.'

He spoke in a metered monotone. 'Look, Ms Gallagher, I can see this isn't going to work out. Why don't I just call my home office and ask them to arrange for me to work this through different channels? Meantime, I'd appreciate your dropping me at a car rental place. I'd like to head over to Weir's place and get started.'

She fumed awhile, knowing she couldn't afford to take him up on the offer, no matter how tempting. Holland would blow a fuse.

'That won't be necessary,' she said finally. 'I agreed to work with you, and I will. No reason two rational adults can't find a way to get along.'

'True,' he said, a little smirk playing on his lips. 'But it does take *two*.'

Quinn glowered at him. 'Our common interest is Eldon Weir. Let's stick to him, shall we?'

'Fine. That's why I'm here. Anyway, if you insist on staying with this case, you should know as much as you can about Weir. There are a number of things you won't find in his file.'

He sipped his tea and folded his hands on the table. His expression became rapt and solemn.

'Weir was adopted in infancy by a couple from Queens. They were too old to be acceptable to the legitimate agencies, but they were desperate for a kid, so they made private arrangements. Paid some shyster a bundle to get them a healthy, white infant. Baby looked perfect, but the Weirs noticed from the beginning that something wasn't quite right.

'Even as an infant, he was difficult and impossible to predict. He'd be mute and stiff for hours, then he'd fly into these uncontrollable rages. Later he had problems with other kids, sent a couple of his little playmates to the emergency room. And he started several fires in the house.

'But his parents didn't want to talk about the problems or even acknowledge them. The Weirs figured it had to be something they were doing wrong, so the guilt and shame kept them quiet most of the time. But once, the mother broke down and confessed the whole mess to a neighbour who was willing to talk to me.'

'Did you interview Mrs Weir also?' Quin said.

'She's long dead. So's the father. They were killed a few months apart in very freaky accidents. She was electrocuted in the bathtub when a fan fell in the water. Mr Weir supposedly fell asleep in his car with the motor running and died of asphyxiation. At first, both deaths were viewed as suspicious, but the investigations didn't turn up anything conclusive, and eventually the files were closed.'

'Are you saying you think Weir murdered his parents?'

Levitsky turned up his hands. 'The cops didn't even consider it because he was so young, but frankly, nothing that ghoul did would surprise me. Not at any age.

'The mother's sister took Weir in after the deaths,' Levitsky went on. 'Dear little Eldon was about eight at the time. For a couple of weeks, Aunt Gloria kept finding small dead animals in the backyard. She blamed the family cat until one day, she happened to look out the kitchen window and saw her nephew playing near the bird feeder. While she watched, Weir trapped a robin. For a few minutes, the boy stroked the bird and talked to it. Aunt Gloria was thinking how sweet it was, when Weir opened his mouth and bit off the birdie's head.'

Quinn winced. 'Didn't she do anything about it?'

'You bet. She went hysterical, called the pediatrician immediately. He told her it was probably an aberration. Isolated bout of childish bad judgement. Said she should ignore it.'

'You think he could have been cured at that point? Stopped before it went further?'

The agent frowned. 'Maybe, but I doubt it. Weir's violence has deep, stubborn roots. Probably a mix of rotten genes and some early, powerful reinforcers: abuse, neglect, who knows? No one's been able to trace his birth parents or the baby broker who brought him to the Weirs. But whatever

53

happened was the formula for the kind of sadistic cruelty that's rarely been seen in a so-called human being.'

'You mean the Buckram girl's murder?'

'For starters. The newspapers didn't get all the gory details, but I kept at it until I was able to piece them together. Weir treated the whole thing as a bizarre experiment. He kept the same kind of lab report he was learning to write at the time in seventh grade science. The detectives found a detailed log Weir made of every aspect of the crime from planning to execution. He was especially careful to record the details of the victim's torture and death: the terror sounds she made, exactly how far she was able to move in her attempt to escape after each stage of the dismemberment. He wrote about it as if he were observing a fruit fly. That's how he came by the nickname, "Professor Pain".

'The investigation and court proceedings were kept secret because of Weir's age, but the cops involved will never forget the particulars. Weir kept Jenny Buckram locked up in an abandoned warehouse while he went about his business. Never missed a day of school. Went home in the afternoon for milk and cookies. Showed up on time for dinner. Sick monster.

'Took him six days to finish the kill. Guy's got a God complex. Does his bloody work in six days, and on the seventh, he rests and reflects on his handiwork.'

'That's all pretty gruesome. But I can't see that it makes any difference in the way I handle Weir.'

Levitsky caught her eye. 'It should, Ms Gallagher. I'm telling you the guy's inhuman. Capable of anything. To him, torture is an interesting exercise, a game. He likes to observe how people react when they're in excruciating pain, and he likes getting away with murder.'

'If you're telling me again to be careful, Mr Levitsky, let me assure you again that I'm no fool. I've handled plenty of dangerous criminals, and I'll do the same with Weir.'

'I'm telling you Weir's different, Ms Gallagher. And I'm telling you you'll have to be more than careful.'

'Meaning?'

Levitsky looked grim. 'Meaning you listen hard for the sound of the bell. And the second you hear it, you come out swinging.'

8

The tube muffled his voice to the elastic wailing of a slide trombone. The sound came from below, a tickling vibration at the base of her spine. Abigail could not make out the words, but the cadence was teasing and strung with threats.

She'd tried to stay silent, but she couldn't contain herself any longer. 'Let me out of here,' she screeched. 'You have to let me out!'

Magically, the voice changed shape and direction, rising in a crisp whisper from behind her left ear. He was always doing weird things like that. Things she couldn't begin to explain or comprehend.

'You must find your own release. Seek and discover the way.'

'You stop it, or I'll tell. I swear I'll tell everything if you don't let me out right this minute. I don't care what anyone thinks.'

She listened to the ringing aftermath of her ultimatum and the thunder of her pulse. Not a sound from him.

Had he left?

She couldn't take this any longer. Her body ached from the cold and confinement. Terror gnawed at her belly and rumbled in her bowels.

'Please. Please let me out!'

She heard flapping. Bats?

God, no! She hated those ugly things. Stinking night demons that circled and struck, insinuating their claws and gluing their stickum into your hair so you had to be shaved bald to get rid of them. Steph had told her about a bunkmate that had happened to in summer camp. Took a whole year for the girl's hair to grow back, and then it came out mud brown and stringy.

'You have to let me out of here. I can't breathe!'

The flapping grew louder and took on tone. Abigail

realized the sound was coming from him. He was dry chuckling in that nasty way of his. The cackles built to loud mocking laughter. She was drowning in the noise. Suffocating.

'Shut up. Shut the hell up!' she cried. 'I hate you, you hear me? I hate your damned guts.'

Sobs of frustrated fury welled up and consumed her. Tears streamed down her cheeks and soaked the neckband of her T-shirt. 'Please, please. I can't stand this another second.'

'Sssh.' His voice had changed again. Now it wafted in a spectral mist from the bottom of the tube. 'You must find the way. Seek and discover. It's simple. Think.'

She struggled to pull herself back in control. What was he talking about? The tube was solid, inescapable.

But no. That couldn't be. Somehow, he'd gotten her inside this thing which meant there had to be a way out, an opening. Abigail extended her hands again and started testing the metal. From the centre of the top lid she worked her way out and then down in slow, methodical sweeps. The tube was solid to the limit of her downward reach.

Forcing herself to remain calm, she used the toe of one sneaker to pry the other off from the heel. Feeling with her bare toes, she continued examining the metal wall. Near the base of the cylinder, she discovered a tiny indentation. Tracing its course, she determined that the seam ran the entire perimeter of the tube.

Abigail shimmied downwards until she was able to plant her feet against the base. Bracing her hands and forearms against the sides, she pushed down as hard as she could.

Nothing happened.

'Damn it to hell!'

'Search and discover,' his voice came again. 'If one way is blocked, you must shift your mind in a fresh direction.'

Scrunching down further, she bent her knees and tried to kick out the bottom. Spikes of pain shot up her legs and pierced her hip sockets.

'I can't do it. It won't move.'

'Seek and discover, child. Consider the configuration.

Remember, form follows function. Function dictates form. Matter and mind. Artifice and actuality. One and the same. Indistinguishable.'

He wasn't making any sense. Lunatic was teasing her. Playing mean games with her mind. Trying to drive her as nuts as he was.

She wanted him dead. Gone.

From the beginning, she'd had vivid fantasies of his succumbing to some disgusting disease or getting fried by lightning or falling into the ocean and having his guts ripped out by sharks.

But now she decided she was capable of actually killing him. She could squeeze her fingers around his chicken neck until he choked blue. Or she'd take one of Poppa's antique rifles from the glass case in the lobby and shoot off his head. Abigail knew where the key was hidden. She'd seen Maisie take it out once so she could clean inside the case. Boom, and his sicko brain would be blown to tomato splat. That was exactly what he deserved.

Die, she thought. Hurry the hell up and die.

'Think.' His voice was a hammer now, striking in angry insistence. 'You must reason and discover. Otherwise, you'll be no further use to me, and I'll be forced to discard you like the others.'

'Stop it,' she screamed. 'Let me out, or I'll kill you! I swear I will.'

'Hush,' he rasped. 'This is only the first test. The simplest. You must wrap it in your mind. Work it through. Consider function and form. Remember artifice and actuality. Rise above the illusion. Everything is illusion; illusion is every-thing.'

Gobbledegook nonsense.

'I would not have chosen you if you weren't capable. You can and must succeed. Succeed or perish. You decide, Abigail. You are the architect of your fate.'

He was crazy. Trying to make her crazy too. But she wouldn't let him. Somehow, she'd get out of this prison thing. Again, she pressed her feet against the base of the

58

tube. She strained until her muscles quavered and lapsed.
But the tube refused to budge.

The tube.

Form and function. Other tube-shaped objects started
drifting through her mind: toothpaste, hand cream. Could
that be what he meant?

Breath held, she braced with her arms and pressed her
feet out against the side walls of the cylinder. She twisted
her legs in a slow, counterclockwise motion. With a squeal,
the bottom yielded, loosening like the screw top on an olive
jar.

A few more turns, and the base of the tube would come off.
Soon, she'd be out of this disgusting place. Then she'd find a
way to get past him and escape.

She kept turning the bottom. The floor of the tube was
wobbling now. With a hollow clang, it fell away.

Peering down, Abigail searched for a trace of light. But
the wall of darkness extended beyond the container. There
seemed no end to it.

How could that be?

She squirmed down through the open base. But instead of
freedom, she found herself trapped in another container.
This one was square with heavy canvas sides, and the air
was even thicker and heavier than before. She considered
returning to the tube, but before she could, the canvas top
closed above her head. She was overpowered by a musky
scent and the bee hum of a motor.

His words came back to her. She'd gone through the first
test. The simplest. So now there would be others.

9

The troopers confronted Reuben Huff at the kitchen door and spirited him into the office for questioning. Nora and Charlie were left in the company of Mrs Bollard and Mrs Bollard's mouth.

The woman prattled on and on about her ingrate sons, her inconsiderate tenants, and her osteo-arthritis, all of which, as Nora understood it, were somehow interrelated.

Nearly an hour passed before DeSoto led Huff back into the living room. Merriman lagged behind, large and unwieldy as a pool float. 'His story checks,' DeSoto told them. 'I don't think he knows anything about your little girl's whereabouts. You want to tell them what you told us, Mr Huff?'

'The whole thing again?' Huff sighed. 'Hate to repeat myself the way some people do.' He shot a pointed look at the landlady.

'That place of yours is a regular disgrace, Reuben Huff,' she grumbled. 'Ought to be ashamed.'

'Ought to know something before you say something. That'd be a refreshing change,' Huff countered. He slumped in an easy chair and began to recount his version of events.

Earlier in the week, Huff's upstairs neighbour had fallen asleep and left the water running in the tub. Huff had been out playing poker as he did two or three nights a week. By the time he returned several hours later, the water had soaked through the ceiling into his living room, bedroom and closet and drenched his carpeting. To avoid the expected hassle of involving the landlady, the neighbour had offered to cover the cost of materials and pay Huff to fix the mess himself.

Mrs Bollard sniffed. 'Some nerve. Happens to be my building, you know. Thought you'd have the courtesy to tell me about a thing like that.'

'Fine,' Huff said. 'I'm telling you. Want to take care of it yourself? Be my guest.'

'I didn't say that, Reuben. I simply said it's courtesy to keep me informed.'

'No disrespect, Ma'am. But you wouldn't know courtesy if it came up and bit you on the ass.'

The landlady's eyes bulged, and she reddened in splotches. Ignoring her, Huff continued his story. He was planning to start the repairs as soon as the ceiling and floorboards dried. Until the work was completed, he was staying with his Uncle Marvin Huff in Wilmington. The job was bound to be messy, so he'd taken all his clothes with him and stored the rest of his things in a friend's garage.

Merriman reported that he'd contacted the friend, the upstairs neighbour, and the uncle. All three had confirmed Huff's story. According to the uncle, Huff had shown up shortly after the time Nora encountered him at the courtyard door. He hadn't gone out again until early this morning when it was time for work. No phone calls made or received. Nothing unusual about his behaviour. At least, nothing unusual for Reuben.

The caretaker seemed bored. He told his story in a listless drone, working a coin between his fingers as he spoke. 'Think I can go now?' he said finally. 'Got a truckload of chores to see to.'

'One more thing, Mr Huff,' DeSoto said. 'You told Mrs Brill she wouldn't find her daughter in her room. How did you know that?'

Huff searched the ceiling for an answer. Scratched his nose. 'I say that?'

'Yes, when I met you at the courtyard door,' Nora said. 'How did you know she wasn't there? Did you see her leave, Reuben? Did she tell you anything? Please try to remember.'

'Must've heard me wrong, Mrs Brill. Haven't seen Abigail in awhile now. Couple of days, at least. Been real busy with the summer changeover chores.'

'But you said . . .'

'Nope. Don't remember saying anything like that. Why

would I, given I haven't seen the girl? Must be you misunderstood. You done with me, officer? Like to get started on those chores before the day gets away from me altogether.'

'One more thing, Reuben,' Mrs Bollard said. 'I expect your place to look like new. Good as you found it, you hear?'

'No problem. Didn't find it all that terrific.' He turned to Nora and tipped an imaginary hat. 'Hope Abigail turns up real soon, Mrs Brill. Nice little girl, that one is. Real sweet and pretty. Sorry I can't help.'

Mrs Bollard trailed Huff out the door. The troopers stood, preparing to leave as well.

'Wait,' Nora said. 'No matter what he says, he knew Abigail wasn't in her room. I remember his exact words. For some reason, he's not telling the truth.'

Something passed between the two men. 'We'll keep our eyes open,' Merriman told her with a languid nod. 'I'm sure she'll be back before you know it.'

'Kids run away all the time,' DeSoto added. 'My son used to pack up his things once a week, minimum. Every time my wife said no to something, off he'd go. She'll get tired and come home on her own. You'll see.'

Charlie draped an arm across her shoulders. 'I'm sure they're right, honey. Hugh ran away for three days once. We were planning a big party to celebrate, but then he showed up.'

After the troopers left, Nora went to the house to clean up and change for her ten o'clock appointment with members of the tourist board. Her head was pounding, and her eyes were on fire. She'd go crazy if she sat around waiting for news of Abigail. Charlie could reach her if he heard anything.

With half an hour to kill, she headed to her studio to collect the proofs she'd developed yesterday for the board's new brochure. As directed, she'd spotlighted the state's contrasts: majestic peaks and verdant valleys, farms and industry, quiet country inns and sophisticated ski resorts. She'd taken several of the shots at the Brill family inn and the surrounding neighbourhood. Portraits of serenity.

Looking through them now, Nora was stung by the bitter irony. She had believed her daughter would be safe here. She'd thought nothing bad could ever happen in such a picture-book setting.

Only last weekend, Abigail had followed her around while she took most of these shots. With a guilty pang Nora remembered how she'd tuned out the child's incessant whining and complaining. She hadn't wanted to hear any more about how perfect life would be if only Abigail could go live with her daddy.

The truth was that Abigail's precious father was only precious in the small measured doses he was willing to dispense. Ray was a perfect holiday parent, all gifts and fun and special occasions. He'd never agree to take Abigail on full time. That would be too much like responsibility. Responsibility was Raymond's starter pistol. He bolted at the very idea.

But Nora could never tell Abigail any of that. The child would have to learn her father's limitations, and her mother's, first hand. So rather than listen to grievances she was unwilling to answer or refute, Nora had lost herself in her work.

Taking pictures had always been her best escape. Through the lens, the world was reduced, ordered in select swatches. She could trap a shadow. Freeze a moment. Banish ugliness beyond the careful confines of her chosen reality.

As she often did when armed with her Nikon or her antique Hasselblad, she'd focused on the snips of time and space she found most appealing. Abigail's gripes had been exiled to the outskirts of her attention with the other unpleasant things: dead trees, storm clouds, mud slicks, litter, road kill.

In a couple of shots, she'd even managed to catch the little girl in an errant smile. She'd snapped one as Abigail completed a double flip on the path to the vacant house up the hill. It was a moment to bronze, the child beaming with satisfaction. Now, Nora thought of the instant that had followed, when the contented gleam had yielded to an angry pout and sullen accusations.

'You don't even want Daddy to come see me. All you care about is being with Charlie and this dumb place.'

Maybe if she'd been more understanding. Maybe if she'd listened harder.

Useless regrets. She couldn't go back. Next time, she'd know better. She'd be patient and sympathetic.

If only there was a next time.

Almost nine. Time to leave for her appointment. Nora searched the desk for an envelope large enough to hold the proofs. Nothing in the drawers, but she kept extra supplies in the closet near the door. She was rummaging through the stationery boxes when the buzzing started.

Closing the closet door, she traced the din to the darkroom. The timer she used to monitor the developing process had gone off. Strange. Then, somehow she must have set it with a stray move while collecting the proofs.

Passing the row of metal trays, she noticed several enlargements still soaking in print-fix solution. Not like her to be so messy or careless.

She plucked the ruined papers from the chemical bath, wadded them together, and held them over the tray to catch the drips. She was about to deposit the soggy mass in the garbage when she spotted a clear image on a paper corner sagging from the bottom of the clump.

A bare foot.

Her heart hammered as she recognised the pointed toes. The delicate dancer's arch. The braid of coloured threads fastened around the ankle by a beaded safety pin.

Abigail's foot.

With trembling fingers, she pried the paper edges apart and smoothed the rumpled glossies over the edge of her worktable.

There were four eight-by-tens, all shot with ultra-sensitive film so the images were grainy. All four were nearly identical except for the facial expressions. One showed the child with her eyes closed and her lips pursed in concentration. In another, she had the startled look of a deer trapped in the glare of headlights. The third had captured her with her lower lip curled in a pout and her eyes brimming with unshed tears. She looked terrified in the fourth, her mouth distended in a soundless scream.

The rest of her seemed stiff and unnatural. Her arms were pinioned to her sides, legs locked in extension. She was wearing the clothes from yesterday, jeans and a tie-dyed T-shirt. Her red windbreaker was tied around her waist. Only one foot was bare. On the other, the sneaker was caked with a mucky substance and sprinkled with hair-like debris.

Nora suppressed a whimper. Her baby looked so dirty and dishevelled. There were dark streaks on her cheeks, and her silken hair was clumped and matted. But there were no other visible signs of injury. No physical signs of pain in any of the shots either. Nora knew Abigail's hurt look only too well. Her eyes misted with detachment, and there was a resigned set to her mouth.

Heart hammering, Nora hung the prints to dry and ran to the inn to get Charlie. She found him in the office, going over the books. In a breathless rush, she told him about the snapshots.

'Maybe it wasn't Reuben, but someone took her, Charlie. He must have left those pictures to prove it. She's in the clothes she wore to school yesterday. Come, I'll show you.'

On the way to the studio, he asked a dozen questions. True, the discovery was eerie and illogical. But Nora didn't try to explain away his scepticism. He'd see for himself.

Charlie followed her into the studio. The place looked looted. Drawers protruded from the desk, the contents spilling over. The desk top was littered with papers. Through a crack in the closet door, the displaced boxes of supplies looked ready to topple. Whoever had left the pictures of Abigail must have been searching for something.

Quickly, Nora led Charlie to the darkroom. She flipped on the lights and pointed him towards the row of prints.

He walked over and stared at the four hanging papers. A moment later, he turned and took Nora in his arms. He held her close, stroking her hair. 'Oh, honey. It'll be okay. You have to try to get hold of yourself. Maybe get some sleep . . .'

'What are you talking about?' She wrestled out of his grasp and strode to the drying rack. The papers were positioned exactly as she'd left them. But the images were gone. They hung in a taunting row: four stark, accusatory blanks.

10 On the way to Weir's place, Levitsky grilled Quinn about the special security arrangements. He was surprisingly knowledgeable about the fledgling science of electronic surveillance. But then, the man was amazingly well-informed about most things, for a fool.

From the sketchy information Quinn was able to provide, the FBI man recognised that the professor's device represented a new generation in monitoring technology.

Weir's movements were being recorded on a constant-trace basis. Quinn was able to show Levitsky her copy of the baseline print-out from the professor's first morning in the renovated house.

'Interesting,' the agent said as he flipped through the pages. 'Man keeps pacing, pacing. Tense, restless.'

Quinn remembered Weir's relentless patrol of the living room. 'He does act like a caged animal.'

'That's no act. I'm glad to see they're not relying on random computer calls alone. Something tells me the professor would find a way to slip through the cracks in that system with no strain at all.'

'Come on, Levitsky. The man's not superhuman.'

Quinn had been given a short course in electronic surveillance when she joined the parole department. The plastic monitoring bracelet was fitted tight to the offender's wrist and secured with welded steel rivets. Any attempts to loosen or remove the device would sound the alarm at the central Telsol computer and a 'Wristlet Tamper' message would register at once on the client's incoming status record. Enough to sound an instant alarm.

The raised portion on each bracelet had a unique configuration that precisely fitted the receptacle in the offender's phone-answering apparatus. That and the voice-verifier system ensured against stand-ins or substitutions.

Sounded fool-proof to Quinn. And the monitoring expert from Burlington had assured her that no parolee had managed to violate the restraint in the six years since the state's first electronic watchdog was installed.

'Anyway, whatever he might have been able to do with a simpler system, he hasn't got a chance with this one,' Quinn said. 'It's fail-safe.'

'So was the Titanic.'

'Cute, Levitsky. Here we are.'

She swung into the driveway and stopped in front of the gate. But before she could step out to open it, the agent grabbed her by the wrist.

'Wait. I didn't realise we were this close. Don't let on that I'm here, okay? You draw him out. I'll lie low.'

'Why?'

'I want to observe him before I go in. After we pull into the driveway, call him to the door. I'll circle around behind those bushes near the front. When you're ready to leave, raise a hand and I'll meet you back here.'

'Is all this cops-and-robbers business really necessary? If you're here to interview the man, why not get it over with?' *Do it and get lost* is what she wanted to say, but Quinn's mother had raised her better than that.

Levitsky scowled. 'If it weren't necessary, I wouldn't waste my time or yours. Now can we get started, or should I make those other arrangements?'

'All right, okay. May I have my arm back, please?' Or am I expected to sacrifice that in service to my country too?'

He released her so abruptly she bumped her head on the side window.

Dolt. Quinn was tempted to give him a piece of her mind. Lord knew he could use it.

'Sorry,' he murmured. 'You okay?'

Muttering Gaelic obscenities, she parked the car inside the gate and approached the staked border. The living-room curtains were still drawn. No sound from inside.

Trying to ignore the FBI jerk who was stalking around like a cartoon cat burglar, Quinn positioned herself the required distance from the staked boundary and drew a deep breath. She was about to call Weir's name when the front door opened.

'Miss Gallagher? How delightful to have you back again so soon.' The professor's mouth was drawn in an enigmatic smile. His blank eyes narrowed in a questioning squint.

'I was in the area. Thought I'd stop by to see if you needed anything.'

'How very kind. Thanks, but no. My requirements are quite modest.'

'Is that so?' Quinn narrowed her eyes in unconscious imitation and waited for Weir to revert to the leering foul-mouthed creep he'd been yesterday.

But he held the mask of innocence. 'Yes. As you know, I've been incarcerated for quite some time. One learns to do without. All part of the process of paying one's debt to society.'

'What's the game, Mr Weir?'

His murky eyes widened. 'Why, do I seem somehow different to you, officer?'

'You bet. All of a sudden you're trying to impersonate a person for some reason.'

Quinn stared into the phoney ingenuous face. So this was what Levitsky meant when he talked about the man's being unpredictable. Shifts and changes. *Now you see him . . .*

At least this assignment wasn't going to be dull.

Weir blinked and pursed his lips. 'Forgive me, officer. I'm afraid I don't understand.'

'That's fine. The important thing is that *I* understand, Weir. And I do – perfectly.'

'I hope so. I detest being misperceived. It's a burden I've borne for as long as I can remember.'

'You poor thing. Pity I left my violin in my other purse.'

'I don't expect your sympathy. All I ask is fairness. Justice. That's all I've ever asked.'

Justice and a little girl to dismember. The man's needs were modest indeed.

The seeing-eye dog lumbered up and assumed his place at Weir's side. The professor extended a hand and stroked between the huge animal's ears. With each caress, his arm muscles rippled like brook water. There was an eerie similarity between the two beasts. Chill, unwavering stares. The lethal stillness of predators on the scent.

'It's been swell, Mr Weir, but I'm afraid I've got to run along now. Have to check on my other boys and girls.'

'Must you, officer? No time for tea? It does get lonely.'

For a moment, Quinn stared into his unblinking eyes. They were devoid of soul or feeling. Dead cold.

'Thanks anyway, but I'm afraid I'll have to pass.' She held up a hand to signal Levitsky that she was ready to leave. 'Bye now, Mr Weir. See you real soon.'

Weir tensed. 'What was that?' he said.

'What?'

He cocked his head and scowled. 'There.' He pointed an accusatory finger towards Levitsky's hiding place behind a tuft of shrubbery. 'That foul smell. What putrid creature did you bring with you, officer? What game are *you* trying to play?'

Flustered, Quinn could not fathom the source of his suspicion. Her hearing was excellent, and she hadn't caught a sound. Levitsky was well out of scent range.

'I don't play games. You're imagining things. There's no one here but you and me.'

Weir issued a bloodless laugh. 'How true. It is no one. Less than no one.'

Quinn started for the car. The professor's smirking presence was a cold mass behind her.

'Stop. Don't leave yet.' His words curled from behind, stopped her short. 'There is a way for you, Miss Gallagher, but not this way.'

'If you want me to understand what you're saying, you'll have to speak English.'

'Come closer, then. This must be strictly between us.' His finger beckoned, undulating like a charmed asp.

Quinn turned and edged a few steps closer. 'What?'

'If you wish to truly know me, you must follow the path.'

'Thanks anyway, but I told you, I'm not all that inter-ested.'

'Oh yes you are. And I'd be willing to guide you. I'll be

your teacher, Miss Gallagher. Your mentor, if you will. I have chosen you, you see. You can be the first to know it all, everything. And the knowledge will serve you well, especially with the current turn of events. But it will take careful observation. Sense and struggle.'

'Nice of you to offer. But unfortunately I'm way too busy to sign up for any lunatic lessons right now. So if you'll excuse me.' She turned again and started towards the jeep.

'You alone can know me.' His voice was an ethereal hum inside her head. 'You will; you must. There is no choice, you see. We are bound, you and I. We hear the same melody. It drives us both.'

Quinn paused, but decided not to waste words. Nut cases, she was surrounded by them. Trying to ignore his urgent whispers, she continued to the driveway.

'The path to discovery,' came the breeze behind her. 'You must discover the path. You must before it's too late for both of us. Before the damage is done.'

As she opened the car door, Levitsky materialised beside her and slipped in first. He slid over to the passenger side and sat staring towards the house. The professor stood poised behind the line of string.

Quinn glanced from Weir to Levitsky and back again. Both looked mesmerised.

She tapped the G-man's arm to break the spell. His startled expression dissolved to a studied neutral.

Quinn opened her mouth to speak, but Levitsky gestured for silence. With difficulty, she held her tongue until they were past the string of shops on Main Street. The guy made her want to shriek.

'Look, I don't know what's going on, but it seems to me Weir isn't the only one playing games here. There's something more between you and the professor than simple scientific interest.'

'What makes you think that?'

'Fine. Forget it. As long as it doesn't get in my way, I don't give a damn if you two are old tango partners.'

'Nothing I do will get in your way. My job is to help with

monsters like him. And I can if you'll let me. What did he say to you when he called you back towards the line?'

Quinn had no interest in giving Weir's creepy statements any weight or significance. Not worth repeating.

'He told me he doesn't like surprises. Says I shouldn't bring any more guests around unless I've given him notice. I guess he wants time to get his hair done and set the table.'

'Okay, Gallagher. Have it your way. You don't want to tell me. I can't force you.'

Levitsky was silent awhile, staring out at the blur of passing trees and power lines. 'Just one more unsolicited bit of advice. Whatever he says, no matter how innocent it sounds, if it comes out of that man's mouth, figure it means trouble.'

11

He was able to read her mind.

Abigail felt thirst, and a plastic cyclist's Thermos was thrust into her hand. The water inside was tepid and had a cloying stale taste, but it soothed the raspy soreness in her throat and eased the parched feeling. Greedily, she gulped the contents. And as soon as she put the vessel down, it vanished.

The same thing happened when the vague stirrings in her bladder mounted to a painful urge. She decided she'd rather pee in her pants than beg him to let her go to the bathroom, but she hadn't needed to make either humiliating choice. Suddenly, a metal pail was pressed between the canvas wall and her right hand.

'A slop bucket,' he said, and when he somehow sensed she hadn't understood, 'for a toilet.'

He met all her needs that way. Anticipating. Whatever she craved appeared seemingly out of thin air. A chocolate bar, another drink, a tissue to wipe her runny nose. Wish, and the thing was in her hand or pressed against her thigh or bumped off the stiff canvas beside her hip. Finish, and it disappeared.

'These privileges are for passing the first test,' he said when she was desperate to know what was going on. 'You shall be elevated and properly rewarded as we proceed.'

The whole thing was so bizarre, she feared she really was going nuts. She wondered if this was the way it had happened to her friend Bonita Todd's mother.

Every year, Mrs Todd spent a month or more in bed at their fancy Park Avenue duplex followed by weeks of frenzied shopping followed by sudden trips to New York Hospital where it was rumoured she was injected full of zombie medicines and tortured with electric shocks.

Abigail imagined that the woman was jolted with great searing bursts of current like the boy in a nearby town who'd accidentally touched a live wire after a storm. The picture in the paper had shown the poor kid glued to the power pole. Burned black as a campfire marshmallow.

No way was anything like that going to happen to her. She was determined to get through this with her sanity intact. She'd pass every one of his dumb tests if that's what it would take to get out of this place in one piece.

His words danced through her mind in an unruly chorus of ideas. Form and function. Image and illusion. She tried to concentrate, but her thoughts were as fleeting and capricious as moths. She kept losing her place in the dark silence, veering off in unexpected directions.

Think!

The thing she was in had stiff, canvas sides. Strong canvas like the outer edge of the trampoline at gymnastics. Canvas like the sail on that boat Daddy had taken her on last summer with one of his 'friends'.

This one had been a woman named Tanya with caramel skin, beaver teeth and a laugh like machine-gun fire. Tanya spoke with a Dracula accent, smelled like vanilla extract, and bragged about her beak-nosed brat daughter, Natasha, who'd spent the whole day in the hold with a book of ballerina stories and a bowl of Doritos. Then what could you expect from a girl with no life and that for a mother?

Stuck on the deck with nothing to do, Abigail had narrowed her eyes and stared, trying to figure out what Daddy could possibly see in this Tanya person. But all she'd gotten for her trouble was a squint headache and one of those rare, angry looks from her father that said he knew what she was up to and she'd better cut it out fast.

Fortunately, Tanya hadn't lasted long. Neither had Marjorie Lump Legs or Gabby Gloria or Suzie Frizz-Hair who looked exactly like her mongrel dog but unfortunately did not know how to roll over and play dead.

Daddy had said she shouldn't resent what he referred to as his 'lady friends', that he loved her the best of anyone and always would. But Abigail's objections had nothing to do with resentment. The simple fact was that the women he picked were all creepy gunks. Every one of them. Stephanie said her father was the same way. She said maybe after the divorce, someone else got custody of the man's judgement. Steph could be hilarious, even about things that weren't all that funny.

Think, Abigail. Get your mind on the problem.

Canvas sails drifted through her head. Canvas sneakers. Last year, she'd wanted pink ones like her best friend Jeanine's, but her feet were too fat, a C-width at least, so she'd wound up with another dumb pair of plain white. Ivory, Mom had called them, figuring Abigail was dumb enough to fall for it.

No. Think about the container. This container.

Canvas hammock behind Grandma Brill's house. Canvas cover over the pool.

But it had to be shaped like this thing: a bag, a sack.

She almost whooped with joy when it came to her. It must be a canvas sack like the one Mr Banyon had carried into their apartment building.

A mail bag.

During the week, the postman came while she was in school, but every Saturday Abigail had found an excuse to wait for him in the building lobby. She'd visit with Sol, the tall black superintendent who told great knock-knock jokes and always had a pocket full of gummy bears. Or she'd make a date to meet Jeanine, in front of the building at the time she knew the old man delivered the mail.

Abigail was forever bargaining with the fates for a letter from Daddy. Somehow, she believed her chances would be better if she was on hand when the mailman showed up.

Concentrate!

She closed her eyes and imagined Mr Banyon with his Humpty Dumpty body and licorice gumdrop eyes. She pictured his rumpled uniform and the blue box of dog treats poking out of his jacket pocket and his clunky black shoes with the heels so worn, he walked with rocking-horse steps.

And the mail sack?

Clenching her lids, she envisioned the rolling metal stand and the trio of battered blue bags stained with oily smudges. Each had the top flap and the insignia on the front: a baleful-looking eagle with drooping claws. The overlap was secured with leather straps. They closed like regular belts, the metal stabber thing poked through a hole and the spare dangling.

The image was complete. She could see the thick leather strap over Mr Banyon's shoulder, the bag itself as he took it off the stand and brought it inside, and the pregnant bulge of mail and packages. She could even visualise the riot of envelope colours as Mr Banyon opened the sack, unlocked the bank of steel boxes with one of the keys on his ring, and started plunking stacks of letters into the appropriate slots.

The whole thing was so clear, but Abigail couldn't figure out how to use it to get out of her canvas prison.

He was walking around upstairs. She heard the steady thumping approach, pause, and then plod away.

By the time he came down again, she had to be out of this thing. If she was forced to listen to his loony talk one more time, she'd pull her hair out. Then, she'd have bald spots like that skinny kid, Alex, in social dance class. Abigail couldn't remember the exact tongue-twister name of the disease that had made the boy's hair fall out. Sounded like hello, pizza. But whatever it was, everyone had been afraid it was contagious, so poor, bald Alex always wound up doing the fox trot with fat, droopy-boobed Mrs Schoop, the teacher's wife. They used to laugh behind her back that Mrs Schoop must wear a cross-your-knees bra.

Concentrate!

Abigail banished Mrs Schoop from her mind and reviewed the image of Mr Banyon, hat to shoes, and the sack. She turned the picture around, examined it from all angles.

And than she realised what she'd overlooked.

The creep had inserted and withdrawn all those things: the bucket, the Thermos, the candy, the Kleenex. How?

She had already examined every inch of the canvas. There were no splits or openings like the one she'd discovered in the tube. Each fabric panel was a single, uninterrupted sheet.

But the sides had to be pieced together somehow.

76

Sewn?

With mounting excitement, she shoved her fist into the seam at hand level, where the Thermos and other things had seemed to materialise. Pressing with all her might, she was able to force a separation between the canvas side and back walls. That must have been how he got things in and out of the sack. Some magic.

The opening wasn't nearly big enough for her to squeeze her whole body through. Hooking a finger around one of the exposed threads in the separation, she tugged as hard as she could. She kept pulling until the string ripped her flesh. There was a stab of pain and a sticky rush of blood.

She slumped back, exhausted; stared at the darkness until her eyes went dry. The ache in her cut finger dimmed to a thumping pulse that matched the thumping overhead. Both echoed the sledgehammer pounding in her chest. She couldn't do anything. Nothing worked.

But then she lifted her sneakered foot to scratch an itch on the ankle of her bare one. At once, she felt the rasp of the beaded pin against her ankle bone.

Contorting herself in a tight bend, she was able to slither her hand down to the level of the friendship band Stephanie had braided for her when she first moved to the inn. Abigail snapped the pin open and wrestled her way back to her original position.

Sliding the pin point back and forth over the thick thread on the canvas seam, she was able to fray through several layers. Once the string was fine enough, she broke it apart and unravelled the stitching until the gap was sufficient to let her pass.

Abigail spread the canvas sides and peered out. The light was watery and dim but still startling after the dense darkness.

Gradually, the space stopped shimmering. The canvas sack was in a square room, windowless, but otherwise normal-looking. There was a staircase in the centre and a cot with a bare mattress. The motor sound had come from a small metal box in the corner. Some kind of machine that emitted a growling sound and irregular winks of light.

Abigail looked the space over, wall to wall. Nothing struck her as obviously dangerous.

Still, prickles of fear erupted on the backs of her arms as she slipped through the opening and dropped to the floor with a thud.

She could see no way out except the column of stairs in the centre of the room, and those led directly to him. No windows, no other doors.

Somehow, she'd have to trick her way past him.

Illusion is everything, he'd said. Everything is illusion. Well, she could pretend too. She'd play sick like Aunt Victoria always did when she wanted to get out of doing her job. Maybe then he'd let her go home.

Preparing for the performance, she stretched her cramped limbs and kneaded the soreness from her neck. Shoulders square, back arched, she took a step towards the stairs to call him. His booming voice caught her before she could take another.

'Stop!'

'. . . But I have to tell you, I don't feel well. My stomach is killing me. I'm nauseous and burning up and I think I might have to puke. You've got to get me to a doctor.'

He puffed his contempt. 'You mustn't fritter your energies on subterfuge, child. The next test will require your full concentration.'

'No more!' Abigail railed. 'I'm getting the hell out of here now. Right this minute. You can't stop me.'

She'd go upstairs and run outside before he could catch her. Somehow, she'd get past him. He didn't scare her any more. She was too damned mad.

She could hear his stupid voice, nagging: 'Stop. You must cease. Move no further.'

The hell with him.

She was halfway to the staircase when the voice stopped. Another sound rose in its place: a whistle. So high and sharp, it pierced her head like a spike. Abigail lifted her hands to her ears to block the hideous noise. But the whistling ceased as abruptly as it had started.

For an instant, she listened to the crushing silence. She

was afraid to move and trigger the awful racket again, but she had to take the chance. Anything to get away.

She cleared her mind of everything but the goal: the staircase. Freedom. Her breathing steadied. She trained her eye and mind on the path. Up, out and away. Simple.

Ready, set . . . But when she tried to take a step, her feet wouldn't move. Something was holding her. And this time the prison was invisible.

12

She had to get away.

Nora couldn't bear another second of Charlie's suffocating concerns or Mim's nagging her to rest or Victoria's gushing over the virtues of her shrink. Everything Victoria had or did was the best. It was positively uncanny.

'Dr Grove can help you through this, Nora. Use my name, and I bet he'll fit you in right away. Neil's crazy about me. And so adorable. Don't you think he's divine, Mim? Remember him at the Andersons' Christmas party in that silver Armani suit? To die for.'

Victoria tossed her raven satin hair and arranged herself in a cover pose. Despite the sleepless night and the family crisis, Charlie's sister looked perfect as always. Maybe the woman had had herself laminated.

A white pressure was building behind Nora's eyes. 'I'm going to drop the brochure proofs at the tourist board meeting. Call me there if you hear anything, will you, Charlie?'

She hurried out, ignoring their solicitous protests. She couldn't breathe in this place any more. Couldn't think.

The pressure eased a bit as the inn shrank to a pin dot in her rearview mirror. Driving north on route 100, she opened the vents and angled them so the cool breeze sprayed her cheeks. Then she flipped through the radio stations: news, weather, traffic reports, soft rock. It shocked her to realise that the world continued to spin as if nothing had happened.

Late already, she'd intended to head straight for the tourist board meeting, but she couldn't shake the feeling she might learn something by searching through Abigail's regular universe.

School was in session at Deerfield Valley Regional Elementary. Nora tracked the meandering drive as it circled the sprawling cedar building with its barn-red door and the whimsical roof that sloped in a dozen directions.

Many of the classroom windows were papered with spring scenes: primitive flowers, Easter bunnies, baskets filled with lumpy eggs and tangles of Crayola grass. Seas of heads bobbled in the background. Fidgety children faced off against stern-faced teachers. Slides flashed on a projector screen. On the music-room stage a clump of kids were singing, their mouths agape and trembling like baby birds.

Nora entered through the service bay behind the cafeteria. The building thrummed with activity. Voices. Waves of noise and rock clashes of forced silence. Feet slapped the checkerboard tiles. There was the strike of an angry rebuke. 'No running!'

Dazed by the intensity of the place, she drifted down the central corridor. Abigail's classroom was second on the left. Less than a month ago, Nora had been summoned here for an early-morning conference with Miss Schiffman, Abby's sixth-grade teacher. Lorraine, as she'd insisted Nora call her, was a rangy, rawboned woman with generous features and the pigeon-toed gait of a seasoned jock.

Seated at Abigail's desk, Nora had gone through the samples of her daughter's recent work. Sad pile of incomplete assignments, tests left half blank or marked in rows of random checks, workbook pages covered with doodles.

'I'm worried about her,' Miss Schiffman had finally said. Nora was so grateful, she could have kissed the woman. No threats or veiled accusations. No attempt to pin the blame on the butt of some hapless donkey named divorce or remarriage or relocating or parental inadequacy.

There was a problem. They would work to solve it together. Exactly the approach she craved now. The offer of help. A plan. Something.

Nora was tempted to knock. But she knew Miss Schiffman was not the one to help her this time.

A tall boy in the front row spotted her peering through the bubbled glass panel in the door. He pointed at her and tried to win the teacher's attention. But before Miss Schiffman had time to react, Nora ducked out of sight and left the building.

Next, she drove to the Haystack Mountain ski area. She bumped the car through the empty lot freckled with rain-filled potholes. The mountain was a sorry heap of mud slicks and trampled brush. The abandoned lifts as inviting as a row of gallows. But she could picture the hills as they'd been a few weeks ago at the close of the spring ski season: frosted with sunlit snow and flame-cheeked skiers.

Whenever work and weather permitted, she and Charlie had come here weekend mornings with Stephanie and Abigail. After a bungling run or two, Nora had been content to rest her aches and bruises at the base and watch Charlie and the girls. Though she'd never skied before this winter, Abigail was always first down the mountain, riding the crisp surface with breathtaking grace; trailing a wavy line of tracks and stopping in a sharp shower of risen snow.

Nora had always been amazed by her daughter's physical prowess. From infancy, the child had been agile and swift, unfettered by Raymond's cumbersome size or Nora's comical clumsiness. The most intriguing and intimidating thing about being a mother was the discovery that your child was an entirely separate, sometimes incomprehensible individual.

From the ski area, she circled back towards Dove's Landing. She passed the tiny cafe done out in Bergdorf Goodman shopping-bag colours where Stephanie and Abigail sometimes went for lunch. Nearer to the inn was the strip mall where the girls rented videos, the shop that sold used jeans, the yogurt place.

Beyond the duplex theatre on the Dove's Landing Road, Nora spotted a slender blonde girl in jeans and a red jacket walking alone on the shoulder. Heart racing she gunned the engine and pulled up beside the child.

'Abigail!'

The girl turned. A wave of sickness swept over Nora. The child was a cruel parody of Abby. Longer, thinner face. Pinched mouth. Her close-set eyes were cocoa brown and hard with distrust.

'Sorry,' Nora murmured. 'My mistake.'

This whole futile exercise is a mistake. Useless. This is not going to help me find my daughter.

But what was?

She drove to the municipal offices in downtown Wilmington. She was over an hour late, but the tourist board meeting was still in progress. Slipping into the second-floor conference room, Nora mouthed an apology to the ring of curious faces that turned at her entrance. She took a seat at the long walnut table littered with coffee mugs and note pads.

Catching her reflection in the polished wood, she decided she looked tired but otherwise okay. She kept assuring herself that she was not being irrational, imagining things. There were plenty of plausible explanations for what had happened to the pictures of Abigail: a quirky chemical reaction, faulty processing.

No question the photos had been real. So real the absent images still resonated in her mind. She could see the four distinct expressions. The stiff extended limbs. Abigail's feet, one bare, one in a sneaker caked with mud and hairy debris. She *had* seen them.

'It all boils down to what kind of impression we want to make, people,' Justin Wellacott was saying. 'Do we keep promoting ourselves as a bunch of backwoods bohunks, or are we finally ready to step into the twentieth century?'

Wellacott was president of the tourist board, mayor of Dove's Landing, an old friend of Victoria's, and something of a fixture at the inn's restaurant, where he ate most of his meals. Given a fat cushion of family money, he had no need for a real job, which was fortunate. Rumour had it he'd failed miserably in assorted positions in several Wellacott enterprises. His relatives had finally concluded that Justin had a black thumb for business and encouraged him to seek alternative employment. Ever since, he'd been dabbling in politics, philanthropy, and a variety of other activities where he was likely to do the least financial harm.

'This is Vermont, Justin, not Vegas. You want slick, you're barking up the wrong state,' said Hallie Trumbull, board secretary and a fifth-generation Vermonter from the north country. Satisfied that she'd made her point, Hallie settled her granny glasses on the pinched bridge of her nose and resumed work on her counted cross-stitch sampler.

Wellacott cast his chiselled good looks in Nora's direction. He was a tall man moulded from the same plastic cast as Victoria: perfect hair, perfect features, perfect teeth. Justin had the pristine look of something processed and packed with preservatives. Forty-something and life hadn't yet laid a glove on him.

'Now that our photographer's here, let's take a look at the pictures, shall we? Maybe they'll suggest their own style of copy.'

Nora passed the proofs to the head of the table. Justin tapped them out of the envelope and began distributing them to the others along with his skewed commentary. 'You see here? Does that beg for a snappy slogan, or what? We'll want a few more like that one, Nora. Quirky. Interesting. Stick-in-the-mind stuff.'

Wellacott was the quintessential politician, Spoke in sound bites. Argued opposite sides of a controversy with equal conviction. Exuded all the genuine warmth of furniture in plastic slipcovers. He purchased admirers by the gross and banked favours where they earned maximum interest.

Charlie detested the man. Nora couldn't take him seriously enough to have any particular opinion. Guy was a walking caricature.

And to be fair, he'd done her a number of favours. The brochure assignment had come on Justin's referral, and there had been several others.

'So? What's your read, Nora? You've worked on tourism promotions before. Do we go homespun or full speed ahead?'

'Both can be effective. Depends on what you people decide.' She knew Wellacott expected her unconditional support, but her integrity was well out of his price range.

'Well then,' he said. 'I suppose we may as well put it to a vote. All in favour of hiring that PR firm from Boston to put together a top-notch, reel-em-in campaign?'

Most of the hands shot up. Wellacott made a great show of counting them, though the whole procedure was clearly superfluous. He would never have called the question if he didn't know he had the votes in his pocket. Justin was accustomed to getting his way, whatever it took. Which started Nora thinking.

'All in favour of sticking with the same old stale, pale, zero-growth approach?' Hallie Trumbull's plump hand rose along with two uncertain others.

Wellacott thwacked his gavel. 'Good. It's settled then. I'll contact the PR people right away and get them on the case. Nora, I'd like you to get us those additional shots ASAP. Which about wraps it, folks. Next month's meeting will be in St Johnsbury. You'll host, Hallie? Nothing like those brownies of yours.'

Chairs scraped over the wood-plank floor, and there was a burst of relieved chatter as the board members switched from in-gear to idle. Wellacott made the rounds. Shaking hands. Slapping backs. Flashing his shark teeth. Nora caught his attention and asked if she could speak to him in private.

As the others straggled out of the building, Justin led her down a short corridor to a vacant office. Motioning her towards one of the stiff-sided chairs, he perched on the edge of the desk and folded his manicured fingers.

'What's up? Nothing wrong, I hope.'

'I thought you might have heard, from Victoria. It's Abigail. She's missing.'

His face went taut with shock and concern. 'Missing? How long?'

'Since yesterday afternoon. Please, Justin. I need your help.'

'Yes, of course. Glad to do whatever I can. What happened?'

Struggling to stay calm and sound reasonable, she told him the whole story, begining with her strange run-in with Reuben Huff. She recalled how she'd found Abigail's room locked and empty, the child's missing things, the contents of the note. Hesitating, she decided to include the strange episode with the disappearing images on the snapshots she'd found earlier. Justin might think she was crazy too, but Nora was convinced the pictures were important. Whoever had Abigail must have planted the shots in the studio, which meant they were still in the area as of two hours ago. She clung to that like a life-line. They couldn't have gotten too far away in such a short time.

'And the police have refused to take serious action?'

'Because of the note they're convinced she's run away and she'll come home on her own.' She wiped a tear and faced him. 'Please, Justin. I don't know what I'll do if . . .'

'Ssh. You mustn't even think that way.' He handed her a note pad and asked her to write a detailed description of Abigail including the clothing she'd been wearing when last seen. When Nora finished, Wellacott read it over. 'That should do it. I'm going to make some calls right away. Get things rolling. I'll keep you posted.'

Nora felt a rush of gratitude. Wellacott believed her. He'd pull the necessary strings, and the police would get on the case. 'I don't know how to thank you.'

'No need. Let me get busy on this. Outrageous that they haven't been out searching for her already.'

His look was grave. Angry? First time Nora could remember Justin registering anything close to a real emotion.

Shutting the office door behind her, she heard him on the phone. 'Is he in? Mayor Wellacott calling. Well, you tell him it's an emergency. I don't give a damn if he's with the *Pope*. I need to talk to him right now – immediately.'

Finally, things were in motion. Wellacott would get the police involved, and they'd find Abigail.

They had to find her.

13 Jake Holland had reassigned part of Quinn's caseload, so she'd have additional time for Weir and the FBI man. But most of too many was still plenty. The majority of her clients were slated for bi-weekly visitations, and each one required a written follow-up report. Levitsky or no Levitsky, she refused to fall hopelessly behind schedule.

She'd offered to drop the agent at a location of his choice, preferably remote, but he'd opted to tag along while she made the rounds. Quinn decided to view him as a nasty cold, something unavoidable and unpleasant that one simply had to tolerate until it went away.

Leaving Weir's place, she headed south towards Brattle-boro where one of her parolees, Lizzie Turner, worked at the Hair and There Beauty Salon on Western Road. Lizzie had earned her beautician's licence through the continuing-education programme at the Chittendon Prison where she'd served fifteen months of a three-year sentence for promoting prostitution.

Like many convicted felons, Lizzie had trouble grasping the reason for her arrest and punishment. As she saw it, she'd run a kind of emergency-relief programme for testosterone victims. How could she possibly be held accountable for what went on behind locked doors between consenting adults? Okay, so some of the adults hadn't exactly been adults, and the consents been purchased for a hundred bucks or more an hour. Still made no sense to Lizzie that those people from the DA's office took the whole thing so seriously, especially given how many of them had been customers. *Satisfied* customers, Lizzie was always quick to add.

Morris 'Melonhead' Muldowsky was next on Quinn's list. Muldowsky was a Pillsbury Doughboy clone: round, spongy, and baby bald. Melonhead's criminal record was slightly longer than the Nile. His offences ranged from fraud to theft of services to racketeering and grand larceny. After Muldowsky shook her hand, Quinn always took a moment to count her fingers.

Melonhead's last business endeavour, before it was rudely interrupted by a two-year stay at Rutland Correctional, had been relieving elderly widows of the burden of their inheritances. Now he was a minimum-wage pump attendant at the Gulf station in the centre of town.

The visits were mostly routine. Quinn questioned each parolee to see if there were any problems, real or imagined. Then she dispensed the requisite advice or admonitions and made the necessary notes to herself and the file.

Jail provided a certain perverse relief from the standard aggravations of outside existence. Former inmates often found it difficult to cope with forgotten annoyances like bills or queues at the supermarket or relatives who were no longer made to magically disappear at the end of scheduled visiting hours. Some ex-cons had a subconscious desire to return to the comforting confines of the penetentiary and acted accordingly.

At each stop, she checked with her client's employer to make sure things had been going well on the job. Lizzie Turner's boss was satisfied. Lizzie was a charmer, Quinn was told. Woman had a particular way with the hair salon's male customers, which was certainly no surprise. Muldowsky's boss complained that Melonhead had an attitude. Nothing new there either.

While Quinn made her visits, Levitsky waited in the jeep. He spent the time reviewing Weir's records. Obviously, the agent found the file fascinating. He barely reacted when Quinn got back in the car and drove to the next stop on her list.

Lyle Ackley, sentenced to two-and-a-half to ten for child molestation, was working in kennel maintenance at the Brattleboro Veterinary Hospital. Armed with a shovel, Lyle spent his day mucking out the cages of the pet hotel's four-legged guests. Suitable occupation for a person of

Ackley's character. Would have been perfect if they'd paid the creep a percentage of what he collected.

A mile down the road, Molly Stark was a book-keeper for the South Vermont Dairy Goat Association. Molly had shot her husband in the upper thigh after catching him on the conjugal Castro with a neighbour's Swedish au pair. The original charges had been plea-bargained down to simple assault, and she'd served eighteen months of a four-year term. The jailhouse joke was that Molly should have pulled an extra year for the bigger crime of poor aim.

Next on the list was Quinn's most exasperating client, Dudley Chambers. Dud was a sweet guy and extremely gifted with his hands. He was a genius at carpentry, mechanics, engineering; could fix or fabricate anything. But he had this little problem with his judgement.

Ask Chambers to wait in the truck while you and your pals in ski masks make a quick stop at the bank, and Dud couldn't see any reason to turn you down. Ask him to do you a teeny favour and drive your unmarked truck to a warehouse at three a.m., and Dud figured it was the least he could do for a friend.

Dudley's bad judgement deteriorated further when mixed with a fifth of Wild Turkey, and liquor was Dud's answer to most every question. Quinn figured he'd taken another headlong leap off the wagon when she stopped at the Photo Lab on Main Street in Wilmington and the manager informed her that Chambers had not reported for work this morning and hadn't called.

Levitsky glanced up from his reading when she returned to the car sooner than expected.

'Problem?'

'I'm afraid so. One of my clients suffers from an occasional bout of bourbon amnesia. I have to go administer the cure.'

Dud Chambers lived in a room over a private house garage two blocks from the camera store. His battered pickup was parked in front, and the shades in Dud's room were drawn. Quinn climbed the wooden staircase on the side of the garage and pounded on the door.

When he didn't answer, she knocked again and waited.

Counted to five – slowly. Then she backed to the edge of the landing, got a running start, and rammed the door with her shoulder. The flimsy lock gave way, and her forward momentum sent her hurtling halfway across the stuffy room.

Chambers was sprawled on the bed snoring like a buzz-saw. He looked about as appetising as something forgotten for months at the back of the refrigerator. Smelled worse.

Breathing only when absolutely necessary, Quinn half-filled the rust-stained sink with cold water and added the melted contents of a plastic trash basket. Apparently Dud had used the receptacle as an ice bucket while there was still something left to chill in the bottle. Now a quart jug of Old Grandad lay empty beside the bed, and Dud was the one with a tankful of gas.

Chambers' face was a map of spidery veins, his nose a knob of broken capillaries. Quinn pried open a puffy lid exposing a murky pink eyeball that was travelling in no particular orbit. Chambers groaned and smacked his lips. His breath was a spoiled beach at low tide.

Fortunately, the man was no giant. Quinn was five-five, one-twenty. She calculated that he had no more than a couple of inches and thirty or so pounds on her. Soaked in booze, the weight was a little harder to manage, but she was able to haul him off the bed and ferry him the six feet to the sink. Once there, she supported him from behind and let him dip from the waist like an oil derrick.

There was a minor tidal wave as his face smacked the full basin. Water sloshed over the sink sides and onto the floor. Took a couple of minutes for the wet cold to cut through all that anaesthetic on the rocks, but then Dud came up sputtering and flailing like a hooked fish.

'Whazzat? Whoozit? Whashappenin? Getawayfrommeee!'

Quinn backed off and gave him ranting room. In short order the tirade was played out. Chambers stood facing her with his head hung and his eyes downcast.

'Sorry, Miz Gallagher. Guess I did it again.'

'Yup, you sure did.'

'Damn. I'm stupid.'

Quinn sighed. 'What am I going to do with you, Chambers? I ought to just drive you right back to Rutland and throw the key away. No passing go, no two hundred dollars.'

Chambers kept eyeing the floor. 'You say so, I'm ready to take my medicine, Ma'am.' He stuck his hands out, wrists together.

Quinn bubbled her lips. 'Don't you get it, you big jerk? If I wanted to send you back, I would have the first time I found you pickled. Your parole's almost over. Less than a month left to go. Can't you just straighten out and behave yourself for twenty-seven more days?'

'You mean you're gonna give me another chance?'

'This is absolutely the last time. I swear it. One more slip, and you can go rot in that jail forever for all I care.'

He smiled and his craggy face lit up. 'Hey, thanks, Miz Gallagher. You're a real nice lady. Real nice.'

'You watch your mouth, buster. Don't you dare call me nice.'

'Okay, sorry.'

Chambers was grinning like the fool he was. But Quinn couldn't discount the guy's other side. He regularly rescued bikes and toys from sidewalk rubbish heaps and fixed them up for poor kids. He'd spent hours modifying old Mrs Lewis's house so she could get around after her stroke. Refused to take a nickel for the work. On one recent visit, Quinn had made an offhand mention of Bren's preparing for the upcoming softball tryouts. By the time she returned the following week, Chambers had rigged an ingenious contraption the boy could use for solo batting practice.

'You screw up, I'll haul your dumb butt in personally. You hear me, Dudley Chambers? I'm not laying myself on the line for you again.'

'Yes, Ma'am. Promise I'll be good.'

'No bourbon or whatever else happens to call your name from the package-store window, promise?'

'Scout's honour.'

'And you'll go to your AA meetings, regularly?'

'There's one in half an hour over at the Congregational. I'm on my way.'

Quinn looked him over and took a whiff. 'Better wait for tomorrow. Someone lights a match near you, the Congregational could be blown to Kingdom Come.'

Chambers grinned and saluted. 'Whatever you say. I sure owe you, Miz Gallagher. Ever you need something, anything at all, you just holler.'

'I'll keep it in mind. For now, all you can do for me is get yourself straight and stay that way.'

'Oh, I will,' he said, with all the sincerity of a puppy promising never again to soil the rug. 'You have my word.'

Levitsky was not in the car. Quinn walked to the corner and spotted him in a phone booth half a block down on Main Street. She caught his eye and tapped her watch impatiently. But he took his sweet time finishing his conversation and meandering back in her direction.

'You up for lunch?' he said. 'There's a place down that way.'

Quinn's stomach rumbled in response. 'I guess.'

'Listen, this afternoon I'd like to take a run up to St Albans. There are some loose ends in Weir's records I want to clear up. Thought I'd do that and then approach him for the interview tomorrow. Okay?'

Guy was too much. 'Obviously you don't know St Albans, Mr Levitsky. One doesn't just take a "run up", as you put it.'

'I know that. I just got off the phone with the warden's office. They're expecting us.'

'I'm not talking about making an appointment, I'm talking about a three-hour drive.'

The discussion was interrupted by the chirp of Quinn's beeper. She kept Levitsky in her sights as she went to the phone booth and dialled the number on the pager's display: Jake Holland's number.

Perfect timing. Whatever else Jake was calling for, he was going to get an earful of complaints as a bonus. Quinn had plenty to tell him about this Bernie Levitsky character. Man was unreasonable, made outrageous demands.

She was set to do her best whining. But something in

Jake's voice derailed her. She listened with a mounting sense of horror. Hanging up, she directed her leaden feet in Levitsky's direction and tried to dismiss the impossible implications.

'What's wrong?' Levitsky said. 'You look horrible.'

'That was Jake Holland,' she said. 'He wants to see us immediately.'

'He say why?'

Quinn's stride was frantic. Levitsky kicked into a near run to keep up. 'He say why?' he repeated. 'What the hell's going on?'

She got into the car and gunned the engine. She wanted to throw something, or someone. Damn this. Damn everything.

'What is it?' Levitsky said. 'Would you please tell me.'

Quinn turned to him. Her eyes were ablaze. 'A few minutes ago, Jake got a call from the mayor of Dove's Landing. Weir's parole to the area was kept quiet to avoid upsetting the neighbours, but the mayor was told. Of course, he was assured it was absolutely safe. That's why he consented to let Weir move to the Waldorf in the first place.'

'And?'

'And now a little girl is missing.'

14 In an awkward crouch, Abigail ran her hands over her feet. Nothing seemed to be holding her, but she was stuck somehow to the concrete floor.

A couple of inches in front of her was a thin red line that ran in a large circle around the room, almost touching the side walls. What was that for? The cold seeped up her bare foot in a spreading rash of gooseflesh. She felt brittle as glass.

'No more!'

'This is a critical test,' he said. 'You must pay strict attention.'

'What did you do to my feet? Let me go!'

'All right. There! You are released. But you mustn't move forward. Not a step over the line.'

She lifted her sneakered foot and rotated it in a cautious circle. Same with the bare one. Icy numb, but no longer bound in place.

Better.

'The solution is revealed in the story I'm about to tell you,' he said. 'The answer is clear. Obvious. You must pay attention to the tale, first word to last, and respond accordingly. Do you understand?'

'Please, I can't do this any more. I don't feel well – honest. You've got to let me go home right now.' She was desperate to get home, to be with her mother. Abigail could almost feel the comforting circle of her mom's arms. She hugged herself and wished.

He spoke in a soothing singsong. '. . . Once there was a beautiful, fair-haired princess who lived in a lovely crimson castle. The princess was so smart and enchanting, she captured the fancy of the cruel, ugly ogre in the dark kingdom beyond the castle's walls.

'The princess knew the ogre couldn't touch her as long as she remained within the safe confines of the castle. But she

94

longed for freedom. Hours each day, she dreamed of running in the woods, drinking the sunlight, caressing the wind.

'Recognising the princess's desire, the ogre decided to draw her to her own destruction with his tantalising spells.

'First, he tempted her with the most glorious flowers. He knew how the princess loved the pretty blooms, so he offered them in wild, flaming masses. Dahlias and zinnias, cosmos and shasta daisies, all so sweet and inviting the princess ached to run through them and press them to her face and pick bunches and bunches. Behold!'

Suddenly, Abigail found herself at the edge of a huge, breathtaking garden. Thousands of brilliant flowers quivered in the haze of a resolute sun. She closed her eyes to block the incredible image. But she could still hear the papery blossoms rustling in the toasted breeze. And she was enveloped by their scent, so rich and sugary, it made her nose itch. Opening her eyes again, she stretched her finger towards a giant yellow dahlia that was exactly like the hybrid Mim had developed and named 'Sunny Abigail' after her. But before she could make contact, the field of flowers vanished with a jarring pop and she felt a screaming pain.

Abigail recoiled. She stuck her finger in her mouth to ease the sting. 'Hey! That hurt!'

He ticked his tongue. 'I told you. The ogre wove wonderful spells. Illusions of the first order. But they were all to entice the princess. She had to learn to rise above them, to *transcend*.

'Meanwhile, the ogre was determined to fool the princess into a deadly error. And he presented her with the most seductive of all temptations.'

There was a creaking sound. Abigail turned to the source and saw a tiny gap opening in the wall. It grew slowly, allowing a sliver of daylight that stretched to a sword. Through the split, she could see a stand of budding trees and a small white house in the distance.

Freedom.

Her heart hammered. The opening was getting bigger. A slim column now. In a few seconds it would be large enough for her to squeeze through sideways. Then, she'd make a run for it. Someone had to be in the house. Smoke curled from the chimney, and a truck was in the driveway, idling in a shimmer of engine fumes.

'Is the princess smart enough to see the trick? Or will she be fooled by the ogre's illusion? Does she understand that the only escape is *transcendence*?'

Abigail steeled herself. Her muscles were tensed to the burning point. His voice came from upstairs and across the house, so she'd be able to run through the opening before he could reach her. Once the wall slid apart another inch, she'd get the hell out.

But why was he letting her go?

Was it another rotten trick?

She thought about what he'd said. There was the ogre. Clever as the princess and trying to tempt her to her own destruction.

Was the danger real, or was he just trying to fool her into straying outside the red circle? She stood frozen by uncertainty. Her finger throbbed. Was the invisible burning thing all around?

Careful to stay behind the line, she untied the red windbreaker from around her waist. Holding it by one of the cuffs, she flicked the rest into the forbidden area.

Instantly, the distant sleeve went up in a rain of sparks. There was the acrid stench of scorched chemicals.

Abigail recoiled from the red line. The ruined sleeve of the jacket was burned black and trailing licks of smoke.

Huddled against the canvas sack, she started to cry. The sobs gathered force, and she made no attempt to restrain them. She wept until nothing remained but syncopated tics of leftover grief to break the crackling silence.

With the tail of her T-shirt she mopped her face. She ached for home and hugs and familiar faces. She could almost feel the sweet comfort of fresh sheets and fluffy pillows turned to the cool side and the breeze ruffling the lacy canopy over her bed.

Tomorrow Steph had promised to give her a rollerblading lesson. Or was it today? Everything was so mixed up.

All she knew for certain was that Daddy would be at the inn any time now. She had to be there when he showed up. Otherwise, he might think she wasn't interested and leave again without ever seeing her. Abigail would die before she'd let that happen. That weirdo mean creep was not going to keep her from her daddy.

The void in her belly began to fill with rage and a stony resolve. She was the clever princess. No sick, rotten ogre was going to keep her prisoner in this ugly place.

Abigail remembered what he'd said. The answer was in the story, in the words.

The crack in the wall stopped growing. There was a hush followed by the mocking pulse of his bat laugh. She blocked it out and concentrated hard on remembering exactly how he'd told the tale. It came to her in teasing pieces. Ogres, spells, temptations, danger.

Dancing thoughts, butterfly dreams. She was struggling to sort it out when exhaustion overcame her in a warm, black rush.

15 Jake was trying to act calm about the meeting with Mayor Wellacott, but Quinn could tell his nerves were as frayed as hers. Waiting for the mayor's arrival, he checked the coffee urn a dozen times, rearranged the conference-room furniture, and made four trips to the men's room. He even refused to take a call from his cherished Marilyn.

'Tell her I'll get back to her later. I want to be sure everything's in order before Wellacott arrives.'

'This is not a bar mitzvah, Jake,' Quinn said. 'If the mayor doesn't like the arrangements, maybe he'll do us a favour and leave in a hurry.'

'Promise me you'll hold that temper of yours, Quinn. I need to know I can count on you.'

'I'll be the model of civility, Jake. Don't worry. I have no interest in making this any worse than it already is, believe me.'

'I mean it. You can't blast off on this character, no matter what he says. No matter how outrageous he acts.'

'Relax. You make it sound as if I'm some unpredictable force of nature. I assure you I'll be the consummate professional.'

Levitsky coughed to cover a chuckle. Quinn heard it anyway and responded with all due restraint.

'Who do you think you're laughing at, you know-it-all, bigmouthed, opinionated, overbearing creep?'

'Quinn!' Holland's mouth was a circle of horror.

'It's okay, Jake,' Levitsky said. 'Ms Gallagher is just being her regular, consummate professional self.'

'That's it. Consider yourself under a gag-order for the duration of the meeting,' Holland told her, his face aflame. 'Not one unauthorised word. You read me?'

'Yes, Jake.'

'Not a peep. Not a gesture. No faces, no nothing.'

'I said, all right.'

Quinn would find some way to stay mute. If necessary, she could amuse herself with castration fantasies featuring agent Levitsky and Brendon's batting machine.

Minutes later, the mayor of Dove's Landing descended on headquarters trailing cosmetic fumes and a chill air of arrogance. His wardrobe was obviously expensive, but singularly uninspired: knife-edged grey gabardine slacks, silk shirt, cashmere blazer with monogrammed gold buttons.

Without waiting for an invitation, he positioned himself at the head of the conference-room table and clasped his manicured hands. Quinn was not one to make snap judgements, but it was obvious the guy was humourless, absurdly impressed with himself, and a world-class sonavabitch, not to mention vapid and materialistic and probably fixated on his mother.

Jake started to make introductions, but Wellacott dismissed the gesture, along with Quinn and Levitsky, as irrelevant.

'I'll keep this short and to the point, Holland. My only reason for coming here was to let you know I hold you personally responsible for Abigail Eakins' disappearance. Anything happens to that little girl, it's your neck.'

'I can appreciate your being upset about the child, Mayor,' Jake began. 'We all are. But I don't see . . .'

'Then I'll paint you a picture,' Wellacott snapped. 'Dove's Landing is a safe, peaceful community. I haven't had a serious crime in my town since the day I took office. Now you bring this . . . this animal to live in the midst of my good citizens, and suddenly a lovely, talented child is missing. A child who happens to belong to dear personal friends of mine. You will answer with your job and more, Mr Holland. Unless that little girl is returned unharmed, and quickly, I'll sue you and everyone involved for all you're worth and more.'

Holland tensed, but he didn't blow. 'I can assure you there's been no breach of Weir's security,' he said, 'but I've ordered a thorough search of his person and property to double-check. Special agent Levitsky here is from the FBI. He and several troopers will participate along with Ms Gallagher, Weir's parole officer.'

Wellacott eyed Quinn and sniffed. 'Figures.'

Quinn bit her tongue. Hard.

'Obviously, what all of us want is to find Abigail Eakins,' the FBI agent said. 'With your authorisation, I can offer full bureau support in that regard, Mayor Wellacott. Nothing gets our people fired up like a possible kidnapping. All I need is for you to say the word, and I'll make the call.'

'You'll do no such thing. I will not allow a bunch of pistol-packing strangers to come into my town and frighten people to death. Our state troopers are perfectly competent to handle the investigation.'

'Then let the Bureau work with them,' Levitsky suggested. 'Our resources . . .'

'I said no. You have a problem with your hearing, Agent Levitsky?'

The G-man kept his calm too. Incredible.

'Frankly, I'm not impressed by your precious Bureau,' Wellacott said. 'Offhand, I can think of a dozen cases where your people didn't find missing children until they were well past saving. Our troopers have agreed to undertake a full-scale search-and-rescue operation: tracking dogs, helicopter sweeps, the works. They are more than capable of managing this case without your so-called resources.'

He turned to Jake. 'By the way, Holland, *I* will select the troopers to search Weir and the house. Obviously you have a vested interest in finding everything in order. Levitsky and the girl can go along if you like, but it'll be under my people's supervision. I'm not about to let you trump this thing up in your own favour.'

Jake reddened. 'If that will help convince you of Weir's innocence in this, fine. Use whoever you like.'

Wellacott puffed his lips. 'Convince me? Hardly. Your little search is for nothing but effect as far as I'm concerned. I'm not familiar with the mumbojumbo monitoring system Weir is on, but I want whatever read-outs or records you keep so I can have them examined by an outside expert. Get them to me by noon tomorrow.'

'All right,' Jake said.

Quinn could not believe Jake would just sit there and take it. The man was threatening to ruin them because he felt like it. Facts didn't matter to him. Neither did the missing child. All he cared about was covering his own overprivileged behind.

'You'd better hope that child is found pronto,' Wellacott said. 'Or you'd better start thinking about new careers.' With a contemptuous nod, he stood and left.

Jake pinched the bridge of his nose and slumped in his chair. 'So it looks like we prove Weir's clean to the mayor's satisfaction. Or we deal with the consequences.'

'Nonsense,' Quinn said. 'He has no right to lay this on us.'

'Maybe not,' Jake said, 'but apparently he intends to do so anyway.'

'You should have bent over and asked him for a kiss,' Quinn said. 'Who does he think he is anyway?'

But Jake refused to be baited. 'He thinks he's filthy rich and extremely well-connected,' he said glumly. 'As I understand it, the family owns one of those cosy international conglomerates with interests in dozens of industries. Over the years, Wellacott tried his hand in a number of different businesses, but his performance was less than stellar to say the least. Guy's reputed to have a reverse Midas touch. Turns gold into garbage. So the family has encouraged him to be a career dilettante. Politics is the latest in a long list of short-lived passions.

'Rumour has it he's got his eye on much higher office,' Jake went on. 'What he needs is a springboard to national fame and glory, and this situation would do perfectly. Has all the potential elements: drama, pathos, public outrage. When Wellacott decides it's strategically the right time to break the news that Weir's in town and a child is missing, the press will swarm on it like a plague of locusts.'

'There's got to be something we can do besides bowing down to that pompous fool.'

'I wish,' Jake said, 'but I'm afraid all we can do is stand

behind Weir's security measures and continue with business as usual.'

'But it's not right. Why should we let some pedigreed jackass come in here and push us around? He admitted he doesn't even know about Weir's security system. Maybe if he did . . .'

Levitsky caught Quinn's eye and flashed a loaded look. Quinn tried without success to catch his meaning. He mugged again, but she still didn't get it. Finally, he gave up and turned to Jake.

'We'll be in Dove's Landing first thing tomorrow. Want us to bring Wellacott those tapes from the perimeter cameras and the tracings from Weir's monitor?'

'Actually, that'd be a big help, if you're sure it won't be out of your way.'

'No problem,' he said.

Quinn stiffened, but she didn't argue. Holland was upset enough already. So was she, for that matter. She got to her feet and shrugged into her jacket. 'Don't worry, Jake. It'll all work out.' The assurance was as much for herself as Holland.

'That it will, one way or the other,' Jake said.

Quinn eased the stranglehold on her temper as they left the building. 'I don't mind dropping off those tapes, Levitsky. But in the future, let me do my own volunteering, will you? Maybe it slipped your little mind, but it's my car we're driving in and my schedule you took it upon yourself to rearrange.'

He stopped in the centre of the parking lot. 'You still don't get it, do you? Holland has no choice but to keep a low profile, but that's not going to make this mess disappear. There are ways to try to confirm or deny Weir's involvement in that child's disappearance. If he's really clean, your office is off the hook. If he's not, we can do something more effective than play ostrich. In either case, I'm sure you don't want to hand Weir or the mayor any advantages.'

'Why didn't you say all this to Jake?'

'Because if you weren't so blinded by that chip on your

102

shoulder, you'd see that Jake's hands are tied. Wellacott's set this up so Holland can't make a move without tripping a political land mine. If he acts as if he suspects Weir, he strengthens Wellacott's case against him. I'm willing to pick up the slack. I can do some digging and pretend it's all part of my study, but I'll need co-operation from someone in your office, and it can't be Holland.'

'So I'm elected.'

Levitsky didn't answer. He just stood there in the centre of the lot. Then no further discussion was necessary. Quinn had a giant stake in this. Much bigger than she cared to admit, even to herself.

'All right, Levitsky. I'm in.'

'Good.' Walking towards the jeep, Levitsky laid out the plan; proposed several tedious ways to test Weir's guilt or innocence in the missing-child case. Some of it sounded like a giant pile of busy work to Quinn, and she wasn't too shy to tell him so.

The agent listened and shrugged. 'The difference between you and me, Ms Gallagher, is that I'm willing to work my way through a problem, step by step. I'm willing to learn from what I hear and see and read and make considered, reasoned judgement. You prefer to fly by the seat of your pants.'

'No. The difference between you and me, Mr Levitsky, is that I'm willing to mind my own business.'

A muscle twitched in his cheek, but his expression didn't waver. 'Fine. You're right. It's nothing to do with me. I simply thought you might want to pursue this logically, and I was stupidly willing to stick my neck out and get involved. But by all means, forget it. It's not my butt on the line here.'

Quinn was steaming. One thing she couldn't stand was a person who was absolutely right and knew it. She blew a mammoth breath. Enough to put out most fires, though not quite sufficient to douse her own incendiary temper.

'All right, Levitsky. You win. If you're sure all this is necessary, I'll play it your way.'

'You say it like you're doing me a favour.' Wry chuckle.

'You know, Gallagher, you're absolutely the most impossible woman I've ever met.'

'Thanks, Levitsky,' Quinn said with a smile. 'I try my best.'

16

Quinn could hear them downstairs.

'Bend over, Weir. Now spread 'em.'

'Certainly, officer. Whatever you say. Is that *wide* enough? Can you see *everything*?'

While an armed state cop and two corrections officers from the Rutland Prison conducted Weir's strip-search in the den, Quinn, Levitsky and another trooper appointed by Mayor Wellacott had split up to inspect the house. The team was under orders to go over every inch of the place and the prisoner with a nit comb.

'Now hike up the family jewels, Mr Weir. One at a time.'

'Yes, officer. You feel free to look as *long* and *hard* as you like.'

'Yeah, I can hardly take my eyes off you, Weir. Fascinating, really. Looks exactly like a dick, only smaller.'

Quinn chuckled. The work did have its moments.

But this particular moment paled quickly. There was nothing amusing about the situation. As Jake had explained it, the local child who'd disappeared fit the profile of Weir's earlier victims: same age range, same blonde hair and slim, athletic build as Jennifer Buckram and the murdered child in Bennington. Most damning of all, the missing girl lived at the inn directly down the hill from Weir's house.

Easy grabbing distance.

Weir's bedroom was carpeted in a grey wool berber. The dresser, nightstands, and bed frame were finished in black lacquer. Recessed lights in deep silver sockets cast ominous shadows on the pearl grey walls. Forced air heating wafted through metal grilles at ankle level.

Quinn rifled every drawer and cabinet, checking for false sides and bottoms and making certain no contraband had been taped to the frames. Next, she removed the haphazard clumps of clothing from the dresser. In addition to his numerous other virtues, the guy was a grade A slob.

Methodically, she lifted each garment and shook it out. She checked pockets, cuffs and seams. Weir favoured black shirts and trousers in flowing fabrics. Costumes. His scent clung to everything, dark and musky.

She cringed at having to touch his things. All too intimate and repugnant. Too much like touching the beast himself. The drawers revealed small personal secrets. He knotted his socks in pairs. Wore silky briefs, all black. Had no jewellery except an ancient gold pocket watch on a chain. It bore an uncanny similarity to the one Quinn had inherited from her grandfather. She flipped open the case and discovered a yellowed snapshot of a man inside the cover. Had to be Weir's father or grandfather, she thought.

Downstairs, the body search was still in progress. 'Open your mouth wide, Weir. Lift your tongue now.'

'Whatever you say, officer. Whatever you'd *like*.'

'I'd like to step on your fucking head, jerk. Now cut the wisecracks and do what you're told.'

Finished with the drawers, Quinn turned over the bed-side braille clock and examined the radio. She felt the charcoal comforter for suspicious lumps and stripped it off the bed. There were a couple of stiff stains on the silver bottom sheet. Pulling that away, she ran a palm over the mattress and flipped it to check the underside and examine the box spring.

'Tongue down now, Weir. Now stick it out. Further.'

Only a few garments hung in the closet: a black cotton robe, a thin khaki jacket, the standard court-appearance suit in a deep convict blue. The single white shirt had a soiled collar and sweat stains under the arms. Quinn checked the shelves, top and bottom. She scrutinised each of his three identical pairs of black oxfords, noting the dried muck and debris he'd picked up in the Waldorf's yard. Feeling inside the shoes, she winced at the slimy dampness and fetid smell.

No sign of loose boards or fake panels in the closet or anywhere in the room. No acoustical tiles or dropped ceiling

106

or other obvious place to store forbidden tools or weapons or even the most compact corpse. She unscrewed all the electrical plates and removed the metal grilles over the heating ducts to search underneath. Found nothing but yawning tubes caked with dust.

'Now spread your toes, Weir,' came the voice. 'Raise your arms over your head. Higher.'

From other parts of the house she heard furniture scraping across the floor, tapping sounds, the clatter of dishes and silverware as one of the troopers checked out the kitchen. Levitsky had volunteered to inspect the outside perimeter of the house and the basement. Quinn had the whole upstairs. Fun city.

Finished with the bedroom, she moved on to Weir's bath. Another mess. The glass shelf over the sink bore a jumble of soaps, prescription vials, shaving equipment and brushes matted with hair. Wet towels were heaped on the floor beside the porcelain tub. Weir had dropped his dirty clothes between the tub and toilet, not bothering with the large wicker hamper under the window.

Disgusted, she forced herself to test every tile and crevice for false fronts and hollows. She emptied the medicine chest and probed for loose panels. She inspected the toilet tank and checked for fake joints or inserts in the pipes. The waste basket was empty except for a couple of blank sheets of crumpled paper.

Having gone over the spare bedroom, bath and linen closet, her final assignment was the attic. Quinn pulled down the folding staircase mounted up through the linen closet ceiling. Climbing to the top, she found a string dangling from a porcelain socket. A tug activated the bare bulb and cast the cramped space in a puddle of yellow light.

She heard scurrying. Mice. The flimsy boards over the floor joists were thick with droppings and dust. Cottony webs draped the air vents and the hulking skeleton of an ancient fan. This was the only part of the house that still showed its age and history.

Before it was renovated for Weir, this place had stood empty and neglected for decades. Ironically dubbed the

Waldorf-Astoria, the dump had been adopted as mischief-central by local adolescents. They'd come here to drink beer or play hooky or wait for tempers to cool after report cards arrived at home. Here, Quinn knew from her own highly forgettable experience in a similar small town hovel, countless virginities had been lost or stolen or, at least, temporarily misplaced.

A month ago, after Langdon Industries completed negotiations with the absentee owner, the house had been boarded up and patrolled until the kids gave up and relocated.

The trapped heat in the attic settled on Quinn like a shroud. She had to stoop to avoid knocking her head on the squat ceiling. Playing her flashlight from wall to wall, she spied the standard house entrails: electrical wires, ducting, metal flues. Nothing worthy of closer inspection, she decided. No way a blind man could negotiate the space in any event. There were large uneven gaps between the plywood sheets over the joists. One false step, and he'd put a foot through the ceiling of the room below.

She backed down the flimsy stairs and hefted them to their original position.

'All clear upstairs. You finished down there?' she called.

There was a flurry of activity, but no answer.

'Okay for me to come down?'

'Yup,' came a voice. 'It's fine.'

Quinn took the stairs two at a time, eager to get out of this place. She didn't like breathing the same air as that animal.

One of the state cops was finishing his inspection of the living room. Levitsky was still bumping around in the basement. Quinn headed for the den to tell the trio with Weir that she was leaving. The view from the doorway stopped her dead.

Weir was naked. At the sound of her approach, he flashed a lascivious grin and executed a coy, little bow. Quinn turned away quickly, but not fast enough to avoid the repugnant eyeful: the curly thatch of hair on his tattooed chest, the ragged line leading to his thick middle, the

108

dangling tube of pale flesh below, twitching in the first stages of arousal.

'Hey, hope that thing of yours isn't loaded, Weir. Bet that'd be a serious parole violation, wouldn't it, Ms Gallagher?' said Ralph Norman, the paunchier of the two state troopers. The others started to laugh, their giggles spawning fat gales of hysteria.

Quinn was trembling with rage. Not trusting her voice, she stormed out of the house. Fools had no idea of the damage they'd caused with their idiotic stunt. Weir had been allowed across the line. Not just allowed, invited. They'd given the beast licence to view her as fair game for ridicule and harassment.

And all for what? Moronic macho posturing. A stupid sophomoric dirty joke. Another cheap shot at a favourite target? When the hell was it going to stop?

Venting her fury, she drove towards Rutland at breakneck speed. Quinn was daring some anonymous trooper bastard to stop her. She'd smile real pretty and run the sonavabitch over. Those idiots with Weir weren't the only ones who enjoyed a good laugh.

By now, the tale was probably top ten with a bullet on the police-band hit parade. She didn't even bother to tune in and find out. She tested her options and trashed them in turn. Damned story was going to spread like the plague no matter what she did. She could already imagine the snide remarks and nasty asides she'd have to endure. She'd been through it all before. More times than she cared to consider.

Trying to cool off, she stopped at the diner for an iced tea. Sat awhile. Shredded an entire holder full of napkins. Considered all the possible ways one could assault a deserving soul with a long-handled spoon.

The diversion didn't work. When she turned into the lot at headquarters an hour later, her blood was still at a roiling boil. Her cheeks were hot, temper loaded with the safety off. The first person who opened his mouth to her, or even thought about it, was damned well going to be sorry.

Jake's office door was ajar. Through the gap she spied Bernie Levitsky spewing his side of a heated conversation.

Quinn took a seat and waited for the talk to wind down. The FBI man would be a perfect place to dump the cargo of unclaimed rage she was hauling.

The discussion continued, the words hurled like live grenades. Quinn couldn't see Jake, but she wondered what had Levitsky so riled. His jaw was jutted forward, body hunched in a pugnacious stance.

Moments later, Levitsky's temper erupted.

'You stupid jackass,' he said. 'What the hell's wrong with you pulling a stunt like that on her?'

There was a mumbled reply.

'Fine. You want it, you got it.' Levitsky shot a sharp uppercut followed by a staggering roundhouse right to the other man's midsection. There was a blown-tyre sound, a startled groan, and the unseen man hit the floor with a thud. Levitsky stood back panting and rubbing his knuckles.

Quinn raced in to her boss's aid. But the man sprawled on the floor nursing his wounds was not Jake. She recognised the pork-bellied wreckage as Ralph Norman, one of the strip-searchers from Weir's house. His supercilious smirk had yielded to an egg-sized swelling on his lip. His nose was bleeding, and his right eye was the size and colour of an individual blueberry soufflé.

Quinn paused and shoved her hands in her pockets. 'Taking out the garbage, Mr Levitsky?' said Quinn.

'Thought I should. You don't take it out, it starts to stink.'

'How true. In fact, it was stinking already.'

The trooper creep hauled himself up and dusted his rump. 'You're a fucking maniac, Levitsky. I've got half a mind to call your fucking boss and fucking tell him.'

'That's a fact, scum. You do have half a mind,' Levitsky said.

Norman skulked out, mumbling. 'Fucking lunatic. No fucking sense of humour. Whole thing was a joke, for chrissakes.'

Quinn heard him still muttering as he passed outside the office window. 'Maniac thinks he's John fucking Wayne.' She waited until he was safely out of earshot.

'Where's Jake?'

'I don't know. He was gone when I got here.'

'Lucky thing,' Quinn said. 'He likes us all to play nicely together.'

'So do I, ordinarily.'

Quinn couldn't help smiling, but she did her best to cover it with a mock yawn. 'I know you meant well,' she said. 'But I can fight my own battles.'

'I don't doubt that, Ms Gallagher. But since he was begging for it, didn't seem right to turn the guy down. You okay?'

She shrugged. 'Fine, if you don't count being the state's number one laughing stock and the fact that it'll take me a month with Weir to get back to where I started. What was the final word on the search?'

'Everything was squeaky clean.'

'That's good news. Now all we have to do is wait for Hurricane Wellacott to blow over.'

'I'm not so sure he's going to, Gallagher,' Levitsky said. 'You know you can still beg off this case. Especially with what's happened.'

'Wrong. What's happened makes it even more important for me to stick with it. The Little Miss Muffet act doesn't fly real well in this business. Believe me, I know.'

'This isn't about appearances. If Weir starts thinking he's got you at a psychological disadvantage, he might decide to see how far he can push it, alarm or no alarm.'

Quinn didn't bother answering. There was more at stake here than the FBI could begin to imagine. She was on this case for the duration, whatever the consequences.

17 When Nora returned to the inn, she found Charlie in the office working on the blueprints for the overhaul of the town's summer theatre complex. The plans had shrunk in inverse proportion to the state's budget overruns. A dance studio had been scrapped. Ditto the proposed outdoor amphitheatre. Instead, the focus had fallen on renovations to the main building with its large-capacity auditorium and complex backstage and storage facilities.

Charlie had nothing to report about Abigail except a barrage of solicitous follow-up calls from the friends and relatives they'd contacted last night. Still no word from Raymond.

'Guy's never been around when you needed him. No surprise he isn't this time.'

'Please, Charlie. Let's not play that stuck record again. Not now.'

Nora told him about her meeting with Justin Wellacott and the mayor's promise to get the police on the case.

'Wellacott's an ass,' Charlie said.

'Maybe so, but he's willing to help.'

'Justin's not interested in helping anyone but Justin. He's just trying to play the big shot to impress you. It's obvious he's got a thing for you, Nora.'

'That's nonsense,' she bristled. 'Anyway, I don't give a damn what his motives are. All I care about is finding Abigail.'

'I understand, honey. But it's a mistake to count on him.'

'I think you're wrong,' she said. 'He may not be Mr Wonderful, but he's a man of his word.'

'Right, and his word is "bullshit".'

Nora flushed with anger. 'At least he's willing to do something.'

'Meaning I'm not?'

112

'Well, you aren't, are you? You think Abigail simply ran away, and I'm nuts.'

'No, I don't. I think you're upset.'

'Of course I'm upset. If you gave a damn about her, you would be too.'

He looked slapped. 'I'd do anything for you, Nora. For both of you. You know that.'

'All I know is I want my little girl back, and I'll take my help wherever I can find it.'

He tried to wrap her in his arms, but she stiffened and pulled away. 'Justin wants some additional shots for the brochure. I'm going to get on with it. If I don't keep busy, I'll go nuts.'

'Please don't shut me out. What can I do? What do you want?'

She caught the mix of sorrow and bewilderment in his eyes. Turned away. What she wanted was obvious.

'I'll be back in a while.'

Eyeing the mess in the studio, she decided she lacked the will or energy to put things back in order. Avoiding the four blank glossies still hanging from the drying rack, she stuffed her lenses and extra film in a case, strapped her Nikon around her neck, and started walking the property.

She didn't know what she was after. Quirky? Interesting? Justin Wellacott had made himself perfectly unclear, which probably meant he had no idea what he wanted either.

Fine with her. The best shots came as surprises. Fleeting moments when light, camera, and action blended in a magical stew. You couldn't plan or recreate the scenes. Nora had learned that the hard way early on, when she'd tried to rectify mistakes or rearrange nature to suit some preconception. The results had been stiff and disappointing, like heavy-handed makeup or a phony political smile.

Which made her think again of Justin Wellacott and Charlie's reaction to the mayor's offer to intervene with the police. How could Charlie be jealous of that? And even if he were, how could he put some petty resentment above finding Abigail?

Impossible.

Charlie wasn't like that. True, he had a possessive streak, but until now Nora had found it more flattering than onerous. The man was sweet, steady, giving. Or so she'd believed.

But then, she'd been wrong before, dead wrong about Raymond. So she knew she was capable of making mistakes. In Raymond's case, she'd made a huge one: about six-five, two-fifty, with size fourteen feet and an extra-extra-large ego.

She smiled despite herself. Falling for Raymond had been dumb and ultimately disastrous, but certainly defensible. When he put his mind to it, Ray was a baited line. Irresistible until it was way too late. You didn't realise the pretty lure was filled with poison until you'd already swallowed the hook.

But none of that had anything to do with Charlie. The two were worlds apart. Different species.

She was approaching the small lake behind the ring of cabins. In the towering tufts of marsh grass along the bank lay an overturned canoe. A pair of broken sunglasses, a tube of designer sunblock and a weatherbeaten issue of *Esquire* were tangled in the scrub beside the boat. This entire portrait of a yuppie shipwreck must have been buried all winter under a blanket of snow.

She shot the arresting composition from several angles. Eye glued to the viewfinder, she then snapped the sun-dappled surface of the lake and the lovely gazebo on the far shore. Reuben Huff had already slapped a fresh coat of white paint on the lattice walls and started on the deep green roof. Soon the sides would be twined with wisteria and purple clematis.

Charlie had proposed to her in that gazebo. It was a long Brill family tradition, he'd told her at the time, dating back several generations.

Could that possibly have been last summer? Seemed a lifetime ago that they'd met at a mutual friend's fortieth birthday party in a SoHo loft. Between the main course and the cake they'd drifted together and stuck like quick-bonding glue.

114

Less than a month later, he'd brought her here to meet his family and see the inn. She'd fallen almost as hard for the place as she had for Charlie. She loved the serene setting, the best of nature in continuous live performances. Sceptical city friends had warned that Vermont was where the suicidal went to die of boredom, but to Nora the place had all the pulse and vitality of midtown, minus the switchblades.

Listening now, she caught the low, throbbing backbeat from the pool motor in the equipment shed beside the lake. Huff had uncovered the pondlike pool in the centre of the courtyard last week, part of the process of readying the inn for the busy summer season.

Another steady beat emanated from the fan in the greenhouse where Mim's herbs and flowers shot flames of vibrant colour. Immediately after the first thaw, the groundsman had turned the soil in the gardens and beds. In a month or so, Mim would begin overseeing the planting of seedlings and flats and the transfer of her prizewinning hybrids from the ancient greenhouse.

Here, all the seasonal changes were made with the automatic ease of a familiar dance step. In their Manhattan apartment, every minor repair and alteration had required complex arrangements and a sacred visitation from that urban deity: the building superintendent.

Nothing had been simple or natural in the city. Before they'd moved to Vermont, Abigail had grown up thinking that vegetables grew in the supermarket bins, that a proper groundcover was uncracked cement, that air was smelly grey stuff you consumed only as necessary and then at your own risk.

So many things had seemed risky. Then maybe it was her constant worry and vigilance that had kept Abigail safe in Manhattan. Here, Nora had felt too protected, been too trusting.

Pushing aside the futile recriminations, she took shots of the greenhouse and the silent stone courtyard. From a rise behind the inn, she used a telephoto lens to shoot the abandoned old house up the hill. Turning back towards the gazebo, she spotted the solitary figure in the distance. As she was trying to decide whether to walk over or turn away, he waved and called.

'Hey, hello! Come on over here.'

She trudged over the spongy ground towards the old man. By the time she reached the front yard of Mim's house, Poppa had settled down in one of the Adirondack chairs and started perusing the *Dove's Landing Daily*

'Poppa?'

'Yes? Help you?' Like an old radio, he could be ice clear or lost in static.

'It's Nora. Charlie's wife, remember?'

'Charlie? Charlie's not married.'

'Yes he is, Poppa. To me. We had the wedding at the inn Christmas Eve, remember? You made that wonderful toast.'

He was a blank. Murky gaze, head cocked like a curious dog.

'I'm Abigail's mom.'

'Oh, Abigail.' He brightened. 'How's that little honey? Haven't seen her today.'

Nora hesitated. 'She'll be back soon.'

He patted the chair beside him. 'Sweet child. You've done a fine job with her. Girl's got manners, shows respect. Not like some. And smart too. Only showed her my antique gun collection one time, and she can recite all the years and models by heart. Even remembers which went with what war. Real honey, that one.'

'Thanks. She thinks the world of you. And she loves your Vaudeville stories.'

He chuckled. 'Thought I was the bee's knees when I ran off to travel the circuit back then. Some Mr Showman I turned out to be. Knew a couple of tap routines, a few comedy bits. Figured I was headed straight for the big time. Wound up doing the soft-shoe backstage with a broom most nights. Don't tell that part to the kids though. Kids want happy endings.'

'So do grown-ups,' Nora said.

He set a weightless hand over hers. You could almost see

him seeping away. Losing substance like a leaky raft. Nora met his gaze. Hard to believe he was the same commanding presence rendered in oils over the parlour hearth. From the painting, Nora knew he'd been the source of Victoria and Stephanie's striking good looks. Now he was frail and faded to the nameless colour of furniture left for decades in the sun.

'I know about Abigail's running away,' Poppa said. 'Heard Mim talking about it with Maisie. Funny how people are always talking around me or over me. Guess they figure I'm a dotty old fool who doesn't hear or remember, so they don't pay me any attention. She'll come home soon. You'll see.'

Nora knew not to upset him with her doubts. 'I'm sure she will.'

'He was the worst of them, you know. Picked on Abigail right in front of me like I'm too old and feeble to do anything. Never carried on with her like that when anyone else was around. Made me so mad. I could see how scared of him she was.'

'Scared of who? Who picked on her?'

He blinked. Ran his fingers over the paper, so they came away black. 'Don't see running away's going to solve anything, but I can't blame her wanting to be out of reach of that rotten creep. Way he was always teasing, acting crazy. Like to pay him back in kind, I'll tell you. Ought to take one of my old muskets to him, see how he likes playing a rabbit on the run. Serve him right.'

'Are you talking about Reuben Huff?'

'Rubin? Hmm. Went to high school with an Ed Rubin. That who you mean? Big pea-brained bully? Bad skin? I ever tell you about the time Ed Rubin deliberately tripped me in the hall when I was on the way to Civics class? Stupid ass knocked my front tooth out, so I had to get a bridge. I was a just a little squirt then. Didn't start really growing till I was fifteen, you know. Shot up a mile that year . . . You ever take a cruise?'

Snap, and he was gone.

'Please,' Nora said. 'Tell me who frightened Abigail. It's very important.'

'Abigail? Is it after three now? Have to take my pills at three. Mother'll scream if I forget.'

She took his hand. 'It's early, Poppa. Mim will be back soon. She'll get your pills, okay? Try to remember about Abigail. Who was she afraid of?'

'Mim? You got any nickels? Gotta call that girl. We've got a date later. Stepping out, with my baby . . .' His eyelids drooped, and he settled in a light snore.

Nora ached to push him further, but she knew it was futile. She'd seen Mim struggle any number of times to prod him back to lucidity when he'd dropped over the edge. Couldn't be done.

Collecting her equipment, Nora started towards the studio. She'd come back and question him again later. If the old man was right, the key to Abigail's disappearance might be someone at the inn. Alibi or no alibi, maybe Reuben Huff was involved after all.

Or maybe it was someone she hadn't yet considered.

Her mind swarmed with the possibilities: staff, guests, neighbours. So many people came and went in this place. Any one of them could have had access to the little girl.

Nora was so preoccupied, she didn't notice the long black Lincoln turning into the drive. Slowly, the insistent honking poked its way into her consciousness. It was followed by the smack of the car door and the sound of an unmistakeable voice calling her name.

She shaded her eyes and watched as he ambled over the soggy ground in her direction. Less than a year since she'd last seen him, but Raymond seemed different. Nora couldn't place the change until he got closer. Once before, she'd seen that look in his eyes.

Once had been more than enough.

18 Raymond strode over the lawn like a duelling gunman at high noon. His eyes blazed fury, and his hands were balled in fists.

'What's happened to Abby, Nora? Where the hell is she?'

'So you got the message.'

His eyes narrowed. 'Hell, yeah, I got the message. Middle of the night, I get a call from my mama. Poor woman can hardly get the words out she's so worried. Tells me Abby's gone. Doesn't know what happened, for chrissakes. So I try calling here, and all four lines are busy nonstop. Three goddamned hours I kept calling, until I finally gave up and got in the car.'

'How'd your mother manage to find you?' Nora said.

'What difference does that make? All that matters is where's Abby. You hear anything yet? She all right?'

'I don't know.' Nora couldn't look at him. Raymond had a way of kicking out her pilings when she was at her shakiest. One of his more endearing talents.

'You don't *know*? What the hell kind of answer is that?'

'An honest one. She's been missing since yesterday afternoon. We're doing the best we can to find her.'

He raised his palms and eyed the heavens. 'You hear that? They're doing their best.' Narrowing his eyes, he spoke through a cage of clenched teeth. 'Anything happens to that little girl, you'll answer for it, lady. She's your responsibility.'

'Is that so? Funny, I thought she was *your* child too. Then maybe I was mistaken. That would certainly explain your pretending she doesn't exist most of the time. Forgetting little things like support cheques.'

He came at her like a tidal wave. For a second, she thought he was going to hit her. She'd never forget the one and only time he had. Hauled off and caught her on the side

119

of the head with a cupped palm. Immediately, he'd gone mushy and repentent, but the damage was done and irrevocable.

For a week afterwards she'd been plagued by a hollow clanging in her ear. Nora had heard those bells the entire time it took her to hire the lawyer, change the locks, and have his things picked up by a group collecting for earthquake victims in Soviet Georgia. The marriage had been dead for quite a while. Time to give it a proper burial.

'Don't hand me that crap,' he said. 'You know I love Abby.'

'Yes. And so do I. Look, the last thing I need right now is a fight with you or anyone, Ray. I'm worried sick.'

He met her eye. Softened. 'Me too. Shouldn't have blown off like that. Sorry.'

'Why be sorry? It's what you do best.'

'Guess I deserve that,' he said. 'You're right. Fighting's not going to bring Abby home. Tell me what's been going on. Must be something I can do.'

They walked to the gazebo and sat on opposite benches. Nora shivered with cold and exhaustion. Raymond slipped off his striped cotton sweater and tossed it over her shoulders. Thing was big enough to sleep six.

Nora had repeated the details of Abby's disappearance dozens of times, but it was different telling the story to Raymond. Watching his face, Nora could see that the big galoot was hurting. True, he didn't love Abigail exactly by the books, but he did love her.

'None of it makes any sense,' Nora said finally. 'The note makes it seem as if she ran away. But then there were those pictures planted in the studio.'

Raymond frowned. 'That picture business sure sounds peculiar. You say they went blank?'

'You don't believe me either.'

'All I said is it sounds peculiar.'

'Damn it, I'm not crazy. I know what I saw.'

He patted down the air between them, urging her to settle with it. 'Easy. I'm not arguing. All I'm saying is it wouldn't altogether surprise me if she did run away. Some of her letters caught up with me a couple of weeks ago. Can't remember her ever sounding so miserable.'

'Letters?'

'In the car. Want to see them?'

He loped off towards the parking lot. Waiting for him to return, Nora reflected miserably on all the screaming signals from Abigail she'd conveniently managed to ignore. Poor kid had tried a dozen ways to tell the people she loved how desperate she was. *And my lame response was to plan a week's vacation in New York.*

And Raymond's had been worse. A couple of weeks since he'd gotten the notes, and he hadn't even bothered to call. How could he be so reckless with his daughter's feelings?

Watching him return like a carefree cowpoke on the range set Nora simmering. By the time he made it back to the gazebo and handed her the pile of pastel envelopes, she was at a boil.

She read the letters without comment. They were full of anguish. Abigail had begged Raymond to come to Vermont and take her to live with him. Several times she made reference to something at the inn that she couldn't stand any more. Same thing she'd said in her note.

When Nora finished reading, she flung the stack of letters at Raymond. 'Why didn't you call and tell me about these?'

He shrugged. 'Figured you knew something was wrong, Nora. She was right here with you, after all. You've got eyes.'

'And you've got a damned big arrogant mouth, Raymond Eakins. I don't see any father-of-the-year medals on your overstuffed chest. If all you came for was to blame and criticise, you're welcome to get lost.'

She stood up and started for the house. He caught up and grabbed her by the elbows. 'I'll go when I see Abby safe. Not before.'

'Take your hands off me.'

'We're gonna figure out how to get along until this thing's over.'

'Fat chance.'

Nora tried breaking loose, but he had her in a vice-like

grip. She flailed and cursed, tried to kick back at him, but he wrenched out of the way. Whipping her head around, she tried to catch at him with her teeth. On a perverse level, Nora was enjoying the battle, venting some of the trapped steam.

'You're a big, fat pain in the ass, Ray Eakins,' she stormed. 'Now let me go.'

'I am not fat,' he said. 'That's all muscle.'

'The only muscle you've got is between your ears.'

'You mind your mouth, you midget. Cut the insults, or I'll . . .' His mock-serious expression crumbled, and he started to laugh.

The giggles were contagious. 'You'll do what, piggy porker?'

'You take that back, you tiny little bitch. Take it back, or I'll tickle you.'

'You wouldn't dare,' she said.

Fighting words. Immediately, he honed in on the deadly ticklish spot on the right side of her waistline.

Nora shrieked her protests. 'Stop it. You stop that this minute, you big bucket of flab!'

He kept it up until both of them were convulsed with hysterical laughter.

'Puff-ball, blubber-belly.'

'Miserable munchkin.'

They were breathless, screeching insults, greedy for the chance to forget that Abby was missing, that something was deadly wrong, that they'd both failed their daughter. Nora was running out of fresh lines when Ray suddenly let her go.

'You giving up? Getting soft in your old age?' His smile warped into a spasm.

'What a face,' she said. 'Hey. You okay?'

But he didn't seem to hear her. The grimace tightened. With a convulsive shudder, he grabbed his shoulder and crumpled to the ground.

'Okay. Enough. That's not funny,' she said.

Nora leaned over him. His lips moved, but no sound emerged.

'Ray? Are you okay? What's wrong?'

'Something got me,' he breathed. 'My back.'

'One of your more convincing practical jokes, buddy.' She put a hand under his shoulder. 'Come on, you big lard. Get up.' She tried to give him a boost, but her palm skidded over a warm, sticky substance. Prickles of shock scaled her back as she withdrew her hand. Her fingers were slicked with blood.

But how?

There was shouting in the distance. Tracking the sound, she saw Poppa approaching. One of his antique rifles was tucked under his arm. Smoky residue wafted from the barrel.

Sparks of terror erupted in Nora's mind.

'Poppa, what happened? What did you do?'

He walked closer. Shaking his head, he leaned and squinted at the large huddled figure on the ground.

'Shot the sonavabitch,' he said with a wry chuckle. 'Should have done it long ago.'

19 Preoccupied with the Wellacott mess, Quinn was already late when she remembered her promise to pick up Brendon after band practice. She sped the distance to the Post Road Elementary School despite Levitsky's attempts to slow her down by hitting his imaginary brake. Guy was clutching the upholstery like a life-line. Barrelling into the deserted school driveway, she spotted Bren's school bag and French horn at the kerb.

No sign of her brother.

Her pulse quickened as she stepped out to look for him. The world was full of child-snatching maniacs. And worse.

'Bren!'

No answer.

Levitsky came up beside her. 'You see if he's inside. I'll check around the back.'

Quinn walked to the front entrance and jiggled the knob. The door was locked. No cars left in the lot. How could she have been so damned careless?

She thought of her mother. Always on the dot, always a step ahead of weather conditions and impending illnesses and the enormous little hurts of childhood. As a parent, Quinn wasn't even such a hot sister.

The building was dark except for the fuzzy red glow of the exit signs at the far end of the main corridor.

'Bren?' she said in a pinched voice. 'Come on, tiger. Where are you?'

She drew a deep breath and tried to see beyond her mountain of apprehensions. Maybe he'd gotten a ride with a friend. Or Mr Bell, the band teacher, might have decided to take Bren home with him. Would have been the responsible thing to do. Then, what the hell did Quinn know about responsible?

'Brendon!' she called. 'Hey, Levitsky? You find anything.'

'Yeah. Back here.'

124

Heart thumping, she raced through the playground to the rear of the school. Why hadn't the FBI jerk called her right away? She pictured Levitsky huddled over her brother's broken body. Attempting mouth-to-mouth.

Instead, in the glare of the waning sunlight, she saw Brendon and the agent hunched side by side in identical poses, heads bowed, knees slightly bent, fisted hands perched beside their right shoulders.

'That's it exactly,' Levitsky said. 'And then you say the magic phrase. Keep repeating it to yourself.'

'Okay,' Bren said. 'You sure it works?'

'Always has for me.'

'All right. I'll give it a try.'

Levitsky retrieved a tree branch from the edge of the field and handed it to Brendon. With minor coaching, the boy resumed his ready stance and took a few practice swats at the air.

Levitsky strode a distance away, staged an elaborate warm-up, and tossed a rubber ball in Bren's direction.

Quinn tensed in reflex, waiting for the missile to zip past her brother untouched. Bren's mouth was pinched, eyes glued to the approaching target. If guts and effort were all it took, the kid would be a major-league all-star by now. Quinn saw his tongue boring into his cheek. Almost time.

Now!

With a neat pop, he connected and sent the ball skipping towards Levitsky. The FBI man caught it and shot Bren a look of mock dismay. 'Hey, I thought you said you couldn't hit a barn door with a load of hay.'

Bren's grin was enough to light a night game. He lowered the branch. 'Guess it was the trick.'

'That helps, but *you* did it, my man. Good cut, would've been an easy single,' Levitsky said. He turned to Quinn. 'Okay if we try one more?'

'Guess so.'

Levitsky revved up and hurled a fast slider. Quinn cursed under her breath. Creep could have used a little restraint. When she practised with the kid, she was always careful to hurl them in straight and easy. Bren would never be able to touch a hot-dog pitch like that.

But the little mug swung his makeshift bat hard and level and sent the ball whizzing over Levitsky's head. Guy had to be near six-four, but he kept his arms down and made a great show of lurching backwards while he let the hit pass him and roll to a stop somewhere beyond a hypothetical second base.

He shook his head. 'I'd have to say that'd be a double, at least, buddy. What was that thing you said about the barn door and the hay again? Is this kid a ringer or what?'

Bren was carbonated. 'You have a catching trick too?' he said. 'Can he stay for dinner, Quinn? Please can you, and we could practise more after?'

'I don't think so, Bren. Mr Levitsky's had a very long day. I bet he can't wait to get back to his hotel and spend a nice, quiet evening all by himself.'

Levitsky beckoned her to a whispered conference. As Quinn listened, she could almost hear her plans for a long, lazy soak and a hairwash gurgling down the drain.

She turned to Brendon. 'Mr Levitsky and I have a lot of work to do tonight, kiddo. We can all eat together, but I'm afraid it's back to business after that.'

'Okay. Can we bring in pizza?' Brendon said.

'I guess.' Quinn loved cooking as long as someone else did it.

'Sounds good to me,' Levitsky said.

Bren retrieved his book bag and French horn from the kerb and hopped in the back of the car, leaving the coveted front seat for the FBI man.

'What do you like on your pizza, Mr Levitsky?' Bren asked. 'You're the guest.'

'It's Bernie. And whatever you like's fine with me: mushrooms, peppers, chocolate chips. Anything but anchovy. Okay?'

'Perfect.'

When Quinn turned to check on Bren's seat belt, he caught her eye and winked. So the little character liked Bernie Levitsky of all people.

Bren wasn't instantly adept at most things, but he was an excellent judge of people. Almost uncanny. Whenever possible, Quinn gave her brother some time alone with a new guy while she loitered upstairs. All it took was ten minutes or so for the kid to get a fix on the subject and compose his review. When she came down, he'd flash her an ice-cream face or a broccoli puss or something in-between. Most often, he was absolutely on target.

But clearly, he was not infallible. The instant affinity for Special Agent Bernie Levitsky confirmed that. Quinn didn't loathe the man as much as she had on first meeting, but he in no way made her think about silver patterns.

True, he wasn't bad to look at, but neither was Ted Bundy. And he did have a way with kids. But then, so did most of the terminally immature. Quinn shook her head and cancelled all further silent debate on the subject. It would be a black day indeed when she was desperate enough to search for redeeming virtues in the likes of Bernie Levitsky.

'Luigi's or Sorrento's?' she said.

'Sorrento's stinks,' said Brendon.

She swung onto the street and headed downtown towards Luigi's. Levitsky and Bren spent the ride discussing baseball, basketball, and football. The talk turned to tennis as she pulled into the garage. Comforting to know their interests weren't confined to team sports.

'How about you come over tomorrow night, and we'll practise some fielding?' Bren said. 'I can lend you a mitt.'

'If it's okay with your sister.'

Quinn felt a swipe of resentment, but she kept it to herself. Coaching Bren happened to be her department, and she didn't appreciate being displaced. But she resolved to be grown up about it. She waited until Bren and the G-man were locked in discussion to stick out her tongue.

'You a rightie?' Bren asked. 'I've got my grampa's old glove from the minors. Gramps played triple A ball two seasons. Would've had a spot on the Sox the next year, but he hurt his elbow. Stupid Nicky Dibble wouldn't believe me until I showed him Gramps' picture in that old newspaper article.'

Kid was pumped. On the way up the stone walk, Quinn set a hand on his shoulder and tried to turn down the volume. 'Easy, honey,' she whispered. 'You don't want to blow a fuse or something.'

He scowled. Silent warning that she was to behave herself. Not act like someone's mother, for heaven's sake. Especially not in front of his brand-new tin hero.

She unlocked the door. 'I'll get the table set. You wash up, Bren.'

He looked murderous. Next she'd be talking bedtime or something equally unspeakable.

'I'd like to clean up, too,' Levitsky said. 'You show me where?'

'Sure, come on.'

They trudged up the stairs in tandem. Bren aped the agent's loping gait and bemused expression. 'Want to see my baseball-card collection? I've got complete sets of the Red Sox from eighty on. Mint condition.'

'Sounds great, but it'll have to be another time. Your sister and I have to get to work soon.'

Levitsky had convinced Quinn that they should view the tapes from Weir's perimeter cameras before turning them over to Wellacott.

Quinn saw Levitsky's point. But she was not looking forward to the task. There was a monstrous stack of tapes to watch. More than two days' worth, Quinn calculated. Even with the miracles of fast forward and strong coffee, it was going to be a very, very long night.

20 Quinn awakened with a start. She had fallen into one of those dense sleeps that trample the line between dream and reality. If not for the telltale ring of nap drool on the sofa cushion, she would have doubted she'd been asleep at all.

The room was dark except for the television screen, where wind-tossed trees and birds in ragged V-formation fluttered around the silent carcass of the Waldorf-Astoria.

Levitsky passed a mug of coffee under her nose like smelling salts. Quinn took it. Had a sip. Liquid mud with one sugar. Needed at least three and probably a side of detergent to make it near palatable.

Quinn tested her muscles. Sat more or less upright on the couch. 'You see anything worth worrying about?'

'Couple of question marks. I'll show you.'

He extracted the current tape from the VCR and rummaged through the marked stack for an earlier one which he raced through to the halfway point. When the picture cleared, Quinn saw a man in a down vest and a baseball cap standing at the split rail fence. His face was obscured by the low-riding bill of the cap. He stood immobile for a few seconds, tossed some pocket trash on the ground, and walked away.

Levitsky hit the remote button for stop action. Backed up the reel and replayed the scene again. In the background Quinn noticed that the living-room curtains remained closed. The man in the cap hadn't gotten anywhere near the house and hadn't made any visible contact with Weir.

'Probably nothing,' Quinn said. Obviously it hadn't raised enough interest at Central to inspire any follow-up. Quinn would have been notified if it had.

'Probably. But I don't think we can afford to overlook anything in the least suspicious.'

Next, he showed her snips from a pair of reels. Quinn

watched, trying hard to concentrate. They were moving pictures, but you'd hardly know it. Trees and birds, lawn and house. A dirt-coloured rabbit, as animated and interesting as a rock, could have claimed star billing.

'That's scintillating stuff,' Quinn said.

'You don't see anything strange?'

'Not unless you mean that bad-ass bunny. You think he might be an accomplice?'

'Look again,' Levitsky said. He ran both clips once more. Quinn was getting a tiny bit impatient.

'Okay, I give up. What's the mystery?'

'Watch the shadow of that big oak next to the house.'

Quinn concentrated on the tree's shadow as Levitsky ran the segments again. In the first one, the stretched mirror-image of the trunk ran almost horizontally across the lawn. The second showed the dark mass cast against the front of the house on the diagonal.

'So?' she said. 'I still don't get it.'

'Supposedly, those reels were shot at the same time on consecutive days. Seems to me the shadows should be at more or less at the same angle.'

Quinn's brain was still pre-heating. 'Then why do you suppose they aren't?'

Levitsky hitched his shoulders. 'Could be a number of reasons. Problem with the timer on the cameras. Mistake in the markings on the reels. Maybe some odd cloud formation played tricks with the sun's angle.'

'In other words, it's probably nothing too.' It had to be nothing. Weir could not have taken that child.

'I hope not. But again, I don't think we can shrug it off without further study. I took some soil and other samples at the Waldorf that I'm planning to pass to my boss at the bureau for analysis. I'd like to send copies of these as well.'

Quinn shrugged. 'Not much time for that. Jake promised he'd have these to Wellacott this morning.'

'There must be someone who can make us duplicates on a rush basis.'

Quinn thought of the perfect person. 'In fact, there is, and his shop isn't far from the Waldorf. I'll drop you at the Waldorf for your interview and go see him.'

She went up to shower and change. Fifteen minutes later, she was dressed in fresh jeans and a white blouse. Semi-formal. Leaving the bedroom, she spotted herself in the mirror over her dresser. No good news there. Her thick red hair was a frothy mess, skin pasty pale, green eyes puffed and red-rimmed.

Still, the shower had revived her somewhat. She decided she was almost up to the Herculean task of waking Brendon for school. But when she peeked in, his room was empty. Downstairs, she found him in the kitchen with the FBI man.

Levitsky was at the stove, surrounded by bowls and utensils, flipping pancakes. He'd ditched his blackboard-coloured bureaucrat suit for distressed denims and a work shirt. Quinn couldn't help but notice that the guy had good shoulders and an excellent rear. Pity to waste such quality buns on a jerkburger.

'You shouldn't have gone to all that trouble, Mr Levitsky.' Translation: the last thing Quinn needed was some crock with a Betty Crocker complex trashing the kitchen.

'No trouble.'

She caught a sloshing sound from the washing machine. Bren's sheets again. Too bad.

'Hey, slugger,' she said, surreptitiously rearranging his sleep-crazed hair. 'How was your night?'

'Great. I had a catching dream. Bernie told me how you can dream about something you're having trouble with, and from then on, you've got it licked. Can't wait to see if it works.'

'Interesting concept,' Quinn said with a pointed scowl at Levitsky. Big-mouth had no right filling the kid's head with such nonsense.

'I know it sounds crazy,' Levitsky said. 'But I had a backhand dream once. Changed my game completely.'

'How nice for you.' What the guy really needed was a

131

personality dream, she thought. Or one where he suddenly reached maturity.

Quinn downed a cup of the fresh coffee Levitsky had perked, and started on a stack of his flapjacks soaked in syrup. Tasted wonderful, but she couldn't recall whether sweets and carbs were good for her or poison under the circumstances. There was some complex nutritional formula for avoiding the surges and lows that followed a mostly sleepless night, but she was way too tired to remember what it was.

They dropped Brendon at school and drove to Dove's Landing. On the way, Quinn wanted to work out the day's schedule, but Levitsky was circling in a solo orbit. Guy had the tight, focused look of a runner on the blocks.

She didn't try to reach him again until they were nearly past the line of shops on Dove Landing's Main Street. 'How long will you need for the interview, Levitsky? I'll take care of copying the tapes, see some clients, and come back for you.'

'Should take all morning for starters. If it goes well, I'll need another half-day session or two. But before you leave, I'd like you to run a little interference for me. I've found it helps to have someone familiar approach the subject and warm him up a little before I go in.'

Quinn tensed, remembering her last encounter with the professor: the leer, the naked body. She would have liked to keep her distance until that episode had time to get nice and stale. Maybe longer.

'What would I tell him?'

'Nothing specific. Just that you've brought someone to meet him. Say I'm a friend.'

'That would be stretching it.'

'Stretch it then. It's for a good cause. The more we can learn about monsters like Weir, the better chance we have of protecting society from them.'

She drew a breath. 'Okay. Wait here. I'll signal you when I'm done.'

Quinn killed the engine at the gate. The Waldorf stood dim and quiet under a sullen sky. Approaching the house,

132

she battled with a vacant, shaky feeling. Had to be fatigue, she decided, refusing to consider that Weird Ellie or any of this impossible situation might be having an adverse effect on her.

A yard from the stakes, she stopped and called Weir's name. No response from inside, so she cupped her hands beside her mouth and raised the volume.

'Mr Weir? I need to talk to you. Open up.'

She heard a vague skittering inside. Sounded like the seeing-eye dog padding back and forth, his nails tapping a rhythm on the wood floor. He chuffed a couple of times and fell silent. Funny how the beast was sometimes vigilant, sometimes oblivious.

'Mr Weir?'

There was a long silence. Quinn turned and shrugged at Levitsky. He shot her a questioning look. But she shook her head in the firm negative in response. The professor had to be there. Unthinkable that he'd slipped away.

She called again and was toying with the idea of a serious panic when the door finally inched open. Weir stood with folded arms and a guarded expression.

'Do forgive me for keeping you, Officer Gallagher, I was . . . indisposed.'

Quinn drew a breath. 'I've brought someone to meet you, Weir. A friend of mine.'

His brow peaked. 'What friend? And for what purpose?'

'He wants to talk to you. He'll explain.'

'No, officer. *You* shall explain. Who is this so-called friend, and what exactly does he want with me?'

Quinn cursed under her breath and motioned frantically towards the car. Got nothing back, so she decided it was time to punt.

'He's a scientist. Doing some kind of research. Really, he can tell you about it much better than I can. Here, he's on the way.' She signalled again and finally heard the reassuring slam of the car door.

As soon as the FBI man arrived at the staked boundary, she backed out of the conversation and let him take over. Quinn listened as he aimed his practised pitch at the professor's ego. Levitsky described his study's potential benefits to mankind, implied that Weir's contribution could enlighten the scientific community and improve the human condition. He kept spouting the terms Weir liked best: unique, fascinating. The professor clung to his scepticism, but he finally allowed Levitsky to manoeuvre him inside the Waldorf. As the door closed behind them, Quinn let her shoulders droop and headed for the car.

It was a short hop to downtown Wilmington. A bell jangled as she entered the Photo Lab. This time, Dud Chambers was on the job. Quinn slalomed through the displays towards the rear stockroom. Dud was hunched over a piece of equipment, listening to light rock on the radio.

'Morning, Dudley. How's it going?'

Guy jumped half out of his skin at the sound of her voice. He tossed a rag over whatever it was he'd been working on and faced her with a guilty grin. All Quinn could see was a slim rectangular shape shrouded by the ragged cloth.

'Miz Gallagher? Hi. Something wrong?'

'You tell me.'

'Nothing wrong here,' he said. 'Just busy. I'm doing this project for a guy. I'd show you, but he asked me to keep it top secret.'

'Nothing illegal, I hope?'

He looked crestfallen. 'Course not. You're never going to trust me, are you?'

Quinn rolled her eyes. 'Don't you get sensitive on me, Dudley. Anyway, I do trust you. Enough to let you handle an emergency job for me. I need copies of these three tapes right away. Can you do that for me?'

He brightened. 'Sure thing.' He took the tapes out of the bag and dropped one in a viewer. He ran through several minutes of film and frowned. 'What's this about, if you don't mind my asking?'

'I'm afraid that's top secret too, Dud. Should I wait or come back?'

He viewed the start of the second reel. Tensed.

'Problem?' Quinn said.

Chambers shot her an anxious look. 'No, Ma'am. I'll make the copies right away. Shouldn't take more than twenty minutes or so.'

'I'll take a walk and be back then.' As she left, Quinn stole another glance at the cloaked rectangle in the storeroom. She was curious, bordering on suspicious. But at the moment, she had far bigger worries than Dud Chambers' penchant for stupidity.

Once she had the copies, she was slated to drop the tapes and tracings off with Mayor Wellacott. Quinn knew she was going to have to hold her tongue hard around that man. Otherwise, she could be signing herself up for a very powerful enemy.

That, she thought, and a great deal of satisfaction.

21 Abigail snapped awake. There was an odd creaking sound. Tracking its source, she saw that the gap in the wall was shrinking. She had to escape before it closed altogether.

Ogres, princesses, castles, spells? If the answer was so obvious, why couldn't she see it? There was no time to figure out his stupid story. Already the opening was visibly smaller.

For some time, she hadn't heard any noises from upstairs. No thumping or witch cackles. Maybe he'd turned the burning thing off and gone out.

Picking up what remained of her scorched windbreaker, she began casting it over the crimson line at intervals. At every attempt sparks shot from the centre to the borders of the red circle. Same thing near floor level. But when she flicked the jacket up high, at shoulder height, there was no chemical stench or pop of embers. She tried again, flinging the jacket overhead like a cowboy's rope. Nothing.

Abigail had a mental image of the bad place. It was shaped like a giant cake.

No way to get around it. The crimson line ran too close to the walls. Even scrunched sideways, she'd stick out into the fiery area. Her only chance was across the top. That's what he must have been hinting at when he said she had to rise above it. 'Transcend' must mean the same thing.

But how?

She studied the ceiling. Between the beams was a tangle of pipes and wires. The pipes were for hot and cold water, the wires for TV and telephone. She knew that from tagging along when Sol the caretaker went to work on the boiler in the apartment-house basement.

Sol had taught her how you could tell the hot water pipe, which connected to the red valve, from the cold, which ran to the blue. Between knock-knock jokes, he'd bragged about the strength of the copper piping and how it would probably hold up longer than the building walls. So she thought it likely that the line would bear her weight.

The gap was contracting further. She had to hurry.

Abigail tracked one copper vein as it ducked through holes in the beams to the shut-off valve on the far wall. The valve was blue, which meant she'd located the cold pipe.

By bending her knees and springing upward as she did to mount the uneven parallel bars in gym, she was able to grasp the greenish tubing. Holding fast, she waited a second. No dangerous sagging. It would hold her.

Working hand over hand, she approached the red circle. Before entering the forbidden zone, she bent her knees, brought them up between her arms, and let her head dangle beneath her. In that awkward position, she began quickly hand-walking the pipe over the danger zone.

Her arms felt pulled and dull. Blood rushed to her head and thundered in her temples. She imagined the bad place pulsing beneath her, waiting to zap her to dust.

Don't think. Hurry!

Working as fast as she could, she slid her hands in a frantic rhythm across the pipe. Afraid to slip, she clutched the chill metal so hard her fingers cramped.

Her arms threatened to give out, but she fought past the pain. There was still a small breach in the far wall. She had to make it in time. Panting, desperate, she scurried the rest of the way across the burning circle. Dropping to safe ground, she allowed a tiny triumphant cry.

'Yes!'

She raced to the gap in the wall. Now it was only a few inches wide. Edging sideways, she squeezed into the gap and began forcing her way through.

The opening was so narrow she could barely move. Trying to compress herself, she sucked in a breath and held it, contracted her muscles. Still her flesh was scraped and squeezed hard against her bones.

Slowly, she forced her way through the tiny aperture. The wall was still coming together. What if she got stuck? Crushed.

Terrified, she pushed harder; strained with all her might until she popped loose like a champagne cork.

She was out.

Too frightened to look back, she tugged off her remaining sneaker and started running towards the white house in the distance. She raced across a level stretch of land dotted with woodpiles and large heaps of litter. Stones and dried grasses lacerated her soles, and her calves ached from the shock of the compacted ground. Her lungs were scorched by low, laboured breaths. Tears streamed from her eyes.

Across the field, she darted to the left and sought the cover of a densely wooded area. Here her footing was cushioned by a carpet of damp, matted leaves. The spongy earth emitted the ripe scent of mould and rotting matter. Watching the ground for errant branches and skittering animals, she sprinted through to the other side.

Emerging, she saw she had only one more grassy rise to negotiate before she reached the white house. It was an easy run but at the crest she would be exposed, clearly visible to her captor if he happened to glance out the window.

The white house looked safe and inviting, but Abigail didn't want the people inside to spot her before she had a chance to check them out. You couldn't be too careful. You couldn't be careful enough.

Dropping to the ground, she began creeping up the gentle slope. The tall grasses were stiff and abrasive, but they would keep her hidden from view in both directions.

Soon she was scratched all over: forearms, palms, the tops of her feet. The grasses clawed her cheeks and pulled her hair. But she was numb to everything except the electric fear sizzling in her gut like a live wire. And all she could think of was getting to safety.

There would be a phone in the house. She could call the inn, and Mom or someone would come for her. Once Abigail was out of that maniac's reach, surrounded by safe people, she'd tell everything and the police would lock him up forever like the dangerous loony he was. No one would treat him like such a damned important big shot anymore.

At the top of the rise, she paused and took a quick look back. No one was coming after her. At least, not yet.

The rest of the way was easier. Shaded by the hill, the ground on the down slope was muddy and soft, the grasses sparser and more pliable. She fairly slid down the gentle incline towards the white house. Abigail had the urge to curl up and roll the rest of the way, but she couldn't risk being out of touch or control. Not for a minute.

A postage-stamp lawn surrounded the white house. The truck still idled in the driveway, now belching plumes of sooty exhaust. Abigail crouched low and bolted towards the rear of the building.

Pressed against the whitewashed siding, she waited for her heart to settle and listened for people sounds. She detected a rhythmic murmur, so faint she couldn't decide if it was someone talking or the rumble of a motor. She'd have to get closer to tell, maybe peek in a window.

No way to do that from where she stood. A screened porch covered in thick plastic sheets for the winter, ran most of the width of the rear. There were two tiny windows beyond, bathroom-sized, but they were well above her eye level. Trying to scramble up the siding and trim would be too risky. If she fell, someone inside would be able to hear.

Peering around the corner, she spotted a larger pane of glass at perfect viewing height. It didn't look large enough for a living-room window. A kitchen, maybe. Or possibly a den, she thought. Whatever it was would do. The house was so small, she could likely see as much as she needed from any decent vantage point.

She padded soundlessly to the window. Shading her eyes, she looked inside. The place was dim and silent. It reminded Abigail of Granny Eakins' house in Charleston: dark, heavy furniture with crocheted doilies on the arms; sombre lamps with yellowed shades; needlework samplers in shadowbox frames; knitted afghans everywhere; lots of books. A cinnamon tabby was curled in front of the blackened brick hearth where the fire was flaming its last in fitful spurts.

No other signs of life. But there had to be someone home. Otherwise, why would the engine be running in the truck?

Abigail strained to listen. Holding her breath, she pressed her ear against the glass.

Again, she heard the steady murmuring. A pump? She had to know what it was. If the house was empty, she'd find a way to sneak inside and use the phone. It was impossible to know how close she was to the nearest neighbour or what she'd find once she got there. She had to call for help before he discovered she'd gotten out and came after her.

Dashing to the opposite side of the building, she peeked into the kitchen. The cabinets were dark wood, the walls papered with a faded print. Potted herbs lined the sill over a sink jammed with dirty dishes.

Stepping closer to the window, she held her breath and listened. The murmuring was louder now. Closing her eyes, Abigail focused on the sound. A rhythmic beat. It grew stronger and clearer as she waited. Soon, it was unmistakeable: the same thumping she'd heard in the prison house.

Immobilised, she saw a large dog lumbering into the kitchen. Behind him, a mass of shadow moved in the hall.

Abigail clamped a hand over her mouth to keep the scream inside. Breaking through the dread, she turned and ran headlong for the cover of the woods.

It had never occurred to her that the white house might belong to him too. From now on, she had to think everything through, consider every possible danger. She wondered if any place was absolutely safe. She wondered if she'd be able to trust anything or anyone ever again.

22 Quinn spent twenty excruciating minutes pacing the streets of Wilmington. Nothing to do, nothing to see. No intriguing shops or serious eccentrics or startling occurrences. Everyone appeared semiconscious at best, dogs included. Whoever invented quaint, idyllic New England towns should be sentenced to a long stay in one of them, she thought.

When she returned to the Photo Lab, she found the duplicate tapes and originals on the counter. In the storeroom, Dud was back working on his secret project, too engrossed to notice her arrival. Quinn called a thank you, scooped up the tapes, and left.

She drove directly to the Town Hall in Dove's Landing only to learn at the information desk that Mayor Wellacott was not in yet and rarely arrived before eleven. Eager to try to convince the pompous jerk to get off their backs, she decided to check on a few clients and return later.

A cluster of her charges worked in Manchester, which had been revived from financial coma a decade earlier by concentrated applications of factory-outlet stores. Now the business district was a powerful tourist lure with its bounty of designer discounts, manufacturer's overruns, seconds and thirds.

Quinn, who found shopping nearly as enjoyable as root canal work, had made one sincere attempt last Christmas to mine the fool's gold in Manchester's bargain bins. Half a day of dazed browsing, and all she'd managed to pick up was a nasty headache. No extra charge.

It took three passes through the congested mark-down mecca before she was able to nab an undersized parking space. A few determined bumps in forward and reverse and she managed to enlarge the opening enough to accommodate her jeep.

Ron Poltrack, paroled after serving most of a three-year

stint for racketeering, was waiting tables at the Magic Dragon Chinese restaurant. No problems there. Poltrack had logged plenty of food-service experience on kitchen detail at Chittendon.

Len Salvatore, who'd been sent up for securities fraud, had been hired to work the cash register at the Designer Coat and Suit outlet half a block from Cole Haan shoes. The assignment had been arranged by the transitional team at the Rutland Prison over Quinn's outraged objections. But so far, no sticky fingers in the till or, at least, none that had been detected.

Next on her list was Andrew Rodman, an acknowledged leader in the credit-card forgery business. Rodman was a crossing guard and part-time cafeteria aide for the school system.

Quinn found him in front of the Junior High, wielding a stop sign on a stick. Guy was fizzing about a potential deal he'd been approached about for movie rights to his life story. Quinn hated to burst his balloon, but she felt compelled to remind him about Son-of-Sam-based laws that would prohibit him from profiting from his crimes.

Ever the schemer, Rodman instantly hit on several promising loopholes he was sure he could slip through on his way to the bank. Guy was so confident, he even talked about getting Quinn a bit-part in the film. Prison did not often rehabilitate, but it did offer inmates ample time to plot a future of better quality crimes.

From the school, she phoned headquarters. Jake Holland had no particularly interesting news on the missing Eakins child. All the evidence continued to point to a simple runaway, but that still wasn't likely to douse Mayor Wellacott's flames.

Quinn tried to sound upbeat and encouraging though her heart wasn't at all in it. She and Levitsky had agreed not to tell Holland anything about their sideline investigation unless they found hard evidence of a problem. Poor Jake was on aggravation overload already. And Quinn knew precisely how that felt.

On the return trip to Dove's Landing, she started seething again about Mayor Wellacott and his impossible demands. Why should a decent guy like Jake be saddled with such a heap of undeserved aggravation? And why should she? One well-placed kick of Wellacott's custom boot and she could be back in that black hole again. Quinn had worked too damned long and hard to climb out.

At the skinny Victorian building that served as Dove's Landing's Town Hall, she parked behind a stretch Cadillac with a waiting chauffeur at the wheel. Had to be the mayor's. Not many people travelled in such style in Vermont. At least, not while they were still breathing.

Once a private home, the municipal building boasted several cosy touches: organdy sheer curtains, wooden window boxes, a brass lion's-head knocker on the door. Off the entrance foyer were doors marked 'Hall of Records' and 'Licence Bureau'. Through a fire door at the right, a narrow corridor carpeted in blue plush led to the mayor's office.

Wellacott's secretary sat in a homey alcove at the corridor's end filing her nails and listening to an oldies station on the radio. She was a buttercup blonde with inflated lips and improbable blue eyes. On her cheek was a faux beauty mark in the shape of a tiny black heart. Her blouse was so sheer, Quinn could almost read the use-and-care instructions on the boob job. But it was a perfect complement to the black wristband skirt, seamed stockings, and stilt-heeled purple pumps.

'Is the mayor in?'

'You got an appointment?'

'No. But he's expecting these.' Quinn held up the carton of tapes and tracings. 'From Jake Holland.'

'Fine. I'll see he gets them.'

'Nope. I've got to hand them over personally. Strict orders.'

'Sorry,' she said. 'That's impossible without an appointment. The mayor's real busy.'

'This will only take a minute.'

'He hasn't got a minute.'

'Then I'll give him one.'

By then, their voices had risen well above sea level.

143

Wellacott's office door edged open, and the mayor's head poked through. Guy bore an amazing resemblance to Barbie's boyfriend, Ken. Had all the sex appeal of wax fruit.

'Problem, Dawn?'

'I brought those tapes and tracings you wanted.'

'Oh yes, come in.'

The office was a generous rectangle lit by crystal chandeliers and ornate silver sconces. It was resplendent with museum-quality antiques, priceless knick-knacks, and modern masters.

He put the carton down and worked his eyes in a brash march over Quinn's peaks and valleys. 'Your name again?'

'Quinn Gallagher.'

'Gallagher? Any relation to Fast Eddie Gallagher?'

Quinn flushed hard. Her father's early reputation as a hell-raiser had led to the hideous mess after the accident. It was the last thing she wanted to think about right now, or ever. With a noncommittal shrug, she raised the conversation to higher ground.

'I'm glad to have a chance to talk to you again, Mayor Wellacott. I wanted to give you my personal assurance that Eldon Weir had nothing to do with that little girl's disappearance.'

'Well now, you can't imagine how relieved I am to hear that, Miss Gallagher. I feel *so* much better.'

'I'm sure you would if you understood the specifics of Weir's security system. I'd be glad to take you to the Waldorf and explain everything.'

Wellacott shook his head on a scolding negative. 'I am not interested in assurances or excuses or guided tours, Officer Gallagher. You want me to let up on this thing, find Abigail Eakins.'

'There's nothing any of us would rather do, Mayor Wellacott. But from everything I've heard, the child ran away. The troopers are convinced of that. She even left a note. How can you possibly try to hold us responsible?'

'The troopers do not speak for me or my office. I'm not at all interested in their convenient, premature conclusions.'

144

'I don't get it,' Quinn said. 'Why are you so determined to believe Eldon Weir kidnapped that little girl?'

'I don't need to explain myself to a low-level nobody. Now, if you'll excuse me . . .'

'But it's ridiculous.'

Wellacott's shoulders stiffened in the expensive suit. 'Exactly who do you think you're calling ridiculous?'

'Don't see anyone here but you and me, Your Royal Tightass.'

As soon as the words were out, Quinn regretted them mightily. It was not smart to infuriate the rich and heinous. Fun yes, but definitely not smart. From what Jake had said, Wellacott wielded more than enough power to make her life miserable at best.

'That will be all, Miss Gallagher. There's the door. Use it.' His voice was icy.

'Look, I'm sorry. I didn't mean that. This whole business has everyone on edge. We're both on the same side here. What do you say we shake hands and call a truce, okay?'

He held himself in stiff control. 'I *said*, that will be all.'

Quinn let herself out and strode past dippy Dawn without comment. Several choice remarks leaped to mind, but she knew she'd done more than her damage quota for the month already. Someday, somehow, she'd have to figure out how to disconnect the auto-pilot feature on her tongue.

Checking the time, she expected she'd have to wait for Levitsky. But on her way to the Waldorf, she spotted him talking on the pay phone under the green-and-white-stripped awning in front of Emma's Luncheonette.

His back was to her. Quinn strode closer and cleared her throat, but the agent was oblivious.

Quinn hadn't been to the luncheonette since new management had taken over and renovated the place several months earlier. Peering through the window, she admired the change. Place was airy and sunlit, the front inset with a broad span of polished glass. The main room had bleached plank floors, round tables with chequered cloths, ceiling fans, and a deli counter packed with appealing salads and cold cuts. At the back, a slim terrace was cantilevered over a rushing splinter of the White River. Looked like a good bet for lunch.

While she waited, she caught his end of the conversation. Apparently, the interview with Weir was not going well. The professor's responses had been riddled with glaring inconsistencies. When Levitsky finally got fed up and called him on the lies, Weir had clammed up completely.

For a few seconds, Levitsky went silent, listening to the person on the other end.

'Usually I would in this situation, Mel,' he said finally. 'Obviously, if Weir won't get real, I can't include him in the study results. But I'm afraid there may be way more at stake here than the study.'

Quinn tensed. Had Weir said something about the missing child? Please no!

'No, nothing definite,' Levitsky told the receiver. 'But I picked up a couple of things that convinced me it's worth digging deeper. I'm putting together a package for the lab, and I'm going to keep at him. Problem is, I don't think he'll talk to me now no matter how hard I push.'

There was another pause.

'Look,' Levitsky said. 'You know a woman would have a better shot . . . Yes, in fact, he has a female parole officer. But I can't allow her to get involved.' He listened again, his expression clouding over.

'No way, Mel. Out of the question,' he said. 'She's not trained to handle a thing like this. You're talking about a one-on-one grilling at close range with Weird Ellie here. That's no stroll in the park, even for an armed expert.'

Another pause.

'No, that's not the point. In fact, this one's the type who'd stick her head in a lion's mouth for effect. But just because she's one of those volatile redheads with no sense doesn't mean we offer her up as a human sacrifice. You have to get me someone from the Bureau . . .

'I don't care about rules or protocol, Mel. We're talking about a possible kidnap here. And, if Weir's involved, we're talking about a killer with a six-day attention span. I

146

understand we're not officially on the case. But who gives a damn about "officially" when a kid's life is on the line?'

Quinn retreated a few steps and cleared her throat again, this time to eliminate the outrage. She'd show the creep exactly *who* had no sense. 'Hey, Levitsky. You almost through? I'm starving.'

He turned and held up a finger. 'Right, Mel. Yes. See what you can do, okay? And you'll check on those other things? Good. Speak to you tomorrow then. Right. Bye.'

Hanging up, he forced a smile. 'I'm pretty hungry myself, Gallagher. Here all right?'

'Fine. How about outside where we can talk in private?' Chilly day, but the terrace was steeped in sunlight.

A pudgy waitress trailed them through the rear door to the terrace, wiped the table, and set two places. The sun toasted Quinn's back, and she felt her bones thawing.

'My name is Suzy,' the waitress said handing them menus. 'I'll be serving you today.'

'We'll need a minute,' Quinn said.

Suzy gave them sixty seconds exactly. Before Quinn could begin grilling Levitsky, the waitress was back with an order pad.

'We're not ready yet,' Quinn said. 'We'll call you, all right?'

'Sure. Take your time.' The waitress backed away, ogling Levitsky as if he were one of the specials and she hadn't eaten in days.

Quinn waited until the waitress was well out of earshot.

'So, how'd it go with Weir?'

'Fine. Pretty routine.'

'Is that so? So Weird Ellie opened right up to you, did he?'

'Most of them do.'

'Boy, am I ever glad to hear that, Levitsky. I have to tell you, I didn't think Weir would take to you right off like this. Didn't I read somewhere that child molesters are more comfortable talking to women authorities?'

'Not all of them.'

Quinn liked watching him squirm. But she knew better

than to push it too far. She didn't want to risk rousing his suspicions.

She kept remembering Weir's whispered offer to lead her on a guided tour of his secret self. Could be the monster was blowing smoke, but given what she'd heard on Levitsky's end of the call, she had to take him up on it. She had to find out what, if anything, Weir knew about the missing girl. She had to be certain that he'd had no part in the disappearance.

In a hideous way, she was convinced Weir's actions belonged to her. If he'd kidnapped that child, she'd be tried with him and sentenced to the same life sentence.

It couldn't be. He had to be innocent in this.

But Quinn could almost hear him recording the findings of his bizarre experiments: *Stage one – the subject is bleeding profusely. Her screams have a strained quality* . . .

She could almost feel the stones and brickbats of her furious fellow citizens. Pummelling her, beating her down again. After all, what can you expect from Fast Eddie Gallagher's girl? She's nothing but a serious screw-up, just like her old man.

'Think I'll try the club sandwich,' Levitsky said. 'You?'

Quinn pretended to study the choices, but her mind was elsewhere. She knew what she had to do and how she would have to go about it.

Motioning the waitress, she wondered what she should have for lunch. All of a sudden, she was not at all hungry.

23 Nora sat on the lawn near the gazebo, cradling Raymond's head in her lap. He was chalk pale. Dusky troughs rimmed his eyes, and his lips were a bloodless blue. A piteous whimper pulsed from deep in his throat.

She listened for the sound of approaching sirens. What was taking so damned long?

'Hang on, Ray. Help is coming.'

He moaned and tried to move. Pain deformed his features, and a shiver wracked him like a train barrelling through a tunnel. Reaching over, Nora retrieved the striped sweater she'd dropped when he was hit and draped it across his chest and shoulders.

'Where's the damned ambulance already?' she said. 'Hurry up.'

Charlie came up beside them. He looked dazed. He'd seen Mim and Poppa to their house, called their doctor, and left them in Maisie's care.

'How's he doing?' Charlie said.

'Not well. How about your folks? Are they all right?'

'Hardly. Mim's a wreck, blames herself for not keeping a closer eye on Poppa. The old man's always wandering off, but we never imagined he could get in any real trouble. Meanwhile, my father's carrying on like a lunatic. Thoroughly delighted with himself. Keeps blithering about how he should've shot the bastard long ago. Mim's terrified that if he sounds like that when the cops get here, they'll lock him away in some loony bin.'

Raymond groaned. Nora blotted his clammy forehead with her sleeve and held his hand. The skin was damp and feverish.

She was numb with shock. The walls of her world were caving in, crumbling to dust. What terrible thing could happen next? First Abigail. Now Ray and Poppa.

Abigail. She thought of the little girl coming home to find her cherished father hurt. Or worse. No, that couldn't be. Raymond had to be all right.

Finally, a siren's scream pierced the ominous hush, and Nora spotted a row of flame-capped vehicles speeding towards the inn. Moments later, an ambulance careened through the lot followed by two police cars and an emergency van from the volunteer EMS squad in Wilmington.

Several of the guests had congregated in front of the main house to gawk and speculate. Charlie gestured, and the emergency vehicles bumped over the footpath towards them.

One of the medics, a slight, squat-jawed man with lumpy skin, crouched to check Raymond's pulse and blood pressure while his moon-faced partner questioned Nora.

'Gunshot?'

'Yes. Will he be all right?'

'Calibre of the gun?'

Nora looked at Charlie.

'It was an antique,' he said. 'Civil War vintage. No idea what calibre. I didn't even think we had ammunition for it.'

'One shot only?'

'Yes. Please, will he be all right?'

The medic kneeling beside Raymond log-rolled him onto his side to check the wound. Gnarled fingers of blood stretched across his shirt. With a frown and a cursory inspection, the emergency worker tore away the fabric and taped a large gauze compress over the site.

'Will he be all right?' Nora repeated. 'Is he going to make it?'

The EMS man gave her a look. 'That's for the docs to say. Only thing I can tell you is he's damned lucky he didn't catch it a few inches lower. Would have been all over in a big hurry.'

She shuddered, and Charlie moved nearer her side. The pie-faced medic rolled up Raymond's sleeve to start an IV. Nora winced as the needle slithered under Ray's skin.

She didn't recognise the quartet of troopers straggling over the lawn. Her stomach churned. What would they do to

Poppa? Could they really hold the poor old man responsible? Mim would perish of the guilt if he was forced into an institution.

One of the troopers, a large man with a flat top and a pencil moustache, crouched beside Raymond and the medic.

'Well, now. What have we got here?'

'It was an accident, officer. He didn't mean it,' Nora said.

'He's not himself,' Charlie said. 'You have to understand.'

'Whoa,' the trooper said, looking up at them as if he'd just been informed of their existence. 'What do I have to understand? Who didn't mean what?'

Raymond forced his eyes open and fixed his disjointed gaze on the officer. His voice was a grainy whisper. 'Me. I didn't. Didn't think the damned thing was loaded. Stupid.'

'What?' Nora tossed him a puzzled look. His response was a cautionary squeeze of her finger.

'Tripped and dropped the damned gun,' Raymond rasped. 'Who'd have thought it'd go off like that?'

The oversized cop scratched his new-mown head. 'You saying you shot yourself in the back? That's some trick, mister. One for the books, I'll tell you.'

Raymond started to laugh, but a pain squeezed him serious. 'Damn, that hurts. You got something I can take?'

'Not till they look you over at the hospital. Sorry, pal,' the medic said.

The officer squinted at Nora. 'That true what he says? He shot himself?'

She shrugged. Hot colour infused her cheeks. Lying had never been her strong suit. 'It happened so fast . . .'

'Who could make up something like that?' Charlie said.

'Shot himself in the back.' The trooper clacked his tongue. 'Amazing. Every time I think I've heard the craziest, crazier comes along. Guess that's it then. You boys ready to take him over to County?'

'All set.'

A trio of medics hefted Raymond onto the wheeled stretcher.

'Can I ride with him in the ambulance?' Nora asked.

'I'll go,' Charlie said.

'Thanks, but I'd better. He doesn't even know you.'

'Then we'll both go.'

'No. I need you to stay in case anyone calls about Abigail. Anyway, Mim and Poppa need you here.'

Again, he got the same lost-puppy look he'd affected when Nora told him about asking Justin Wellacott to help her find Abigail. And again, she ignored it. There was no shortage of real problems. No reason Nora could see to invent any.

'I'll call you as soon as I know anything,' she assured him.

With a collective grunt, the medics and two of the troopers shifted Ray onto one of the ambulance litters and carefully strapped him down. Nora climbed in and sat beside him. The hatch closed, and they started towards the hospital.

As the ambulance bumped over the muddy footpath, Raymond went cheesy pale and fresh pearls of perspiration erupted on his brow. Nora blotted them away and stroked his forehead.

She felt a reflexive tug of affection. Ray had always been a giant bundle of perplexing opposites. Taking the blame for his own injury, letting Charlie's father off the hook, was typical of his sweet side. So was the way he looked and acted when he was around his daughter, all lion's pride and unbridled love. Nora smiled, thinking of that and his several other sparkling positives. Man could be charming, funny, gentle, understanding.

But then there was the other Raymond: the one-man cock fight complete with squawks, razor claws, and flying feathers. And there was Raymond the Oblivious, who could inflict giant wounds on the people he loved most, trampling the most delicate emotional turf like an elephant on an ant-hill. Countless times, Nora had seen him do it to Abigail. Forget a special occasion. Shatter a prized promise. Leave her sad, broken, and bewildered.

If only there had been a way to keep him grounded. But Raymond's moods and interests were subject to change without notice. That was another Raymond altogether: Raymond the Kite. Eventually, you got tired of pulling and

152

coaxing and simply let go of the string. Otherwise, it would snap on its own eventually, and so might you.

He had lapsed into a fitful unconsciousness. Nora smoothed his hair and watched his eyes work under his lids. He looked so soft and innocent, big overgrown baby.

None of his thoughtlessness had been spiteful or intentional, she knew. He was the product of an angry, punitive father and a mother too cowed and diminished to defend herself, much less her son. Given what he'd told Nora of his turbulent childhood, he'd turned out better than one might have predicted. Somehow, he'd retained the capacity for loving and giving. True, it was often buried under nine yards of prime Georgia bullshit, but it hadn't been lost altogether.

Nora shook her head. Here she was, making excuses for him again as she had for years before she finally came to her meagre senses and showed him the door. Intentional or not, Ray's slights and tempers had inflicted real pain, especially on Abigail. Yes, the child adored him still, forgave him anything. But Nora had seen the slick of hurt in her eyes when Raymond disappointed her. Seen it too many times. You fire shots at someone, they bleed. Mistake or no.

Which curved her thoughts back to Poppa. He'd mistaken Raymond for someone else. Nora was sure it had to be the same person he'd said was frightening Abigail. She tried to figure out who most resembled Ray in size, colouring or both. Reuben Huff was nearly as tall as him, as were Hugh and Justin Wellacott and Jory Albert and Sam Albrecht who delivered the produce and on and on. Add similar looks or colouring or clothing and the list stretched to a discouraging spot east of infinity.

Beyond that was the fact that Poppa's eyesight was almost as flawed as his memory. He might have been reacting to an imagined resemblance or none at all. Given the state of his mental processing, he might have been reacting to an imaginary affront by an altogether imaginary offender. If Abigail had been frightened by someone at the inn, why wouldn't she have said so? The little girl had never been shy about sharing her problems.

Nora glanced out the window as the ambulance turned into County General and followed the signs to Emergency Receiving. Inside the glass doors, two orderlies were waiting. Someone had called ahead.

24 On the return trip to Rutland, Levitsky told Quinn he had calls to make and a courier coming to his hotel to collect the duplicate tapes, the copies of the monitor tracings, and a number of other items he wanted analysed at the FBI labs in Quantico. After last night's video marathon, he planned to turn in early. Good, Quinn thought. That would give her all the time she needed.

She dropped Levitsky at the Rutland Holiday Inn and hurried home. With any luck, she could get what she needed and be on her way before Bren got back from school. During the week, she'd have no trouble getting a sitter on short notice. Everything was slipping nicely into place.

The basement was jammed with the displaced remains of her beloved four-room walk-up in Boston's Back Bay area. Swallowing hard, she picked her way through the dusty jumble of sofas, chairs, rugs, lamps, dressers and tables.

The memories stung. Quinn had adored that apartment, loved the space and the solitude. It was the first time in her life she'd been totally on her own. Answerable and responsible to no one but Quinn Gallagher. No parents, no roommates, no keepers, no partners, not even a potted plant to make demands or pout at her inattention.

Yes, she enjoyed friends and family. But she'd treasured her independence as well. Revelled in it. When Daniel came into her life, she'd even held him at a cautious arm's length. She would never allow him to leave a change of clothing in her closet or a spare razor in her medicine chest.

Quinn knew how such incursions escalated. First, it was the razor. Next thing you knew, platoons of Budweiser were bivouacked in your refrigerator, and battalions of large sweaty men in uniforms had invaded your television set.

She shook her head to clear the cobwebs. This was no time

155

for silly reveries. She wanted to be done with this and gone before Bren showed up and started asking hard questions.

Beyond the heaped furniture were stacks of at least two dozen taped boxes. Some held books, kitchenware, and other miscellany from her place in Boston. The rest were filled with certain of her parents' things that Quinn had packed away for a variety of reasons shortly after moving back to Vermont.

Three years since she'd touched the boxes, and Quinn had no recollection of what was in which. Selecting a stack at random, she tore off the tape strips, blew away the dust, and began rifling through the contents.

The first carton contained some of her mother's precious mementos: a wedding veil, a dried orchid corsage, a bundle of letters from the year her father was stationed overseas in the Army, yellowed snapshots.

Next was a box of baby things: clothes, blankets, albums detailing her early accomplishments and Bren's. Quinn smiled at her mother's hopeless sentimentality. She'd saved carrot-red curls from their first haircuts, kept several of their baby teeth, their first shoes. There was even the raggedy blanket scrap Quinn had loved to death in infancy and Bren's precious pacifier, sucked to near oblivion.

The bottom carton in the stack contained some of her father's prized possessions. Eddie Gallagher's attachments had been far more pragmatic than his wife's. He'd held onto his favourite sweater, a pair of hip waders, his flame-orange hunting gear, and the proud basics of his trade: his detective's shield, his police department I.D., several medals and citations for bravery. Quinn found what she was after at the bottom of the box.

Stuffing the contraband into her jacket pocket, she went upstairs, found a pocket recorder and several blank cassettes, and arranged for one of the Ostrow twins from down the block to stay with Brendon.

The girls, Trish and Terry, seemed identical to Quinn, but Bren knew the critical differences between them. Trish made the terrible hot dogs; Terry did the burnt burgers. Quinn couldn't remember which he protested louder about, so she didn't state a preference when Mrs Ostrow answered the phone. Chances were she'd be back before dinner anyway. She knew anything she threw together would be fine with Brendon, as long as he didn't have to eat it.

With her radar detector suctioned to the dash board, she made a record run to Dove's Landing. She didn't want to arrive too late or stay too long. To anyone at Central Headquarters viewing the live feed from the Waldorf's perimeter cameras, the visit had to appear as routine as possible.

When she turned through the gate, she spotted Weir at the window, his blank eyes blazing through the near-drawn drapes. Halfway down the drive, she parked at a calculated angle, so the jeep would block the view from the right-front perimeter camera to the house. That was the one trained on the door. Once she was nearer the house, she'd be invisible on the closed-circuit monitor.

Walking slowly so that anyone watching at Central would have plenty of time to confirm her identity, she circled the car to the blind side. A yard from the staked border, she hesitated out of habit and a nip of fear. There was an expectant stillness about Weir, the charged immobility of an arched cobra. But she kept telling herself she was on top of the situation. Ready, willing, and unstable.

Quinn kept a leery eye on the professor as she stepped over the warning string and approached the door. Her mouth parched. No big deal, she kept telling herself. He was nothing.

Answering her knock, Weir's lips warped in a sneer, and his nostrils flared. The dog stood beside him, hazy eyes trained on Quinn.

'Miss Gallagher? To what do I owe the pleasure of this unexpected visit?'

'I have to talk to you, Weir.'

'Why certainly. Come in.'

With a dramatic sweep of his braceleted arm, he directed her towards the ring of leather sofas in the living room. As Quinn crossed the threshold, the dog bristled and growled.

'There, there, Darling,' Weir said, settling a hand on the

animal's broad back. 'Miss Gallagher is a guest. You mustn't treat her so rudely.' He stroked behind a peaked ear and worked a sinewy slab of fur through his fingers. 'Darling means no harm, officer. It's just that she's grown quite attached to me. And terribly protective. Everything will be fine so long as nothing makes her think I'm being threatened.'

Quinn took another step, and the growl gained weight and menace. 'Shut that animal up, Weir. Call her off.' Quinn knew the dog had been bred for gentleness and trained for obedience. But an animal was an animal.

'Of course, Miss Gallagher. Sssh now, sweetheart. You're frightening our visitor.'

The dog went still, but the grey eyes glistened with raw enmity. Sidestepping the beast, Quinn sat at the edge of one of the sofas.

Weir followed and paused behind the adjacent couch.

'So delightful to have you in my humble abode at long last, Miss Gallagher. Might I get you a cup of tea? Take your coat, perhaps?'

'No, I'm fine.' She placed a hand over the reassuring weight in her jacket pocket. She was better than fine; she was prepared.

'Well then? What is it you wished to discuss?'

Quinn measured her words. She agreed with Levitsky that it was all gamesmanship with the professor. Deadly diversions.

'I've been thinking a lot about what you said, Weir. You're right. I am curious about you, and I'd like to take you up on that offer you made. I do want to know you.'

Lazy nod. 'Yes. I know.'

Quinn waited, impatience nagging like an unscratchable itch. 'So? Can we get started?'

He was playing with her. Mouse in the trap. See how it squirms. 'You do disappoint me, Miss Gallagher. We've already begun, don't you see?'

'What's next then?'

Weir ticked his tongue. 'I told you it will take time, Miss

Gallagher. Careful observation. Sense and struggle. You must find the path and follow it.'

'Okay, Weir. Forget it. I thought you had something to tell me, but obviously, I thought wrong. I don't like being jerked around.' She stood to leave. The dog edged towards her, a rusty crackling deep in its chest. 'Call her off.'

'Down, Darling. There, there.'

The beast snarled and bared its teeth.

'I said, call her off!'

'She won't hurt you. Will you now, sweetheart?'

The Alsatian edged closer. A froth shimmered on its drawn muzzle. Closer.

Quinn's hand trembled as she groped for the bulge in her pocket. She slipped her fingers inside, and went numb with horror.

The thirty-eight was gone, replaced by a crystal ashtray. The dog was still coming at her.

Quinn raised the glass weight. She'd use what she had.

Weir clapped his hands. Instantly, the dog dropped to the ground and rolled on its back like a playful pup, tongue lolling. The professor knelt, felt for the creature, and patted her downy underside.

'Good girl,' he crooned. 'That's my sweetheart.'

Quinn felt a pinch of relief, but she still faced the bigger danger. She thought of Weir's cool, clinical detachment as he logged the effects of his tortures. Professor Pain. Investigating the limits of human endurance, enjoying his victims' slow painful demise.

'Hand it over, Weir,' Quinn said. It took every shred of resolve to rid her voice of the tremor.

'Oh? Are you missing something, Miss Gallagher?'

'Now.'

He turned up empty palms and a face limp with ingenuousness. 'If you tell me what it is you've lost, I'll be glad to try to help you find it.'

'The gun, Weir. Give it to me or . . .'

'Oh that.' He flapped a hand. 'Slipped my mind. I put your weapon on the dining table for safekeeping. A loaded gun is so terribly dangerous, Miss Gallagher. Especially around unpredictable criminal types who might turn such a thing against you. That's why there are strict regulations banning parole people from bearing arms, as I'm sure you know. I am truly surprised that you'd be so reckless. Shocked.'

On rubber legs, Quinn went to the dining room. The metal nose of her father's revolver was sticking up in the middle of the silk floral centrepiece. But how the hell?

Clutching the loaded piece in her hand, she made her shaky way towards the door. This little excursion had been a stupid, terrible mistake. But it was over. She would get the hell out and pretend it had never happened.

Weir's voice caught her as she gripped the doorknob. 'Find the melody, Miss Gallagher. That's the foot of the path. You already have everything you'll need for the journey. Discover the melody first, then you can proceed from there.'

She turned and peered into his cold, empty eyes. 'I'm done, Weir. That stunt you pulled was the fat lady singing. We stick strictly to the basics from here on. All other bets are off.'

'That's a pity, Miss Gallagher. I thought you were eager to find that missing child.'

Quinn froze. 'You have her?'

'Of course not. How could I?'

'Then you know who does?'

He shook his head with maddening slowness. 'No, officer. I don't know *who*. But if she's been kidnapped, I know by *what*. You can't find anything if you don't know what you're after. But I can guide you. Advise you. Help you catch his scent.'

Quinn hesitated. 'The police are convinced she ran away. What makes you think otherwise?'

His face warped with amusement. 'Oh I don't. It's you who thinks so. You and your nosy, suspicious friend from the FBI. Then it's prudent not to take chances, I suppose. Especially given all the unsavoury elements in our society. Abigail Eakins might well have been taken, if you think of it. Pretty, blonde child. Talented and intelligent. So very desirable to so many, I'd imagine.'

She took in the smirk, the attitude. He was still tugging her strings. Well, she wasn't about to dangle and dance for the creep.

'I've had enough, Weir. I'm done.' She strode out of the house, slammed the door behind her, and filled herself with fresh air.

She wasn't playing his games. No more. From now on she'd do her job by the book and keep her distance. Playing hero in this situation wasn't going to prove anything except her own terminal stupidity. Weir wasn't giving anything away. Probably had nothing to give in the first place.

Or did he?

She was haunted by that impossible possibility. And she was haunted by the picture the cops had circulated of the missing child. Cute blonde kid, trusting blue eyes. A pony tail, for chrissakes. The girl wasn't much older than Brendon. This could have been him.

She could still hear Weir's voice wafting on the breeze. Coming at her from impossible angles as if he were smoke curling through the building walls. The words were teasing, seductive.

Pretty blonde child. Talented and intelligent. How did Weir know all that about the missing girl? And how had he learned the child's name?

25 Nearly two hours had passed, and still no word about Ray's condition. Nora had spent the time pacing the overheated Emergency waiting area, leafing blindly through medieval magazines, and trying to wheedle information out of the snow-haired receptionist, who now refused to make eye contact.

Since they'd wheeled Ray into treatment, Nora had been plagued by horrific images. She pictured him bleeding to death, having convulsions, suffering cardiac arrest. She could almost hear the emergency room doctors bickering over whose turn it was to inform the next of kin as they closed his sightless eyes and drew the sheet over his head.

The clerk in Admissions had presumed she was Raymond's wife, and Nora had declined to correct him. It was odd being referred to as 'Mrs Eakins' again, but she thought they might be inclined to keep her better informed if they thought she was married to the victim. If she didn't hear something soon, she expected she'd wind up in one of those veiled cubicles herself. Tragic victim of spontaneous combustion.

She approached the desk again, set her elbows on the Formica surface, and folded her hands like a penitent. She knew she must look and sound like a crazy woman: wild-eyed, dishevelled, her clothes rumpled and streaked with Ray's blood. But nobody was moved to take pity on her and tell her what the hell was happening with Ray.

'Please, please, can't you call in there and see what's going on?' she asked the white-haired woman. 'It's been forever.'

The woman nudged the bridge of her bifocals and sighed. 'I told you, Mrs Eakins, if I could, I'd be glad to. But I'm not allowed to interrupt the trauma team. You wouldn't want them distracted from critical procedures to answer the phone, now would you? Try to relax. I'm sure the doctor will be out any minute to talk to you.'

Nora resumed her restless patrol. Glum clusters of the ailing and their anxious escorts dotted the square, antiseptic space. A small child with a canine cough was defoliating a potted palm near the entrance while his mother emptied her purse of crumpled receipts and used Kleenex. In the centre of the room, a dishevelled old woman with ulcerated ankles was interviewing herself. A large gypsy clan was encamped around an elaborate picnic near the bank of phones. Nora circled around them and dialled the inn.

Charlie answered. She told him that things at the hospital were still on hold and asked for an update from his end. No news yet about Abigail. When Nora asked about other calls, he grudgingly reported that Justin Wellacott had stopped by to say that the police were out searching for the child in force. In addition, the troopers assigned to the case had phoned. They were on their way to the inn to examine Abigail's things and begin interviewing the staff and guests.

Charlie assured her that things with his parents were under control. Poppa had finally calmed down with the aid of a stiff tranquillizer, and Mim seemed over the worst of the upset. She'd already taken steps to avoid a repeat performance. The gun collection was now locked away in the storage closet near the wine cellar. Mim had hidden the key where Poppa would never be able to find it. She'd also begun rescheduling some of the inn's personnel, so the old man would be under constant supervision.

'Mim hates having to treat him this way, like a child.'

'What's the choice?'

'That's what I told her. Meanwhile, you've been there for hours already. Can't you get through to someone and find out what's going on? Everyone's in this hideous limbo around here.'

She sighed. 'It's not exactly Disneyworld here either, Charlie. I'm doing the best I can.'

'Maybe there's someone we can call, then. Mim's got an

163

old friend who's been very active in fundraising for the hospital. Should I ask her to . . .'

'Wait.' A storm was brewing inside the treatment area. Nora heard the tangle of approaching voices and had a feeling this had to be about Raymond, 'Something's up. Gotta go, Charlie. Bye.'

He was still talking as she dumped the phone in its cradle. Nora hurried over and positioned herself at the doors. No way to get closer. The lock had to be released by an electric switch behind the reception desk.

She was trying to think of a way to sneak inside when a wedge of frantic people burst through to the waiting area. Raymond was at the centre of the throng, his gaze level, mouth set, making his determined way towards the exit. His escort included a large orderly, two beefy male nurses, a small Oriental doctor, and a young man with patent-leather hair whose badge identified him as Director of Patient Relations. Except for Raymond, everyone was chattering in frantic chorus.

'Ray?'

The gloss-haired man from Patient Relations fell out of step and drew her aside. 'You here with Mr Eakins?'

'Yes. What's going on?'

'They were able to remove the bullet and clean the wound under local anaesthetic. It wasn't too serious, but he's lost some blood, and there's always the risk of infection in cases like this. He really should stay with us for a couple of days, minimum. We were trying to arrange a bed, but he got himself up and dressed and refuses to listen to anyone.'

Raymond had stalled at the exit. 'Let's go, Nora.'

'You sure about this?'

'Don't I look sure?'

Raymond detested doctors and hospitals. Remembering how difficult it had been to coax him to show up for Abigail's birth, Nora was not at all suprised by his present perfor-mance. Nor was she tempted to argue. With Abigail mis-sing, she didn't have the strength or patience to concern herself with Raymond's obstinate stupidity.

164

She addressed the gel-cap from Patient Relations. 'Don't worry. You can't be held responsible if he's a stubborn fool.'

'But I explained to him, this kind of injury is highly unpredictable. It's really not advisable for you to leave so soon, Mr Eakins. I have these orders from the admitting physician that say . . .'

Nora nodded. 'You have all that in writing?'

'Orders,' he said. 'And a statement advising Mr Eakins of the possible consequences if he leaves against medical advice.'

'King Kong here will read them word for word and memorise them, especially the part about possible consequences. And he'll sign that he's leaving against doctor's orders. Won't you, Raymond?'

He heaved an impatient sigh. 'Whatever it takes to get the hell out of this place. Don't see what's the big deal. I'm absolutely fine.' Forgetting himself, he tried to reach for the papers with his right hand. The movement made him wince and cry out.

'Right. I can see exactly how fine you are. Come on, I'd better get you settled somewhere before you get any dumber. We can call and make arrangements from the inn.'

'Hate to be any trouble.'

'No you don't. You love it.'

They drove to Dove's Landing in silence. Charlie greeted them at the inn's front door. 'Raymond? Are you all right?'

'Sure. No big thing.'

'Come in, come in. Am I ever glad to see you.'

Raymond proffered a left-handed shake. 'Good meeting you, Charlie. Heard all about you from Abby.'

Charlie took the hand and gripped it. 'You too. How can I ever thank you for saying the shooting was an accident? I'm sorrier than you can imagine that you had to go through all this. You really all right?'

'Good as new.'

'Like hell, he is,' Nora said. 'They wanted to keep him for a few days at least, but he refused. Big baby's scared to death of hospitals.'

Charlie frowned. 'Then you'll stay right here with us, and

Doctor Gordon will keep an eye on you until you're fully recovered. I'll put you in Sugar House One. It's our nicest suite.'

Nora scowled at Charlie, but he was oblivious. At least he could have consulted her before inviting Ray to convalesce at the inn. Maybe it was the correct thing to do, but she wasn't so sure her ex-husband was covered by the etiquette books. Not even as a footnote.

'I'll show you there,' Nora said grudgingly. 'You should get off your feet.'

'No, let me,' Charlie said. 'There's something I want to discuss with Raymond anyway.'

Nora let it go, but she couldn't imagine what the two of them had to talk about. If it were something about Abigail, she certainly thought she should be included. Whoever invented men had definitely not ironed out all the kinks.

'This way,' Charlie said.

'Right behind you.'

Victoria breezed in as the pair disappeared down the hall. She was freshly coiffed, expensively scented, and radiant with auto-adoration, cosmetics or, more likely, both.

'What's with you, Nora? You look like nine miles of bad road.'

'It's been quite a day. I'm afraid I have some disturbing news.'

Nora waited until Victoria shed her floor-length mink, fluffed her hair, and arranged herself on the chintz sofa in front of the gleaming copper hearth where she could enjoy her reflection at will. Mim had set a trio of African violets on the side table. The flowers were a perfect foil for Victoria's eyes. The leaves matched too – bilious.

'Justin stopped by earlier, and he said not to worry about Abigail,' Victoria said. 'He's made sure the cops put finding her at the top of the list. They know all the places kids go to hide when they run away.'

'This isn't just about Abigail.' Nora chose the words carefully. Victoria was not the great empathiser, true. But, still, it *was* her father who'd pulled the trigger.

She did register a hint of shock at the story, but she

recovered with record speed and reacted by touching up her lip gloss. 'So Abigail's famous daddy's finally shown up? When do I get to meet him? Abby showed me his picture. Pretty cute, and I do adore a southern drawl.'

'Don't bother unpacking your hunting clothes, Victoria. Raymond's only here to recuperate.'

'Don't you worry, sweetie. I'll be gentle with him, I promise.' She feigned a yawn. 'Oh, my, I am positively exhausted. Can't imagine what's wrong.'

Nora could well imagine. The dinner crowd would begin arriving in under an hour. Victoria had almost no time left to incubate her nightly malady.

'Better rest up in a hurry then, *sweetie*. I will not be able to cover for you tonight.'

'Did I ask you to?' Victoria hitched her brow indignantly. She had scooped up her mink and was about to make her exit when Mim came in leading troopers Merriman and DeSoto.

With difficulty, Merriman wrested eyes from Victoria and nodded in Nora's direction. 'Wanted to stop by and let you know we finished looking through your daughter's things.'

'And?' Their business-as-usual detachment was driving her mad.

DeSoto read from a pocket notebook. 'Abigail's savings passbook showed a fifty-dollar withdrawal three days ago. Day before that, she had an English assignment to write a journal entry about her feelings. Hers was about not being able to stand it here any more and how she was planning to run away. Everything certainly points to her having left voluntarily.'

Mim placed a hand on Nora's shoulder. The day's events had pinched her face with exhaustion. She looked frail and weary. 'They're going to find her, dear. That's all that matters.'

Nora was too wrung out to argue. 'If there's nothing else, would you please excuse me?'

DeSoto shut his notebook and tucked it away. 'Nothing else. We'll be talking to some of the workers and guests, see if anyone knows where she might have gone. Meanwhile, the entire force has her picture and they'll be keeping an eye out for her.'

Nora brushed past them and out into the chill of the thickening twilight. A mizzle of frozen rain had begun to fall. Already, the ground was glistening with icy patches. In this part of the world, winter was slow to surrender.

Careful with her footing, Nora crunched through the lot, passed under the double archway and strode across the stone courtyard. Beyond the line of guest rooms, she made her way towards their cabin. She dreaded the emptiness inside, the deafening echo of Abigail's absence.

In the cabin Nora went through the rooms flipping on lights, television, radios, anything to challenge the screaming hollow inside that threatened to expand and consume her.

She climbed the stairs, wanting to make sure the detectives had left her daughter's room intact. It seemed critical that the child find things exactly as she'd left them when she finally came home.

Soon, she thought. Please let it be soon.

The bedroom door was open. Arms folded to hold herself together, Nora entered. She'd expected a mess, but everything appeared in perfect order. The bed was smooth under the lacy canopy, the drawers neatly shut. On the maple bookshelves, the rows of gymnastics trophies and young-adult novels were exactly as Nora remembered them. Under Mim's watchful eye, the troopers had even placed the jumble of school books in two neat stacks.

She was drawn to the composition book marked 'English'. Abigail had never shown interest in keeping a diary, though Nora had encouraged it as a good place to plant thorny emotions. As a child, she'd often kept a journal herself, mostly a self-indulgent litany of wishes and complaints. She'd found it especially helpful to be able to inscribe the unspeakable when she had a gripe against her parents.

Opening the book, she turned to the dated entry the detectives had mentioned. She stared at the page in disbelief. The words, the writing, even the multiple erasures were exactly the same as the note she'd found on the day Abigail disappeared. The only difference was the teacher's comment in the margin and the tick that ran into Abby's writing.

Nora's heart started to pound. The whole crazy business started clicking in place. Abby hadn't written it as a note at all. Her kidnapper must have made a copy of this journal entry with the teacher's notations carefully covered up and planted it to make it seem as if the child had left of her own will.

She had to show both copies to the troopers. Once she did, they'd have to believe that this was more than a simple runaway.

Racing to her room, she searched the dresser and the nightstand. Where had she put that note? She pulled things out of the drawers, dumped piles of clothing on the floor, worked in an anxious frenzy.

Get a grip, Nora. She backed away and drew a measured breath. *This is not the way. Be methodical. Think.* Outside, sleet pelted the windows. The sound grated on her, made her even tenser.

Go back to that night. Think it through!

Slowly, she remembered finding the note in Abby's room and putting it in her pants pocket. During that first night after the child's disappearance, she'd read the thing a million times. But she hadn't seen it since.

Rifling through the closet, she pulled out the black slacks she'd worn that night. Charlie had brought the pants and a sweater to her from the cabin so she could change out of the black cocktail dress she'd worn to work at the restaurant. Uttering a quick prayer, she stuck her hand in the trouser pocket. The folded paper was still there. Retrieving the English binder from Abigail's room, she raced out of the cabin.

In her eagerness to rush the evidence to the detectives, she skidded on an icy patch and came down hard on her palms and knees. Ignoring the shock and the burning soreness, she forced herself upright, brushed off the binder, and continued on in a strained hobble towards the inn.

Mim was at the reception desk. 'Oh, my. What happened, dear? You're bleeding.'

Looking down, Nora saw the ragged bruises on both filthy knees. Her tights were ripped; both palms of her hands were raw and oozing.

'I fell. It's nothing. Where are Merriman and DeSoto?'

'In the office. But . . .'

Nora barged in. The troopers were interviewing Jory Albert.

'Sorry to interrupt, but you have to see this right away,' Nora said. 'Jory, would you excuse us?'

The bartender shrugged. After he left, Nora triumphantly placed the binder and the folded note on the desk. 'I knew there had to be some logical explanation. Whoever took Abigail made a copy of that journal entry to eliminate the teacher's comments and planted it to look like a runaway note. See for yourself. They're identical.'

Merriman opened the spiral binder to the page with the journal entry. DeSoto stood at his side while Merriman slowly unfolded the note. Both men frowned, exchanged a look, and turned to Nora.

'What? What's wrong?'

Merriman pressed his lips in a seam as he passed the paper across the desk.

Nora picked it up. Desperate, she turned it over and over in her hand. This was a nightmare, insane. The message was gone. There wasn't a single mark on the page.

26 Fleeing the white house, Abigail raced for the cover of the woods and crouched panting behind a clump of brambled vines. Fear beat inside her like the wings of a frantic bird. He could be anywhere. Might come after her at any time. How was she ever going to get home?

She was starving, filthy, frozen so deep her bones rattled. A frozen rain was falling. It was only going to get colder. Bleaker. More impossible.

Soon it would be night, black and thrumming with danger. Abigail knew it was babyish, but she still feared the dark, saw it as a gargantuan cave full of dread, formless dangers.

The thought was enough to get her moving. She pressed through the woods and came out on the far side. From there, dense brush blocked her view of the white house and the idling truck. That had to mean he couldn't see either.

Emboldened, she pressed on. Soon, she scaled a post-and-rail fence at the edge of a mammoth stretch of cultivated fields. The farmland extended endlessly in measured drab brown squares and beige rectangles. The monotony was unbroken except for the meandering fences and an occasional cluster of grazing cattle.

Squinting through the deepening shadows, she searched for signs of life. At first, she saw nothing. Then, far ahead, a light flickered. Staring hard, she wished and waited until she spotted the flash again. The sinking sun bouncing off metal, she thought. Maybe the top of a barn.

Following the blinks of glare, she continued through the grid of fields as quickly as she could. Her feet were raw and she was fast running out of energy.

Soon, the source of the intermittent light came into view. Abigail's hopes plummeted as she viewed the sprawling squat building with its barred windows and corrugated metal roof: a chicken coop.

One of her classmates in Miss Schiffman's room was a farm kid, and the sixth grade had been invited to visit on a recent field trip.

The entire place had made her retch. Dung heaps and mud everywhere, stinky animals roaming around making googly eyes and gross noises, the incessant clamour of machinery. But nothing had been worse than the coops. Her gorge rose at the memory of the stench, the disgusting bins of dirty feed, droppings everywhere. Abigail had kept her opinions to herself, but she couldn't imagine how anyone could live anyplace as revolting as a farm. Manhattan was paradise by comparison.

No way she could hide in that chicken coop. She'd rather risk freezing in the pelting drizzle.

She continued, her pace diminished to a limping hobble. She was on the verge of tears when she spied a ramshackle equipment shed. The door was unlocked. Trembling with relief, she slipped inside.

Typical farm warehouse. The place was jammed with rusted tools, cast-off bikes and baby carriages, the carcasses of ancient farm equipment. She picked her way through stacks of old books and magazines, nests of abandoned pots and pans, canning equipment, broken toys and wrecked furniture. In a dim corner, she found two mouldy blankets and wrapped herself in them. Nearby, under a pile of seed catalogues, she discovered a pair of old army boots.

Gingerly, she slipped her damp battered feet inside. The boots were huge, so big they didn't pinch her torn, bruised flesh. But the leather was dry and cracked, the insides caked with filth. Abigail took a few tentative steps. They were better than nothing, though not by much.

Rummaging through the shed, she discovered other dubious treasures: a moth-eaten shawl, a pair of garden gloves stiff with dried mud, a couple of Nancy Drew books with cracked bindings and pages the colour of tea.

Abigail loved detective stories. Overhead, the rain drummed on the roof. Thinking she'd read to pass the time

172

until she dried out and warmed up, she sat on the carriage mattress and opened one of the volumes. But she was too hungry to concentrate. Her stomach fisted and made sandpaper sounds.

Huddled in her blanket cocoon, she got up and started foraging again, this time for food. A long, frustrating search yielded nothing but a few desiccated nuts, an empty set of spice canisters, and a tin half-filled with a yellow powdery substance. She took a taste, but the powder was bitter and stung. Abigail spat on the ground and wiped her tongue on the blanket.

Pressing open the door to the shed, she peered outside. The sky had dimmed. Time was getting away from her. The main house couldn't be far away now. She had to get there before nightfall and find a phone.

Wrapped in the blankets, she left the storehouse and squinted against the pelting swirl of frozen drizzle. Soon she spotted the barn and a trio of towering metal silos. Past those, she finally came upon the farmhouse, a two-storey red building with forest-green trim.

Approaching with caution, Abigail observed several hopeful signs. There were two tricycles on the lawn and a gaily painted swing set. In the backyard laundry was hung on a tree-shaped metal contraption. She spotted baby clothes, women's underwear, Snoopy sheets, a couple of plaid flannel shirts, pairs of white socks dangling in size order, dishtowels. Someone had neglected to bring the wash in before the rain, and now everything was soaked dark and heavy.

But the hanging laundry meant a real family lived here: kids and parents. It had to be safe. Clumping in the heavy boots, Abigail hurried to the front door and knocked. No answer. Hammering on the wood frame, she prayed for someone to come. She jiggled the knob and tried to force it open, but the door was locked. Same with the windows. The shades were drawn so low, she couldn't even see inside. Nobody was home. which explained the neglected wash.

On the front porch were two wicker rockers with pale

puffed cushions. Abigail angled the fronts together and crouched behind the makeshift fortress. Huddled in the blankets, she was reasonably warm. Her hunger had abated, replaced by a dull ache and a queasy feeling.

Through a small opening in her blanket cocoon, she watched the long dirt drive for an approaching car. A couple of times, she mistook the whip of the wind for engine sounds. Once, she was positive she detected the flash of a metal truck grille bumping down the road, but the image evaporated.

The sky was peppered with needles of rain. Before long it would be dark. Then she'd have to face the fat, silent belly of the night, the part Abigail always burrowed under her covers to escape.

But surely the people from the house would be back long before that. If they had gone away on a vacation or something, there wouldn't be washing on the line. With little kids, they were bound to return early from wherever they were.

She clutched that tiny piece of logic like a lifeline as the sky deepened to a dismal ash colour. Closing her mind to the gathering menace, she kept staring at the road.

Where were they already?

Maybe they'd gone somewhere for dinner. That was probably it. Abigail pictured a strapping man in striped overalls sipping the last of his coffee and signalling for the bill. She imagined a trio of chunky little kids being zipped into their jackets and herded to the family van by their slim, timid mother. Now they were climbing in the car. The motor was turning over, and they were backing out of the space.

The fantasy evolved in satisfying detail, transporting Abigail to the warm centre of a reassuring farm family.

The Johnsons, she named them. Gerald and Maude Johnson and their children: Gerald Junior, Lisa, and baby Jeanine. The little one was probably asleep in her car seat by now. Young Gerry was teasing Lisa the way he always did, pulling her braids and tweaking her nose while the

174

parents' heads were turned. Lisa whined, but the grownups paid no attention. Farmer Johnson was intent on the weather forecast, thinking about how he'd have to bundle up when he got up to do the milking at four a.m. The missus was wondering if she should wait until morning to bring in the saturated wash.

Abigail could see it all: kids, van, sleeping baby. She imagined Mr Johnson turning onto the farm road, anticipating sleep with an extravagant yawn.

Abigail had shut her eyes for a clearer view of the fantasy, but suddenly she detected a flaming glare and heard a hideous flapping sound. Forcing herself to look up, she spotted a huge black capsule in the sky. A sword of light projected from its underside. Icy raindrops danced in the beam.

A helicopter.

The chopper trailed in slow swipes over the lawn in front of the farmhouse. Soon, it honed in on her hiding place and hovered there. Huddled deep in her blankets, she held her breath.

For a breathless crush of time, she was caught in the cruel wash of light and the blustery gale from the rotors. But finally, the light released her and the wind eased as the chopper edged away.

Relieved, Abigail watched the giant metal bug retreat. She'd be all right now. She could wait for the Johnsons to come home and rescue her.

The helicopter was moving steadily over the farm. She saw it approach the barn and pass beyond. Next, it passed the three silos and headed in the direction of the storage shed where she'd found the boots and blankets. She was about to turn her attention back to the road, when the chopper ceased its forward progress.

It hovered in the distant sky, the conical beam trained on something directly below. Then, slowly, unmistakeably, it started to descend.

Maybe he'd seen her after all? Was he landing to come and get her?

The helicopter was sinking fast. In seconds it disappeared behind the line of buildings. The engine sputtered and went still. A booming voice arose to fill the silence.

He was calling her name.

27

Raymond was in rare form. Even bruised, bandaged, and blunted by painkillers, that man knew how to work a room.

Too restless to stay in the suite, he'd drifted into the parlour less than an hour after their return from the hospital. Ray had wanted Charlie to take him out to search for Abigail, but Nora, Charlie, and his injuries had joined forces to change his mind. Now he was sprawled on the sofa in front of a crackling fire, propped by needlepoint pillows, draped in a pair of Mim's crocheted afghans, and surrounded by fawning members of the Brill family.

Victoria was playing a designer Florence Nightingale, dispensing canned sympathies while she sized up Ray's escort potential. While Poppa slept off the effects of his tranquillizers, Mim had stopped by to make sure Ray was comfortable. She'd stayed to hang on his every word and witticism. Stephanie was conducting a cross-legged vigil at his oversized feet. The teenager regarded him with Abigail's brand of dewy adulation. Even sullen Hugh had deigned to hang around and grunt an occasional contribution to the group.

And then there was Charlie. After a year of expressing nothing for Ray but unbridled resentment, the last thing Nora had expected was for the two men to become fast friends. But she'd caught them passing meaningful looks, winks, infuriating asides. Worse, she had the distinct sense that she was the place their minds had met. No, she was not paranoid. But that didn't mean they weren't talking about her.

She found the whole cheery scene infuriating. How could they all be having such a grand old time while Abigail was missing? True, she had laughed earlier with Ray, but that had been a reflex, a release of trapped steam. There had been no pleasure in it. As long as Abby was gone, there could be no pleasure in anything.

While the others giggled and gabbed, hideous images flashed in Nora's mind. In vivid stills, she saw Abby hurt, terrified, startled, screaming for help. She pictured the bare foot and the dirty sneaker. The stiff limbs and fisted hands from the snapshots that had gone blank.

If only she still had those pictures. She ached for the rest of them to appreciate the danger. They were convinced that Nora was simply being hysterical, imagining things. Over the edge with irrational worry. *How could they be so calm?*

Raymond was finishing one of his big-one-that-got-away stories. He loved bragging about all his breathless near-misses: fish, women, fame, fortune. He especially enjoyed describing the giant deals he'd lost by a hair. This one involved an Arab financier and a massive shipment of pricy Italian sports cars. As usual, the transaction had disintegrated at the last minute over an ethical disagreement. Naturally, big Ray had walked away with his oversized principles intact. He finished the tale with a stolen punchline Nora recognised from a TV comedy special.

The Brills dissolved in appreciative laughter and clamoured for an encore. Nora used the cover of the commotion to slip away. She was in no mood for a party.

Restless, she hurried through the frozen rain to the studio and slipped into the darkroom to develop the rolls of film she'd shot earlier for the tourist brochure.

Mechanically, she filled the trays with developer, print-fix, wash, and cleaning solutions. Out of habit, she set the clock for each stage of the process though her internal timer told her when to pass the film spool from one chemical bath to the next.

Having exposed only two rolls, she decided to enlarge all the pictures for Justin Wellacott. Lacking an expert eye, it was difficult to make any sound judgements from the tiny images on contact sheets or grainy proofs.

She left the darkroom and scrutinised the work under the unforgiving light of her desk lamp. The results were decent. No errant shadows or disappointing quirks of composition to mar the shots. But flipping through the prints, she had the annoying sense that something was amiss.

She went through the stack again, but she couldn't define the problem. Giving up, she decided to pass the prints to Justin as they were. If he found anything lacking, he wouldn't hesitate to demand a reshoot or reprocessing.

As she was about to leave the studio, Nora realised there was still time to kill before the dinner shift. She didn't relish going to the cabin where everything struck her as a taunting reminder of Abigail's absence. And she definitely didn't want to return to the inn for more of Raymond's investiture and inaugural ball.

All she wanted was her little girl.

Folding her arms across her chest, Nora ached for one of those priceless moments when she would hug Abigail and revel in a hot-soup infusion of pure, uncomplicated love.

She recalled one particular incident when Abby was about two years old. For months, the marriage had been bumping over especially rough terrain, and Ray had shown no interest in repaving. That night, after hours of futile sparring, he'd stormed out of the apartment and slammed the door.

Nora had settled on the couch for a good cry. Abby had been asleep, but soon Nora heard the child pad into the room. Nora was struggling to compose herself when Abigail's arms slipped around her neck and a tiny hand rubbed soothing circles on her back.

'No sad, Mommy. All better.'

The memory evaporated as the lights flamed on in the inn's living room and washed across the front porch. From the studio door, she saw Reuben Huff cross to light the outside lamps and the corridor sconces in the guest wings. The first staff cars pulled into the lot.

Shivering, Nora knew she'd been drifting in aimless circles, struggling to avoid all the ugliness that had seeped into her world. This tranquil place, this new marriage and big, close adopted family had promised to make everything all better. Ease all the hurts. Fill all the yawning voids in her world and Abigail's. Instead, everything had fallen to ruin like the old, abandoned house up the hill.

Gazing at it now, Nora spotted a dark grey Wagoneer jeep with an official medallion on the rear backing out of the Waldorf's driveway. An attractive young woman with a puff of ginger hair was at the wheel. She appeared to be staring through the sweeping windshield wipers at the darkened building.

On impulse, Nora snapped a picture. Funny how people found that old dump so fascinating, Nora thought. Herself included.

Peering at the dilapidated house now, Nora experienced a recurrence of that same odd sensation she'd felt while examining the prints for the tourist brochure. Something wrong.

Troubled, she turned back into the studio and rummaged through her desk drawers until she found a magnifying glass. Forcing herself to sit and be methodical, she began scrutinising the photographs again.

Amplified by the lens, the detail was startling. She was able to read the date on the magazine near the overturned canoe. She could see the brush marks and several tear-shaped drips on the freshly painted gazebo. In the court-yard, she spotted hairline fractures in two of the patio stones. Tiny seeking tips of the season's first weeds poked up through the soil in the border beds. The trim on Mim and Poppa's windows had the blistered look of sunburned skin.

She studied another shot of the canoe, several of the greenhouse, the pool shed, the courtyard from a different angle, the lake. Near the bottom of the pile, she came to the photos she'd taken of the covered bridge up the hill and the ones she'd snapped of the Waldorf.

Since moving to the inn, Nora had taken dozens of pictures of that charming, spooky place. In Manhattan, abandoned buildings were quickly claimed as crack dens, shooting galleries, squalid nests for squatting vagrants, dark lairs of unthinkable evil. Here, kids appropriated such sites to store fantasies, brew mischief, hide, and heal. Legends sprouted in the silence. Myths and rumours flourished among the weeds. Dumps like the Waldorf were precious community resources.

Then it came to her.

Through the magnifying lens, she could see that the place had undergone some deliberate tending. Comparing the new shots to the last ones she'd taken of the building, she confirmed that the wild grasses, now mowed low and level, had been a knee-high dead tangle a week ago. Fresh panes glistened in place of the several shattered windows that had added to the building's delightful seediness. Dangling spans of the rotted split-rail fence had been replaced.

Nora frowned. Why would anyone want to tamper with the Waldorf's endearing imperfections? Not much had been done, but someone had definitely authorised and funded the improvements. And they weren't only on the outside.

Heavy drapes hung at the living-room windows. They were drawn nearly shut, but through the small opening, Nora saw the edge of a white sofa, a span of pale carpeting, and an end table with a china cup and a newspaper on it.

Someone was living in that house.

Clutching the photo, she put in a call to May Dunkelman, a member of the tourist board who owned the area's largest real-estate firm. May checked the directory of houses for sale and recent property transfers. The Waldorf was not listed.

Bristling with curiosity, Nora dialled Justin Wellacott's office. The mayor was gone for the day. Nora asked his secretary if she knew anything about the Waldorf's facelift and occupation, but the woman was no help. At first, Dawn, whose accent was an odd hybrid of Northern Maine and the South Bronx, denied any knowledge of the renovations. Then, in mid-sentence, she suddenly recalled hearing that the absentee owner was fixing up the abandoned house for rental.

Checking the time, Nora was sure she'd be able to get better information from Justin when he came for dinner. She had to find out who'd moved into the Waldorf. Whoever it was might have seen when and how Abigail left the inn.

Wellacott monitored every burp and hiccup in this town.

181

His standing reservation was for seven. Most nights, he arrived at six or six-thirty and had a drink with whatever potential votes he happened to encounter at the bar.

Nora ducked through the drizzle to the inn and stationed herself at the reception desk to wait for him. Laughter drifted in from the living room where Raymond was still holding court. From the snatches she caught, he was into the name-dropping portion of his routine. He was up to the rock stars, which meant he'd already recited the roster of Hollywood heavies and media moguls he counted among his two or three thousand close personal friends. For once, Nora was grateful for Chef Villet's outraged interruption.

The group around Raymond went mute when the temperamental cook stormed in and started ranting.

'Quiet! *Silence!* No one can create with such a noise,' he sputtered. 'This is madness. *La folie!* The strawberries are *ordure*. Fit for pigs. And I will not put my beautiful lobster bisque in those tureens. Fingerprints all over. A disgrace. If this is how you choose to run your restaurant, you will run it without me, Monsieur Brill.'

'All right, Etienne. Calm down. I'll take care of everything,' Charlie said.

As usual, Nora marvelled at Charlie's restraint. Villet was a massive pain in the derrière. But he was also the mainstay of the inn's prizewinning kitchen. He'd been with them a year – a very long year, Nora imagined. Charlie had been discreetly trying to replace him from virtually the day he arrived, but so far, no luck. Not many top chefs would agree to be consigned to the north boondocks.

'No more!' Villet ranted. 'Not again. I can not tolerate such . . . such *paresseux!*'

Under stress, Villet's English often failed him. Unfortunately, his tongue did not. He unleashed a flood of French expletives, and a pox of scarlet blotches erupted on his neck.

'All right, Etienne. That's enough. I said I'd see to everything.'

Villet swerved on his petulant heel and stormed out of the room.

Ray's audience reluctantly dispersed. After the last of

182

them had left, Raymond hauled himself off the couch and trudged down the hall towards his suite. Grateful for the silence, Nora waited for Justin to arrive. Hopefully, he'd be able to tell her about the Waldorf's new occupant. In a tiny town like Dove's Landing, neighbours were supposed to be known quantities, all part of a comforting, familiar weave.

Wellacott breezed in about fifteen minutes later sporting a cashmere blazer, silver flannel trousers, and a silk paisley ascot. He brushed the beads of rain from his shoulders and drew a bracing breath. He was wearing his signature scent: a custom blend of citrus, musk, and money. Crossing to the desk, he caged Nora's hand between his palms.

'Nora, my dear. How are you holding up?'

She questioned him about the progress of the search. So far, no leads. The troopers were still out questioning townspeople. The reconnaissance helicopters and dog teams would continue searching until Abigail was safely returned. Nora had heard the chop of the rotors on her walk. Small comfort.

'We're going to find her, my dear. It's just a matter of time.'

Time. Another night of endless, creeping seconds. More jarring nightmares of Abby plummeting through the gaping earth to black oblivion. Screaming for help Nora was powerless to give. Reaching, begging.

At the thought, panic looped around Nora's neck, shutting off the air. An electric rash of fear scaled her spine. She couldn't stand it any more.

No more!

The room was whirling. She groped for a handhold. Flailed in impotent desperation. Struggled to breathe.

Suddenly, she felt hands. Shaking. A sharp, insistent voice was pulling at her.

'Nora? Stop it now! Get a hold of yourself.'

She managed tiny sips of air, ordered her muscles to ease. The panic began to back away. Her fingers uncoiled with the creaky reluctance of rusted hinges. Better. But the air was slicked with an eerie sheen, and the walls trembled.

Maybe they were right. Maybe she was losing her mind.

'Nora?'

Justin was staring at her, his face warped with astonishment.

'My word, Nora. What happened? Are you all right?' he said.

'Yes. I mean, no. Of course I'm not all right. How the hell could I be? I want Abigail. I need my baby!'

He looked as if he'd stepped on a rattler. Obviously, he couldn't begin to comprehend her despair. There was no way to explain fear and anguish to a jewel-encrusted hunk of plastic like Justin. Why waste words?

The spell of panic had left her numb and worn out, but she was over the worst of it. Back in reasonable control. Justin was eager to withdraw from the unpleasantness, but Nora remembered why she'd been waiting at the desk and stopped him.

Struggling to sound calmer, she asked about the changes at the Waldorf-Astoria and the new tenant. Wellacott wasn't able to add much to what she'd heard from his secretary. There had been talk of a possible rental, he said. The owners, an elderly couple living in Florida, had hired local contractors to make the necessary repairs. If the house had already been leased, he knew nothing of the arrangements. But he promised to ask around and let Nora know what he'd learned.

As he left her to go to the bar, she was puzzled by his offhand attitude. It wasn't at all like Justin to be uninterested in anything to do with Dove's Landing. He treated the tiny town as his personal property, which it mostly was. Hard to imagine he was barely curious about a new resident.

Then so many things she'd taken for granted had proven to be dangerous mistakes. If she ever awoke from this monstrous nightmare, she'd have to start over from the beginning and try to separate the wishes from the truths.

A party of four entered in a puff of rain-soaked cold. Wearily, Nora rose to greet them.

28 Quinn was in no mood for more surprises, but she collided with several on the trip home. Five minutes north of Dove's Landing near the town of Bondville, the rain yielded to a light scatter of snow. Flurries weren't all that rare for Vermont in late April, but the flakes soon multiplied, fluffed like popped corn, and began to dance in dizzy spirals.

Zero visibility would have been an improvement. Quinn inched along, feeling her way for the next couple of miles, until she emerged from the freak squall into a world of startling clarity. No rain here; not a cloud, though looking over her shoulder she could see the wall of dark weather to the south. Ahead the sky was navy lacquer and sprinkled with stars. Firm winds and the tumbling temperature polished the air to a dazzling glimmer.

Without incident, she followed Route 30 to the junction of Route 7 North. Then, a few miles south of East Dorset, she hit a tangle of stalled traffic, mostly jeeps and pickups, honking their frustrations like a gaggle of aggravated geese.

The line of cars stretched well beyond the limits of her vision. Stepping out, Quinn searched for a clue to the problem, but caught none. Flipping to the police band on her radio, she was accosted by the standard squawks and static blips before a dispatcher from the nearby town of Danby barked through to report a jackknifed milk tanker.

Familiar with the exasperating pace of local operations, she eased onto the grassy central reservation, negotiated a tricky U-turn, and doubled back to leave the highway. The meandering secondaries and back roads took her miles out of her way, but at least she was getting somewhere. At the town of Pawlet she cut east and reconnected with Route 7 beyond the tie-up.

Clear road ahead, so she nudged the accelerator, and

suctioned her radar detector onto the dashboard. If she made up some of the time she'd lost, she'd be able to get home in time to have dinner with Brendon. A hefty dose of childish silliness and enthusiasm would be exactly the cure for what was ailing her.

That, and a working brain.

How could she have been so dumb? She'd let Weir get the better of her. Let him *get* her to be more precise. If he'd been so inclined, she'd still be at the Waldorf-Astoria, playing the bleeding lady in one of Professor Pain's world-famous slice-and-dice shows.

But he'd let her go for whatever reason, and she intended to make the reprieve permanent. No way would she ever let down her guard around that monster again. Quinn never made the same mistake twice. No need, given her talent for inventing fresh ones. She kept reliving the creepy encounter. *How had he known so much about Abigail? How had he known the child's name?*

She was making excellent time. No traffic. No warning blips from the radar detector. Trees and power lines melded in a satisfying blur. The jeep was no hot rod, but the old girl did respond nicely to encouragement.

Ten miles to Rutland; ten minutes until Bren's usual dinnertime. Quinn nudged the gas harder. Her reward was a whistling rush of displaced wind followed closely by the wail of a police siren.

A light flashed in her rearview mirror, and she heard the trooper's voice booming through a roof-mounted speaker, ordering her to pull over. Knowing such devices were not very popular with the cops, she reached over to detach the radar detector and stuff it in the glove compartment. No surprise that the thing hadn't sounded a warning: Quinn had neglected to plug it into the cigarette lighter.

She rolled onto the shoulder and the state car pulled up behind her. Quinn knew it would take the trooper a couple of minutes to run her plate number through his on-board computer. She used the time to test and discard a number of improbable excuses: sick relative, job emergency, house on fire, labour pains, cat up a tree.

Nope. The only one up a tree was Quinn Gallagher herself. What the hell else was going to go wrong?

The trooper was getting out of his car. Trying to feign innocent nonchalance, Quinn kept her eyes dead ahead until he was even with her door. When she turned to smile pretty and try to charm the guy, he aimed a million-watt flashlight directly into her eyes.

Slowly, the initial blindness yielded to a grainy vision of giant floating dots.

'Yes, officer? What's the problem?'

A grunt voice issued from one of the dots near the top of the blur. 'Problem is you were doing eighty in a sixty-five zone. Licence and registration please.'

Quinn groped for the items he'd requested. When she deflected her gaze from the beam, the floating dots followed her.

He kept the unrelenting light on her as he inspected the cards. Handing them back, he chuckled.

'Step out now, Ma'am. You been drinking?'

'No.'

'How many drinks you had exactly?'

'None.'

'We'll see.'

Quinn opened the door. Damned flashbeam stuck to her like flypaper.

'Can you please turn that thing off?' she said. She was familiar with the state-police procedure book. Giving the suspect a sunburn was not standard.

'Oh, I will. But first I'd like you to put your arms out to the sides, touch your index fingers to your nose in turn, and recite the alphabet.'

Quinn felt a trifle foolish, but she obeyed. Damned light was so distracting, she almost forgot what came after the L-M-N-O-P part.

'Now, stand on one foot, close your eyes, hold your arms out at your sides, and sing, "I'm a Yankee Doodle Dandy".'

The light was driving her crazy. But suddenly, a bigger bulb snapped on in Quinn's brain. She knew this cop: the voice, the bulk, the imbecilic sense of humour. It could only be one so-called person.

A murderous rage bubbled in her gut. She wanted to castrate the creep. Make him swallow his flashlight whole. She wanted to slather his face with Alpo and introduce him to Weir's dog. But she was able to keep a grip on herself in the interest of a much nobler purpose: revenge.

The gun was in her right pocket. She slipped her fingers casually into her left one and found the better weapon.

'That's you, isn't it, Ralph Norman? I didn't recognise your voice right away.'

He snickered. 'You shoulda seen your face, Gallagher. Scared like you were in front of a fucking firing squad.'

'You pulled me over for a joke? Is that what you're saying?'

'Gets real boring waiting out here for yuppie New Yorkers to come along in their Beemers. Can't see nabbing locals when it's such fun fingering those rich snots. Anyhow, I saw you pass, figured I'd stop you and see if you'd gotten over your temper tantrum.'

'You mean you pulled me over, flashed that light in my eyes for ten minutes, and gave me a drunk test just for fun?'

'Got you again, didn't I, Gallagher? Have to tell you, though, you were funnier when we tricked you into walking in on Weir's strip-search. Should've seen your face when you got a load of that guy buck naked.'

'You thought that was funny, Ralph?'

'Course I did. It *was* funny. Pretending to nab you for speeding was funny too. Lighten up, lady. Life's too short. Where's your sense of humour?'

Quinn bared her teeth. 'Oh I have one, officer. Absolutely. It's just that different things strike me as funny. For instance, I'm going to fall down laughing while you're roasting on the spit over the fire I set for you at Internal Affairs. And it'll double me over to watch you sweat bullets during the sexual-harrassment suit I'm going to bring against you. Don't worry if you don't have the whole amount of the judgement in the bank, Ralphie boy. I'll be satisfied with a lien on your house and an attachment on your salary until it's paid off.'

He blanched. 'It's your fucking word against mine, lady. So don't waste your time. Cops stick together.'

Quinn let her face fall and hesitated a nice, long time. 'Gee, I didn't think of it that way.' She held the forced frown as she slipped into the jeep and turned the engine over. Edging onto the highway, she poked her head out the window and smiled. Stupid lard had already ambled halfway back to his cruiser.

'You know what, Ralphie boy, you've got it wrong. It's *your* word against yours. You see, I got our whole chat on tape. Think of it, Norman, you enormous, abnormal nerd. You just hung yourself with your own stupid tongue.' She held up the cassette and gave it a jaunty wiggle.

Ralph Norman flushed scarlet and lunged towards the jeep. But while he was still out of range, Quinn pulled out her father's gun and shot a warning round at the rising moon. The guy did a confused little dance, flailing around for his next move. Before he could realise that chasing her in the cruiser was his only chance to get the tape, she took aim and shot out his front tyres.

Quinn fired a final round of howling laughter. 'Now that's what I call funny, Ralphie boy. That's, as you'd put it, *fucking* hilarious.' She hit the accelerator and bolted onto the road.

Though she was sweat-soaked and wrung out from her trials with Weird Ellie and Rotten Ralph, Quinn suddenly felt wonderful. She whistled the rest of the way home. The sky and the roads stayed clear.

Opening the door, she called for Brendon. No answer, but she caught the drone of someone on the phone in the den. Listening harder, she heard the popping sound of Bren batting at Dud Chamber's practice contraption in the backyard. Neither snow nor sleet nor dark of night stayed that pipsqueak from his appointed quest.

After hiding the gun and the incriminating tape in a safe place, she headed for the yard. Her victory over the fool trooper had her in a celebratory mood. A splurge on a white-cloth restaurant seemed appropriate.

Out the kitchen door, she spotted Bren at the batting

device: poised, intent, grimy. She watched as he took a couple of studied cuts. No question, the kid seemed more fluid and put together. Bugged her to think Levitsky would probably try to grab the credit when she'd been practising with the squirt for years. But then the only important thing was Bren getting the reward he deserved.

Enjoying the view, she let him continue for a couple of minutes until she sensed a natural break in the action.

'Hey, slugger. Looking real good.'

Bren nodded. Smiled. Took another swat.

'Think you can tear yourself away for dinner at your all-time favourite restaurant?'

'The Sirloin Saloon?'

'None other.'

He frowned. 'Tell you in a minute.'

Bren dropped his bat and dashed into the house. Quinn waited, stumped. Kid loved that hokey place with its giant slabs of juicy cholesterol, cottony rolls, three-mile salad bar, and lethal desserts. Why would he hesitate?

The question answered itself as her brother re-emerged with Bernie Levitsky in tow. Quinn's spirit slipped its cable and plunged to the sub-basement. Seeing the agent was a head-on crash with reality. The little girl was still missing. Quinn's neck was still firmly in the noose. She had screwed up royally with Weir and possibly killed whatever chance she'd had to get at the truth. What the hell was there to feel good about?

'Brendon didn't expect you back until later,' Levitsky said. 'I was going to call a cab and take him out for a bite, but since you're here, we can play it any way you want.'

What she wanted was to make the agent disappear, but she knew precisely how that would play with her brother. 'I thought you were going to stay at the hotel and turn in early,' she said.

'I was, but then I remembered I promised Big Bren here that I'd help him practise his fielding tonight.'

'Oh.' So the guy kept his promises. Quinn knew where and how she'd like to pin the medal. 'Guess we can all go to the Sirloin Saloon then.'

'Whatever Bernie wants.'

Levitsky ruffled the kid's hair. 'You're the man of the hour, champ. Your choice.'

Bren dashed upstairs for a shower, and Quinn ambled into the living room to wait. She was hoping to lose Levitsky for a while, but no such luck.

Determined to ignore him, she picked up an ancient *Newsweek* from the end table and tried to get herself interested in an article about the anticipated outcome of the presidential election two years earlier. She could feel Levitsky's eyes on her, as intense and irritating as wretched Ralph Norman's flashlight.

Finally, she looked up. 'Yes?'

Levitsky crossed his legs and leaned back. 'You're the one who has something to say, Ms Gallagher. Not me.'

'No I don't.'

'Yes you do.'

'Since you obviously know it all, Levitsky, why would you need me to tell you anything?'

'I don't. But I thought you might prefer it that way.'

She puffed her contempt. 'You're so full of hot air, it's amazing you don't float away.'

Levitsky just sat there. Relaxed. Unhurried.

'You went into the Waldorf to talk to Weir,' he said.

Quinn flushed. 'Why would I do a dumb thing like that?'

'Because you're reckless and impulsive, and you thought you'd have a better chance with him than I did.'

She felt the blush intensify. She wanted to kick herself and him, though not necessarily in that order.

'I'm tired, Levitsky. If it's all the same to you, I'd prefer you put off my inquisition and beheading until tomorrow, okay?'

'All I want to know is what happened with Weir.'

'Nothing happened. I didn't say I was at the Waldorf.'

Bren was on his way down the stairs. Levitsky lowered his tone to a whisper. 'You'll tell me later.'

'There's nothing to tell.'

'Oh yes there is,' he rasped. 'And you can start with the part about how he took away your gun.'

29 'Abigail! Abigail Eakins?'

The voice was drawing closer, honing in on her. If she waited much longer, she'd be trapped in her hiding place. Ditching the blankets, she fled the farmhouse porch and ran through the frigid drizzle as fast as she could in the clumsy, oversized boots. To reach the access drive she had to traverse a span of perilous open field.

'Abigail! Say something. Answer me, Abby. Come on now.'

The drive was much slimmer than she'd expected, barely wide enough for a car. Protruding twigs and snarled brush further narrowed the way. The path was bordered by towering trees. High overhead, their limbs arched together casting thick webs of shadow on the murky ground.

'Abby? Say something, and we'll come for you. It's okay, honey. You'll be safe with us.'

She plunged ahead. Closed her mind to the dizzying shadow stripes that lashed her face. Blocked out the skittering creatures and stalking hulks of unseen menace. The greater danger was behind her. The gathering darkness was nothing compared to a maniac armed with airless tubes and invisible fires and paralysing ghost fingers that could grab you and lock your feet to the ground.

She strained to avoid jutting stones and jarring furrows. Once, she came down hard in an unexpected groove and wrenched her ankle. There was a cracking sound, and a bolt of pain. But several tentative steps later, it eased to a nagging soreness.

'Come on, Abigail. We know you're here. Tell us where you are.'

We. Us.

It did sound like two different voices, but she wasn't fooled for a second. She knew he could send his voice skipping like a pebble on a pond, slip it to unexpected places like a coin under a trio of revolving nutshells, stretch it paper thin or weight it to a giant vat of wet gravel. He could change his tone, accent, mood, intentions with the ease of a finger snap. He'd done it to her in the tube thing and again in the canvas sack.

Games and tricks. Phony newspapers and secret pictures. Fake fires and dead rats. A chant looped through her mind, echoed in the rhythm of her run: *I won't let him trick me. Never, never again. Never, never. I'll die first.*

'Abigail!'

Her ear caught the breathy rush of a passing car. She was nearing the road. The voice behind her was dimming, almost inaudible now.

She followed the drive as it circled a massive oak and scaled a gentle incline. At the peak she came to the farm's entrance. A rusted fence girdled the property. The gate was bordered by a cow-shaped wooden sign and a battered mailbox. Beyond to the right was a wooden stand with the legend 'Maple Syrup for Sale' etched on the side.

The road was not much broader than the dirt drive and hardly better tended. Cracks and ruts marred the surface, and the shoulder was heaped with scabrous patches of the sand spread to tame slick winter roads.

Miles of nothing stretched endlessly in both directions. Facing the desolate landscape, her lungs burning as she struggled to catch her breath, Abigail was assailed by the wet piercing chill. Her torn T-shirt was soaked. She regretted leaving the blankets on the porch. They might have slowed her down, but now she had nothing to keep her dry or warm.

What next?

Freezing, starved, and sore-footed, she didn't relish the prospect of walking on indefinitely in the rain in pursuit of the unpredictable unknown. She had no idea which might be the better direction. Could be miles either way before she came upon a house or another farm.

But she couldn't stand here forever.

She set out towards the left. But a few feet away, she was

stalled by the hacking sound of approaching helicopter blades. He'd given up on the farm and gotten back in the chopper. Aiming towards the road.

Hide!

Racing for the maple-syrup stand, she pried open the flat wood panel that served as a door, tugged it in place behind her, and crouched out of sight.

The booth was a drafty, gap-toothed construction of flimsy planks and crossbeams. Abigail huddled in the corner on the warped plywood floor. Arms around her calves, knees pressed to her chest, fingers woven, she couldn't stop trembling. The helicopter hesitated above the stand, worked its searchlight in a lazy sweep, and finally drifted away.

Outside, another car passed with a wind surge and a piercing flush of rain-salted headlamps. She imagined herself riding in its lavish comfort, soothing music on the radio, toasty heat wafting through the vents.

Once she was dropped off at the inn, she'd sneak in and surprise everyone. Warmed her like a bulb in her belly to think about all the kisses and hugs and welcomes and happy tears. Mim would fix her a huge mug of her special hot cocoa with marshmallows, Mom would fetch her furry slippers and terry robe from the cabin, and they'd all sit in front of a fire in the copper hearth. Abigail would tell them the whole story. Everything. How sick, mean, and demented he was. All he'd said and done to her. The only thing she might leave out was the part about how she'd gotten home by hitching a ride.

Mom had warned her thousands of times about getting into cars with strangers, talking to strangers, strangers in general. Abigail knew the rules: not to make eye contact or answer questions or do favours no matter how innocent the situation seemed. Not to take anything or give anything including the most trivial personal information like your name or your birthday.

The gory hazards were all over the news: murder, rape, kidnapping. Daily, there were stories about children struck by those horrors in their most horrific forms. So many

194

stories, Abigail's response had dulled from electric dread to numb, clinical curiosity.

Once, on a Saturday night sleepover, she and Jeanine had spent half the night speculating about the victims of such crimes. Nearly all of the fresh-faced kids over the nasty captions in local tabloids were honour students or star athletes or extremely popular and good-hearted or all of those things and very religious to boot. Not one of them had a reportable flaw.

At about three in the morning, when they were both drunk with exhaustion, stuffed with munchies, and deeply ensconced in the mandatory giggle phase of any really serious discussion, they'd decided that the best defence against such a sinister fate was avoiding perfection at all costs. No problem for Abigail, who had a mental block against maths and had tried smoking with Bonita Todd in the fifth grade. None for Jeanine either, who suffered memory lapses about homework and sometimes ditched school for a particularly important episode of *All My Children*. Anyway, they'd decided, neither of them was all that fresh-faced.

No matter what Mom said, avoiding strangers didn't guarantee a thing. Abigail knew her tormentor. Worse, he knew her. He could read her fears, gauge her weak points, entrap her with her own shortcomings. A stranger would be a breeze compared to him.

Another car passed. Hitching was really the only way, she decided. Mom would never have to know.

Pushing out the door plank, she stepped outside. The fierce, frigid wind had risen, and the rain had solidified to stinging snowflakes. The right side of the stand provided some meagre protection, and Abigail waited there for another car to come. Seemed forever until a fuzzy light loomed in the distance. The headlights gained form and intensity as the car approached, but she couldn't bring herself to stand exposed in the road and heft her thumb.

Several minutes passed before another car zipped by: a little red sports number. Abigail promised herself that she'd signal the next one, but when fresh lights materialised down the road, she saw they were the massive double beams of a truck. A car seemed safer.

Took forever. Finally a misty sheen invaded the far edge of her vision. This car was moving in near slow motion, giving her plenty of time to hoist her nerve and get herself in position.

Waiting, she rehearsed the proper pleading expression and the optimal crook of her thumb. The car was still some distance away, but she could tell it was a long, dark, polished road-boat like Daddy's Lincoln.

Exactly like Daddy's. A sharp knocking started in her chest. Her mouth turned to blotting paper. Could it be?

She tried to contain her excitement. Sense told her there were plenty of shiny, black Lincolns. The person at the wheel was invisible in the dark interior. Might be anyone.

But instinct said it was Daddy. He'd probably heard she was missing and come to find her. Exactly what he'd do. And she knew exactly what he'd say: 'Abby Gail, where've you been, girl? Come on in out of the cold now.'

She was grinning so hard, her face hurt. In a second, she'd be safe in Daddy's car. Wrapped in a major hug. Giggling to one of his hilarious stories.

Skipping onto the road, she raised her arms and started waving frantically. He beeped in response. Her insides were jangling. Spring-loaded feet, trampoline bones, heart so happy it threatened to pop like a gum bubble.

'Daddy!' she screamed. 'I knew you'd come. I just knew it!'

Her yelling intensified as the Lincoln slowed even more. She was so nutsy impatient, she was tempted to run and hurl herself on the hood while the car was still moving. She wanted to squeeze the metal, plant wet kisses all over the snow-frosted windshield.

'Hurry up! Stop already. Hurry up, Daddy!'

As the car rolled to a stop, she raced around the front, tugged open the driver's door, and prepared to fling her arms around her father's neck.

But what she saw rooted her in shock. The maniac had come for her. And she'd run right to him.

30 Back from the Sirloin Saloon, Levitsky borrowed Quinn's rain poncho and spent an hour in the floodlit backyard tossing fly balls and hot tips at Brendon. Finished, the pair came in flushed with the cold and dripping a dark trail of slush off their raingear. In the kitchen, Levitsky whipped up a hot froth of some milk-based concoction. At her brother's urging, Quinn had a taste. Damn. Delicious.

Marilyn Holland was forever nagging Quinn to find herself a man who could cook. So this one could. Unfortunately, he didn't do all that much for her appetite.

When the clock struck bedtime, Brendon pitched her an offhanded goodnight and motioned for Levitsky to accompany him upstairs. As executive in charge of tuck-ins, Quinn suffered a swat of envy. She'd always known that she'd be evicted from the core of Bren's universe eventually. But the other woman was not supposed to be six-four with beard stubble.

She heard them overhead: trampling feet, squealing bedsprings, laughter, a long whispered conference that wafted with teasing clarity through the heating ducts. Seeking distraction, she flipped through the cable channels. She was up for a horror movie or a cooking show. Entertainment equivalents to Quinn. But she found neither.

Ten minutes later, Levitsky plodded down the stairs. Before he could make it to the den, Quinn zapped the set back on by remote and feigned rapt interest in a home-shopping show. Only thirty-two fifty for a ceramic whatsit with an extremely captivating doodah on top. Real bargain. The host was down to the last three hundred units, warning in dire tones about limited supplies and lost opportunities. Quinn figured she'd better excuse herself and phone in her order before she missed out.

But Levitsky stood blocking the doorway with crossed

arms and a bemused expression. Guy was too damned single-minded and determined for Quinn's taste. Made her want to ram him like a tackling dummy. Too bad she needed the job.

She settled for a sour expression, which he studiously ignored.

'What I need is a blow-by-blow of everything Weir said and did from the moment you entered that house. Don't leave anything out no matter how unimportant it seems to you.'

'Are you on that Weir business again? Where'd you get such a crazy idea, Levitsky?'

'It's written all over you.' He worked from the bottom up, pointing and delineating. 'The clippings stuck to your shoes are from the Waldorf's front yard: blend of zoysia grass, rye, and wild clover mowed with the blade set at two inches. Those dog hairs on your pants are from Weir's pooch: five- or six-year-old German Shepherd with a pinch of Collie and a dash of black Labrador. Poor thing has a case of doggy dermatitis, which accounts for the flaking at the follicle level and the unseasonal shedding. Your jacket pockets are stretched out, which tells me they were recently stuffed with bulky objects. From the particular bagging in the right one, I'd lay odds on a gun and ammunition, probably a forty-five from the size and angle of the sag, though I won't venture a guess about the make or model. Can't say much about the bulge in the left pocket either, though it was obviously a rectangle, heavy for its size. Maybe a tape recorder or a portable radio.

'Most telling of all, when you came in you were sweating bullets, and it's been the coldest April twenty-fifth on record. Word is there was frozen rain and a snow squall further south. You're not ordinarily a heavy perspirer, not even when you're enraged, which is most of the time. So obviously you had yourself quite a scare.'

Quinn was incredulous. Not only was the guy a walking x-ray machine, but he had the audacity to sit there, stripping her naked, making a total fool of her, and he wasn't the least bit smug. Not a hint of triumph in those

198

Bambi eyes, not a twitch of arrogance on the full-lipped mouth, not a pinch of superiority in the lean, athletic body. If only she had something heavy and dangerous to throw at him.

'How the hell do you know so much, Levitsky?'

'I find it impossible to forget things, Gallagher. Even things I'd rather not remember. I read something, hear or see something, it's with me for keeps. Can be a curse or a blessing. But right now, I'm more interested in what stuck with you from your visit with Weir.'

She glared at him, then slumped in the chair and clicked off the TV. 'All right. I admit I went to the Waldorf. From certain things he said before, I thought Weir might be willing to talk to me. Tell me what he knows, if anything. It was a stupid idea.'

Levitsky didn't argue.

'I got nothing and nowhere. So let's forget it, shall we?'

He shook his head in a firm negative. 'No, Ms Gallagher. We're not going to forget it. I want to hear everything. Every detail, no matter how trivial it seems to you. Your approach was all wrong, but I applaud your instincts. If that little girl was snatched, I'd lay odds that Weir was involved, directly or indirectly.'

'How could he be? He has no way to get out of the Waldorf or communicate with the outside.'

'Obviously you're no surer of that than I am, or you wouldn't have risked your fool neck going in there. So please, tell me exactly what happened.'

Quinn recognised the voice of reason, and she found it absolutely infuriating. She wanted to deny her own nagging suspicions. Maybe if she pretended hard enough that the whole mess didn't exist, it would go away. *But how had Weir known the little girl's name?*

'You want me to start with the butler opening the door and the waiter passing those little canapes on a doilied tray? The gravlax was really outstanding.'

'I've got all the time in the world, Ms Gallagher.'

'Then why don't you go out in the world and use it, Mr Levitsky?'

He sighed. 'Look, I know you don't like me. You've made that exceedingly clear. But this isn't about you or me or us. It's about an eleven-year-old girl who could be in terrible jeopardy and an evil sonavabitch who just might slip and give us something we can use to get her back. So why don't you tell me what happened with Weir first, and then you can beat up on me all you like. Okay?'

Quinn lost the stare-down. Guy was right. Why was he always so goddamned right?

He sat opposite her. She told him about the disastrous visit. Levitsky took a while to digest the tale.

'He talked about a melody?' he said finally.

'Yes.'

'And he said you already have everything you need to go from there?'

'Yes.'

'Those were his exact words?'

She rolled her eyes and sputtered like a leaky tyre, but Levitsky was oblivious to her irritation. Quinn wondered if he'd catch on if she slipped her fingers around his neck and squeezed.

He mulled things over a while longer. 'It's obvious then.'

'What is?'

'Think, Gallagher. If he says you already have everything you need, what must he be talking about?'

'You mean his corrections file?'

'Exactly. And if he's pointing you to his file, what would be the sensible place for us to start digging? Where do you think we'll find the so-called "foot of the path" he talked about?'

Quinn was getting worried. She was actually starting to follow the guy's reasoning.

'Start at the end and work backwards, you mean?'

Levitsky's face stretched in a slow, satisfied grin. 'Not bad, Ms Gallagher. You might have the makings of a logical being after all.'

'Watch it, Levitsky,' she said. 'I told you. No insults.'

Levitsky managed to reach Will Darmon, the warden from the St Albans Prison, at home. When he heard that the subject was Eldon Weir and a missing child, Darmon agreed to squeeze them into his packed schedule in the morning as long as they could be at the facility by ten.

To make it, Quinn would have to rouse Brendon over an hour early and deposit him at a friend's house. She asked Jason Stutey's mother for the favour, hoping that Jason's premiere collection of Nintendo cartridges would help lure the kid out of bed.

No such luck.

Boy didn't so much as twitch during her entire rendition of Brendon-at-the-bat. Not a flicker when the frenzied crowd roared to its feet. Time to haul out the heavy artillery.

She hefted the mock megaphone and segued into her world famous Yogi Berra imitation.

'It's a banner day here at the stadium, ladies and gentleman. The big man, Gallagher the Great, one of the few living legends still alive today, is on hand to help us retire his number. No one deserves this honour more than everyone's pal Gallagher. Big Bren has done more for, to, and with the sport of baseball than anyone in the history of the game. So now join me in giving a rousing Gallagher-Stadium welcome to the battiest batter ever – Brendon the Tendon Gallagher!'

She hooted and whistled and cheered and gesticulated and acted the general fool until he relented and slipped out of bed. Then she yapped and chuffed like a hyperkinetic dog to keep the kid moving. Skinny arms aloft, waving at his frantic fans, he padded across the hall into the bathroom.

Once the door was shut and the water running, she peeked under the covers. No damp spots. A miracle drought.

Quinn was delighted for the kid, but she knew not to say anything. It was his call. If Bren wanted congratulations, he'd ask for them.

Which he did not. When he slogged into the kitchen still yawning and rubbing his eyes, his only request was for French toast and fresh squeezed juice. Then he regained sufficient consciousness to realise who was preparing the meal and padded to the pantry cabinet for the Wheaties.

After breakfast, Quinn dropped him at the Stuteys' and drove to the Holiday Inn to fetch Levitsky. He was waiting at the kerb, engrossed in a three-page fax. When Quinn beeped to catch his attention, he quickly folded the papers and stuffed them into his briefcase.

The town of St Albans was in the northwest corner of Vermont. Not far from the Canadian border, it was way further from Rutland than Quinn thought any place had a right to be.

She had long resented the sheer size of her home state. Scenery-starved tourists never tired of Vermont's appalling glut of rolling pastures, snow-sugared mountains, and virgin forestland. Quinn found the endless sprawl of loveliness highly inconvenient and extremely boring.

She had much preferred compact Boston with its nerve-jolting noise and frenzied pace. She missed the nice, sardine-packed feel of an urban hub. Reared with a surfeit of numbing rural calm, Quinn had fast become a fan of rapid transit. People who bumped and jarred one another like too many packed molecules in a jar; neighbours who didn't know your name much less your business; blessed anonymity.

Predictably, Levitsky studied the verdant landscape, issued a contented sigh, and made the typical tourist observation. 'It's so beautiful here.'

'Oh really? What do you like the best about it, Levitsky? My particular favourite is the roads. It's a little known fact, but Vermont happens to have the premier pothole collection in North America. We also generate the nation's largest crop of cattle manure. And if you want to talk skiing, we export more torn ligaments than any other state and almost double the number of fractures, plenty of them compound. You ever have one of those where the bone cracks like a dry twig and sticks up through the skin?'

That killed the conversation for the next couple of hours during which Quinn fiddled with the radio, unsuccessfully searching for a decent station. Another of the Green

Mountain State's well-kept secrets was that all those damned green mountains fouled up the TV and radio transmission. Fouled up Quinn's mood too.

She wanted to find the easy listening station she'd stumbled over several times in the last couple of days. Dud Chambers had it on in the Photo Lab, and dippy Dawn from Wellacott's office had been tuned to it as well. Nice play list, all sixties and seventies. Quinn remembered the call letters from a station identification announcement: WCCR. But she didn't know the frequency, so she pressed the 'seek' button about four or five thousand times.

'What are you looking for?' Levitsky said through clenched teeth. 'Maybe I can help.'

Quinn turned off the radio. She knew when she was being annoying, and much as she enjoyed making the G-man uncomfortable, she was starting to get on her own nerves as well.

The final leg of the trip wound north on the Veteran's Memorial Highway through Colchester, Chimney Corner and Checkerberry Village. Quinn found the endless string of tiny towns with precious names utterly depressing. Her spirits didn't begin to improve until they came to the sign announcing that they'd entered Georgia Center, which meant they'd soon be in St Albans and finished with half of this interminable trip.

Like most local towns, Georgia Center featured a minuscule library, an elementary school, farm stands and antique shops. After a few blocks, the standard crop of centre-of-town colonials yielded to the customary spread of outlying dairy farms.

The town's sole distinguishing trait was the Langdon Industry factory complex near the town line for Alban's Bay. It was an unsightly sprawl of commercial buildings surrounded by chicken-wire fencing and capped by a fat cloud of Langdon's premier product: air pollution.

'That charming place is brought to you by same dear folk who gave us Eldon Weir,' she said as they passed.

'Stop,' Levitsky said.

Quinn chose not to hear him. She wasn't interested in prolonging this endless trip.

'Would you please stop?'

Quinn would have continued her scrupulous disregard, but Levitsky made that extremely difficult by reaching over and wrenching on the emergency brake. The jeep howled like a wounded bull and bucked to a halt.

'What in the hell do you think you're doing?' Quinn screeched.

'I asked you to stop,' he said. 'I want to look at that factory. Now would you please back up? It'll only take a minute.'

'How about I leave you right here, and you can look all you like, Levitsky?'

'Pull up next to the gate. I'll be able to see what I need to from there.'

Seething, Quinn sped in reverse to the factory entrance. Drove her crazy that she couldn't get a rise out of this man. Brilliant, unflappable people like him made her want to throw a good old-fashioned tantrum.

Levitsky stepped out and scrutinised the industrial complex for several minutes. Quinn tried to see what he found so captivating, but it was all cement, metal chunks, and plumes of stinking exhaust to her.

Slipping back into the jeep, Levitsky nodded for her to proceed. His eyes were aimed in her direction, but his mind was obviously elsewhere. Quinn was dying to know what, if anything, he thought he might learn from observing the repulsive place. But she wouldn't give him the satisfaction of asking.

More juvenile spite.

Quinn knew she'd been behaving badly since the man's arrival, but she was powerless to stop. Soon, she thought, all this would be over and he'd be out of her life forever. She'd get back to normal, or as close as she'd ever been.

A Levitsky-free life. Funny how she couldn't imagine exactly how that was going to be.

31 St Albans, officially known as the Northwest State Correctional Facility, was a low brick structure, sombre and forbidding. Jutting off the main building were two wire exercise pens and several boxy concrete constructions built as an after-thought to house vocational programmes. The prison was buttressed by a ten-foot fence capped by a double coil of razor wire. At intervals along the border were manned watchtowers and giant rotating spotlights.

The prison was ranked as a closed facility, medium security. The designation called for a secure external perimeter, armed perimeter patrol, restricted inmate move-ment within the institution and armed escort whenever a convict had reason to go outside. Quinn knew that offenders deemed in need of tighter strictures were shipped to maximum-security penitentiaries out of state, but from the look of this place, it was hard to fathom what breed of animal would require a more fearsome cage.

Knowing the rules, Quinn left her keys in the glove compartment. Levitsky deposited his hotel key there as well along with his FBI-issue Smith & Wesson 10mm semi-automatic and a twenty-two calibre pistol from the ankle holster Quinn had failed to notice earlier. All prisons prohibited visitors from carrying weapons or keys inside, either of which might be snatched by an inmate and put to unfortunate use.

In the main lobby they waited for the guard, a stocky flaxen-haired woman, to check their names and identifi-cation against the warden's roster of approved visitors for the day. Next, they were directed to pass through a rectan-gular metal detector.

Quinn went first and got the green light. When Levitsky stepped through, the light flashed red and a buzzer sounded.

'It's very sensitive,' the guard said. 'Better empty your pockets.'

Levitsky dumped his change on the counter, but the detector was not appeased. Next, the guard had him remove his belt and boots. Sometimes there was metal in the heels, she explained. But even barefooted and beltless, he triggered the alarm.

The guard was clearly enjoying the show. Quinn stood by, miffed at the silly delay, while Blondie and Levitsky bantered about strategy.

'Guess there's nothing left to lose but your jeans, Mr Levitsky. Sorry, rules are rules.'

Levitsky hesitated. Then, when Quinn thought the dolt was actually going to drop his denims, he thought of the sunglasses in his shirt pocket. They proved to be the culprit, and the detector finally gave him clearance.

The prison's circulatory system was regulated from a glass-walled observation booth at the building's core. Inside the bubble, a guard monitored three tiers of small video displays that provided a constant view of all internal and external doors. The same guard controlled the building's electronic locks by remote to ensure that no two adjacent doors were ever left open at the same time.

Airlocks, small corridors secured at both ends, served to further stanch any easy flow of inmate traffic and segregated visitors from residents. On the way to the warden's office, Quinn and Levitsky were stalled three times until the guard in the observation deck deemed it safe to open the airlock doors and let them pass. Behind them, the doors clanged shut with the hideous ring of finality that had led to such places being called 'the slammer'.

Warden Darmon's office was in the centre of the administration wing. A uniformed assistant ushered Quinn and Levitsky inside and introduced them to Darmon, a stocky man with steel-blue eyes and hair the tone and texture of vanilla ice cream. His gaze lit for an instant on Quinn's lanky figure before landing on Levitsky.

Clearly the G-man had been deemed to be in command of the visit, which made Quinn's teeth itch. But it also freed her from having to offer their complex requests and explanations. She was glad to sit by while Levitsky told Darmon about the missing child and Weird Ellie Weir's possible connection to the case.

Listening, Darmon scrawled several notes to himself. When Levitsky finished his pitch about wanting information on Weir for his study, the warden dialled an internal extension.

'You free for a couple of minutes, Brooks? Good. I'm coming over with a couple of people. It's about Eldon Weir. Right.'

Hanging up, he stood. 'I'll take you to meet Brooks Harper. He'll be able to fill you in.'

Quinn and Levitsky followed him out of the office wing, through an airlock, down the corridor housing the mess, laundry and library, through a second airlock, and up a short flight of metal steps.

Darmon's knock brought a short, ferret-faced man with flowing chestnut hair to the door. He had a pencil moustache, dramatic bearing, and an accent thick as London fog. 'Brooks Harper,' he said, extending a graceful hand. 'Do come in.' Guy sounded as if his mouth were full of marbles and someone had planted a clothespin on his nose.

From the nature of the clutter, Quinn could see that the room served a variety of functions. She spotted an eye chart, posters touting the twelve-step programme of Alcoholics Anonymous, computer training manuals, enough annotated Bibles to arm a large study group, and brochures detailing the probation department's community reintegration procedures.

'Brooks is in charge of our Violent-Offender Unit,' Darmon said. 'He supervised Weir during the time he spent with us. I'll leave you in his capable hands, Agent Levitsky. Officer Gallagher.'

After Darmon left, Quinn and the agent took Harper's cue and cleared the rubble from a couple of chairs so they could sit. Quinn displaced heaps of props and costumes. Levitsky moved stacks of books and assorted art and craft supplies.

'So what's Weird Ellie gotten his nasty hooks into now?' Harper said.

Something passed between the men. 'Officially, nothing. Unofficially, I'm not so sure,' Levitsky said finally. Then to Quinn, 'Harper knows Weird Ellie as well as anyone. I think he ought to have the straight story.'

'Up to you, Levitsky.'

'You can trust me to keep my mouth shut, Officer Gallagher. I'm British.'

Levitsky told him about Abigail Eakins' disappearance. He described the proximity of Weir's house to the child's residence and ticked off the other damning coincidences, most notably the physical resemblance between the missing girl and Weir's earlier victims. Quinn had heard the story so many times, her mind drifted. But it snapped back to attention when Levitsky mentioned a new piece of information.

'When I was at the house for Weir's search, I noticed something odd on the door mat. I took scrapings and sent them to the Bureau lab for analysis. The results aren't all in yet, but last night the technician faxed me his preliminary findings. He thinks the sample was a heavy concrete mixture, much higher than average crushed-stone content. Raises some very interesting questions if further testing confirms his first hunch.'

'Wait a minute, Levitsky,' Quinn said. 'The Waldorf was just renovated. Couldn't Weir have picked up the concrete mix there?'

'No,' Levitsky said. 'As I mentioned, it was heavy concrete, industrial grade. Laid over a steel-rod reinforcing base, a surface poured with this stuff would be strong enough to hold an eighteen-wheeler. Nothing like that would be used in a single-family residential construction. Way too expensive. Even in industrial projects, this particular blend would only be used where there's an unusual stress load. Say a factory with heavy machinery or a parking lot or a multi-family dwelling.

'To be doubly sure, I called the general contractor who handled the Waldorf's restoration. He told me the only masonry work on the job was some repair of the front walk. The subcontractor used a standard sand and gravel mix there.'

Quinn wasn't giving up so easily. The guy needed to be wrong every so often. Everyone deserved that basic human pleasure.

'So what's to say the concrete wasn't tracked onto the mat by one of the contractor's men from another job? Or why couldn't it have been brought in on any visitor's shoes? For starters, there was the whole search team.'

'All good points and all possibilities I've considered. Unfortunately, we also have to consider the possibility that Weir tracked the sample in on his own.'

Harper frowned. 'He's always been a slippery sort, that Weir. Can't say I was ever convinced there was any security tight enough to hold him. You ever hear about the time he shook up the entire Rutland Prison?'

Neither of them had.

'Happened six months before he was transferred here. Weir was in the sex-offender programme, scheduled to attend a therapy session. The guard in the main control station spotted him approaching, found his name on the list of approved session attendees, and admitted him to the central airlock. The guard swears Weir was right there, between the two locked doors. He turned away for a split second to check a monitor, and when he looked again, Weir had vanished.

'The general alarm was sounded, the building secured, and all exit points blocked. Off-duty personnel were called in to help with the search, and reinforcements were brought in from Chittendon. Every inch of the place was combed, but not a trace of Weir.

'The warden didn't know what to do. He didn't want to panic the public, but he couldn't allow Weir to slip further away if he'd somehow managed to escape. The governor and the corrections commissioner were both consulted and both agreed that the internal search should be continued for two more hours before going outside with the news.

'No sign of Weir by the deadline, so the warden picked up

the phone to notify the media and the state troopers. But before he could finish dialling, who should stroll into his office but Weird Ellie in the nasty flesh.'

Harper allowed a theatrical pause, then continued.

'The man was all wide-eyed innocence. Couldn't imagine what all the fuss was about. Claimed he'd been feeling poorly and spent the entire afternoon sleeping in his cell.'

'Is that possible?' Quinn said.

Harper shrugged. 'I'm afraid we'll never know for certain. You see, the alarm had triggered an emergency backup recording of all the prison's video displays. The warden ordered the films impounded, positive they'd disprove Weir's story. He was so certain he'd get the goods on Weir, he invited several high-level state officials and the district attorney to witness the viewing. They were all hoping to stretch Weir's sentence with an attempted escape charge.

'But instead of showing the prison exits, all the reels were full of kiddie cartoons: Rocky and Bullwinkle, the Flint-stones. Rather embarrassing, to say the least.'

Levitsky drew a breath. 'How come there was no report of that in Weir's file?'

Harper shrugged. 'I'd suppose it was one of those things easier forgotten. Imagine how such a report would read. "At thirteen-hundred hours on February fourth, inmate number nine-three-five-one-seven-oh-three made raging asses of the entire prison staff." '

Levitsky sighed. 'That would about cover it. And now I'm afraid he might be making raging asses of the rest of us.'

'Then he must be stopped,' Harper said. 'Especially if he's within any possible reach of a young girl. For Weir, that's the trigger. The very notion of a slim, blonde girl and he starts ticking like a time bomb.'

At first Quinn had been glad to let Levitsky do the talking, but he'd spent nearly fifteen minutes circling the central question. She pointedly checked her watch.

'Why don't you ask him about the melody, Levitsky? I'm sure Mr Harper hasn't got all day.'

'I was getting to that, Ms Gallagher.' He shot her a hard

look and turned to Harper. 'Please forgive Officer Gallagher,' he said sweetly. 'She's herself.'

Quinn glowered at him, but he refused to shrivel. Instead, he repeated Weir's strange statements with cool, professional detachment.

'He said, "find the melody, discover the melody, that's the start of the path." He said he heard it beginning again. And he mentioned that the discovery would take sense and struggle. Does that cover it?'

She allowed a tight nod of affirmation.

Harper was nodding with far greater gusto. 'Never heard it called a melody before, but I'd wager he was talking about the concept at the very heart of our rehabilitation programme.

'We work with a select group on the Violent-Offender Unit: a particular breed of murderer, rapist, and armed robber. These men have been caught in a repeating pattern of savage behaviour since childhood. But few have the slightest notion of why they act as they do or, more critically, how to control themselves.

'Our approach focuses on dissecting the sequence of events that leads to the violent outbursts. We look at exactly what triggers the rage. There are the externals, such as Mr Weir's particular fetish for slender, fair-haired girls. And there are the more elusive internal factors: a skewed sense of injustice, imagined disrespect or mockery, self-loathing.

'Inmates on the unit spend a great deal of time reconstructing their crimes. We draw pictures, write up inciting incidents, describe the route to violence in key words and images. And then we act out the trigger situations until they've lost their mystique and power.'

Levitsky listened raptly. 'I've read about your programme. You base it in psychodrama, right?'

'Precisely. For many of these men, acting proves the breakthrough. They come here incapable of assessing or expressing their own feelings. Playacting their crimes in a neutral, controlled setting allows them to examine what was happening underneath the explosion. They also learn to empathise with their victims. Helps prevent recurrences.'

Quinn had a preposterous image of a circle of angst-ridden serial killers, sipping herb tea and dabbing at their teary eyes as they confessed their most intimate emotions.

'That approach can't possibly work for everyone,' she said.

'Correct, Ms Gallagher,' Harper said. 'The method is entirely worthless with the true psychopath. Feelings can't be exploited where none exist, after all. We attempt to keep those sorts out of the programme, but every so often a clever pretender manages to slip through. Participating in programmes like mine sits well with the parole board, so inmates are highly motivated to enrol! Given sufficient ingenuity, one can learn how to pass the selection tests and respond appropriately to treatment, so that even a total lack of conscience is virtually impossible to detect.'

'Is that what you think happened with Eldon Weir?' Quinn asked.

'I can't say for sure, but I'd be willing to bet Weir manipulated his way into and through the programme,' said Harper. 'Man's quite an accomplished actor, in fact. So good, it's difficult to catch him at it. Even when he dares you to try.'

'And the melody?' Levitsky said. 'Where does that fit in?'

'As I said, he must be referring to one of our central notions. It's easier to show than tell.'

Harper crossed to a storage closet behind a free-standing bulletin board across the room that was peppered with aphorisms: 'When in doubt, don't. If you don't know where you're going, you may miss it when you get there. Fly in a rage and you'll make a lousy landing.' Quinn was halfway through the cliché collection when Brooks Harper emerged from the closet wearing a frightful mask. It was the face of a garishly coloured beaked creature with hideous black eyes.

Transformed, the little man emitted a series of horrific shrieks and advanced towards Quinn and Levitsky with clawed fingers and the gnarled posture of a prehistoric beast. Reflexively, Quinn gasped and recoiled.

Harper stopped and removed the mask.

'Sorry to startle you, Ms Gallagher. It's difficult not to view this monstrous thing as real, which I suppose is why it's so effective. In the programme, we use this as the symbol for the murderous wrath buried in all of us. In those who've resorted to murder and mayhem, that fury has risen to the surface and broken loose. We teach violent inmates to recognise the first symptoms of that deadly process and do whatever they must to keep the rage safely locked away.'

'How does that relate to Weir's melody?' Levitsky said.

Brooks Harper straightened the grotesque mask on the back of his hand.

'This creature represents that rage, Mr Levitsky. We call it the Deathbird. And its summons to violence is the Deathbird's song.'

32 Fuelled by nervous energy, Nora had spent most of the morning straightening the mess in the studio and catching up on her backlogged work in the darkroom. Twice, she'd taken a break to go to the house and try questioning Poppa, but he remained hopelessly disoriented. Not a speck of recognition at the mention of Abigail or the child's tormentor. Not a hint that he had any idea who Nora was, or Charlie for that matter. His eyes were glazed, face an empty room.

'Please, Poppa. Please try to remember who was scaring Abby. Was it one of the staff? A guest?' She'd asked everyone else at the inn. Only Poppa had seen Abby teased and tormented.

As Nora questioned the old man, Maisie looked on, her moon face taut with sympathy.

'Sorry, honey,' the housekeeper said. 'Mr Brill's been that way since the doctor came by yesterday. Seems he's having trouble shaking off those tranquillisers. Doc Gordon says it could be another couple of days before he snaps out of it altogether. Impossible to say exactly.'

'You'll call me as soon as he starts making sense?' Nora said.

'Course I will. Glad to help out any way I can. Doesn't feel right around here without that little girl. I just know she'll come walking in any minute. Feel it in these old bones of mine.'

'Are you sure you have no idea who Poppa was talking about? You never saw anyone teasing Abby? Frightening her?'

Maisie shrugged her pillowy shoulders. Woman was built like a snowperson, round on round. 'Nope. Nothing like that. She always got along real well with Stephanie. Like sisters, those two. And Hugh hardly looked at either of the girls. Doesn't mind much of anything or anyone, that one.'

She frowned. 'I'd bet old Mr Brill was just imagining things again. Man's done a heap of imagining since he took sick.'

'But Abby wrote in her journal that something here was upsetting her. She said she couldn't stand it any more.'

'Maybe she meant she was missing her city friends. Or being lonesome for her daddy. Abby never stopped going on about how she had the best daddy in the whole world. Bet that was it. Makes no sense otherwise. Why would anyone pick on a sweet little girl like her?'

'I don't know. But Poppa specifically said someone was scaring her. And I don't think he was making it up.'

'Poor old thing doesn't know what he's about most of the time, much less anything else.' Maisie smoothed a stray wisp of hair from the old man's brow and wiped a line of spittle from his lip. 'Want some juice, Mr Brill? How's that sound? Think I'll go fetch you a nice big glass of fresh orange. You hardly ate a thing at breakfast.'

Nora returned to the studio, but she soon ran out of things to do. Exhausted but anxious to keep busy, she went to the inn and entered through the kitchen door. Too early for the lunch shift, the place was deserted. But there was never a shortage of chores. Beside the sink was a heap of silver gravy boats and serving pieces in need of cleaning. Retrieving a cloth and polish from the base cabinet, she tried to lose herself in the mindless task.

And she did so with reasonable success until her attention was caught by a volley of voices from the adjacent office. From where she stood, she recognised Ray's elastic drawl interspersed with Charlie's no-nonsense New England. Nora was drawn closer, like metal filings to a magnet, until she was able to catch the gist of their conversation.

They were discussing her state of mind, trying to decide the best way to deal with what both men saw as her worsening instability.

'Woman's always been a worrier,' Ray said. 'Any time Abby had a sniffle or a splinter, Nora would go stark raving nuts. I was forever telling her to take it easy. Kid isn't made of glass, for chrissakes. But you know how some mothers get.'

There was a conspiratorial silence.

'She was a mess about moving Abby to Vermont,' Charlie said. 'She worried about the school, friends, the climate, you name it, even though Abby was pretty calm about the whole thing.'

'Typical.'

'Things went beautifully at first, but Nora kept waiting for a problem. I can't say I was all that surprised when Abby started acting up. She had to sense Nora's anxieties.'

Ray ticked his tongue. 'Don't mean to tell you your business, Charlie, but I'd hook that woman up with a good shrink, and fast. Seeing how little things set her off, it's no surprise she's all loose screws and marbles over Abby's running away.'

'I agree with you. But I've already suggested she see someone, and so has Victoria. She won't hear of it.'

Raymond sighed. 'And she says I'm pigheaded. That woman could out-stubborn a mule.'

'I don't know what to do, Ray. I'm really worried about her.'

'Don't fret. We'll put our heads together and think of something.'

Nora was mad enough to play ring toss with the good china. She was tempted to barge in and bash their heads together. But given that they'd already deemed her certifiable, such behaviour would be redundant.

She snuck out the kitchen door and sucked in a chestful of the crisp morning air. The sky was ice blue, hung with wisps of cloud. There was a chorus of chirping birds and the mechanical drone of tractors cultivating crop land on the adjacent farm. She caught the low thump of Reuben Huff's hammer from the storage shed and the angry exchange from the side yard where Chef Villet was busy abusing the produce supplier.

The local list of people and places she wanted to avoid kept growing. There was Villet, creepy Reuben Huff, vapid Victoria, and Hugh the obscure. There was the cabin, especially Abigail's room with its accusatory silence and

216

taunting memories. And now there was Cowboy Ray with his improbable sidekick, Charlie Brill.

Charlie's buddying up to Ray struck Nora as unthinkable disloyalty, especially under the circumstances. Now, of all times, she needed her husband's undistracted attentions. She craved his ready shoulder and empathetic ear and the reliable circle of his arms. But he was unavailable to her, wholly preoccupied in some primitive rite of male bonding with an exceptionally primitive male.

How could Charlie do this to her?

She felt so achingly alone. Then the truth was she had nobody. Mim was preoccupied with Poppa. Victoria was absorbed with Victoria. And Stephanie was a child, too sweet and innocent to be burdened with Nora's problems.

She couldn't even call her mother in Florida. Normally, Mom was an excellent, sympathetic ear. But for the past month she'd been grappling with serious health problems: angina and high blood pressure, terrifying tests and tricky medicines. Nora had resolved to spare her the stress of Abigail's disappearance. At least, she'd spare her as long as possible.

Which, given Charlie's affiliation with Ray, left exactly no one. Nora would have to stand on her own through this ordeal. Lucky she had big feet.

Refusing to waste time on self-pity, she went to the studio and put in a call to Justin Wellacott at the Town Hall. By now, he must have gotten a read on the Waldorf's tenant. As soon as she had more details, she'd make sure the troopers interviewed whoever it was about Abby.

Justin's secretary left her on hold for several minutes. Then the mayor came on the line and kept her holding in a different pattern. On the surface, he was his usual smooth self, but she detected a rare edginess underneath. He grew jumpier still when Nora cut the small talk and questioned him head-on about the Waldorf's occupant.

'You mean you think someone's living there?'

'We talked about it last night, Justin. Remember? The place has been renovated and someone's moved in. You said you'd find out about who it was and let me know.'

'Oh gee, sorry. Must've slipped my mind. Let me check it out and get back to you. I'm up to my ears today, Nora, but I should have an answer for you tomorrow or the next day latest, okay?'

'Does it really have to take that long? You could make a simple call, and . . .'

'Now, now, my dear. I understand that this whole thing with Abigail has you anxious and overwrought. But I can't simply drop everything.'

'All right. I'll wait to hear from you.' She hung up quickly, not trusting what she might say otherwise. Nora didn't believe for a second that he'd forgotten about the new occupant at the Waldorf. For some inexplicable reason, he was lying to her. But much as she wanted to call Justin's bluff on the ridiculous charade, Nora couldn't risk alienating him. Not when he held the power to keep the troopers searching for Abigail.

Leaving the studio, she stared up at the Waldorf. The drawn drapes gave the place an air of taunting mystery. Made no sense that she couldn't get a rapid fix on the tenant's identity. If the person in that house had seen anything at all that could help the police find Abigail, Nora wasn't about to wait for Justin or anybody else.

Chef Villet was still outside arguing with the produce man in fractured English liberally spiced with rage. The strawberries were garbage, the avocadoes fit for swine, the lettuce was a felony, and the lack of baby squash merited a beheading at the least. Villet took his produce very seriously.

Sneaking into the kitchen, Nora rummaged through the refrigerator and threw together a platter of pastries and cookies left over from last night's dessert. To fill the empty spaces, she added a few pieces of fruit and several of Villet's infamous chocolate truffles. The effect was no *Gourmet* cover shot, but it was more than adequate for a neighbourly gesture of welcome.

She heard the door slam and the roar of the produce truck's engine, which meant that Chef Villet was headed back to the kitchen. Nora slipped out through the dining-

218

room door. Passing the office, she noticed that Raymond and Charlie had left. They'd probably gone to check out the local loony bins and see which might have a spare bed for a photographer with a broken focus. Pity Poppa hadn't shot Ray in the mouth. Heaven knew it was a more than generous target.

Balancing the ungainly platter on her right shoulder, Nora left the inn through the front door. She crossed the porch and strode through the front yard and parking lot to the side of the adjacent road.

There, she waited while a sedan and two delivery trucks passed, navigating the pocked pavement at a crawl. She eyed the Waldorf up the hill, grim and lifeless.

Repositioning the tray over her forearms, she crossed the road. The platter was a large awkward oval that dug into her abdomen as she stretched her fingers to grasp the opposite edge. But going back to get something smaller meant inviting a run-in with Chef Villet. She'd rather tote an elephant than deal with that Gallic grenade.

Clutching the platter, she plodded up the meandering dirt slope towards the covered bridge. The access road was a minefield of ruts and frost heaves. Nora peered beyond the tray to monitor her footing, but twice she misread the hazards. Once, her foot turned in a furrow and she came down hard with a shock of pain that made her eyes water. Nearer the rickety bridge, she caught the tip of her sneaker on a hillock. Lurching forward, she narrowly avoided a fall by grabbing the splintered side rail at the entrance to the bridge.

In the process, she dumped half the goodies on the ground. Setting the platter down, she arranged the remains as artfully as she could. Looked a little sparse, but it would have to do. She wasn't about to turn back.

The rickety bridge groaned and cracked underfoot. Far below, the river spur, swollen with the spring thaw, churned and clashed against the boulder-lined basin. With startling clarity, she imagined Abby falling through the flimsy footbridge, flailing in the frigid water, bashing against the rocks like a rag doll. Stepping off the bridge onto solid ground, she felt relieved.

But as she stood facing the Waldorf, the relief was displaced by an odd foreboding. With all the time she'd spent observing and photographing the old dump, she'd never had the least desire to get any closer than reasonable camera range. Nora knew that hordes of local teenagers invaded the place regularly to party or hide or both, but she preferred to keep her distance. Such houses were best left untouched, except by one's imagination.

Still, thinking of Abby, she forced herself to continue. The Waldorf commanded a decent view of the inn. This mysterious new neighbour might have witnessed something important on the day Abigail disappeared.

Nearing the fence, Nora noticed the green mesh tacked between the rails and the fresh posts that had been installed to replace the rotten ones. Juggling the tray, she managed to open the gate and step inside.

Noting that the drapes were drawn, she hesitated. It was after eleven, but the new neighbour might still be asleep. She didn't relish waking some stranger, especially when she was after the stranger's co-operation. Nora stared at the house a while, wondering whether it would be prudent to leave and come back later.

Then she recalled that the drapes had been closed, or nearly so, in pictures of the house she'd taken in the middle of the afternoon. Could be the new tenant had some odd aversion to daylight.

Slowly, she approached the building. She rebuked herself for being silly, imagining spooks and goblins inside. More likely, some kindly retired couple more comfortable by lamplight had taken the isolated place. Or maybe it was a young, amorous couple. That could explain the drawn drapes as well.

Gripping the platter, she drew a breath and strode towards the building. She had no patience for any nonsense, her own included. She'd simply march up to the front door, ring the bell, and introduce herself. No hesitation, no excuses.

220

She was determined. Confident. Nothing was going to stop her. But suddenly something caught her foot and she was unceremoniously dumped on the sodden ground.

The remaining contents of the pastry tray were scattered in the new mown grass. Nora's rump was sore and mud-soaked, her dignity badly bruised. She had never been all that graceful, but in the last couple of days terror and exhaustion had turned her into a human pratfall. How could she be so clumsy?

Then she noticed the line of stakes and the slender string drawn between them. That was enough to trip anyone. Nora couldn't fathom the placement of the barrier or its purpose. Feeling uneasy, she looked up.

She felt the gaze before she spotted the eye peering through a tiny slit in the living-room drapes. It was coal dark and unblinking. Turning away, she suppressed a shiver.

Rising quickly, she refused to be cowed. She didn't need the cookie platter or any other excuse to walk right up and ask this new neighbour for information about her little girl. Abigail had been missing for three days. Finding her was all that mattered.

Approaching the house, she kept her gaze fixed on the ground, watching for other booby traps. She sensed she was still being observed. Why didn't the person at the window simply acknowledge her presence and open the door?

No matter. Nora wasn't about to stand on formalities or worry about feeling welcome. She brushed her muddy shoes on the door mat and raised her hand to knock.

But the action was stalled by a wailing siren and the sight of a police car barrelling down the dirt road towards the Waldorf's gate. As the car turned in, Nora recognised Detectives Merriman and DeSoto. They were yelling for her to stop.

221

33 The police car lurched to a halt at the end of the driveway. Merriman and DeSoto burst out and charged at Nora like crazed buffalo.

'What is it? Did you find Abby?'

Each man grabbed her by an elbow and steered her firmly away from the house.

'Please,' she said. Her voice was tiny, terrified. 'Is she all right? Is she hurt? Whatever happened, you have to tell me.'

At the car, Merriman paused to catch his breath.

'What's going on?' Nora said. 'Please!'

'There's no news about your daughter, Mrs Brill,' the big man rasped. 'Nothing yet.'

Nora wrestled free of DeSoto's persistent grip. 'Then why the hell did you come barging over here like that? You scared me half to death.'

'Sorry. Didn't mean to,' Merriman said. 'We spotted you from the road. Wanted to head you off before you stepped into any trouble. Guy living here called headquarters soon as he moved in. Warned us to keep people away. Seems he's real eccentric. Paints pictures all day long. Likes his privacy way too well, if you know what I mean. Regular Howard Hughes type.'

'Yeah,' DeSoto agreed. 'Guy wanted to know if he could post "No Trespass" signs and asked about the state's laws on shooting intruders. We didn't want you to wander into some craziness and maybe get hurt.'

Nora blew a breath. 'He can't go around shooting people for stopping by to say hello. This isn't the Wild West.'

'True,' DeSoto said. 'But he sounds like the type who'd blast away first and worry about the consequences later. Guy is set on being left alone, whatever it takes.'

She gazed at the house. A solitary eye still glinted through the gap in the drapery. Weird.

222

'All I wanted was to bring him some desserts. Unfortunately, I tripped on that stupid string and everything went flying.' She nodded towards the row of stakes and the scatter of sweets that had already attracted a flock of gluttonous crows.

Merriman strode over and retrieved the empty platter from the ground. Nora's mishap had dislodged one of the stakes. The trooper poked it back in its hole and tamped the surrounding soil with his heel.

'Thoughtful of you, Mrs Brill. But not such a hot idea in this case.' He twirled a finger at his temple. 'Man's a crazy artist. Hates being interrupted and doesn't care much for people. Waste of time trying to be neighbourly to that kind. Come on. We'll drop you down the hill.'

'That's not necessary. I'll walk.'

A look passed between them. 'If it's all the same to you, Ma'am, we'd rather see you safely home,' DeSoto said.

'That's silly, detective.'

'Let us be silly then. Goes with the badge.'

Seeing it was futile to argue, Nora allowed them to ferry her to the inn in the police car. She watched from the lobby until they backed out and disappeared down the road. For insurance, she watched the grandfather clock and forced herself to wait ten extra minutes.

When the time had elapsed, Nora stole out of the inn and dashed across the road, ducking out of sight beneath the sprawl of wild shadbush whenever she spied an approaching car. She was more determined than ever to have a talk with her new neighbour.

From what the troopers had said, he was definitely not the type to co-operate with a door-to-door squad of inquiring detectives. She couldn't shake the image of that steely eye at the window. Maybe he'd been staring out that way when Abby was taken.

The troopers might not be willing to twist the man's arm, but she had no such inhibitions. Somehow, she'd make him tell her what, if anything, he'd seen. As Ray had so sweetly put it, she could out-stubborn a mule.

Unimpeded by the tray this time, she hurried up the

slope, ran through the covered bridge, and raced towards the split-rail fence. But before she could unlatch the gate, another state police car materialised on the access road. Her heart sank.

The car braked beside her. At the wheel was one of the troopers who'd come to the inn to investigate Ray's shooting. In clipped tones, he ordered her away from the property, not bothering to blunt the edict with explanations.

'You don't want to go in there,' he said.

'And why is that?'

'Sorry, Ma'am. Orders.'

'Whose orders?'

'Best to move along now. Thank you.'

He idled at the gate, monitoring her reluctant retreat. Nora kept glancing over her shoulder, hoping he'd lose interest and take off, but he was tracking her like radar.

At the covered bridge, she paused and changed direction. She followed the dirt road towards Main Street, passing the police car without comment or regard. Soon the inn would be crawling with staff and lunch guests. Nora needed some space and time alone to think.

Emma's Luncheonette was empty except for the rangy brunette behind the deli counter and the stubby blonde waitress who was passing from table to table slowly filling sugar bowls and napkin dispensers. Nora sat in the far corner at a table for two and ordered a Diet Coke.

Through the glassed front wall she had a view of the Waldorf's roof and a clear bead on the approach road to the inn. First one staff car, then a pair, and soon a stream of assorted vehicles made the turn off Main Street, climbed the gentle incline, and veered in at the inn's wooden signpost.

Nora saw Mim pull up in her ancient finned Cadillac followed closely by Charlie and Ray in the inn's pale blue van. Reuben Huff's Nova dipped and swerved over the pothole obstacle course. Victoria zipped up in her flame-red Nissan, honking insistently at the seafood delivery truck plodding in front of her. Woman was in a fat hurry. Probably late for one of her soaps.

'Anything else I can get you? The chicken salad looks real nice today.'

The chunky blonde waitress had come up beside Nora's table armed with an order pad.

'No, thanks. I was wondering though. Has the new tenant from the Waldorf been in here at all?'

'Didn't know there was a tenant. Who'd want to live in that creepy place?'

The tall brunette behind the counter flashed a triumphant look. 'See, Suzy. What'd I tell you?'

'You've met him?' Nora said.

'No. Haven't even laid eyes on whoever it is. But a few times when I was closing up last month I noticed people working on the place, so I knew something was up. Suzy figured it was just emergency repairs. But then I saw the furniture truck about a week ago. No emergency needs furnishing, right? And it's been real busy over there ever since.'

'Busy?' Nora said. 'That's odd. I heard the man was a hermit.'

The brunette chuckled. 'Gets plenty of visitors for even a real friendly hermit. Lots of comings and goings.'

'Local people?'

'Nope. Strangers,' said the brunette. 'Wouldn't surprise me if it was some kind of celebrity living there. Most of the cars had official state medallions.'

Suzy nodded. 'I noticed one of those tags on that cute guy's car. The one who came in with that snippy redhead.'

Nora wondered if the blonde was talking about the same ginger-haired woman she'd seen driving out of the Waldorf late yesterday. That one had been alone.

'Was she a young, pretty woman? Drove a jeep?'

'I wouldn't call her pretty exactly,' Suzy said. 'Pretty nasty maybe, but that's about all.'

'Meow,' the brunette said. 'She was good-looking all right. Big green eyes, real fair skin, great shape. Thin, like

Katharine Hepburn's. You just wish it was you with that tall curly-haired hunk, Suzy, my friend. You're just jealous.'

The blonde reddened. 'Get out, Gloria. Who asked you anyway?'

'What kind of official state cars were they?' Nora persisted.

Gloria flipped up her palms. Woman's hands were huge. Twin hams. 'No idea. I noticed one of those metal medallions on the rear of their jeep, but I didn't catch what it said. You, Suzy?'

'Nope.'

'Course you didn't,' said Gloria. 'You were too busy ogling that curly-haired guy with those broad shoulders and big brown eyes of his.'

'And the dimple in his chin,' Suzy crooned.

'You see?'

And she did. Suddenly Nora remembered the picture she'd snapped of the redhead leaving the Waldorf. Excusing herself, she paid the bill and left.

Skirting the inn, she hastened to the studio. The picture of the redhead in the jeep was still in her Nikon. Prickling with impatience, she extracted the half-exposed film and started the tedious steps in the developing process.

Checking the still-damp negatives, she found the one of the woman in the jeep. She printed and enlarged the shot and took it to her desk.

The camera had caught the medallion at an angle. Even under the magnifying glass she was unable to make out the tiny letters under the official state seal. Could be any department.

Blowing the print up further, she was able to read the letter 'R' in the centre of the word and parts of the two adjacent characters, a slanted line on the left and a half moon curve to the right. Doodling on a memo pad, she wrote down a number of possible combinations: A – R – C, M – R – O. She couldn't tell how many letters were missing on either end.

Nora stared at the letter clusters until they started to blur. So damned frustrating. Then, on a sudden inspiration, she retrieved the phone book from her supply closet and hastily paged through to the 'Government Offices' section in the blue pages.

As she perused the list, she tested each department name against the triple letter combinations she'd written on the pad. Nothing worked through the first column or the second. Halfway down the third, she finally came to an entry that contained one of the letter trios on her list: Department of Parole.

Her mind was racing, but she forced herself to go through the rest of the listings. There were no other matches.

Forcing herself to stay calm, she scrutinised the photo of the medallion on the jeep under the magnifier again. No doubt about the 'R' or the shape of the adjoining letters. The visitor at the Waldorf had to have been from the parole department.

Suddenly, so many things made sense. Patrol cars appearing out of nowhere. The absurd story about a nutty artist demanding that the state police protect his privacy. And what kind of painter worked with the drapes drawn?

Her heart was hammering. A paroled criminal is housed in the Waldorf, and suddenly her little girl disappears. Abigail might have been right there, held in that spooky house all this time. Nora could almost hear the child's desperate whimpers, her pleas for help.

Her first impulse was to run to the inn to tell Ray and Charlie, but she resisted. They'd think this was merely another of her paranoid fantasies. Nora couldn't bear to be humoured or patronised again. She wouldn't waste the words or the time.

And she wouldn't waste time calling the police either. They were part of this nightmare. As responsible as the man in that house. Thinking of all the official lies and evasions, Nora was outraged. They didn't give a damn what happened to Abigail. She was the only one who cared enough to take this seriously and do something about it.

In her supply closet, she found the box of razor-sharp craft knives she used for trimming. She chose two of the largest blades and slipped them into her pocket. If Abigail was in that house, Nora would get her out.

She was halfway out the door when the studio extension started ringing. She would have ignored it, but calls were never relayed to her there. Whoever answered at the inn knew to enter any messages in the inn's daily log and leave her a note. In the past, too many portraits and delicate processing manoeuvres had been ruined by an ill-timed call.

The ringing persisted. Had to be an emergency. Something about Abigail? Her hand quavered as she lifted the receiver.

'Yes?'

'Nora Brill?' It was a male voice, husky.

'This is she.'

'Abigail Eakins is your daughter?'

'Yes. Who's this? What do you want?' Prickles of fear were scaling her spine.

'Name's Eric Wise. Saw your girl hanging around on the street in front of my apartment. She looked kind of lost, so I went out to see if she was okay. Wouldn't talk to me at first, but after a bit, she came around. Told me she ran away, and she's ready to go home. She was afraid to call you. Thought you'd be mad. So I'm doing it for her.'

'Is she all right?'

'She was cold and hungry when I found her, but otherwise fine. You want to come get her?'

'Of course. Right away. Please, can I speak to her?'

'You could, but she dropped right off on the couch soon as I gave her something warm to drink. Kid's out like a light. That's why I'm talking low.'

'I'm on my way then. And thank you so much. I don't know how I can ever repay you.'

'No need, Ma'am. I have kids of my own.'

She wrote down the address and detailed directions. Abigail had somehow wandered to Burlington, about two hours north of Dove's Landing. Nora's head swarmed with questions, but they could wait.

For now, nothing mattered but getting to Abigail. Thank god, her little girl was safe.

34 Quinn was anxious to leave St Albans. The prison thrummed with the noxious aura of the Deathbird. She couldn't shake the vivid guise of that appalling invention: the horrific stew of garish colours, the machete beak, the black eyes sharp as blades. Those eyes could slice into her, lay her open. Bare her own boiling font of lethal rage.

But Levitsky wasn't finished with the place. He asked Brooks Harper to show them Weir's old cell on the Violent-Offender Unit. Quinn couldn't see the point, but she didn't argue. Though she'd never admit it, she was extremely impressed by the agent's canny observations and keen insights. Guy had a sharp eye, was exceedingly intelligent too, for a fool.

Harper escorted them to Section C. Here, a dozen cramped cells jutted off a dim corridor. Several of the unit's residents were lounging in their bunks. A few stared openly as Quinn passed, but she was spared any lurid comments or lewd gestures. Harper's boys were far better behaved than most of the rabid animals on parole she'd had the displeasure to know.

Eldon Weir's old cell was at the far end of the hall near a small TV lounge. Harper gently evicted the current occupant and invited Quinn and Levitsky to go in and look around.

Jailhouse poems and jungle philosophies were scribbled on the mud-yellow walls. There was a metal-framed bed with a skimpy mattress, a rusted sink/toilet combination, a slim locker with a battered door, and a writing table stippled by the scraps of light that squeezed through the window bars. Finding the air unfit for prolonged consumption, Quinn made a polite circuit of the space and stepped out to join Brooks Harper in the lounge.

'So what do you think?' he asked.

'Personally, I prefer something with a lake view and a jacuzzi.'

Harper smiled. 'Unfortunately, few of our guests stop to consider the quality of the accommodations when they book a room here.'

Levitsky asked to be locked in. Harper summoned a guard with a ring of keys and excused himself to make a call. For the next ten minutes, Quinn dawdled in the hall waiting for the agent to finish his inspection.

Having grown up with a detective father, she was accustomed to the waiting. Plenty of nights, Quinn had sat with her mother in uneasy silence, pretending not to watch the door. Knowing her father was out sifting society's dregs for some dubious treasure, hoping he wasn't fated to fall in the process. He was always gone more hours than they expected. Always far longer than he'd planned. Levitsky reminded her of her dad in that way: painstaking, methodical, single-minded.

Fast Eddie had never been the headstrong, brainless carouser his moniker implied. He was a good man: solid, steady, big-hearted.

True, he'd done his fair share of heel-kicking as a young man, but he'd given up the passing lane decades before the accident. Strongest thing Quinn had ever seen him quaff was a light beer with a deli sandwich or a sip of sherry on state occasions. But he'd raised enough hell, or at least talked about raising enough, to ensure that his legend well outlasted his youthful appetite for excess. That, and his outsized pride had been his undoing, and nearly Quinn's as well.

Eddie Gallagher was an imposing man, brick solid. Because of his appearance he'd been saddled with a reputation for limitless strength and vigour. Eventually, he had come to accept the general belief that he was impervious to fatigue or sickness or most mortal limitations.

That's why he'd always been the first called for all-night stakeouts, first on the list for overtime and overwork and the empty satisfactions that flowed from being too much to too many at way too much personal cost.

Quinn had noticed the tremor in his left hand months before she had the courage to mention it, and then only to her mother. The response had been a helpless sigh and a roll of Mother's world-weary eyes. Go try to tell that man anything. Waste of words.

His only concession to the worsening palsy was to shove his hands ever deeper in his pockets. No matter how hard Quinn and her mother cajoled, the man wouldn't hear of anything as demeaning as a check-up.

Check-ups were for infants and automobiles. Doctors made a person sick, hospitals were for dying, medicines helped no one but the drug companies. And none of the above was necessary in any event given that there was nothing wrong with him. The shakes were nothing, ditto the blurred vision and the spells of dizziness and the headaches so fierce he went green-pale from the pain.

The night it happened, her parents had gone to a party at the Hollands'. Fast Eddie had appeared a bit unsteady towards the evening's end, and another guest had offered to drive the Gallaghers home. Insulted by the suggestion that he was in any way incapable, Quinn's father had loudly refused.

Half a mile from home, her parents' car vaulted the central divider and crashed into an oncoming station wagon. Both cars exploded in flames. Witnesses held that the Gallagher's car had been weaving before the crash, moving like drunken revellers on a conga line.

Quinn's parents were both declared dead at the scene. The driver of the wagon, a woman in her late twenties, died in the ambulance. Her three-year-old daughter lived for three days before succumbing to massive head injuries. The five-year-old son suffered permanent paralysis and extensive brain damage. Only the baby, a boy under six months old, had escaped serious injury when he was thrown clear of the wreck.

Before the cause of the crash was officially determined, the deceased Eddie Gallagher had been tried, convicted, and slain again by the press. Friends attested that he'd left the Hollands' party with slurred speech and a staggering gait. Brothers on the force, whose loyalty did not extend to where they believed Fast Eddie had gone, offered reporters graphic descriptions of his mythic bouts with the bottle.

'When Fast Eddie is in his cups, there's no reasoning with the man,' one declared.

The story had sparked national media interest and fanned a fire-storm of public outrage. Police were supposed to protect and defend, not bowl down innocent civilians with a lethal vehicle as the ball.

Fast Eddie Gallagher fast became the symbol for police irresponsibility and unthinkable abuse of public trust. One widely circulated cartoon showed the long arm of the law with its elbow bent on a bar and a bottle of vintage poison clutched in its fist.

Any initial sympathy for Quinn and Brendon quickly evaporated. Bren was taunted by schoolmates. The position Quinn had been promised on the Rutland police force mysteriously disappeared. Committed to the move, she'd already submitted her resignation to the Boston force, where she'd spent five years banking seniority and good will as a vice-squad detective. A hiring freeze made her resignation irrevocable. Quinn decided she'd find some way to manage. But the lost job turned out to be the least of her worries.

An ad hoc citizens' group pressed to have Eddie Gallagher's death benefits revert to the victim's widower and surviving infant. The grieving husband filed a fifty-million dollar lawsuit against Quinn's parents' estate, the Hollands, the City of Rutland, and the State of Vermont.

The plaintiff's lawyer deemed Jake and Marilyn responsible under so-called Dram Shop laws against serving alcohol to the intoxicated. The suit held the city and state at fault under the theory that Fast Eddie's superiors had known of his drinking problems for years and provided no counselling or rehabilitation.

Quinn had faced personal and financial disaster at a time when she was too overwhelmed with grief to do anything but capitulate. She'd even started to believe that all the anguish was deserved. Hearing so much damning comment about her father, she'd begun to doubt what she knew to be the truth about the man.

Without Jake Holland's guidance and support, she would have folded under the strain and quietly suffered the consequences, possibly for life. But Jake had helped her harvest the truth. There had been no alcohol in Fast Eddie's bloodstream. Nothing but over-the-counter pain medications. Two independent labs refuted the coroner's preliminary findings. Holland squeezed the papers to print retractions and convinced the corrections commissioner to offer Quinn a vacant slot in his parole office.

But even now, three years after Jake had helped her expose the facts and regain her footing, people still remembered and believed the lies. She was forever bearing the barbs, facing the contemptuous looks. It was the same expression that had crossed Mayor Wellacott's face when he asked if she was related to Fast Eddie. And Quinn had felt the old familiar swell of fury.

Someday, somehow, she'd find a way to eradicate the stain from her father's memory, and hers. Eldon Weir was not going to get in the way. Quinn could not let that happen.

Brooks Harper returned, and moments later Levitsky knocked to signal he was ready to be released. As he emerged from the cell, Quinn tried to read his expression, but if he'd unearthed any secrets, the agent wasn't eager to reveal them.

'Anything else I can show you?' Harper said.

'In fact, there is,' Levitsky said. 'I'd like to see Weir's materials from your programme sessions.'

Harper frowned. 'Warden Darmon nagged me for months to get rid of all those old papers and such. Kept going on about how the lot of it was nothing but rubbish and a fire hazard.'

As Levitsky's face fell, Harper's lit with a puckish grin. 'Fortunately, I didn't listen. Everything ever produced in the programme is stored down below. Come along.'

They traversed a maze of designated living units and fractured hallways. At the rear of the building, Harper tugged open a fire door, and they traipsed down two concrete flights to the basement.

The cavernous underground housed the prison's heating plant, water tanks, central power and alarm circuits and a row of emergency generators. Harper motioned them past the clamorous machinery to a puffed tarpaulin in the far corner. He pulled back the cover, exposing a mountain of papers and files.

The mess appeared impenetrable to Quinn, but Harper was able to cut his way in and excise Weir's contributions in minutes. He emerged from the pile filthy but pleased.

'I think this is all of it.'

Levitsky took the armful of soiled posterboards and pages and laid them out on the concrete floor. Thoroughly engrossed, he crouched and studied each item in turn, making notes on a pocket pad as he went.

Peering over his shoulder, Quinn perused several of what Harper had referred to as 'thought reports'. Inmates in the Violent-Offender programme were expected to provide a written account of any event that aroused their anger. Each incident was titled, illustrated, and dissected to distinguish facts from reactions.

Quinn found Weir's offerings laughable. It appeared that the monster had taken a course in advanced psycho-babble. His reports were full of canned insights. He had a problem with poor self-esteem. Because of early alienation, he made false assumptions about the world. He was over-compensating for lack of self-worth by testing society's limits. Observing others with similar histories, he was able to recognise his own motives. By recording his experiences, he hoped to better understand his anger.

Spread stuff like that on the garden, you can grow prize-winning tomatoes.

Finished, Levitsky stood and cranked his neck to ease the kinks. 'Thanks, Mr Harper. That should do it.'

'Fine then. I'll see you out.'

Quinn waited until they were back at the jeep to pump the agent for information.

'Nothing but bits and pieces yet,' he told her.

'So I'll take bits and pieces.'

'I'd really rather wait until I can put it all together in meaningful form.'

'Well, I'd really rather hear what you have now.'

'It won't make sense to you.'

'How about letting me be the judge of that?'

'You don't give up, do you, Gallagher?'

'Yes I do, Levitsky, as soon as I get my way.'

He laughed, but quickly waxed serious. Quinn could almost see the gears meshing in his tidy little mind.

'Weir told you to find the melody and then follow the path,' he said. 'If the starting line was the Deathbird's song, I figure he had to have left markers we could use to proceed from there. Logically, all he had the means to plant in St Albans were words.'

'Makes sense.'

'Yes, but the trick then was to find the significant words and figure out where they pointed. Examining what he wrote on his cell wall and in the reports, I saw no evidence of a code. None of the standard key-words or code-word ciphers. I did notice, though, that he used a number of words more than once. I figured that had to be the key, simple emphasis by repetition.'

'And was it?'

'You tell me,' Levitsky said. 'I'll give you the list of repeated words from his cell wall, and you see what you make of them. Say the first thing that occurs to you. Free association. Okay?'

'I'm ready.'

He pulled out his note pad.

'Arousal . . . fresh . . . smooth . . . entry.'

'Sex,' she said, surprised as the word popped into her head and out her lips.

'Sex with – ?'

The first thing that occurred to Quinn stuck in her throat. She rummaged for a more acceptable interpretation, but the cupboard was bare.

'With . . . a child,' she said finally, and her cheeks went hot.

236

'My reading too,' Levitsky said grimly.

'Which tells us what?'

'Could be a declaration of intent. Could be a reference to the sex-offender programme he was in at Rutland. I was hoping the string of words he repeated in his thought reports would help me figure it out. But so far, I can't make sense of them.'

'Maybe I can help.'

'Be my guest.' Levitsky read from the pad. 'Recording . . . testing . . . assumptions . . . problems . . . observing.'

'Freddie,' Quinn said after a beat.

'Huh?'

'You told me to say the first thing that came into my head, and that was it: Freddie.'

'So go with it, Gallagher. What comes next?'

For a frustrating interval, her mind was in eclipse. But slowly, a notion formed and came in focus.

'Freddie Fenold,' she said. 'He was this annoying little geek who sat behind me in Chemistry. Knew all the answers. Had severe salami breath.'

'And?'

'Chemistry . . . science. Wait, I have it! It's the scientific method, Levitsky. Remember? Observe a problem, formulate an assumption known as a hypothesis, test, observe the results, record the results.'

He took it in, slowly. Worked it over. 'Scientific method as in research. Interesting. Weir had to do plenty to fake his way in and through the Violent Offender programme. Maybe while he was at it, he also studied ways to escape airlocks and other security systems. Weir's exactly the type to flaunt his trickery. Nice work, Gallagher. Really. Let's get to it.' He got in the jeep.

Quinn's pleasure was marred by confusion. Levitsky's kangaroo leaps of logic had left her at the gate. Scrambling to catch up, she slipped in beside him. She stalled, fidgeting with the keys, edging slowly off the prison grounds, hesitating at the main road.

'Okay, Levitsky. I give up. Where are we going?'

'You tell me, Gallagher. You can work it out as well as I

can. And I must say, that's quite a compliment coming from me.'

Quinn felt a pleasant rush. This logic business was almost as much fun as trashing wretched Ralph Norman.

Eyes closed, she pushed past the knowns and began to visualise the way to go. Sense and struggle. Slowly, it came to her. She could see the next step on the path. If only she knew what they'd find when they came to the end of it.

35 Heading towards Burlington, Nora's thoughts kept skipping back to Eric Wise's voice and instructions. She couldn't wait to get there, to see Abigail again, to hold the child in her arms.

Nora felt as if she were heading to claim a stranger. Picking up a tempting but terrifying package of unknowns.

What chasm of experiences had her little girl crossed since she ran away? How much had she changed? Would Nora still know her? Had she really known her before? What – or who – had made her run away?

As Mr Wise had instructed, she exited 189 at the Route 2 interchange and circled the broad cloverleaf to the Williston Road. She sought comfort in the predictable parade of landmarks. Wise had laid out the path in detail.

'Off the exit, you'll pass the Sheraton on your right. Modern building with a fake copper roof and a trendy restaurant in front. Next, you'll come to a strip mall.'

There it was: Gaines Discount Department Store, Price Choppers, the Mobil station at the far intersection, exactly as Wise had described.

Things were where they belonged. Maybe the world was finally reverting to reasonable order and predictability. When this was over, Nora resolved never again to crave adventure or underrate the value of blessed boring routine.

But the nightmare wasn't behind her yet. There remained so many horrifying questions. Where had Abby slept all these nights? Had she managed to sleep at all without her standard reassurances and night lights? How had she travelled from Dove's Landing to Burlington? Nora's blood froze at the thought of the child hitching rides with strangers. Taking crazy, desperate risks. All to escape some situation she was unable to discuss or defuse. What could be terrible enough to drive a little girl from her family and the familiar to the uncertain arms of strangers?

The whole thing was so crazy. Abby had told Mr Wise she'd run away. Confirmed what everyone except Nora had been asserting since her disappearance.

But then what about those weird photographs? From what Abby was wearing in the shots, Nora knew they'd been taken after the little girl disappeared. So who'd snapped them? And where? And how had they landed in the developing tank in Nora's darkroom?

Then there was the note. Why would Abby have left an exact copy of her journal entry? Could all of it have been the product of Nora's warped imagination? Had she fallen that far out of touch?

Nora evicted the crowd of confusing doubts. Everything would be answered in time. Figured and sorted and tamed. Right now, she had to concentrate on Mr Wise's directions. The last thing she needed was to get any more lost than she already was.

Several blocks down Williston she came to the University of Vermont. On the left was a cluster of highrise dormitories. To the right a row of brick Gothic buildings stretched towards the soaring white spire of the campus chapel.

The road veered left and passed the towering grassy mound that screened the community water supply. More of the college stretched across the road, chiselled greens surrounded by stately buildings. Students passed armed with book bags, bicycles and limitless possibilities. Someday, Nora thought, Abigail would be part of such a universe. With Wise's phone call, the child's future had been magically restored.

Across South Prospect, Williston melted into Main Street. The road crested and dipped towards the glistening expanse of Lake Champlain and the hulking mass of the Adirondacks on the distant shore.

She continued down the hill towards the city's congested core. Traffic seeped slowly through the clotted streets. Jangling with impatience, she inched past South Willard to South Union and finally came to Winooski.

Tense as a drawn bowstring, she turned right and discovered more of the landmarks Eric Wise had listed.

There was a firehouse, a library, a multiplex theatre, a Ben & Jerry's ice cream parlour. A few more blocks, and she'd be there.

Pearl Street was lined with boutiques and trendy restaurants. One, called the Deja Vu Cafe, caught her eye. Passing, she confirmed that it was the kind of place Abigail loved: woody, strewn with plants, warmed by stained glass and muted colours. Epidemic in Manhattan, that breed of eatery was a rare find in Vermont.

Nora imagined sitting at a cosy booth in the Deja Vu opposite her daughter. She pictured Abby's clear blue eyes dappled with candlelight, her cheeks ablaze with warmth, satisfaction, and relief. With the two of them alone, unhurried, the child could begin to unburden herself. They could start the healing.

The route took Nora past the crowded pedestrian mall on Church Street. A group of girls idled at the end of the block. One reminded her of Abigail: slender, blonde, perpetually in motion, flashing a neon burst of laughter. The smile was so like Abby's — open, infectious. Nora couldn't wait to see that smile again.

And the waiting was nearly over.

Her mouth became parched as she spotted Pine Street. Angling into the squat, narrow road, she rehearsed how she'd greet her little girl. She was determined to be calm and comforting. No shrieks or hysteria or declarations of residual despair. No demands to know everything at once. She would be all open arms and unconditional acceptance and limitless understanding. From now on, Abby would have all the time and patience and understanding she needed.

Suddenly Nora wished Ray were here. Abby would be so thrilled to see her father.

Actually, her first impulse had been to bring the big oaf along. As soon as she'd finished talking to Eric Wise, Nora had rushed to the inn, intending to tell Ray and Charlie about the call and ask them to accompany her to Burlington. But from the foyer, she'd spotted her ex-husband and Victoria huddled together in front of the fireplace. The hot current passing between them was unmistakeable. She'd noticed Ray's uninjured paw pawing its way up Victoria's well-toned thigh. Nora turned and left.

She hadn't bothered to analyse her reaction, and she wasn't inclined to do so now. She'd deal with the unthinkable concept of that preposterous pair and whatever else necessity dictated after she retrieved her child.

Three houses from the corner on Pine Street she spotted Eric Wise's place. As he'd mentioned, the building was a large slate-grey Victorian house that had been sliced into apartments.

She parked and approached the building. On the front porch was a double row of mailboxes and a line of labelled buttons. The labels were haphazard, hand-lettered, and hard to read. Skimming the list, she didn't spot the name Wise.

Nora wished she'd asked for his apartment number. But he'd said his name was on the buzzer. Slowly, she reviewed the labels again. Nothing close. No names at all beginning with the letter 'W'. No Eric or initial 'E'.

Stepping off the porch, she rechecked the address against her scribbled instructions. It was the right house: 234 Pine Street. Had to be a simple mix-up on the labels. Maybe Wise's tag had peeled off to expose the old tenant's name.

Nora pressed the topmost button. No response, so she continued down the row. Inside, she could hear the low bleating of the buzzers. But she waited in vain for an answer.

Someone had to be home. Abigail was in one of these apartments. Mr Wise knew Nora was on the way. He wouldn't have gone anywhere.

She was down to the last three of a dozen buttons. She pressed. Waited. A vicious pulse stabbed at her temple.

Two left. She pressed harder this time, as if force could coax a reply. There was an interminable pause. *Abby must be here.*

Only one button left. Nora's finger was poised to push it when a loud bleating sound pierced her terror. Someone was buzzing her inside.

The front door clicked open and she entered a foyer ripe with cooking smells and incense. Directly ahead rose a spiral staircase. Craning her neck, Nora spotted the ring of doors on the second and third floors. They mirrored the four numbered units on the first level.

'Mr Wise?'

Her voice resounded in the silence.

'Mr Wise! Abigail?'

Behind her, a door squealed open, and a short sixtyish woman in a pink shirtdress peered into the foyer.

'Help you?'

'I'm looking for Mr Wise.'

The woman was an older Betty Boop: round, pink, eyes like cartoon circles, bobbed hair the dull black of barbecue briquettes. 'Wise? No one here by that name.'

'There has to be. He called me. My daughter's with him. She's been missing.'

'Easy now. Come in, and I'll look it up in the book. Probably just have the wrong house or something.'

The incense smell intensified as Nora neared the woman's apartment. Inside, the living room was cluttered with display cases and shelves stocked with magic tricks and a variety of new age paraphernalia: books, crystals, essential oils, inspirational books and recordings. A sign on the counter read 'The Impossible Possible'.

The woman offered a spongy hand. 'Name's Alice Murtagh.' She scanned the shop and sighed. 'The store was my husband's. Hard to believe it's more than a year already since he passed. I've carried on with it the best I could. Not well enough, I'm afraid. Mr Murtagh knew everything there was to know about all this psychic stuff.'

She pulled out a phone book. 'Wise, you said?'

'Eric Wise.'

'Sounds familiar.' Alice Murtagh scanned the directory. 'Don't see any Eric Wise. You sure that's the spelling: W-I-S-E?'

Nora hadn't thought to ask. 'He gave me this address. And directions. He told me it was a grey house, centre of Pine Street. This number. My daughter has to be here!'

'Ssh. Take it easy. I collect the rents, so I can tell you there's no Wise or anything close. Must be a simple explanation though. Maybe it's right near here, and the man's unlisted. Bet that's it. I'll call my friend, Greta, at the phone company. She'll check the unpublisheds for me.'

The woman made the call. Hung up frowning. 'Sorry. No Eric Wise in Burlington. Greta tried the possible variations too. Maybe he said Bennington? Bet that's it. Eric Wise. That name sounds so familiar. Can't put my finger on it, though.'

Nora stood dazed while Mrs Murtagh called directory assistance in Bennington. No Eric Wise. Nothing close.

But of course, there wouldn't be. The man on the phone had described *this* house, given her specific directions to *this* place.

Abigail's kidnapper was toying with her. Dangling hope like a tantalising morsel of bait he could set and snatch away. Cruel, rotten sonavabitch.

An anguished cry escaped her.

Mrs Murtagh's saucer eyes stretched wider. 'I'm sure it's all just a simple misunderstanding, honey. You want me to try Wilmington for you, maybe? Or how 'bout Arlington? I'm positive I've heard that name before. Probably drive me crazy 'till I figure it out.'

Nora backed out of the apartment. The scent of incense was suddenly overpowering. She need fresh air; she needed to think . . . 'No. It's no use. No use.'

Her mind was reeling. She had to get back and tell the others. The call proved Abby had been snatched. Maybe if the police finally believed her, they could find a way to track the man from what he'd said on the phone. There had to be something they could do. Some way to find Abby.

She sped back to Dove's Landing, heedless of speed limits. At the inn she ditched the car in front of the main entrance and raced into the lobby. Stephanie was at the reception desk, doing homework. She looked up as Nora ran in.

'What's wrong, Aunt Nora?'

'Where is everyone?'

'Mim's at the Baxter house supervising the painter.

244

Hugh's got detention. Charlie's in the office. Haven't seen Ray or my mom.'

Nora called for Charlie to come to the parlour. Running down the hall, she pounded on the locked door to Ray's suite. Muffled protests came from inside.

'Damn it, Ray, get your pants on. It's about Abigail.'

In minutes, the straggling lot of them collected in the living room. Ray looked like a refugee from a wind tunnel. Victoria emerged minutes later, hastily restored. Reuben Huff appeared as did Jory Albert and Chef Villet and Maisie. Charlie came up beside Nora and took her hand.

In level tones, she told the assemblage about the call from the phony Eric Wise and her trip to Burlington.

'This proves Abby was kidnapped. Maybe the police have a way to trace the call or figure out who made it based on something in the conversation.'

Victoria cocked her head. A wave dipped over her forehead. 'But I was on the desk all morning, Nora. There were no calls for you.'

'Obviously, you had *bigger* things on your mind, Victoria.'

The woman bristled. 'I answered and logged every call. Go see for yourself.'

She did. Nora reviewed all the listed incoming calls. None bore her name. 'So you forgot to write it down. Heat of the moment and all.'

'What I do is none of your damned business, Nora. So you keep your nose out of it.'

'This is about my child, Victoria. If you lose yourself in raging hormones and forget something that could help Abby, that *is* my business.'

Reuben Huff cleared his throat. His overalls were streaked with white paint, and he'd smeared a white line across his sallow forehead. 'Don't mean to get in the middle, but you couldn't have gotten any call at the studio this morning, Miss Nora. It's impossible.'

'What are you talking about?'

'I'll show you.'

The group followed Reuben out of the main house and

through the stone courtyard to the rear archway. The studio was beyond, over a span of muddy ground. The sun was setting, and there was a sudden bite to the April breeze. Huff started to explain as they neared the place.

'I'm doing over that old equipment shed near the pool, like Mr Brill asked. Found some dry rot on the north side. Seeing I had to order lumber and supplies for that, I figured I'd check the other old buildings. That old sugaring shed where you have your studio was top of my list. Building's near a hundred fifty years old. Sure enough, I found some creeping rot on the north face there too. Lumber's due to come day after tomorrow. While I was scraping and doing some prep work, I accidentally snipped the phone line. Decided I'd wait till the job was finished to fix it. Didn't think you'd mind given you don't like getting calls out there anyway.'

They were ten feet from the studio now. Huff led them to the rear of the building and pointed to a length of dangling phone wire.

Nora was assailed by a wave of dizziness. Charlie took her arm, but she wrenched free. Racing inside, she lifted the receiver on the studio extension.

It was dead.

There was no sound but a sharp, keening scream. And the scream was coming from her.

36 Quinn and Levitsky drove to Rutland and parked on the street in front of the minimum security prison near the centre of town.

Save for the wire-capped fence and security cameras, Rutland Community Correctional could have passed for a school or office complex: contemporary brick façade, artful glass accents. The broad entrance portico was bolstered by white columns.

A number of Quinn's clients were Rutland alumni, so she was all too familiar with the place. Well-conceived and exceedingly well-intentioned, the facility had been afflicted by the national prison plague of underfunding and over-crowding. Important programmes had been cut, staffing slashed to a minimum. A worsening glut of inmates had necessitated double-bunking in many of the cells. Forty inmates slept, lounged and passed the time in the gym in what amounted to a large, live-in ashtray.

Quinn was able to gain easy admittance and a general facility pass for herself and Levitsky. She led the agent past the main control bubble, through a hallway crammed with pay phones and vending machines, and down a short passageway to the learning centre, a cramped square that housed the prison library, computer literacy programme, vocational assessment lab, and remedial education courses.

The bookshelves had the look of a badly neglected mouth. Great gaps separated the few remaining volumes. Scanning the sorry display, Quinn was reminded that most inmates viewed possession as nine-tenths of the law and found the other tenth of scant interest. They didn't so much borrow books as seize them in the time-honoured tradition of the repo man and the Internal Revenue Service. Circulation then proceeded according to the fundamental law of prison economics: demand and supply.

Discouraged, she realised that there wouldn't likely be a

reliable record of which if any books Weir had consulted during his stay on Rutland's sex offender unit.

But the obvious hindrance did not seem to daunt Levitsky. He strolled over and introduced himself to the centre director, a birdlike bespectacled soul who was stationed beside the subject section of the card catalogue.

Quinn had met the man, Eugene Peterman, when Dud Chambers was taking a home-study course in TV and radio repair. Peterman sported a bow tie, saddle shoes and an awed expression that intensified on hearing that Levitsky was with the FBI. The agent said he wanted to include information about Eldon Weir's intellectual pursuits in a comprehensive study of violent offenders. Peterman saluted and pledged his co-operation.

'Anything for the Bureau,' he said. 'I'm truly honoured.'

Levitsky fired a number of questions over Quinn's head.

'Do you have Dialog?' he said. 'Lexus-Nexus? Knowledge Index? How do you segregate your on-line fees? And where are the user service charges registered?'

Quinn was pretty certain all of it had something to do with computers, which she definitely did not.

'I'm referring to a number of subscription data bases,' Levitsky explained. 'Anyone with a modem can log on, and they've got four Epsons here equipped with Hayes 1200 bauds and Crosstalk. Since the fees are on a rate-based variable time-and-duration schedule, I thought there might be a record by request key and user ID.'

'Thanks, Levitsky. That clears the whole thing right up,' Quinn said. She'd never met anyone quite so well-informed. Made her ache to ask if he knew how to take a flying leap.

Peterman dutifully listed Levitsky's inquiries and added a few ideas of his own. Weir might have taken a course through the learning centre or by correspondence. He could have enrolled in one of the prison's lecture series or signed up on the circulation list for one of the many special interest publications kept on file at the learning centre desk.

'We have better control over periodicals than books,' Peterman said with a sorry nod towards the denuded shelves. 'We cut the losses some by keeping them under lock and key. And we avoid ordering anything too popular.'

Peterman and Levitsky hashed over a couple of other potential sources of information about Weir's independent studies. There were records kept of incoming inmate mail and a log of visitors. If the professor had signed up for any of the courses taught in-house by community volunteers, credit would be noted in his record.

Peterman promised to gather the requested materials within the hour. Quinn wasn't optimistic. She could think of several ways Weir could have bypassed official scrutiny of his so-called 'research' altogether.

All calls out of the prison had to be made collect, so if Weir had done any investigating by phone, they'd have no way of tracing it. Reading materials might have been slipped to him by a visitor in the large, largely unsupervised fishbowl where inmates congregated with their guests. He might have used uncirculated reference works or picked a fellow inmate's brain. On and on.

'It's hopeless, Levitsky,' Quinn said as they left the learning centre and headed towards Rutland's special unit for sex offenders. 'There are dozens of ways he could have circumvented the system and researched whatever the hell he pleased without leaving any tracks.'

'True, Gallagher. Only you're overlooking the one major fact in our favour.'

'Which is?'

'Which is, Weir told you he'd laid out a path that could be followed. The last thing he'd want is for us to get dead-ended and lose interest. That's why he left two sets of key words at St Albans. He was being redundant on purpose. He wanted insurance in case the cell was repainted or the thought reports got tossed out. It's no fun playing alone, Gallagher, even Weird Ellie's kind of games.'

They found Rita Banks in the rec room, where a scatter of sweaty shirtless inmates were working out with weights. Quinn introduced her to Levitsky as head of the Sex Offender programme and waited out the standard interval of stunned speechlessness. Having consulted with the woman about several clients, Quinn was well past the irony of Ms Banks's appearance. But on first meeting, she'd shared Levitsky's astonishment.

Banks was over six feet of considerable curves capped by an exquisite face and a torrent of honey-coloured waves. Her eyes were the blue of pool water, mouth a sensual bow. Hardly the Rambo type one would expect to find at the helm of a programme for hardened sex abusers.

But in Rita Banks's case, looks were definitely not everything. She sliced through Levitsky's slack-jawed amazement with a steel handshake, a stony gaze, and the firm authority of a lion tamer. He responded as everyone did. Snapped out of his stupor and stood up straighter. Quinn explained that they'd come about Eldon Weir.

'Amazing how many people do,' she said. 'Follow me. We can talk upstairs.'

A short open flight led to her office. As she approached the first riser, the three nearest inmates set down their barbells and backed away. Ms Banks's work wardrobe was unfailingly feminine: a suit or a dress. But no right-minded inmate would risk even the appearance of an errant peek up her skirt. Rita the man-eater, they called her. And most believed that to be a perilous understatement.

The office had soft-blue walls and beige carpeting. The desk top was bare save for a portrait of Ms Banks's trio of pet Rotweillers and the certificate attesting to her third-degree black belt in Karate. There was a mysterious row of pencil slashes on the wall. Scalp count, Quinn figured. Ms Banks sat and motioned for them to do likewise.

Again, Levitsky's explanation for their visit was the half truth about Weir being part of a study he was conducting on violent criminals.

'I was hoping you might have insights about him that aren't in the file,' Levitsky said.

'Actually, I have quite a few,' Rita said. 'We deal with highly delicate matters on this unit. When we first opened, we found that many inmates in need of our services were reluctant to sign up unless we'd guarantee that sensitive information would remain in the programme.'

'Then we'll need to see Weir's file from the unit,' Levitsky said.

'Sorry,' Banks said sweetly. 'No way.'

'This is an important project,' Levitsky told her. 'Of national significance.'

'Earth-shattering, I'm sure, Agent Levitsky. But as I told you, we get requests to study Weir all the time. I can't play fast and loose with his confidential records.'

'I'm not asking you to. I can assure you anything you tell us will go no further. Please, Ms Banks. This is crucial.'

'Then cut the crap, Mr Levitsky. If you want me to let you in on Weir's programme records, you'll have to let me in on the *real* reason you want them. I don't care for horseshit. Not even when it's pitched at me by Uncle Sam.'

Levitsky caved right in. Rita Banks had that effect on people. She listened intently as he talked about the missing child and the overwhelming coincidences that pointed to Weir's involvement.

'Wouldn't surprise me if he found a way to breach the security,' she said when he'd concluded.

'You think he's that brilliant?' Quinn asked.

'He's clever enough,' Banks said. 'But what sets Weir apart isn't his mind, it's a fact of his basic make-up. You familiar with the P-graph?'

Quinn hadn't heard of it and for once, Levitsky drew a blank as well. Rita Banks opened her desk drawer and pulled out a C-shaped metal ring attached by wires to an electronic measuring apparatus.

'It's a simple but ingenious little assessment device,' Banks said. 'This metal ring is called a Barlow gauge. The offender slips it on. We show him a series of pictures and audiotapes designed to appeal to a variety of sexual appetites. And any evidence of arousal is transmitted and recorded.'

'He slips that on his . . . ?' Levitsky grimaced and crossed his legs.

'On his penis, yes, Mr Levitsky. That's why it's called a P-graph. The full name is penile plethysmograph. Allows us to assess the precise nature and intensity of deviant

251

arousal patterns. It's a handy fact that men respond reflexively and honestly to visual and auditory stimulation. We document those responses, and we can tell exactly what we're dealing with.'

Levitsky winced again.

'It doesn't hurt,' Rita Banks said. 'And of course, the testing is conducted with absolute respect for the inmate's privacy and dignity. While it may sound and look primitive, we've found it the most reliable way to get honest information about our offenders' sexual proclivities. Few men are willing to admit they're turned on by young children or pain or animals or punishment or worse.'

'But in Weir's case, we already know it's young, blonde girls,' Levitsky said.

'That's a common misperception that Mr Weir furthers at every opportunity,' Banks said. 'His sexual predilection for little girls is nonexistent.'

Flipping through his chart, she extracted a number of graphed tracings. She pointed to several places where the professor had been present with intensely arousing stimuli: naked women, boys, girls, copulating couples.

'But I don't see any responses,' Levitsky said.

'That's because there weren't any,' Banks nodded grimly. 'Mr Weir was aroused by absolutely nothing we could show or describe to him, Mr Levitsky. Yet, from examination, we know he's capable of normal sexual functioning. And by his own report, we know he's experienced intense responses during his most heinous criminal acts.

'When he applied for this programme, he volunteered detailed accounts of sexual arousal while he victimised those children. And I can assure you he wasn't making it up. But it made no difference that they were young or blonde or even girls for that matter. He purposely chose similar victims in typical Weir fashion, to flaunt his crimes and taunt the authorities.

'The man has no response or preference to any particular human attributes. He's incapable of normal release, and he's incapable of reliving or replacing erotic experiences through fantasy. I've been in the field for fifteen years, and

252

I've never seen anything quite like it. Nothing turns Eldon Weir on but the actual physical act of torturing someone and the fun of getting away with it.'

'I don't see how that would give him an edge over any other garden-variety sadist,' Levitsky said.

'Neither did I at first. But in time I got to know Weir. And I came to understand what drives him. You see you're looking at the arousal pattern of a man who's dead inside most of the time, Mr Levitsky.

'A dead man has absolutely nothing to lose,' she continued. 'And he'll stop at absolutely nothing to feel alive again.'

36 The pillow held Abigail's scent: lemon shampoo and baby powder. Nora pressed her face to the soft cotton case and inhaled the precious traces of her lost child: air Abby had breathed, the aura of her dreams, echoes of her whispered secrets.

She was gone. Never coming back.

Nora sensed it at the core of her being, the place even her own best lies were powerless to reach. It was a heavy longing, a dull hideous ache.

She turned on her side and curled in on herself to compress the yawning emptiness. But there was no way to make it easier.

Her baby was gone.

She'd realised it the moment she put her ear to the dead phone in the studio. None of her hopes had been real. It had all been a product of her desperate imagination: the disappearing pictures, the phone call from Burlington, the duplicate notes.

Hallucinations. Craziness. Nothing was real but that dread recurring vision of Abigail falling through a yawning black gash in the universe. Abby swallowed by dark oblivion. Lost forever.

Behind her, the door creaked open, and she heard the approach of hesitant footfalls. Feigning sleep, she felt the heat of Charlie's fretful gaze and caught the measured tides of his breathing. He stared at her for an interminable time while she focused on staying immobile. Invisible.

She had to keep him and everyone at a safe distance. A touch, and she'd shatter in a million fragments. A word, and she'd scatter like ashes in the wind.

Finally he turned and left the room.

She heard him with Mim in the hall, conferring in hushed, solemn tones.

'Poor darling needs the rest.'

254

'Best thing for her.'

'Think she'll be okay?'

'She will, Mim. She has to be.'

The thought hovered over her, slight and frivolous as the lace canopy over Abigail's bed. What did it matter if she was all right? What did anything matter any more?

Nora had always seen herself as capable and resilient, never one to lie on the tracks and let life run her over. She'd viewed adversity as a challenge, faced the toughest things head on. But she was too weary to battle any more.

And she'd run out of decent reasons.

Her eyes felt grainy and sore. Opening them a crack, she found it hard to focus. Dr Gordon had been summoned to put a chemical end to her hysteria. He'd given her a shot of some unpronounceable drug that instantly filled her head with cotton wadding and liquified her bones. She'd wanted to ask if it was the same medicine he'd given Poppa after Ray's shooting. But she'd been unable to grasp the notion long enough to turn it to words.

In a peculiar way, she envied Poppa. She imagined him beyond pain, protected, able to replace unsavoury realities with selected fragments of his past. Maybe he was better off.

Charlie and Mim trudged down the cabin stairs. The door slammed, and their voices trailed away towards the main house. Nora rolled on her stomach, face scrunched in the Abby-scented pillow, and sought the refuge of sleep.

But the damned tranquilliser wasn't working. Random thoughts assailed her like swarming insects. Poppa. Ray and Victoria. Flying bullets. Laughter running in a bloody stream.

Restlessness finally prodded her up and out of Abigail's bed. She sat at the edge of the mattress until the wavering walls settled. Standing on jelly legs, she countered the threat of dizziness by fixing her gaze on Abigail's trophy-lined shelves.

There was the gilt statue the child had won for her floor exercise in last year's regionals. Beside it was the giant loving cup she'd earned by finishing second all-around in the citywide junior club meet. Five identical statuettes poised in a kick line trumpeted the five consecutive years she'd been honoured as the top gymnast on her team at the Midtown Sports Centre.

Those trophies had been forged from so many hours of plodding exertions, so much iron determination. Nora had always marvelled at how her child pushed through the pain of injuries. Persisted in the face of long odds and looming disappointments. Abby would practise a seemingly imposs-ible move hundreds, thousands of times, until it was imprinted in her bones, natural as a breath.

From the start, the little girl had talked about nationals, Olympics. Nora had discouraged the dreams at first, hating to see Abigail skewered by unattainable ambitions. But in time she'd come around to her daughter's view. Nothing was beyond reach if you stretched long and hard enough. The only unbreachable limits are the ones you impose on yourself.

Nora crossed to the window and hitched it open. The world looked unbearably normal. The gentle sloping grounds, the ring of surrounding cabins, the lake, the gazebo.

The property reeked of spring promise. Syrup spouts and catch pails dotted the sugar maples. Fresh green was edging out the dull winter beige on the lawn. There was the exultant trilling of birds. It all struck her as a rank obscenity.

How could the season possibly change without Abigail? Nora could not let that happen. She couldn't give up no matter how hopeless things seemed to be.

Seated at her daughter's maple desk, surrounded by the child's things and treasures, Nora listed everyone she'd contacted since the disappearance. Had she left anybody out? Overlooked even the vaguest possibility?

Next, she reviewed everything she could remember of the day Abby vanished, beginning with the moment the child came charging through the inn on her way to the cabin after school. Nora could still see the pain etched on Abigail's face as she shoved open the kitchen door and bolted through the dining room towards the rear archway.

Find out how Abigail was on the bus, Nora wrote. *Check with Mrs Schiffman about any unusual occurrences that day in school. Problems with classmates? Other kids? A bad grade?*

Certain from the start that Abby had been taken, she'd never thought to explore reasons why the child might have left on her own. If Nora could figure it out, Abby's motive for running away might suggest where she'd gone.

Maybe she'd headed back to New York for some reason. Was there something going on in the city that Abby would hate to miss? A special meet? Might be worth checking the team's gymnastic calendar with Abigail's old coach. *Call Jeanine again*, she wrote. Maybe she'd discussed some critical upcoming event with Abby on the phone.

The list grew as she considered local people the police might not have thought to question. How about all those visitors to the Waldorf? Official cars. Outsiders. Any one of them might have noticed a little girl on the road alone. Nora could begin by tracking the woman with the jeep. Shouldn't be too difficult. How many young, attractive, redheaded women could there be in the parole department?

Charged with fresh purpose, she picked up her list and left the cabin. At this hour, Charlie would be in the office. With his help, the calls would go faster. She'd recruit Raymond too, unless he'd already been drafted in service to Queen Victoria.

Nearing the main house, she stopped uncertainly. She hated the thought of facing the family, dealing with the pointed looks and solicitous comments.

But she forced herself to continue. She wouldn't get anywhere by running or hiding. That wasn't the way to accomplish anything. Not for her. Not for Abby. Even the toughest, ugliest things had to be confronted.

Steeling herself, she entered the inn through the front door. Mim was on the phone at the reception desk. She looked up at Nora's approach.

'Feeling better?' she mouthed.

'Yes, much.'

The old woman nodded. Nothing more. Grateful, Nora continued through the living room where Stephanie was reading on the couch. The child raised a hand in greeting and went back to her book. Easy.

Nora relaxed. Her outburst was past and forgotten.

As she neared the office, Hugh came loping in from the kitchen. In typical Hugh fashion he passed her with a granite expression and no visible regard whatsoever. Nora could have hugged the little beast.

The only remaining obstacle was Charlie. If he had the good sense and sensitivity to say nothing about her temporary insanity, she'd forgive him everything, even his outrageous alliance with Raymond.

She found him hunched over the blueprints for the summer theatre, making further modifications to suit the project's incredible shrinking budget. Seeing her, he quickly set the work aside.

Nora walked over and settled in his lap. He looped his arms around her, and she rested her head on his shoulder.

So nice. Lazy and peaceful. She could have stayed there indefinitely, but too much needed doing.

'I made a list of more people to call about Abby. Will you help me?'

He pressed his lips to her forehead. 'Of course. Anything.'

'Good. Let's get started.'

She pulled herself up and plucked the list from her pocket. As Charlie looked on, she explained the contacts she thought they should make.

He was a sweetheart. No challenges, no scepticism. When she finished dividing the task, he rose and offered her the more comfortable spot behind the desk.

'I'll use that extension,' he said and walked over to sit on one of the brocade side chairs across the room.

Watching him, Nora felt a surge of warmth. Charlie was still Charlie. They were still together. Soon Abigail would be back. Everything was going to be all right.

258

No more lunacy, she wanted to tell him. *I promise. No more.*

As he started dialling the first number, he propped his left ankle on his right knee. Nora spotted the bottom of his shoe and froze.

The sole was caked with the same hairy debris she'd seen on Abigail's sneaker in the disappearing picture. The image came flooding back. One bare foot, the other in a shoe coated with a thick mortar-like substance and a sprinkle of some fibrous material.

But what did it mean? Could Charlie have been in the same place Abigail was hiding?

The same place the child was being held?

Unthinkable thoughts assailed her. No one had easier access to Abigail and the rest of the inn. Charlie could have planted the note and the pictures and found some way to patch the phony call through to her at the studio. If he'd taken Abby, if he was holding the child somewhere, making Nora seem crazy was the perfect way to douse any suspicions.

Could he have planned it all from the very beginning? Nora recalled their first meeting at the surprise party in New York. He'd been so delighted when she told him she had a daughter.

Too delighted?

Stop!

What the hell was she doing? How far over the edge had she slipped? This was her Charlie. Sweet, kind, gentle Charlie with the spare tyre and caring eyes. Charlie Brill who'd lived forever in the same place with the same reasonably steady people. Charlie who was about as sinister as a stuffed bear.

The pictures weren't real, she reminded herself. And the muck on Charlie's shoes might have come from anywhere. Natural hazard of this area in mud season. Not worthy of a second thought.

Charlie dialled a number. Waiting for an answer, he caught her eye and smiled. Warm, open grin. Nothing stealthy or malevolent or manufactured. She had to stop

this. Had to get herself together and do something construc-
tive to find out where Abigail had gone.

Nora made another silent pledge to somehow get past the
craziness. Then she turned her attention to the list and
started making her calls.

37

Levitsky had logged over two hours at Quinn's kitchen table studying the records he'd got from Eugene Peterman at Rutland's learning centre.

Having perused the pages twice without enlightenment or inspiration, Quinn had decided that her time would be better spent catching up on her badly backlogged weekly reports. She worked opposite the agent, jousting for surface space.

The key clacked in the door lock, and she heard Brendon tramp in and dump his boulder-weight book bag in the hall.

'Hey, Tiger. In here,' she called.

After a pit stop in the powder room, Bren charged into the kitchen, slapped Levitsky's palm, crossed to the refrigerator, and stuck his head in the freezer section. Decent imitation of a cherry Popsicle.

'We have ice cream?'

'Frozen yogurt,' Quinn said.

'Gross.'

Instead, he took a handful of cookies and a glass of milk and headed for his room to do his maths homework.

Levitsky continued reviewing the papers. As he worked, several sheets migrated to Quinn's side, so she gave them a tiny nudge. The pile went flying and hit the floor. Freak wind current, no doubt.

'Please, Gallagher. This is important.' He bent to retrieve the jumble of pages.

'You've been at this for hours already, Levitsky. I told you it was hopeless. Weir probably wasn't referring to his research in the first place. Whole thing is probably his idea of a joke.'

Levitsky's expression flashed in a series of stills: perplexed, curious, beaming with delight. 'That's it. You got it!'

'I did? I mean, I did.'

'Use your phone?'

He went to the den and closed the door. Moments later, he popped his head back into the kitchen.

'You have Rita Banks's home number?'

'Probably in the corrections directory.'

'May I have it please?'

'What for?'

'So I can call her, Gallagher.'

Quinn feigned indifference, though she couldn't fathom what would possess him to phone the man-eater, especially at home. Levitsky was many things, but she'd never imagined that he might be suicidal.

Curious, she paged through the pile of papers again. Eldon Weir had signed out a book on the Civil War and read several issues of *Newsweek*. Peterman had listed the articles, but none of the subjects seemed relevant. The professor had attended a lecture on personal finance and taken a brief course in comparative religion. There was more, but nothing that struck her as particularly enlightening. And what did any of it have to do with Rita Banks?

The call went on for quite some time. Quinn took a couple of casual strolls past the den and pressed her casual ear to the door. But all she caught was an occasional '*mmhmm*'.

When Levitsky finally returned to the kitchen, he was muttering and grim-faced.

'I'm afraid we've hit a wall,' he said.

He told Quinn she'd been right about Weir leaving no traceable trail of a particular line of research. She'd also been correct in suggesting that the professor hadn't been referring to his own studies at all. Which had led Levitsky to the obvious conclusion: Weir had been clueing them to explore research in which he'd been the subject.

Rita Banks had mentioned getting frequent inquiries from professionals interested in studying Weird Ellie. Levitsky had thought it would be a simple matter to contact Ms Banks and find out who'd been given permission to examine Weir while he was at Rutland.

Unfortunately, Weir had agreed to participate in a number of research projects. Rita had mentioned the names of three criminologists, two university psychology departments, an institute for the study of psychic phenomena, and a neurobiologist. There were others, she said, but she couldn't remember them offhand, and she'd have to check her office records.

'I told her tomorrow morning would be soon enough,' Levitsky said. 'No way we're going to be able to reach all these and check them out today.'

'We can try,' Quinn said.

'Yes, but I have a strong feeling it's not going to get us anywhere. There's something wrong here, Gallagher. This isn't the way Weir operates. He's more linear, more direct. A person's fundamental behaviour patterns are as constant and distinctive as his fingerprints. Doesn't add up that he'd send us on such a scattershot expedition.'

Quinn caught his pessimism. She was trying to shake it when her beeper sounded. The switchboard number at headquarters registered on the digital readout.

She called back, bracing herself for more bad news, but she brightened as the operator explained the reason for the summons and patched her through to an urgent caller. The man was reluctant to offer details on the phone, but he said enough to convince Quinn he might well be their ticket out of the mess. Quinn took directions to his house and promised to meet him there as soon as possible.

'So much for that wall, Levitsky. We've got ourselves an informant.'

'Who? What'd he say?'

'I'll tell you on the way. Just let me make arrangements for Brendon.' She crossed to the stairs and called up.

'Hey, slugger. I've got to go out a while. You want Tricia or Tracy?'

'Neither,' came the response. 'Give me a minute. I'll take care of it.'

A beat later, he appeared on the landing. 'Marc's mom says I can come over and spend the night. I can ride my bike. Okay?'

'You bet,' Quinn said and hurried up to pack for him before he could change his mind. Dry sheets, sleepovers. Things were definitely looking up for the kid. Now if they could only tie up the mess with Weir, so she'd feel free to enjoy it all.

Brendon stuffed his things in the bicycle basket and took off down the block. Miracle on wheels. Quinn savoured the view until he veered out of sight around the corner.

Back to reality.

Levitsky was waiting at the front door, briefcase in hand. 'So where to?'

'Burlington. How about you drive? I've put way too much mileage on this carcass of mine in the last few days.'

He took the wheel. Quinn could tell right away that the guy was a lousy driver. Lead foot. Death grip. The jerky, extraneous head movements of a suspicious hen.

'Watch it, will you, Levitsky? Two lanes means you're supposed to pick one or the other, not half of each.'

She waited until he was on the highway to explain their destination.

The caller had been a man named Eric Vise. He told Quinn that he'd grown up with Weir. Their families had been close, and out of some inexplicable sense of obligation, he'd kept in occasional contact with the professor. Vise had visited Weir shortly before his parole, and several things about the man's behaviour had been worrisome.

The professor had seemed distracted and agitated, constantly pacing. Vise said it was exactly the way Weird Ellie had acted before snatching the Buckram child and, later, the girl he'd murdered in Burlington.

Vise said Weir had told him certain things about those crimes that he'd never admitted to another living soul. Inexplicably afraid that Weir would find some way to punish him if he broke the confidence, Vise had kept the awful knowledge to himself. And he'd lived with the terrible guilt that he might hold the key to preventing more tragic deaths.

He told Quinn he couldn't remain silent any longer. Vise said he was almost certain Weir was planning to kill again. He claimed what he knew could help the police prevent the slaughter.

'Let's hope the man is right,' Levitsky said.

264

Traffic in Burlington was thick and sluggish. Several blocks into town, they were stopped altogether behind a double-parked moving van.

'Why don't you go around him, Levitsky?'

'Because there's not enough room, Gallagher.'

'Is.'

'Is not.'

'Move over. I'll show you.'

They changed places. The truck was parked beside an Olds sedan, protruding half the distance to the opposite kerb which was occluded by a large dumpster.

Quinn made the necessary geometric calculations. If she didn't angle too hard around the truck, she'd get through with inches to spare. Confident, she eased off the brake and let her rip.

Which she did. Quinn cringed at the jarring metal tear as the jeep parted company with a sizeable section of its front bumper and half the wheel hub.

She looked over to check Levitsky's reaction, but she didn't catch so much as a smirk or a chuckle. Guy didn't even have the decency to toss her a snide remark.

'All right, Levitsky. Say it.'

'Say what?'

'What you're thinking. That I'm a stubborn mule. That I'm headstrong and impulsive and do incredibly dumb things.'

His gaze was steady. 'So happens I wasn't thinking any of that, though all of it is certainly true.'

'So what were you thinking?'

'Only that I understand.'

'Understand what?'

'Another time, okay? It's complicated. Here's where you make that left.'

They found a vacant space in front of the house. There was a roster of residents beside the door. Nothing approached the name of Quinn's informant.

Levitsky backed away and watched until he spied movement in one of the ground-floor units. He pressed what he presumed to be the corresponding button and they were buzzed inside.

A plump, smiling woman greeted them in the lobby. 'Well, hi there. I'm Alice Murtagh,' she said. 'Help you?'

When Quinn said they'd come to see Eric Vise, her grin yielded to a look of perplexity.

'Funny. Woman was in this morning looking for an Eric *Wise*. I told her there wasn't anyone here by that name. No *Vise* either. So you've come to the wrong place too. Talk about odd coincidences.'

'No. I think we've come to the right place,' Levitsky said. He flashed his credentials. 'Mind answering a few questions?'

'Sure. Ask away.'

She led them into a quirky shop crammed with occult books and new age paraphernalia. Levitsky slowly strode around, taking everything in, as he grilled her about the earlier visitor. Quinn listened in amazement as Alice Murtagh described the distraught mother of a missing child.

The agent kept up his probing as he scrutinised the cluttered store. Mrs Murtagh told them her husband had died suddenly over a year ago in a freak accident.

'Ira was founder and president of the Institute for the Assessment of Psychic Potential. The IAPP, they called it,' she said with an obvious puff of pride. 'I tried to keep up the whole operation after he passed on, but it got away from me. So much paperwork, so many difficult people to deal with. Don't know how Ira managed it all, bless his soul. It's more than enough for me with just the shop. I had the rest of the place converted to rental apartments. Only way I could afford to keep the place.'

Levitsky kept at it. Did she have many customers? How many this week? What had they bought? Looked at? Quinn had no idea what he was after, but she hoped he'd find it in a hurry. The place, the whole bizarre business was giving her the creeps.

What the hell was going on?

She'd never worried about a crackpot shortage, but who'd

266

be cruel and warped enough to play a trick on that poor child's mother? And why would anyone lure her and Levitsky all the way to Burlington for nothing?

The answer overcame her in a flush of rage. Only one idiot had the mentality, means and inside knowledge to pull off a stunt like this.

'Let's go, Levitsky. I have to commit an emergency assassination.'

He didn't seem to hear her. His gaze travelled from the desk to the posted list of shop hours in the window to a shelf near the ceiling filled with antiques: ancient magic tricks, sepia photographs, leather-bound books.

'You have a stepladder?' he said. 'I see something up there I might want to buy.'

'In the basement. I'll go get it.' Mrs Murtagh bustled out of the shop.

Levitsky waited until the door shut behind her. With an outstretched arm, he strained to reach the shelf and grabbed a volume.

'Guess you don't need that ladder after all,' Quinn said. 'I'll go tell her.'

Levitsky stopped her with a look. 'I sent her on purpose, Gallagher.'

'But why?'

He set the book on the desk and started flipping through the pages. Halfway through, a snip of paper fell out. Another soon followed. And then more. By the time he reached the rear cover, there was a hill of odd-shaped paper scraps on the desk top. Hearing Mrs Murtagh return, Levitsky slipped the shreds in his pocket.

'I'll take this,' Levitsky said. 'And I'll need a receipt.'

'Sure, no problem. Another fellow seemed real interested in that book a few days back, but he didn't come for it.'

'Was he a big man with strange eyes, dark hair in a pony tail and a red-ruby earring?'

'Right on the money,' said Mrs Murtagh. 'Guy was like my Ira, knew everything there was to know about magic and escapes and all. Of course, Mr Murtagh wasn't at all a creepy type like this guy. Ira was a prince.'

'Did this man spend a lot of time looking at the book and then climb up to replace it on the shelf?' said Levitsky.

'Now how'd you know that? You psychic too, mister? Amazing how many are.'

'I don't know how psychic I am,' Levitsky said. 'But I am interested in psychic research. You wouldn't happen to have the records from the Institute, would you? I'd love to have a look at them.'

Mrs Murtagh bowed her head like a chastened child. 'Should have kept them. Ira would roll over if he knew I'd gotten rid of them. But all those files took up so much room. Boxes and boxes there were.'

Levitsky shrugged. 'Sure, I understand.'

He thanked Mrs Murtagh and turned to leave, but her words caught him at the door.

'I suppose Mr Erlenkotter would be willing to let you go through the files,' she said.

'Erlenkotter?'

'Pete Erlenkotter. Lives down in Queechee. He was real involved in Ira's work. Jumped at the chance to keep the Institute's files at his place. In fact, why don't I call Pete for you? Be no trouble.'

She used the phone at the desk. Hanging up, she nodded with enthusiasm.

'No problem. Like I thought, Pete will be glad to let you see the records. He said any day week after next will be fine.'

'Week after next?' Levitsky said.

Mrs Murtagh nodded. 'Pete's on the dog show circuit. It's real busy for him this time of year. I caught him on the way out to the airport. He and his shelties won't be back for ten days.'

'Isn't there someone else there who can let us look at the files?'

The woman blinked. 'No, sir. Pete leaves, he locks everything up like Fort Knox.'

Quinn followed Levitsky out and to the jeep.

'What was all that business about the book, Levitsky? What did you find?'

In the car, he pulled out the paper snips and started arranging them on the leather cover of the book. His hand blocked Quinn's view.

'Damn it, Levitsky. Would you just tell me?'

Finished, he moved his hand and pivoted the book in her direction. Quinn stared at the connected paper scraps. Incredible.

With mounting horror she realised that this whole mess was deeper and darker than she could have imagined. And she knew they were fast running out of time.

38 Abigail kept reliving the horror. Standing on the road. Spotting the cat's-eye headlights. Knowing it was Daddy's car. Waiting out the small eternity until it pulled up beside her. Bursting happy.

Then came the wall of black shock as she tugged open the car door and saw who it really was.

Grabbing her roughly, he'd flipped her around backwards. He'd covered her eyes with a scarf and shoved a thick plug of gauzy material in her mouth. Then he'd bound her wrists and ankles together and tugged a rope between them until she thought her back would snap like a bent twig.

He dragged her over and shoved her in the trunk. The hatch smacked shut, stealing the minuscule swatch of light that had managed to leak through her blindfold. The air was thick with rubber and exhaust fumes.

She'd fought back the panic, tried to concentrate instead on where he was taking her. For a while the road was harsh and bumpy. Each jolt worsened the strain on her domed spine and pummelled her insides.

She felt a pinch of relief when the road smoothed. Focusing hard, she tried to memorise the route. Right turn. Wiggle curve. Two quick lefts. Another right. An arc to the left, not quite a turn. Or was it?

So many twists and turns, so hard to follow. The ropes nipped her flesh. The gag made it hard to breathe and impossible to swallow. This had to be over soon. She gave up on trying to memorise the directions and focused on a silent chant. *Please stop. Please no more.*

Finally the car jolted over a stretch of dips and hollows and rolled to a stop. There was a rush of chill air as the hatch wheezed open. Without a word, he cut the ropes binding her ankles. Then he hauled her out of the trunk and dumped her on the ground.

She struggled to stand. Not easy with her hands bound behind her and her feet prickling numb from the tight restraints. Once she managed to get herself upright, he prodded her in the back with some stiff object, urging her to move faster.

Stumbling before him, she crossed ground that went from mushy dampness to a brittle crunch and then to a perilous section littered with sticks and papery rubble. Twice, she staggered, but he caught her before she toppled face first and defenceless to the ground.

He caught her again as she was about to bump into a building wall. Opening a door, he shoved her inside, walked her through a big open space, opened another door, and nudged her down a flight of steps. There, he tugged off the tape holding the gauze plug in her mouth, but left her blindfolded and bound at the wrists.

'Rest,' he said.

There was the sharp clack of his retreating steps and the sound of several locks sliding into place from the outside.

For a moment, she was dumbstruck. He couldn't leave her like this.

'Hey! Let me out of here. Take this thing off. I can't see.'

She strained to listen, but there was nothing. No thumping steps. No clack of heels. No bat laughter.

'Hey!'

Feeling the way with her feet, she found the staircase, climbed to the top, turned her back to the door and tried to work the knob. Locked from the outside. She pounded her hands against the wood until her bones ached, but it was no use.

What if he'd been so mad about her escaping he'd decided to lock her in here and forget about her? He was that mean and crazy. She wouldn't put anything past him.

'Somebody help me!'

But she knew from the weight of the silence that there was no one around to hear her.

Cautiously, she felt her way down the stairs again. Sinking to the cold ground, she stretched her arms and rounded her back until she was able to work her hands under her buttocks and bring them out from under her legs to the front.

The blindfold was tight, but she nudged it up by degrees until it slipped off her eyes and over her head. She recognised it as his scarf, the one he often wore under his coat. Abigail mashed it under her filthy boots and tugged it between her feet until it shredded.

He'd brought her back to the same prison room, but the space was barer now. The tube and the canvas sack were gone. All that remained was the cot and a wooden milk pail in the corner. The gap in the wall was closed and invisible.

Suddenly aware of a burning thirst, she crossed and found the pail full of water. Sinking to her knees, she drank greedily. Satisfied, she dipped her tethered hands in the pail and ran the cool wetness over her face.

Feeling a bit better, she sat on the cot and worked at the wrist restraint with her teeth, tugging at the knot until her jaw ached and her front teeth felt sore and wobbly. Exhausted, she flopped back on the cot.

A few minutes' rest, and she'd try again.

Next thing she knew, she snapped awake. She had no idea how long she'd slept or what time of day or night it was. This prison place had no windows. No doors but the heavy locked one at the top of the stairs. How was she ever going to get out without help?

Then it came to her. Glancing down, she saw it was true. Her hands were free. The ropes that had tied them were gone. He must have returned while she slept and released her.

So he hadn't abandoned her after all.

But her relief was fleeting. What would come next? What insane tests and eerie obstacles did he have planned for her now? She thought about the tube and the sack and the invisible feet holders and the unseen fiery ring. When was it all going to end?

A tiny cry escaped her.

As if he'd heard, the locks clacked overhead and he started down the stairs. Abigail pressed hard against the cot, trying to disappear, terrified of what he was going to do.

But he stopped on the bottom riser. Peering at him through near-shut eyes, all she saw was an inky silhouette in a halo of misty light. How did he make weird things like that happen? Strange visions. Acrobatics with his voice.

'Don't be afraid, Abigail. I've only come to see what you need. Tonight, the princess will have her every heart's desire.'

She kept mute, waiting for the trick.

'I mean it. Anything you wish. Foods, fresh clothing. There must be so many things you want, my dear. All you need do is tell me.'

Abigail didn't move. She wasn't going to make any more dumb mistakes.

'Sceptical are you? Well, then. I'll leave you a piece of paper and a pencil. When you've gotten past your silly resistance, write down all the things you'd like me to get for you. Everything, no matter how frivolous or self-indulgent. This is your opportunity, princess. I advise you to take full advantage.'

He made a snapping sound and the room was awash with brilliant yellow light. She blinked away the shocked sparkles.

Long after he left, she sat on the cot staring at the bright emptiness. Was this another trap? Maybe the pencil would blow up in her face or the paper was coated with some acid stuff. Maybe he wanted her to write the things she wanted so he could use the list to torment her somehow. She could almost hear his mean teasing.

'Think of it, Abigail. Hot cocoa. Sweet rolls and french bread and a whole hazelnut torte with a mound of whipped cream.'

Her belly fisted with hunger and there was a grainy rumble inside. Her mind teemed with luscious cravings, all her favourite dishes from Chef Villet: a mountain of pasta with seafood, juicy duckling with lingonberry sauce.

Hesitantly, she crossed to the base of the stairs. She nudged the paper and pencil with the toe of her boot. When nothing awful happened, she risked a jab with her fingertip.

After a few seconds, she bolstered her nerve and picked

up the writing materials. Returning to the cot, she stretched out and started listing her wishes. She included everything that popped into her head, no matter how far-fetched.

She was the princess. Tonight the princess would have her every wish.

She refused to give a thought to what might come tomorrow.

39 Speeding towards Rutland, Quinn and Levitsky agreed on an action plan. First, they'd notify Holland. Then Jake could report their findings to Mayor Wellacott who could arrange for the necessary trooper support immediately.

Quinn tried to absorb all the impossible fresh developments. Following Weir's trail had led them to the crude paper portrait hidden in the old book. When Levitsky pieced the scraps together, the likeness to the missing child was undeniable: slim, blonde girl with wide blue eyes and a pony tail. No doubt the bizarre paper doll had been designed to represent Abigail Eakins. Abigail Eakins bloodied and dismembered.

The grotesque drawing had been planted in a volume on Harry Houdini, master escape artist. Levitsky's attention had been drawn to the book because of its curious placement directly over the sign on the desk that bore the name of the store. The shop's name was the same as the book's subtitle: *The Impossible Possible*. That fit Weir's pattern of leaving redundant clues. As Quinn drove, Levitsky leafed through the book and read her a number of other interesting items.

'Houdini was a stage name taken in memory of a master magician named Robert Houdin. His real name was Erich Weiss.'

'Vise. Wise. Weiss,' Quinn said.

'Weir's thumbing his nose at us with this Houdini business. Boasting that there's no way we can lock him up so he can't get out. Probably bragging that he's been able to come and go as he pleased all along.'

'But how?'

'I don't know, but it wouldn't surprise me if he took a page from Houdini's own methods and philosophies. According to this, Harry Houdini was a vocal detractor of those of his colleagues who claimed there was any real magic. Houdini freely admitted that all his illusions were just that: illusions.

'He used confederates, doctored his equipment. And then he challenged sceptics to catch him in the act. But the man was so clever, no one managed to expose his secrets even when they were invited to look for them.'

Levitsky found checkmarks next to the descriptions of certain tricks in the book. He read them to Quinn: the sack escape, the barrel challenge, the Cingalese child lift, mind-reading effects, and several others. She was intrigued to learn the simple secrets behind those seemingly inexplic-able illusions. The book also detailed the subtle tricks of muscle flexion the master magician had used to help him slip seemingly inescapable bonds. By tensing while the ropes were being tied, he was able to leave himself the necessary play to wriggle out when his captors weren't paying attention.

Levitsky also read her several highlighted sub-sections in a chapter on the use of confederates. They were the basis of Houdini's success, indispensible.

In the centre of that chapter the agent found a picture of Houdini as a young man that was circled in red. Glancing over, Quinn felt a chill. It was the same shot Weir kept in the cover of the antique pocket watch in his dresser.

But Weir's interest in Houdini was far from the only intriguing discovery Levitsky had made in the shop. The Institute for the Assessment of Psychic Potential, run by Mrs Murtagh's husband until his death, was one of the groups on Rita Banks's list of researchers who'd studied Weir during his stay at Rutland.

Then there was the logo above the store's letterhead which had been retained from the Institute. Levitsky had noticed it first on the back of the posted hours in the store window. The agent had requested a receipt because the logo also appeared on the sales slips.

'It's the same leaf and initial pattern I saw on the gate at Langdon Industries,' he told her.

Quinn was incredulous. It was at Langdon that the

professor had suffered his accidental blinding. In an attempt at restitution, the corporation had arranged and endowed all the complex elements of Weir's highly structured parole: the house and furnishings, the guide dog, the specially designed electronic monitoring system.

'Someone at that corporation must have helped Weir set the whole thing up, including the so-called accident,' Levitsky said.

'But the blindness is genuine,' Quinn said. 'I've seen the medical reports. Anyway, why would anyone help a creature like him? Makes no sense.'

'Maybe it will when we find out who it was. Meantime, we have to get enough eyes and ears on Weir so there's no way he can pull anything more.'

They drove directly to the parole office but found the place darkened and deserted. From the reception desk, Quinn called Holland's home number, but the phone machine picked up. In emergencies, he could be reached by pager.

She dialled his service, left her number, and hung up to wait. Quinn hated the idea of going to Mayor Wellacott without Jake. Holland had to appear properly in charge of the situation.

When the phone finally rang, it was Marilyn Holland. She sounded awful.

'What's wrong?' Quinn said. 'Where's Jake?'

Marilyn said she was calling from County General Hospital. Jake had been in a terrible funk over the missing child case, so she'd arranged a surprise dinner out at an elegant inn hoping to boost his spirits. Unfortunately, the idea had worse than backfired. He wouldn't tell her why, but he'd been terribly nervous and distracted during the meal. On the way home, he'd been taken deathly ill. Trouble breathing, chest pains.

Marilyn had rushed him to the nearest emergency room. At first, the doctors had suspected a heart attack. But tests had uncovered no cardiac irregularities.

'Now they're saying they think it's food poisoning,' Marilyn said. 'You had him paged, Quinn. Is it something I can help you with?'

'No, Marilyn. Everything's under control. You go back to Jake. Give him a hug for me. I'll check in later.'

'All right, dear. Take care.'

They had no choice but to go directly to Mayor Wellacott. Quinn dialled the Town Hall and told the night operator it was an emergency relating to Abigail Eakins' disappearance. After a beat, she was patched through to the mayor's home.

A woman with a thick German accent answered. She told Quinn the mayor was out for the evening. Hearing that it was urgent, the housekeeper suggested they try the dining room at the local inn.

Levitsky phoned ahead and confirmed that the mayor had a seven o'clock reservation. The agent offered to drive to Dove's Landing, and Quinn didn't object. Her brain was swarming. Jake, Mayor Wellacott, Langdon Industries, a sadist with a Houdini complex, that grotesque paper-doll parody of the little lost girl. There were so many impossible possibles to absorb, she doubted she had the head to hold the road.

They arrived in Dove's Landing at 7:30. As they drove by, Quinn cast a murderous scowl at the murky hulk of the Waldorf-Astoria. She imagined Weir inside, revelling in his cleverness. Sonavabitch was not going to get the better of them. Not this time.

The inn was one of those timeless, gracious New England treasures that made Quinn's teeth itch. Pristine white clapboard façade with staid hunter-green trim. Well-appointed interior with a serious chintz and copper bias. All appallingly well kept. The plants were green; the copper was not. Food and decorating magazines were aligned like intimidated schoolchildren on the gleaming mahogany occasional tables. No dust, not even a smattering for effect.

A striking woman was posted at the entrance to the inn's restaurant. Raven hair, incredible eyes, fabulous figure, flawless packaging. Quinn didn't feel a drop of envy. It was more like a tidal wave.

Levitsky, bless his workaholic heart, paid her no particular notice. Instead, he honed in on Wellacott, who was dining alone in a corner booth. Sidestepping the hostess, he manoeuvred his way across the glass-walled garden room towards the mayor.

Quinn loitered at the door. She was delighted to allow Levitsky the privilege of interrupting the mayor's assault on a crabmeat terrine with caviar. Face pinched with annoyance, Wellacott dabbed at the corners of his mouth and trailed Levitsky out to the parlour.

The three of them sat on the cosy ring of chintz sofas fronting the broad copper hearth. A hickory fire scented the air and cast flickering flame shadows on the collection of polished copper vessels that hung around the fireplace. There was a profusion of potted ferns and hothouse flowers in antique ewers. Family oil portraits lined the stuccoed walls, and the ceiling was inset with ancient beams and converted gas lights. The room was scented with wood smoke, lemon oil and potpourri. *House and Garden* stuff. Suitable for a Christmas-issue cover. Ironic setting for so many dark puzzles and demonic possibilities.

Quinn let Levitsky do the talking. The agent recounted their startling fresh discoveries. Wellacott reserved comment though his face betrayed a range of emotions: anger, incredulity, smirking amusement.

'The Institute records are unavailable for a couple of weeks. What we need is a round-the-clock guard on Weir and a comprehensive investigation of Langdon Industries,' Levitsky concluded. 'The troopers have to get on it immediately. Given that the random calls to Weir from central headquarters are nearly all programmed for waking hours, it's much more likely that he'd try to slip away during the night.'

'You have quite an imagination, Agent Levitsky,' Wellacott said. 'Now if you'll excuse me, I have a pressing engagement with Chef Villet's fabulous steak au poivre.'

'Wait a minute. You were the one who thought Weir was involved in the first place,' Quinn said. 'Now we're telling you he is, and you refuse to listen?'

Wellacott stood. 'Not that it's any of your business, but I'm quite satisfied at this point that the prisoner had no part in Abigail Eakins' departure. My experts found no significant irregularities in the tapes from the perimeter cameras or the tracings from Weir's electronic monitor. They've assured me that he's been in that building without interruption since the start of his parole.

'Furthermore, the troopers have uncovered compelling evidence that the Eakins child ran away on her own. There's a note, a recent withdrawal from her savings account and other things. The family is satisfied, and so am I. Abigail will undoubtedly return home on her own as soon as she tires of the foolishness. Now, if you'll excuse me.'

'No, I won't excuse you,' Levitsky said. For the first time, Quinn heard anger simmering under his controlled voice. 'I'm telling you Weir is a danger to you and everyone else in this town. You call in the troopers, or I will.'

Wellacott didn't waver. 'Be my guest. You'll find they will not act in this matter without my authority.'

Levitsky went to the pay phone. He returned ten minutes later, muttering to himself.

'Let's go, Gallagher.'

'What happened?'

'I said, let's go.'

'As I told you,' Wellacott said and sauntered back to the dining room.

Levitsky turned to leave. Quinn followed, firing nasty looks over her shoulder at Wellacott's retreating form. Guy was surprisingly arrogant for a chronic failure. Then maybe it wasn't so hard being a loser when you had a mountain of family money to cushion the flops.

Levitsky stalled beside the jeep and stood staring at the taunting silhouette of the Waldorf.

'So what do we do now?' Quinn said. 'Maybe you can get us some help from the bureau.'

'Not without hard evidence. I've been leaning on my boss, Mel Farmington, since this thing started. His superiors found out he's been helping me crash a local party, and they gave him hell. His hands are tied.'

'Well, ours aren't. Why can't we just go down there and hold a gun to the bastard's head?'

'Because they'd pick us up on the closed circuit cameras, and before long they'd send patrols to find out what the hell we were doing in that house. After they banished us for all eternity, who'd be left to do anything about Weir?'

'What then, Levitsky? What do you suggest?'

'Let me think, will you?'

Her pleasure. Quinn didn't have the first notion of how to proceed. They could hardly provide decent coverage themselves. If Weir had managed to slip his unblinking electronic bonds, what chance did they have with nothing but a couple of ordinary pairs of eyes?

'You trying to tell me you think it's hopeless, Levitsky? White flag time? Because I don't give up that easily.'

'I'm trying to tell you it's time to shut up, Gallagher, that's all.'

Levitsky brooded. Retrieving his briefcase from the back seat, he worked the combination. Inside was a jumble of electronic gadgetry and law enforcement toys: handcuffs, stun gun, night scope, burglar's tools, anti-bugging devices, wire taps, walkie-talkies. He fished out a minuscule metal disc and a small black plastic box with an electronic readout and a sound signal.

'Homing device. Works on a digital VHF tracking system. Used to be geared for automobiles only, but they've managed to reduce the size so it can be planted on a person. Might give us a little insurance. Would be better still if we could find a way to pick up and keep an eye on Weir's monitor signal. If we can somehow get through tonight, I'm sure we can find something we can use in the Langdon connection to make a case for state trooper or even Bureau support before tomorrow night.'

Levitsky detailed the plan. Quinn realised whom they'd have to recruit to make it work. The whole venture would be risky and miles from foolproof, but they were about out of time and alternatives.

A young girl's life might well hang in the balance. And that was far from all.

40 Luck was with them. Quinn found Dud Chambers in his room. He was sober and presentable in denim overalls and a work shirt. His place was neat, redolent of spray wax and ammonia. From the clock radio beside his bed came the soothing strains of 'Bridge Over Troubled Waters'. When she entered, he set down the book he'd been reading: the *King James Bible*.

Quinn drew a breath and offered a silent prayer that Dud's metamorphosis had not impaired his gullibility.

'Sorry to bother you, Dud, but I need a favour.'

'Sure, Miz Gallagher. Anything for you.'

'Great. It's a few minutes from here. Why don't you grab your tools and your soldering iron and your electronic gizmos and we can get right to it?'

Chambers stiffened when he spotted Levitsky in the jeep, but Quinn introduced the agent as a friend from out of town, and Dud seemed satisfied.

On the way, she eased into the business at hand. 'I wouldn't be bothering you with this, Dud, but I haven't been able to reach our monitoring technician.'

She told him she had a client on electronic surveillance, and the equipment had been malfunctioning for the last hour or so, triggering false alarms. She was sure it could be fixed by simply soldering another rivet on the wristlet. Then, if they could test the signal and be sure they'd fixed the problem, Quinn could go home and get a decent night's sleep.

'Otherwise, those clowns from Central will be beeping me every five minutes to report a "wristlet tamper" code. As the officer in charge, I get called first.'

'No problem,' Dud assured her happily. 'Sounds simple.'

On the way, Dud whistled several choruses of 'Bridge Over Troubled Waters', bobbling his head to the rhythm.

Guy was nice and loose until they approached the sign welcoming them to Dove's Landing.

'Hey, where're we going?'

'I told you, Dud. My client is on a monitor and . . .'

'Sorry, Ms Gallagher. I'm not feeling so good all of a sudden.'

He didn't look so well either. He'd blanched and gone clammy. His hands were trembling.

Quinn's diagnosis was acute bourbon deficiency. 'Hang in there, Dudley. Please. This is very important.'

'You got to take me home, Ms Gallagher. I need to lie down.'

Down a fifth was what he probably meant. But Quinn wasn't surrendering to that so easily. She caught Levitsky's eye, and they struck a tacit agreement. Time for Plan B. Dud Chambers would never refuse to help a child.

Quinn confessed the honest reason for their mission. The client was Eldon Weir. Though they'd had the professor on a tight electronic lead, they now suspected he'd found a way around the system and gotten involved in a kidnapping. Quinn sketched some of the evidence they'd uncovered by following Weir's own teasing trail of clues.

If Dud could effectively plant the homing device and find a way to intercept the signal from Weir's monitor, they'd have a decent shot at keeping the monster in check.

Chambers punched his fist, looked pained. 'Sonavabitch. That's the worst. Just terrible. Sure I'll help you, Miz Gallagher. I'll do anything.'

'That's good, Dud. This is important.'

'I know, Miz Gallagher,' Chambers said solemnly. 'Listen, we've got to make a quick stop back at my place first. There's something there I need to do the job right.'

They backtracked to Wilmington and waited in the jeep while Chambers bounded up the wooden stairs to his room. He returned quickly.

'Feeling better?' Quinn said.

'Yes, Maam. Much.'

He clambered back in the jeep, trailing a suspicious aura

of wintergreen breath spray. Quinn chose to ignore it. At least, for now.

Weir registered no surprise when the three of them showed up at the Waldorf. His expression was stony and inscrutable. Framed in the doorway, he worked languid strokes between the dog's haunches.

'Isn't this lovely, Darling? Unexpected guests. Our dear Officer Gallagher and the esteemed Agent Levitsky, is it not? And we have a *new* visitor as well.' He proferred his braceleted hand and sniffed. 'I don't believe I've had the pleasure, Mr . . . ?'

Chambers followed Quinn's instructions and stayed mute.

'Your wristlet's been malfunctioning,' Quinn said. 'I brought the technician to fix it.'

Weir frowned. 'How terribly inconvenient for you. My apologies. Where would be best? Tea perhaps?'

Levitsky and Quinn sat opposite Weir at the table while Chambers crouched at his side, soldering the tiny homing device onto the black plastic monitoring bracelet. Properly installed, it would be indistinguishable from the fastening rivets.

While he worked, Quinn took in the hand-painted ceramic tiles, custom cabinets, and top-of-the line gas stove, refrigerator, and dishwasher. Mighty fancy for a trash dump.

Moments later, Dud hitched a thumb, signal that he was done, and proceeded to the black box beside the phone to check the frequency.

Chambers used a contraption the size of a shoebox, manipulating the dials and levers until he was satisfied he'd trapped the correct signal band. Raising his thumb again, he tipped his head towards the door. Ready to leave.

On the return trip to Wilmington, Dud suffered another sudden bout of malaise. Oily pallor, shallow breathing. The shakes.

'You go right upstairs and get to bed, Dud,' Quinn said. 'And no liquid remedies, you hear? I'll check on you first thing tomorrow.'

'Thanks, Miz Gallagher. Don't know what I'd do without you.'

'Yes you do, Dudley. But don't.'

Back in Dove's Landing, she parked the jeep down the dirt road from the Waldorf, well out of range of the perimeter cameras. They planned an all-night vigil, and Levitsky had claimed the first two-hour shift. He sat in the front seat watching the signal receivers for Weir's monitor and the homing device. Quinn settled in the rear and tried to sleep, but something kept nagging at her.

'What did you mean before when I crashed into the dumpster and you said you understand?'

'Later, Gallagher.'

'No, Levitsky. Now.'

'I meant that, in a lot of ways, you remind me of myself,' he said. 'You never forget. Never forgive. Your whole life is driven by the need to correct the past. So's mine.'

'What is it you can't forgive?'

'It's not important.'

'Must be if it drives your whole life, Levitsky.'

'Cut it out, Gallagher. You make me regret ever teaching you about rational thinking.'

'Then shut up and tell me.'

His grin flashed but quickly faded.

'I was a lucky little kid: solid parents, happy home, love and security. The whole fairytale. Then, when I was about your brother's age, someone took it all away.' He was staring at the monitors, but Quinn caught the sorrow in his eyes. 'That's it.'

Quinn sat up. She couldn't strangle the man lying down. 'Come on, Levitsky. Who took it away? What happened?'

'I can't. Maybe another time, okay?' He cleared the static from his voice and blew his nose. Cute nose. Tipped at the end. A nice beat off-centre.

'Okay, Levitsky. Another time.'

He cast a curious look in her direction. Not used to her being so reasonable, Quinn figured.

'I understand some things too,' she said.

She slept fitfully. Tugging herself awake, she felt surprisingly stiff for a two-hour snooze. Focusing on the dashboard clock, she saw she'd been out for almost five hours. The car was cold. Levitsky was still perched in the front, eyeing the monitors and sipping at a cup of take-out coffee that must be iced by now.

'Why didn't you wake me?'

'You looked too peaceful. Anyway, I'm fine.'

Quinn hauled herself up and stepped out to open the driver's door. 'Go to sleep, Levitsky. It's my turn.'

'Really, I'm not tired.'

'We have a busy day ahead of us, Superman. Go night-night now, and that's an order.'

Reluctantly, he got out and curled up in the back. Soon his breathing settled. Quinn watched the monitors. Flat and nothing. More flat, more nothing. Bored already, she peeked at the sleeping agent. Long-limbed, a gentle edge to the somnolent features, nice smudge of beard stubble, a curl lolled over his forehead. Not entirely unappealing.

But then anything was more appealing than the damned monitors. Flatnothingflatnothingflaaaat. Great insomnia remedy. So effective, she felt as if her eyelids were taking on water. Squaring her shoulders, she sternly reminded herself she was here to watch. Her turn. How had Levitsky stood it for five hours?

Flat . . . nothing. Time was at a stubborn standstill.

Flat. Nothing.

Wait.

The monitor from the homing device was making a funny little noise. So subtle, Quinn took it for a mental hiccup at first. But as she stared, unblinking, the sound intensified. Next, the rhythmic pattern on the other monitor was broken by a series of dips and slashes. Small changes, but undeniable.

She hated to wake Levitsky. Could be insignificant. But suddenly the signal strengthened a notch, and the irregularities in the monitor tracing grew in height and frequency. Still might be insufficient to trigger an alarm at Headquarters, but it was more than enough to set her off.

'Levitsky? Get up. Something's happening.'

He whipped awake. Eyed the monitors. Lifting the receiver from the homing device, he studied the signal sound.

'Let's go.'

They walked in tandem, their shadows stretched and wavering under the bower of bud-laden branches. Dried leaves and brittle twigs crunched underfoot. There was the long trilled whistle of a pygmy owl.

Nearing the Waldorf's gate, Quinn thought of the perimeter cameras and slowed. Levitsky pressed ahead, brandishing his semi-automatic.

'Wait,' Quinn said. 'They'll see us.'

'That's okay. If he's out, we'll want all the help we can get.'

Levitsky paused outside the gate. 'Look.'

Halfway to the house, footprints veered off the flagstone walk. They continued in a steady arc around the side of the house.

The agent drew a penlight from his pocket and trained it on the prints. They followed the trail through the Waldorf's rear yard and over the mesh-lined fence. This side of the property abutted a dairy farm. The tracks continued through a span of fallow pasture and into another section that had been tilled for spring planting.

From behind, Quinn heard the wail of approaching sirens. Good. When they caught up with Weir, the cops would be on hand to haul him into surer custody.

Over a rise, they spotted the farmhouse and the scatter of outbuildings beyond. Plenty of places for the professor to hide and wait. Levitsky wrested his twenty-two from the ankle holster and handed it to Quinn.

'Wait here for me.'

'Fat chance.'

'Then at least let me lead.'

'This one time, Levitsky. That's it.'

She followed him across the open field towards the farmhouse. The footprints changed course and started angling towards the front porch. Quinn's mouth grew parched as she imagined the sleeping family inside. Peaceful, defenceless.

They had to stop Weir before he hurt anyone.

She lengthened her stride to keep apace of Levitsky. Guy could move. They were almost across the field, nearing the house. *Please don't let it be too late.*

But the agent stopped so abruptly Quinn almost ran up his back.

'What the hell?'

'Look at that.'

By the wavering glow of the penlight, she saw the agent's stunned expression. Tracking his pointed finger, she followed the line of prints as they came to a sudden, inexplicable end in the middle of the field. Trailing away in the return direction was another, smaller set of impressions: paw prints. Levitsky played his light along those tracks until they too abruptly disappeared.

'How could that be?' she said.

Levitsky shook his head. 'Illusion, Gallagher. Very black magic. And this time, I'm afraid the trick's on us.'

It came at Quinn like a brick. There was the shrill of gathering sirens at the Waldorf. Weir was probably already greeting the first arriving troopers, brimming with innocent surprise. She and Levitsky would have to answer for their unauthorised appearance at the house in the dead of night, their stalking around armed with forbidden weapons in plain sight of the perimeter cameras.

Their standing would slip below sub-zero. All part of Weir's carefully executed plan to get them and everyone else out of his way.

The professor had arranged a lesson for them. And neither of them would soon forget it.

41 Nora kept fading in and out like a radio with faulty wiring. Dream and reality crashed in her murky mind. Jolts of confusion interspersed with gentle spans of teasing calm.

Before the medication kicked in, she and Charlie had managed to complete her list of calls. But all she'd gained from the exercise was a disturbing sense of the depth of Abigail's desperate sadness. They'd uncovered no single issue or event that might have triggered the child's flight. Abby seemed to be running from an undefined, unbearable melancholy.

Everyone Nora contacted had used the same vocabulary to describe the little girl: down, depressed, changed. Nora had been forced to consider the worst case. Maybe Abby's skid had no external cause. Maybe it was an emotional illness.

Her gut churned at that hideous thought, but she could not dismiss it. Raymond's father had been unstable. Explosive. Driven to mindless rages.

And years ago, her own mother had suffered periods of suffocating despondency. Growing up, Nora had watched the woman downshift and stand at idle, sometimes for days at a time. She'd shuffle around the house in slow motion, never dress past a robe and slippers, stare at whatever happened to appear on the television screen.

Then she'd snap out of it. Go suddenly light again like a room stripped of dark draperies. Fortunately, the condition had resolved over time, vanquished by a good therapist and a better drug.

Which meant Abby could be healed as well. Should be even easier for her. She was a child after all, open, malleable. But they couldn't do anything to help the little girl until they found her. They *must* find her.

Nora slogged out of bed and plodded downstairs. Earlier,

one of the waiters had stopped by with a dinner tray from the restaurant. When it arrived, she'd pushed it away. But now she was moved by a hollow ache of hunger.

The covered dishes were in a row on the counter. Lifting the silver domes, she discovered a bowl of vichyssoise, a tossed salad and a grilled salmon filet ringed with vegetables. There was a dessert soufflé, Grand Marnier from the heady smell of it, and a cup of cappuccino.

Every dish was a masterwork. Chef Villet might be a miserable person, but no one could fault his culinary skill or fabulous presentation. In her first two months at the inn, Nora had put on ten pounds. Realising that at that rate she'd soon be in suitable shape to hover over sporting events, she'd learned to resist the considerable temptation.

But now she felt ready for a bout of serious overindulgence. She hadn't eaten much of anything since Abby's disappearance. Nothing but a forced bite here and there at Mim or Charlie's insistence. She looked and felt gaunt. Empty.

The soup was wonderful, rich and soothing. She finished that and the salad with its luscious walnut vinaigrette and moved on to the main course: baby squash, tiny new potatoes sprinkled with dill, salmon grilled to melting perfection and capped with a subtle sauce.

Finished, she settled back and was overcome by a drowsy wash of satiation. Her eyes drifted shut, but she forced them open again. She had the nagging sense that she'd forgotten something. But what?

Disconnected thoughts pressed through her woolly mind: the mystery resident at the Waldorf-Astoria, the woman from parole. She strained to move in a logical line, tried to deflect the assault of stray notions and the swell of distracting noises outside. But soon the sounds grew too strident to ignore.

Sirens.

The wailing built to a crescendo. Through her shuttered eyes, Nora detected the screaming flash of emergency lights.

Fear iced her bones, and her heart squirmed. Stiff with terror, she made her way upstairs to grab her shoes. She had to learn the reason for the commotion. Maybe it was something about Abigail.

42 An angry crowd of cops and officials confronted Quinn and Levitsky in the Waldorf's front yard. On the walk back from their fools' chase, they'd agreed on a simple, direct defence. They'd had reason to believe there was a problem with Weir, a possible escape attempt. Unable to get official help, they'd driven down from Rutland to have a look around. At the time, the weapons had seemed prudent and necessary. End of story.

And of them.

Mayor Wellacott was on hand to revel in their discomfiture. So was ratty Ralph Norman. The corpulent cop stood nodding in fervent, almost religious assent as his boss brusquely ordered Quinn and the agent to keep away from Weir until their conduct had been subjected to comprehensive official review.

'I'm sure you're well aware that parole officers are strictly forbidden to bear arms, Ms Gallagher. This is an extremely serious offence.' The chief trooper was a bulldog marine type, cropped, clipped and to the point.

'Mr Levitsky is not a parole officer, sir. The guns were his.'

'I'm fully aware he's with the FBI,' Chief Festo said. 'I'm also aware that he's here without official consent or authorisation. You are in clear violation of the compact between local law enforcement agencies and the US government, Agent Levitsky. This does not go down at all well with us. And I'm sure your superiors will feel likewise.'

'I am appalled that you'd get involved here in direct opposition to our wishes,' Wellacott huffed. 'Chief Festo has assured me that if either of you are spotted in the vicinity of this house again, you will be arrested immediately. I suggest you get out of my town at once and stay out.'

'That's fine,' Levitsky said. 'Now that Chief Festo plans to post sentries on the house, we'll be glad to stay away.'

'He'll do no such thing, will you, Tom?' Wellacott said.

The chief trooper cleared his throat. 'Well, actually, he's right. I'm sure you can understand my position, Mayor. The risk is probably minimal, but imagine how I'd look, how we'd all look, if Weir actually did get out by some bizarre twist.'

'I won't have it,' Wellacott spluttered. 'You are to disperse your troops. Weir isn't going any place. You have my personal assurance on that.'

Festo stood at attention. 'Sorry, Mr Mayor. My responsibility is clear in this case.' He ordered three units to stay and watch the house until further notice. 'Sergeant Matthews, I'm putting you in charge of this detail. If there's any change, I'll send word. Everyone else is dismissed. Go on about your business, people.'

Levitsky was waiting at the jeep. But Quinn had some nagging business of her own to attend to. Scanning the crowd, she spotted a cop she knew who lived in Rutland. Signalling the agent to wait, she wandered over to talk to the trooper. She returned shortly with the man in tow.

'This is Hal Trencher, Levitsky. He lives in Rutland near your hotel, and he'll be glad to drop you off. I've got something to take care of before I head home. Condolence call. Friend's sister's mother-in-law. I've put it off too long already.'

'What's going on?'

'I told you.'

'Come on, Gallagher. Don't play games. We're in this together.'

'This is personal, Levitsky. Go.'

After a short, silent deadlock, Levitsky retrieved his briefcase from the jeep. A beat later, he reached in and took the receiver from the signal monitor as well.

'I'm sure you won't be needing this on a condolence call. Right, Gallagher?'

'Right, Levitsky.'

'Promise you'll call me if there's any trouble. Even a hint.'

'Give it a rest.'

'You've got my number.'

'You bet I do. Now go.'

A line of cop cars escorted the jeep to the Dove's Landing town line and then began peeling off in assorted directions. The car ferrying Levitsky was among the last to let go. When those headlights finally veered off and vanished, Quinn eased onto the shoulder and changed course for Wilmington.

On the way, she vented her frustration on the gas pedal, stomping it to the floor. If this particular condolence call turned out as she expected, she was definitely not the one who was going to be sorry.

His room was dark. She parked in the driveway, mounted the outside stairs and pummelled Dud Chambers' door. Silence. She waited, hammered again and called his name. Nothing.

Rearing back, she mustered enough momentum to snap the latch chain, which Dud had repaired since her last break-in. Guy was a wiz at fixing everything except himself. Feeling her way, she found the light switch and spotlit the sorry scene.

Dud was splayed on the floor in a drunken stupor.

Quinn prodded him in the ribs with her toe. Nobody home. Stooping in a crouch, she shook him hard by the shoulders. His response was a porcine snort.

She tried to lift him, but his weight kept shifting in unpredictable bursts like a sack of gravel. Breathing hard, she stepped back and set her strategy on a surer course.

'Hey, Dud Chambers. Fancy seeing you here. Buy you a drink, buddy?'

Dud hefted himself onto all fours and smacked his lips. 'Sure. Double anything be real nice.'

With considerable effort, Quinn was able to haul him off the floor and seat him more or less upright in a slat-backed chair. His T-shirt was sweat-stained, and he'd worried his hair in greasy tangles. His back was bowed, and his eyes had sunk in craters of despair.

'What happened, Chambers? What the hell are you running from this time?'

294

He squinted. 'Miz Gallagher? That you? Nice lady like you shouldn't be hanging out in a dive like this.'

'Come on, Dudley. Tell me what's going on. Why did you get so upset about Eldon Weir being in that house?'

He raised a finger. 'Barkeep, give my friend here whatever she wants. On me.'

'Tune in, Dudley. You've got to tell me.'

Useless. Chambers's eyes were skating in jerky circles.

'All right, Dud. I guess you need a wake-up call.'

She tugged a trio of ice cube trays from the freezer compartment beside the sink. Holding out the collar band of Dud's T-shirt, she emptied one down his back. She dumped the second into the waistband of his pants. Then, she pressed the third tray at intervals along his neck, wrists, ankles and finally, across the soles of bare feet.

Dud jerked and flailed back to consciousness. 'Whoa, cold. Whooo freezing.' He sat bolt upright and his eyes popped. 'Miz Gallagher?'

'Yes. Now tell me. What's the story with you and Weir?'

'Oh God. I'm so sorry. I didn't know. You got to believe me.'

'You didn't know what?'

He drew a trembly breath and mopped his eyes with the back of his hand. 'He said he wanted to help me. I thought it was on the up-and-up. Honest, I did.'

'What are you talking about? Start at the beginning.'

Chambers sniffled. 'Okay. This guy came to see me at Rutland right after my parole board hearing. He was real rich-looking. Wore fancy suits, fat jewellery, the works. Told me he ran some big business upstate. Said he worked with ex-cons, volunteer-like, in his free time. Pleased him to help people like me get back on their feet. Said he wanted to remain anonymous, so no one would make a fuss about it.'

To be eligible for parole, Dud had needed to secure a job and arrange an acceptable living situation. With the man's behind-the-scenes help, Chambers had been able to bypass normal channels and expedite the process.

Dud's sponsor had found and furnished his garage apartment and pulled strings to get Dud hired at the Photo Lab. The man had even arranged occasional odd jobs so Chambers could earn extra money in his spare time. Dud had been working on one such project when Quinn dropped by the camera store to have the tapes duplicated.

'I fixed half a dozen radios for him,' Dud went on. 'My sponsor said they were for this club he belonged to. Group of amateur magicians. He had me rig all the radios to the same open frequency and hook them up so they worked like walkie-talkies. When they weren't transmitting, they were set to sound like a real station, but it wasn't. Just a tape one of the members had put together. I couldn't see the harm in it, Miz Gallagher. Honest.'

'And you dropped one of those radios off at the Waldorf?'

Glum nod. 'Mr Milton told me to stick it on the furniture delivery truck with the rest of the things. Said a friend of his from the club was moving in there.

'I had to order a part for the transmitter. When it arrived, my guy had me drop it off in front of the house in some crumpled paper. I asked him why all the sneaky business, and he told me his friend was funny about strangers.'

'Funny about strangers. Interesting way to describe Weir,' Quinn said.

'I had no idea Eldon Weir was living in that house, Miz Gallagher. First hint I had was when you brought those tapes for me to copy. When I saw that the parole department was filming that old dump, I knew the person living there wasn't just some regular club friend of Mr Milton's.

'I checked around and heard Weir was on house arrest at the Waldorf. Eldon Weir, for godsakes. When you told me a little girl had been kidnapped, I knew it had to be his doing. And I realised I must've been part of it somehow. How could I be so dumb, Miz Gallagher? What's wrong with me?'

Chambers squeezed out two oversized tears. Quinn was almost moved to comfort the dope, but a larger urge to strangle him interfered.

'Who's Mr Milton?'

'Like I told you, a businessman who likes to help ex-cons. That's all I know about him.'

296

'What's his business?'

'Some company upstate. He mentioned the name once, but I can't remember.'

A chilling notion scaled her spine. 'Was it Langdon Industries?'

'Hey yeah. That's it. How'd you know that?'

She persisted. 'Did Mr Milton arrange for you to participate in a research study about psychic powers?'

'Wow, Miz Gallagher. You're even smarter than I thought. I had to sit behind this black curtain and try to tell this guy what he was seeing on the other side. Weirdest thing ever.'

Quinn's heart was doing flips. It was finally coming together. All she had to do was track down Dud's sponsor.

'Where does Mr Milton live, Chambers?'

'Don't know. He always came to see me. Just sort of showed up from time to time.'

She kept digging. 'What's his phone number? How about the make and model of his car?'

Chambers was a blank. Out of questions, Quinn drew a hard breath and tried to proceed with calm Levitskian logic.

'All right. Let's try this another way. Can you get me one of those rigged radios?' If that was the way members communicated, Quinn wanted to be in on the party line.

He snuffled. 'Sorry. Gave them all to Mr Milton.'

'Then how fast can you make me one?'

'I'd have to order the parts first. Takes a few days at least. Specially for that transmitter doodad.'

Quinn clenched all her clenchables: fists, teeth, temper. 'What kind of parts are they, Dud? Can't you take them from the TV or the toaster or something?'

'Sorry. They're specialised. Kind of doohickeys you'd only find in ship-to-shore or police radios. Not too many of those floating around for the taking.'

Quinn didn't know whether to kiss the guy or kick his butt. 'I have a police band on my car radio.'

'You mean it? No problem, then. I can adjust it to catch the club signal in no time. Just let me get my tools.'

When he tried to stand, his legs wobbled like cheap

furniture. Leaning heavily on Quinn, he managed to heft himself out of the chair. He paused a second and shook off a clatter of melting ice cubes.

In awkward concert, they sashayed across the room and over the porch roof to the stairs. She eased him down the wooden flight, a perilous step at a time, and walked him down the driveway to the jeep.

Dud flopped onto the front seat and started fiddling with the radio. Given his pickled condition, Quinn was sceptical that he'd be able to manage the intricate adjustments. But he emerged less than ten minutes later sporting a satisfied grin and a victory signal.

'All set, Miz Gallagher. You want to listen to the club channel, you just turn to the peak of the police band and then down two notches. Nothing to it.'

Quinn took the driver's seat and followed Chambers' directions. When she got to the club frequency, a Carol King number was playing. 'It's Too Late'. She hoped it was not prophetic.

'The members only transmit once in a while,' Dud explained solicitously. 'It'll be hit or miss, specially at night. But you don't need to worry about Eldon Weir any more. I made sure he can't get out of that house and hurt anybody. Good and sure.'

Quinn caught the odd set to his expression and went cold. 'What did you do, Dudley?'

'Did what I had to, Miz Gallagher. Couldn't take any chances, could I? Not when a little girl's life was at stake.'

'Tell me, Chambers.'

'Weir stays in that house, there's no problem. Don't give it another thought, Miz Gallagher. Just put it out of your mind.'

Bounding out of the jeep, she caught him by the sodden neck of his T-shirt and twisted hard. 'Speak, Chambers.'

He tried, couldn't. Hard to speak and choke at the same time. Quinn eased her grip. 'Now tell me.'

Coughing, Chambers raised his hands in surrender. 'Okay. I had a little plastic explosive in my room left over from this rock blasting job I did with a friend. When I heard it was Weir in that house, I had you bring me back here so I could get some. I smoothed it under his wristlet and rigged it so it'd be triggered soon after he broke his electronic lead. Weir tries to escape, he's history.'

Quinn couldn't believe her ears. She felt ready to explode herself. 'Get the hell out of my way, Chambers. I've got to get to him before it's too late.'

She pushed Dud aside and left him sputtering in astonishment. Gunning the jeep, she barrelled out of the drive and tore towards Dove's Landing. She kept imagining the scene. Weir stealing out of the Waldorf, erupting in a poison fireball, reduced to stinking ash and smoking embers.

Might be a fitting end for that monster. But if Weir triggered Chambers' explosives, she feared she'd be stuck for all eternity trying to clean up the mess.

43 Abigail was woozy with pleasure. She couldn't remember the last time she'd had a full belly, felt clean and warm and comfortable.

He'd brought her everything she'd requested and more: rich desserts, soft pyjamas and a fleece robe, furry slippers.

The bath had been the only disappointment. He'd lugged down a basin filled with soapy water, the excess sloshing over the rim. After he left, Abigail had washed herself a section at a time, rubbing with the washcloth until her flesh was tingling. Not a real bath, but better than nothing.

Soon as she got home, she planned to soak for a week. Drift in scented bubbles. Scrub until she was cleansed of him and his stinking sicko jokes.

Finished with all the treats and privileges, Abigail was exhausted but too keyed up to sleep or even close her eyes. Something was about to happen. The little girl sensed it like the pressure dip before a storm. She didn't know whether it would be a good or bad difference, but she was caught in a noose of expectation.

Listening hard, she heard a sharp blipping overhead like a leaky tap. A second sound resonated deep in her bones. Felt like the drum throb of a heavy metal tune.

She couldn't stand the waiting. Whatever it was, Abigail wished it would get started already. Nothing could be worse than the crawling fiends in her memory and imagination. Dead rats. Fires.

When he finally came back down the stairs, it was almost a relief. 'So are you prepared, Abigail? All your wishes fulfilled?'

'Prepared for what?'

'I trust you rested as I said. You will need all your energies.'

'What do you want? What are you going to do to me now?'

At that, his expression went wierd. She'd never seen such a crazy face. Bug-eyed. Toothy. Glinting with vicious mirth. Scared her to ice.

'You have to tell me.'

'Certainly, I'll tell you, my dear. I'll even *show* you. After all, you are the star of the enterprise, the subject of our little experiment. It's all in the interest of *knowledge*, you see. *Enlightenment.* Together, we'll explore the very essence of humanity, probe the mysteries of existence.' He clapped his hands. 'Now, then. We shall begin by recording the baseline data and proceed from there. Be still now.'

She started to tremble as he placed a finger on her wrist, poked at her neck, tugged her eyelids open and peered underneath.

'What are you doing?' The tremors were building to harsh spasms. Wracking her. 'Stop that. Don't touch me.'

'Silence!' He pressed the frigid mouth of a stethoscope against her back. Made several notations on a page clipped to his chart.

All sicko craziness, she kept telling herself. Another dumb wierdo trick. But something in his eyes was terrifying her. Abigail couldn't place it. She only knew she wanted to get away from those eyes and the nameless thing crouching behind them.

'There. I have all I need for the time being,' he said at last. 'You rest until I return, and we'll begin the final test.'

Abigail watched him mount the stairs and disappear into the shadows. The final test, she thought. Only one more, and then he'd be done with her.

44 The road was deserted. Quinn urged the speedometer needle into the end zone. Time was the enemy. She felt the dread drain of seconds, the minutes bleeding away. If Weir tried anything, both of them were doomed to go up in smoke.

Perfect night for a catastrophe. Charcoal clouds scudded across the sullen sky. The moon emerged at fickle intervals. Dizzying kaleidoscope of hope and menace.

Bristling tense, Quinn flipped on the radio. The dial was set to the club frequency. She was about to change channels when an announcer with a pinched nostril voice came on to tout a sale at a used car dealership in the nearby town of Queechee.

'Those babies are going to disappear off the lot. They'll be gone before you know it. And then it'll all be over. Abracadabra.'

The word gripped Quinn like a vice. *Abracadabra.* The station wasn't real and neither was that announcement. It had to be a coded message.

Those babies are going to disappear. Gone before you know it. The meaning was obvious. Weir was planning to leave the Waldorf.

She pressed even harder on the gas. Gritted her teeth. Flares of terror were firing in her mind. *Let me make it before it's too damned late!*

Abracadabra.

And then it would all be over.

45 Still battling the effects of the tranquillisers, Nora traversed the inn's sprawling lawn, stole through the parking lot, crossed the road and hastened up the hill towards the covered bridge. Nearly there, she caught a clear view of the line of cars leaving the Waldorf. Three units stayed behind, and half a dozen men lingered on the front lawn talking.

From the cover of the rickety wooden bridge, she couldn't make out the words, but the ring of faces, illuminated by a scatter of headlights, looked grim.

She wanted to march right over there and demand to know what was going on, but she was stalled by the memory of her last attempts to get anywhere near the house. Last thing she wanted was to be forcibly escorted back to the inn again, evicted without ceremony or explanation by earnest, overbearing cops.

She had to talk to that new tenant, criminal type or no. She had to find out if he'd seen or heard anything related to Abby's disappearance. Nora hadn't been put off by the troopers' warnings, and she wasn't the least bit afraid. With her daughter missing, she felt nothing but the sick ache of desolation.

Camouflaged by the thickets of wild shrubbery along the road, she edged closer. Straining to listen, she was able to field scraps of the conversation. Something about a professor. No mention of Abigail. Then the furore at the house might have been unrelated to the little girl's disappearance. Nothing but a teasing coincidence.

Nora decided to stay out of sight until the last cops had departed. Then she would go in and meet the mysterious neighbour. Whoever, whatever he was, if he knew anything that could help her find Abigail, she was determined to hear about it.

The ring of troopers seemed in no hurry to leave. Nora

ducked around to the blind side of the fence and hunched behind a scraggly line of privet. Soon her legs began wavering from the strain. To still the tremors, she gave in and sat on the chill, mushy ground. After the initial shock, it felt sort of nice. Soothing.

Nora stifled a melting yawn. The final clump of cops was taking forever to peel away. They stood around jawing about the Red Sox, the state of the state budget, a woman named Sally Ann with the build and substance of a blow-up doll.

Nora's eyes were sore and heavy, and her head throbbed. *Get lost already. I need to get in there and question that man.*

There was a static squawk from one of the patrol-car radios. One of the troopers loped over to listen. Ambling back, he flashed a thumbs-up gesture. 'That was a call from the chief's office,' he said as if he'd read Nora's mind. 'We're out of here.'

The remaining men started straggling towards the gate in slow motion. They paused at intervals for added scraps of discussion. *Come on already!*

Her limbs were tingling with exhaustion. Lids lead-weighted. She decided she'd be fine if she allowed them to shut for a tiny second. That was all she needed.

Jolting alert, she felt stiff and disoriented. The patrol cars were gone. No hint of anyone around.

Angry with herself for drifting off, she tried to make out the time on her watch, but fast-drifting clouds blocked the moon's glow. No point worrying about the hour anyway. No matter how late it was, she was going to meet the new neighbour. Nora struggled up off the ground and started for the house.

46

Quinn bolted out of the jeep fifty yards down the dirt access road. Circling the property, she came up even with the front of the Waldorf. Deftly, she vaulted the split-rail fence and approached the house in a deep tuck. She was hoping to evade the piercing scrutiny of the perimeter cameras. Until she had a chance to size up the situation, she had no desire for company.

A yard from the staked border, she was stalled by a reflexive jolt of fear. But the thought of Weir breaking loose and setting off those explosives prodded her forward.

Too risky to use the door. The eye beams of the two front cameras converged at the front entrance. She'd be clearly exposed at Central if she tried that route.

She assessed the alternatives. Towards the rear of the house a window opened into the dining room. Standard builder's fare: two panes over two. From there, she calculated she'd be beyond the seeking watch of both the front and rear cameras. Going in, she'd have the sound-muffling advantage of the plush mauve carpeting. If Weir was upstairs or even at the opposite end of the house, she'd have a decent chance to slip in undetected and take him by surprise.

But then she remembered the dog.

Damned beast was so unpredictable. He could be a snarling defender of the turf or docile, verging on oblivious. Quinn had seen both personalities. Had no idea what made the difference.

So it was a crap shoot. What wasn't?

She stole towards the side window. Peering in, she faced the lowering gloom. Nothing stirred. No glinting dog eyes. No warning yaps or throaty growling. At least, not yet.

She nudged the window frame, and the lower panel slid up without noise or effort. Clambering over the sill, she tuned her ear to filter the bristling silence. Nothing she could see or hear. But she sensed a cold, venomous presence.

He was still in the house.

She pulled the twenty-two from her coat pocket and worked it in a wavering arc in front of her. She planned to keep the weapon securely in her grasp for the duration. This time, Weir was not going to get the better of her.

Padding soundlessly, she made her way through the living room. The moon had lapsed behind a cloud bank. Intense darkness slowed her progress, setting mock obstacles in her path. She waded through a perilous sea of eye-fooling silhouettes. Last thing she needed was to trip over something and give herself away.

Safely past the ring of sofas, she fumbled along the wall for the switch. Given Weir's blindness, light would give her an advantage or, at least, more even odds. Finally, her hand hit the wall plate. But when she flipped the switch, nothing happened. She tried several times, working the lever in a frantic flurry.

Weir must have killed the power.

Quinn stared into the blackened hallway and willed her eyes to adjust. Squinting hard, she was able to define the chunky outline of the monitoring box and its snaking tether to the phone. The staircase rose beyond.

Mounting the flight, Quinn held her breath. *Please no loose risers.* The tiniest sound could betray her. Armed with nothing but this silly little pea-shooter, she wanted desperately to maintain the advantage of surprise. Or was that even a possibility? She thought of the professor's eerie prescience. His claim to second sight.

Did he already know she was in the house? Could he feel her presence the way she sensed his?

Then, halfway up, she heard it. A low sputtering hiss. A sound without identifiable form or substance. Could be nothing. But it scaled her back in a rash of terror.

Her mouth dried. Frozen, she waited for the noise to cease or change into something recognisable. Soon, the hissing muted, and the breathy play of his words looped around her neck.

'The path ends here, officer. You have tracked it to the finale.'

Where was he?

She couldn't locate the words. His voice was a wind squall in the darkness, capricious play of tone and direction. Time to call off the game.

'Show yourself, Weir. Right now. I'm taking you in.'

'But I *have* shown myself, Ms Gallagher. I've exposed the very essence of my heart and soul. Revealed my innermost secrets. And this is my reward? Distrust? Subterfuge?'

Suddenly his voice reared up at her, poked her hard in the chest like an angry accusatory finger.

'*This!*'

Quinn flinched and nearly plummeted down the stairs. Her heart was going nuts, throat a squeezed lemon.

'Put your hands behind your neck and come out slowly, Weir. Right now!' She winced at her own shrill, desperate timbre.

'Oh? Must I sit in the corner, mummy dear? Have I been a naughty boy?'

He rasped the words, tossed them at her from the empty air beside the staircase. Tickled her ear with them.

'Would you like to spank me? I wouldn't mind. Truly, it would be my *pleasure.*'

Enough!

Quinn was not going to stand around like a trapped bug and take this. She was going to win this round. There were only so many places in this house he could be. And she was damned well going to find him.

She continued up the stairs, ignoring his taunts and admonitions.

'Stay away, officer. Far away. You know I cannot be trusted.'

At the top landing she scanned the silent corridor. The door to Weir's bedroom was wide open. Next in the row, the spare bedroom door was nearly shut. There was a closed door at the far end of the hall. Linen closet, as she remembered from the search. The final door was a tiny bathroom, also closed. Making a quick decision, she slipped into Weir's bedroom and searched the shadows.

No one there.

Pressed to the wall, she waited for her pulse to settle. Drew several deep, measured breaths. She needed to think this through, to come up with a workable way to overpower Weir and take him into custody.

From the day of the strip search, she still held a mental map of the house. If only she knew where to start looking, if only she could beat him at his own damned game.

Slowly, it came to her. The Waldorf had a forced-air heating system. Same as the set-up in Quinn's house. Eyes closed, she pictured the design. Ornate metal grilles were set at intervals along the base of the walls. They emitted the warmed air from the basement furnace that circulated through a fat web of ducting.

Sometimes when she was in the den at home, Quinn was treated to Bren's post-bedtime monologue from upstairs. The kid's words resounded through the hollow heating system like a hammer on stone. Same thing had happened the night Levitsky put Bren to bed. She'd been able to hear them talking.

Maybe that was the big magic behind Weir's ability to throw his voice around.

Quinn stooped and groped along the bottom of the wall until she came to one of the heating grilles. She pressed her mouth to the chill surface and issued a throaty rumble.

An instant's wait, and she was rewarded with the desired response. Sharp barking from downstairs to the rear. The dog was in the kitchen. And so, she was sure, was Weir. The furry brute might be unpredictable about strangers, but he kept a constant fix on his beloved maniac of a master.

Quinn snuck out of the bedroom and padded silently down the corridor. She was about to start down the stairs when she was frozen by tentative rapping at the front door. The knocking stopped for an instant, then resumed and intensified.

No response from Weir or the dog. Quinn's reaction was a

paralysis of indecision. Who the hell could it be? Was it one of the professor's confederates? Or might it be help for her?

The front door creaked open, and she heard the tentative pad of footsteps from below. Then came a woman's voice.

'Hello? Listen, I'm sorry to disturb you so late, but I'm from the inn down the hill. It's very important that I talk to you. It's about my daughter.'

The missing child's mother. Quinn's throat closed. *Go away, lady. Get the hell out of here!*

But the footfalls advanced to the centre of the entrance hall. Peering down, Quinn spotted the woman's slim silhouette. What if she wandered into the kitchen?

Quinn bit her lip to keep the warning shriek from escaping. The woman stopped. Quinn willed her to change her mind. *Turn back. Run!* But after a beat, the child's mother moved closer to the stairs and called up. 'Anybody home? Please answer. I have to talk to you.'

As quickly as sense and nerve allowed, Quinn hustled down the steps, grabbed the woman, and pressed a hand hard over her mouth. Her body stiffened.

'Don't make a sound,' Quinn breathed in her ear. 'Come with me. Hurry.'

She dragged the child's shocked mother back up the stairs and down the hall to the spare bedroom. The woman strained for freedom, but Quinn couldn't risk releasing her. Not yet.

'Listen to me,' she rasped. 'There's a very dangerous man downstairs. You have to be quiet. Understand?'

A spike of moonglow had pierced the cloud cover. By the spare wash of light, Quinn saw the woman's expression. Her eyes looked ready to pop. But she nodded stiffly in Quinn's grip.

'You won't make a sound? Promise?'

Again, the woman nodded.

'Okay.' Quinn released her. 'Sorry for the craziness. You must be Nora Brill. I'm Quinn Gallagher. I'm a parole officer. One of my clients has been on house arrest in this place for the past several days. His name is Eldon Weir.'

That said it all. The woman gasped, and her hand flew to

309

her mouth. 'Oh God. Are you saying Eldon Weir took my little girl?'

'I don't know,' Quinn said. 'But if he did, I won't let him get anywhere near her. Abigail's not in this house. And I'm here to make sure Weir doesn't get out.'

Nora nodded in stiff acquiescence. 'Please don't let him hurt Abby. Please.'

'I won't. Duck behind that dresser and stay there. I'm going to try to draw him out.'

'Can't I *do* something?'

'Yes. If you know any prayers, say them.'

Quinn waited until the child's mother was safely ensconced beyond the chest of drawers. Crossing to the wall, she deliberately upended a lamp. It fell with a satisfying clatter. Hunched near the heating grate, she cupped her hands around her lips and spoke in a rasp. 'Damn! I hope he didn't hear that.'

She poised beside the door to wait. Heard nothing at first but Nora's thready breathing. The air bristled with tension so ponderous, Quinn felt it like the press of hands.

Finally, a sound pierced the awful stillness. Footsteps. They were moving towards the staircase. His voice wafted through the vent.

'I can smell your fear, Ms Gallagher. You *reek* of terror.'

She raised a hand to signal the child's mother. It's okay. I'll handle it.

Or would she?

Quinn tensed. He was on the steps now, moving with excruciating deliberation. Her ears were superkeen. Nerves aflame.

He hesitated at the top landing. Then he started moving down the hall. She heard the steps pass his room. Drawing nearer. Only a few feet away.

Closer.

She raised the pistol and aimed it at the door. Her hand quaked in a palsy of fright. Mouth blanched.

Don't shoot until he's close, Quinn. You can't afford to miss.

She waited for the door to open. Her muscles were fisted

and searing. *Come on already. Let's get this over with, you stinking sonavabitch!*

Suddenly, the door burst open. Quinn fired at the dark form hurtling into the room. Three shots, four erupted in a fiery flash. She kept shooting until the empty pistol spat a series of impotent clicks.

Clouds had swallowed the moon. She narrowed her eyes to breach the darkness and kept an eye on the inert heap on the floor. Waited to be sure she'd finished him off. Nothing moved. Good.

Quinn hauled herself out of the crouch. Signalling for the child's mother to stay where she was, she approached the lifeless shape. Looked like a sack of laundry. As she bent over to check his pulse, a thunderous voice caught her from behind.

'That's it, Gallagher. No more. You're finished.'

47

Whirling around, Quinn tried to clip her assailant with the empty gun. But before she could make a move, he swivelled her around, pinioned her arms, and swatted the gun out of her hand.

'I said, *no more!*'

Suddenly, she recognised the voice. 'Levitsky?' Quinn was incredulous. 'What the hell are you doing here?'

She caught the stifled whimper from across the room and remembered the child's mother.

'It's okay, Nora,' Quinn said. 'He's on our side.'

Levitsky released her. She turned to face him and found his eyes flashing angrily, mouth a furious seam. 'No, Gallagher. It's *not* okay. If I hadn't thrown that couch cushion in ahead of me, you might have killed me with your damned loose-cannon act. Don't you get it? This is *not* a game. It's serious, Gallagher. Deadly serious.'

'Is that all?'

'No, that's *not* all. Because of your heroics, Weir's got a bigger head start. The report on the perimeter tapes was waiting for me back at the hotel. The cameras were definitely doctored to cut out big chunks of time during which Weir could slip in and out undetected. The analysis determined that the missing hours were during this time of the night.

'I commandeered a car from the hotel's night manager and rushed right back here. On the way, the signal monitor started sending out some peculiar tracings. Somehow, Weir must have gotten that doctored too. The back door was ajar when I got here, so I figured he was out. I was about to go after him, when I heard the noise from up here.'

'Oh, God. I'm so sorry.'

'You should be, Gallagher.'

'No. You don't understand, Levitsky. We've got to catch up with him, it's worse than you . . .'

Suddenly, there was a distant concussion, and the sky went bright for a startling instant.

'What the hell was that?' Levitsky said.

For a minute, Quinn was too shocked and horrified to speak.

'What was it, Gallagher?' he persisted.

'Chambers rigged Weir's wristlet with plastic explosives. He set off the timed trigger when he broke the electronic circuit. That was Weir. Rest in pieces.'

Now it was Levitsky's turn to be shocked mute. The child's mother broke the silence. 'Please. We have to find Abigail.'

'Of course,' Levitsky said. 'I have a pretty good idea where she's being held, Mrs Brill. I'll go after her.'

'Let's get going,' Quinn said.

He shook his head. 'You've done way more than enough already, Gallagher. I'll go myself.'

Quinn caught his eye. 'Please, Levitsky. I have to come with you.'

Levitsky shot her a hard look. 'Okay, Gallagher. But you'll do exactly as I say.'

'Deal.'

'I'm coming too,' Nora said.

'I can't let you do that, Mrs Brill,' Levitsky said. 'For your sake and Abby's, go wait for us at the inn. We'll bring your daughter to you there. I promise.'

'Listen to him,' Quinn said. 'The man knows what he's doing.'

Nora nodded, not wanting to delay them any longer. 'Please find her,' she said. 'Please bring my baby home.' Eyes puddled with desperate tears, she headed to the inn.

Quinn and Levitsky followed her out, no longer concerned about who might see them. Nothing mattered any more but bringing the nightmare to an end.

48

'Head for Haystack Mountain,' Levitsky said as they bumped down the dirt road. 'I followed up on the Langdon Industries connection. Had a stockbroker friend fax me the company's latest annual report. Langdon makes the kind of heavy cement I found at the Waldorf. The report listed a dozen current construction projects using the stuff, two right near here. We'll try Haystack first.'

Quinn turned onto Main Street and barrelled through the darkened centre of town to the outskirts. She tried to deflect the haunting image of Eldon Weir, decimated in a fiery explosion. She shuddered, picturing him reduced to charred fragments. Right now, he was probably nothing but a stinking scatter of smouldering waste.

Quinn turned onto the highway and zipped past a billboard advertising ski area events. How the hell was she going to support Bren after Jake Holland fired her? She thought a while. Her list of marketable talents was dishearteningly brief. Quinn imagined the 'Situations Wanted' ad: *Outcast parole officer with short fuse seeks highly empathetic employer with equally short memory and exceedingly low standards.*

Lost in bleak reverie, she didn't hear Levitsky at first. His tone had grown fierce by the time it broke through the clouds.

'I *said* turn around, Gallagher. Go to the summer theatre complex first.'

'But we're almost at Haystack.'

'Just do it, will you?'

She made a shrieking left and barrelled back towards Dove's Landing. The remains of the old theatre complex were located at the edge of town.

'Why the sudden change?'

'That billboard we just passed. It said Haystack has golf

314

and tennis schools in session now and a big craft show starting tomorrow. With all those people around, no one would try to hide a kid there.'

The theatre complex had been largely demolished, and the reconstruction was not yet underway. So it was deserted except for occasional visits by site planners and members of the proposed contracting crew. Much easier place to stash a child and keep her presence secret.

Levitsky also pointed out that the nature of the site fit the central theme of the abductors: tricks, illusions, dazzling escapes. All of it pointed to a penchant for the dramatic.

'These lunatics are into showmanship, Gallagher. Where better to perform than a theatre complex?'

'But I thought all the buildings had been torn down.'

'Only one way to find out.'

They arrived in minutes. Set near the north town line, the sprawling theatre-complex property was surrounded by endless stretches of farmland. The theatre had been shut down over six months ago for renovation. Probably hadn't had a casual visitor since, except the occasional grazing cow.

Quinn parked the jeep out of sight behind a wooded area, and they made their approach through the tangle of trees. They tried to move silently, but at intervals their feet crunched loudly in the dense mat of rotted leaves and dried twigs.

The thicket adjoined a sloping meadow. From the edge of the woods, they spied the sparse remains of the theatre complex: a small white caretaker's house across the field and a tomblike structure down the hill.

'You take the house, I'll check that place,' Levitsky said. He handed her the twenty-two, but his eyes were full of hard warnings. 'The gun is for absolute emergencies only, Gallagher. The Eakins girl might be alone, or Weir might have an accomplice holding her. If you see anything at all suspicious, wait and report it back to me. I'll meet you right here in ten minutes.'

'Okay. Ten minutes.'

'No more dumb stunts, Gallagher. You promise?'

'No dumb stunts for how long?'

He touched her cheek. Quinn flushed and felt grateful for the cover of the darkness.

'Watch your back, Gallagher. And no heroics.'

Levitsky took off down the hill. Ducking low to blend with the shadows, Quinn crossed the field towards the still white house.

There, she slowly circled the building, searching for a clear view of the interior. The rear porch was swaddled in near-opaque plastic. Edging along the side of the building, she came to an undraped window. Peering cautiously inside, she spotted a scatter of dark furniture, squat lamps with pleated shades, a blackened brick hearth matted with ashes.

Nothing extraordinary at first glance, but as she stared harder, she was able to make out the symbols in the crocheted doilies on the chair arms and some of the titles on the crammed bookshelves. All magic and occult mumbo-jumbo like the items stocked in Mrs Murtagh's store, 'The Impossible Possible'. She spotted volumes on tarot, numerology, reincarnation, escape and illusion.

Had to be headquarters for Mr Milton's magic club, she thought. Looked like a very select group from the small ring of chairs. Then the dues were well beyond the average budget: payment in blood.

Scrutinising the house through several other windows, Quinn confirmed that no one was inside. On the dresser in a tiny bedroom a working tape recorder was rigged to a crude transmitter. Straining to listen, she picked up a few bars of 'Crackling Rosie'. So this was the source of the club's mock radio station.

Eight minutes had elapsed.

Outside, she stooped into the shadows again and retraced her steps across the field to the edge of the woods. Staring down the hill, she waited for Levitsky to make his appearance. The silence seeped under her skin.

Nine minutes.

Ten, and still no sign of the agent. Quinn trained an unblinking eye on the concrete structure. She decided to give him two more minutes, time that drooped and sagged with excruciating torpor.

Enough.

Clinging to the spectre of the woods, Quinn made her way down the slope. At times, her progress was hindered by tall, wild grasses. Stiff, tearing stalks scratched her hands and raked at her skin through her jeans.

The ground finally levelled, and the abrasive scrub yielded to a flat span littered with construction supplies and debris. Camouflaged by the tree shadows, Quinn surveyed the scene.

There were piles of beams and two-by-fours, sheets of tar paper, battered squares of copper flashing. Abutting the side of the concrete structure were more stacks of supplies: bricks, sand, cinderblock. She spotted sacks of the heavy cement marked with the Langdon brand.

The block edifice was all that remained of the summer theatre's main auditorium. Quinn had brought Brendon here last August for the final series of children's concerts before the place closed for repairs. Then, given the shabby state of the building, the tear-down and rehabilitation had seemed a fine idea. Now, eyeing the creepy grey crypt with its belly full of unknown menace, she wished they'd left the old place alone.

The exterior appeared to be a solid block. No way to peek inside and size up the situation. Maybe she'd find something if she got closer.

She raced across the littered field to the block structure; felt her way along the cold façade. The concrete was cracked in several places, including one vertical break that was far too straight to be accidental. Quinn remembered the grand piano rising magically from the depths at the start of the final kids' concert. The deliberate crack must have been part of a mechanical stage hoist. She tried but couldn't force the wall to open manually. None of the gaps was wide enough to afford a decent view of the interior.

Two more minutes elapsed as she stood trying to devise a workable strategy. Levitsky had left her almost twenty

317

minutes ago. Quinn didn't like the smell of it. Maybe he'd walked into trouble.

She circled to the front of the concrete hulk. There was a crude wooden door in the centre. Quinn eased it open.

Inside was a cavernous, gloomy space. Cold and foreboding. There was a musty smell.

No sign of Levitsky. Seemed as if the place had swallowed him whole. Quinn stepped in and shut the door behind her, forsaking the last swatch of moonglow.

Waiting for her eyes to adjust, she felt her way along. Where the hell was the agent?

Maybe he'd slipped out before she started watching for him and gone off to explore something else on the grounds. The thought eased the knots in her gut and replaced them with sparks of fury. Had he put her through all this terror for nothing? Thinking of the guy perfectly safe and oblivious made her want to murder him.

She turned to leave, but a noise from below stopped her at the door. Sounded like the cry of a tiny kitten, thin and pitiful. Poor little fur ball must have been locked in by mistake and forgotten, probably starving.

Tracking the sound, she moved to the rear of the structure. There was a narrow door at the back wall. Prodding it open, she hesitated. But the mournful meowing drew her on.

'Here, kitty. Don't worry. I'll get you out.'

She started down the stairs. The cellar was even darker than the main level. Engulfing tide of blackness. Quinn groped blindly ahead as she went.

'Where are you, cat? No games, okay? I'm in a hurry.'

Nearing the bottom, she heard a muffled racing sound. Following it quickly across the basement, she reached out to grab the kitten. But what she caught instead was muscle and bone. And by the time she tried to turn and run, a grunting, multi-tentacled beast had her locked in a death grip.

49

He bound her hands and feet and thrust her to the concrete floor. Then he stood back panting.

'Welcome, Ms Gallagher. I've been eagerly anticipating your arrival.'

Quinn recognised the voice, but she could not believe it. Mayor Wellacott?

'You? You're in on this? Where's Levitsky?'

'Right beside you. But I'm afraid the poor man's mind is elsewhere.'

There was a snapping sound, and the cellar flooded with blinding yellow light. Gradually, the quivering ghosts receded and Quinn saw the agent crumpled on the floor nearby. He was face down. A bloody blue welt glistened on the back of his neck.

'What did you do to him, you sick sonavabitch?'

He frowned down on her in dismay. 'My, my. Such hostility simply will not do. Terribly destructive emotion, hostility. Drives people to desperate acts. Anyway, your precious colleague has not been seriously harmed, officer. In fact, no one has been seriously harmed – as yet.'

Quinn stared at Levitsky until she confirmed that he was breathing. Then she surveyed the rest of the grim space: cot, bucket, a large draped object in the far corner. The mayor stood beside a two-tiered rolling cart laden with gleaming medical equipment: diagnostic devices, surgical tools.

His laughter was a demonic trill.

'Your expression is priceless, officer. Sheer disbelief, utter astonishment. I fooled you completely, didn't I? Nice to know my dear cousin Milton failed to corner the market on guile.'

Quinn's brain was bulging with unthinkable thoughts. 'You need help, Wellacott. Turn yourself in right now, and I'll see you get it.'

'Help? How amusing. I am quite capable of attending to my own needs, officer. Always have been, no matter what my family was made to believe. But they'll soon see the light. When I complete this ultimate illusion, everyone will recognise my talents, my powers.'

'You thought you were going to impress people by helping Eldon Weir?'

Wellacott issued a disgusted sigh. 'You have it all wrong, officer. Why don't I enlighten you and save your paltry intellect the exercise. You see, very soon what you know will be of no consequence whatever.'

His face darkened. 'You of all people understand the effects of scurrilous lies. People mocked and ridiculed you too, didn't they, Ms Gallagher? They kept watching and waiting for you to fail like your infamous sot of a father. No one cared a bit about the truth, did they?

'Well, you were willing to put up with it. But I am not one to play the passive victim. My cousin Milton has done everything in his power to hurt and humiliate me. Since we were small children, he has played cruel tricks on me, made me appear foolish and incompetent. He caused me to fail in school, misplaced critical papers, replaced my test sheets with others doctored with the wrong answers.

'After I entered the family business, he continued to engineer it so all my efforts led to catastrophe. Soon, the family didn't want me any more. My own father urged me to pursue other interests.'

He coughed to evict the emotion from his tone. 'I had to regain my rightful place in my family's regard. I had to reclaim my proper position in Wellacott Worldwide. And I needed to do it in a way that my cousin Milton would not be able to discover and thwart.'

Levitsky was beginning to stir. Quinn turned her voice up a notch, hoping to help tug the agent back to consciousness.

'What did you possibly hope to gain by abducting that child?'

'Think, Ms Gallagher. It's obvious. I needed a major crisis in Dove's Landing. By leading my citizens out of the disaster, I would emerge the hero. With all the national hysteria over lawlessness, a criminal menace was the obvious choice. And what would stir more passionate public response than the kidnapping of a young girl?'

Quinn chanced a peek at Levitsky. His eyes were working under the lids. For an instant, they flickered open, and he met her gaze. She read his silent message: *Stall the guy. Keep him talking.*

'But how could you claim any credit?'

He puffed his lips. 'How tiresome of you to be so dense. This is my play, Ms Gallagher. I cast the child as the victim, Weir as the villain, and I enter at the crucial moment as the white knight.'

'So you were just using Weir?'

'Precisely. His very name stirs public hysteria to a higher pitch. Egotistical fool actually believed I was eager to secure his release because I admired him and wished his counsel. He actually believed I shared his bloodlust for small girls. Fool had no idea that he was nothing but a prop.'

Levitsky nodded almost imperceptibly. *Keep him going. Distract him.*

'You must have planned this for years.'

He flapped a hand. 'Not at all. It was quite simple really. Once the idea struck me, I simply posed as my cousin Milton and set everything up in that bastard's name. Had it gone awry, he more than deserved the blame and punishment. But, fortunately, the plan has proceeded with relative ease. I followed my dear cousin's guiding principle you see: illusion is everything, everything is illusion.'

'Everything was a fake? Weir's blinding included?'

'All it took were opaque lenses and a greedy physician. Most everything and everyone is for sale at the proper price, officer. I'm sure you know that.'

Levitsky was squirming in his bonds. Quinn forced herself not to look at him. 'Where are you holding Abigail Eakins?'

Wellacott crossed the cellar and jerked the drape off the huddled form of the unconscious little girl. She was milk-pale, eyes rimmed with dusky circles. Quinn felt a jolt of fury.

'What did you do to her, Wellacott?'

'I've simply seen to it she gets the rest she'll need for her final trial. Poor child faces a considerable ordeal, I'm afraid. She will need every last shred of strength.'

'You're out of your mind.'

His eyes widened. 'Oh no, officer. You misunderstand. This isn't my preference at all. The truth is, I find such brutality tiresome and distasteful. But I must recreate Eldon Weir's atrocities in convincing detail. Think it through, and you'll realise I have no choice.'

Quinn eyed the items lining the supply cart: scalpels, retractors, fanglike probes. Tools the madman intended to use in the little girl's mutilation.

And hers.

'Let me guess,' Wellacott said with a devilish smile. 'You're wondering about your own destiny, am I correct? Well, it would be unthinkably cruel of me to keep you guessing. Cruel and unnecessary.' He lifted a blade and passed it over the ball of his thumb. A bloody line appeared, but Wellacott was oblivious.

'Naturally, you and Agent Levitsky must pay the ultimate price for your meddling. After I see to the two of you, I've only to eliminate the child's mother and Grandfather Brill and my few associates, and I can be done with this tiresome business. Silence a handful, and my secret will be secure forever.'

Levitsky was slowly shifting his position. Wellacott turned as if he'd detected something.

'Who worked with you at the inn?' Quinn said quickly. 'Someone had to help you set up the kidnapping.'

'Who do you think, Ms Gallagher? Let's see how clever you are.'

She wasted some time pretending to ponder. 'The caretaker, Reuben Huff?'

'No, no, officer. Not close. It was the chef, Etienne Villet. Thoroughly wretched man. No scruples whatever. Detests females. He was perfect for the job.'

322

She thought about the professor's sudden disappearance from the Waldorf. 'What about Weir? Did you eliminate him so he couldn't talk?'

'Eliminate? Certainly not. Not yet. The child has to be dealt with first, don't you see? What is wrong with you, Ms Gallagher? Haven't you any brains at all? If the child were discovered by some unfortunate chance, I'd need Weir alive to assume the guilt. I've arranged it so he would then meet his end while being taken into custody. Poor bastard would be shot during a foolhardy escape attempt.'

So Wellacott didn't know about Weir's escape or the explosion. Nearly as intriguing, the mayor had one of the troopers in his pocket. Quinn would have made book on which one.

'Ralph Norman is in on this too?'

Wellacott nodded. 'Much, much better, Ms Gallagher. I knew you weren't a total idiot. Probably won't surprise you to hear that Trooper Norman was my most reasonable purchase. The man sells himself quite cheaply. I suspect he found the whole enterprise appealing apart from the financial reward.'

Levitsky's eyes were open now. He struggled to a sitting position. Wellacott shot him a murderous look. 'Soon, Agent Levitsky. Soon I'll put you out of your miserable existence.'

Levitsky ignored the maniac. 'You okay, Gallagher?'

'Yes, Levitsky. You?'

'Fine. I keep thinking about that magic phrase I taught Brendon. He ever tell it to you?'

'Silence! You'll talk when and if you're instructed to,' Wellacott snapped. '. . . Now, where was I? Oh yes. Trooper Ralph Norman. That man has a real taste for meanness and evil. He coached me on highly effective ways to intimidate the Eakins child. Very useful. Pity he won't be around for further projects.'

Quinn tuned him out and tried to figure out what Levitsky was trying to say. Bren had told her the agent's magic phrase. But how could she use it now?

Wellacott went dreamy for a moment, as if he'd forgotten his lines. He tapped his sculpted cheek. 'What was I saying?

Oh yes, and the chef. Now, having to dispose of him is a real pity. Villet is a sanctimonious prick, but his cooking is sublime. I arranged for him to be hired at the inn, you know, though the Brills never suspected a thing. As I thought, his presence in the kitchen has come in quite handy. When I need to temporarily disable someone like Grandfather Brill or your meddlesome boss, Jake Holland, I have the chef serve up the appropriate special: succulent breast of free range chicken with a tasty arsenic sauce.

'I met Villet years ago at the Culinary Institute in Poughkeepsie,' Wellacott went on. 'I was studying there in anticipation of opening a chain of restaurants for Wellacott Worldwide. Another enterprise that was undermined by my wretched cousin Milton.

'But in that instance I emerged with something of considerable value. You see, Eldon Weir was taking courses at the cooking school as well. He was enrolled under a false name, but I recognised him from the press he'd gotten in the Bennington child mutilation case.

'I was in a pastry class with both Weir and Villet when the plan came to me. Suddenly, I saw how all the elements of my vindication could be prepared and served up in a delectable stew.'

Wellacott's grin faded and his eyes narrowed to blazing slits. 'If not for your interference, it would all be done by now. I'd already be basking in public adulation, parlaying my popularity into higher office. The State House first. Then the Senate. And before long, The White House. I would be the most successful Wellacott in family history. But you, the two of you, set out to ruin everything. Just like Cousin Milton.'

He spat his words. 'You stinking, cowardly liars and usurpers. I'll rip you apart, tear you to bloody shreds.'

Rearing back, he landed a vicious kick in the centre of the agent's spine. Levitsky moaned and crumpled.

Wellacott turned to Quinn. She edged backwards but, bound as she was, she couldn't move nearly fast enough to escape him. In a breath, the mayor was all over her, screeching, making animal noises. He exuded a ripe, fetid scent.

'Get the hell off me, you maniac.' She brought her knees up hard and caught him in the face. There was a sick crunching sound and a gush of blood.

Wellacott staggered backward, hissing like a wounded snake. Quinn caught the crazy glint in his eye as he lurched towards the cart and grabbed a scalpel.

With a desperate groan, Levitsky flung himself hard against the cart. It caught Wellacott in the shin, knocking him momentarily off balance.

But the mayor was fuelled by the molten rage of a madman. Quickly regaining his balance, he butted the cart back at Levitsky, catching the agent on the side of the head.

Still wielding the scalpel, he came at Quinn. The frail remains of the agent's voice pierced her terror.

'Remember the trick, Gallagher. The book; the magic phrase. Remember.'

Wellacott was savouring the moment, wriggling the scalpel towards her in a languid dance.

'I'm going to gouge out your eyes, officer,' he chanted. 'And then I'll carve your insolent tongue and feed the slices to Weir's dog.'

'The *book*,' Levitsky coughed.

Quinn struggled to remember what Levitsky had read her from the Houdini book: tricks, rigged escapes. How the hell could any of that help her now?

Wellacott was teasing the scalpel towards her neck, slashing the air in slow, menacing arcs.

'And then I'll lop off your head, Ms Gallagher. Your skull will be my first trophy. Long overdue. Imagine your flesh-less, blind skull on my mantelpiece, officer. Cleansed of course, and filled with daisies.'

She needed time. From his semi-stupor, Levitsky was still muttering encouragements.

'Remember the trick, Gallagher. The magic phrase.'

She strained against the ropes binding her hands, pulled until her flesh felt sore and torn. What was Levitsky getting at? The so-called magic phrase played through her mind.

'I think therefore I am.' *Cogito Ergo Sum.*

Bren had fallen for it. Descartes' precursor to 'The Little Engine That Could'. Hocus pocus. Confidence in a jar. I think I can. I can, or I'm a dead woman.

Illusion is everything; everything is illusion.

The scalpel was so close, she felt the icy promise of its impending caress. Wellacott worked the blade above her neck in a teasing dance, closer by agonising degrees.

Nothing to lose. Nothing and everything.

'Watch out, Levitsky! Behind you!'

Wellacott whipped his head around. Quinn flopped flat on her back and butted her bound feet into his midsection. As he fell, the scalpel clattered to the floor.

Contorting her fettered hands to one side, she was able to dig into her pocket and clumsily extract the gun. But before she could take aim, Wellacott came at her in a grunting charge and knocked the pistol from her twisted grip. Grabbing her by the shoulders, he bashed her head against the cement floor. She was losing focus, slipping under the force of the blows when she heard the strange, mocking voice.

'*I know about this scheme too, Cousin Justin. I'm going to ruin it for you like I did all the others. You'll see.*'

Wellacott released her. 'Milton? Is that you, you stinking bastard? Where are you?'

He stood and pivoted in a lurching circle. 'Where the hell are you? Show yourself, you rotten slime. You'll never hurt me again. I'll make it so you can't.'

'*No, you won't, Cousin Justin,*' came the voice. *Everything you do will be a failure, a joke. I'll keep destroying everything you do until the day I die.*'

If Quinn hadn't seen the subtle movement of Levitsky's lips, she wouldn't have believed the words were coming from him. He was able to change his tone, toss his voice like a curveball. Another trick he'd learned from Houdini's book? She had no idea what the agent was doing. But through the vicious pounding in her head, reason told her to shut up and let him do it.

'*You want to stop me, Cousin Justin? The only way is to*

kill me. But you don't have the nerve, do you, you miserable failure? You wouldn't dare murder me. Wouldn't dare.'

Quinn saw the rage quivering in Wellacott's hand. 'That's always been the only way to beat you, hasn't it, you bastard?'

Ducking to the floor, he frantically retrieved the pistol. 'You'll never hurt me or anyone again, Milton,' Wellacott said. 'You'll be dead and forgotten.'

Quinn tensed, anticipating the shot, imagining the searing pain of the bullet as it pierced her chest. But as she watched in horrified astonishment, Wellacott stuck the gun barrel into his own mouth and squeezed the trigger.

50 Levitsky drove the jeep. Quinn sat in the back cradling Abigail Eakins' head in her lap. The child was murmuring, edging back to consciousness.

They'd decided to take the little girl home immediately. After a cursory examination, Levitsky was confident the trip wouldn't harm her. Home would be the child's best medicine. And they were anxious to escape the concrete bunker with its lingering stench of death and madness.

'What do you think he dosed her with?' Quinn said.

Levitsky shrugged. 'Probably not cimetadine. Too bitter. Could be stelazine or chlorpromazine or a large dose of something like trimeprazine tartrate. That's colourless and odourless and easy to hide in food. Whatever he used, it was probably intended to be short-acting. I'd bet Wellacott wanted her alert and aware for the big, bad finale. Guy definitely liked to play to an audience.'

'How did you figure out that "Cousin Milton" was nothing but Justin Wellacott's evil alter-ego, Levitsky?'

'There were pictures of the Wellacott founders and corporate chiefs on the first page of the Langdon Industries annual report. No cousins listed. No relatives named Milton Wellacott. But I didn't put it together until I was poking around the remains of the summer theatre. The truth hit me right before Wellacott did. Pretty dumb of me, huh?'

Quinn stroked the little girl's forehead. 'One thing you're definitely not is dumb, Levitsky. Pharmaceuticals, medicine, electronics, psychiatry, forensics, ventriloquism. Is there anything in the world you don't understand?'

'Yes, Gallagher. I definitely don't understand you.'

They were nearing the centre of town. Everything looked so still and serene. Levitsky passed the line of darkened shops on Main Street and angled up the inn's access road. The little girl awakened. Terror squeezed her voice.

'Who are you? What's going on?'

'Shh. It's okay, Abigail,' Quinn said. 'You're safe now, sweetie. Another minute, and we'll have you home.'

They turned into the inn's lot and stopped at the entrance to the main house. The place was steeped in gloomy slumber. But that was about to change.

51

Quinn drove away from the inn in dazed silence. Behind her was the electric aftermath of the family's joyous reunion. Abigail was safe. Having her back blunted all the pain and grief. The family was shocked and outraged at Mayor Wellacott's insane duplicity, but the worst was behind them. For those people, the waiting and worrying were finished. The evil aura could be excised from their everyday existence and, in time, forgotten.

But she knew the mess was far from over for her and Levitsky. The agent would have to answer for his unauthorised interference in a local case. Quinn would have hell to pay for her disastrous mismanagement of Eldon Weir and Dud Chambers and Lord knew what else. She stopped the jeep beside his borrowed car down the road from the Waldorf.

'So I suppose you'll be heading back to FBI-ville,' she said.

'Nothing more for me here. I suppose I'll take the first flight out tomorrow.'

'Okay. I'll give you a ride to the airport.'

'No thanks, Gallagher. You get some rest. I'll take a cab.'

She deflected a stab of disappointment, tried to sound upbeat. 'So what do you plan to wear to your beheading, Levitsky? I thought I'd go with basic black to match the blindfold.'

'I doubt I'm in for anything like that. I'll probably get my wrist slapped, that's all. There's a serious shortage of impossibly single-minded agents willing to risk their stupid necks for the cause.'

Quinn killed the engine, grabbed the car keys from Levitsky's slackened grip and tossed them in the black hole at the bottom of her purse.

'Before either of us goes anywhere, you're finally going to

tell me why. What stole your happy home and gave you such a passion for nabbing monsters like Weir?'

'Later Gallagher, okay? It's been a long day.'

'It'll be a whole lot longer if you don't tell me. Now speak.'

He shot her an exasperated look. 'All right. My father died when I was a baby. About a year later, my mother met a terrific man and remarried.

'They had a little girl together. They were so happy. We all were. Everything was near perfect until he took it away.'

'He who?'

'Wish I knew. My sister, Emmy, was only seven at the time. One afternoon, she was walking home from school as usual, but she never showed up. No witnesses, and the body was never found. There was a huge search for her at first, armies of local volunteers. But eventually, they gave it up.

'Everyone forgot it in time, except my family. We couldn't think about anything else, kept hoping until it was impossible to hope any more. My mother couldn't ever get past it. Less than two years later she died in her sleep. No one could explain it medically. Thirty-eight years old, and she'd just lost the will to live.

'My stepdad felt responsible, worthless. He started drinking heavily. Took him longer, but eventually, he killed himself too.'

'I'm so sorry, Levitsky.'

'Me too, Gallagher. And I'm sorry for what you went through. I heard about the nasty business with your father. I know how it feels to have the rug pulled out from under you.'

'Impossible to put into words,' she said.

'Exactly. There are no words for it. Only the need to fill the void.'

'And it mostly fills with poison,' Quinn said.

'Unfortunately, that's true. Now can we go and get some sleep?'

'We can try.'

The agent watched as Quinn fished in her purse for the car keys. She dug through the standard minefield of stray hairs, used tissues, ossified restaurant mints, pocket change. She started removing some of the rubble and setting it on the dash. Wallet, card case, one of Bren's action figures with a missing leg, a nearly toothless comb. Sticks of gum. Antacid tablets. Lip gloss. Hand lotion. As she was despairing of ever finding the damned keys, Levitsky stuck his hand into the perilous depths and plucked them out. When he handed the set to her, their fingers collided. Quinn's felt singed.

'Thanks, Levitsky. I couldn't find them.'

'Sometimes it's toughest to see something when it's right in front of your nose.'

'True.'

'Bye, then, Gallagher.'

'Right. Bye, Levitsky. It's been . . . interesting.'

'True.'

Quinn watched as he walked the few feet down the dirt road towards his borrowed car. She felt a sinking sense of loss. Had to be the lack of sleep. Anything less than six hours, and she wasn't at all herself.

'Bye, Levitsky,' she told his retreating form. 'Have a nice life.'

52 Abigail issued a squeaky yawn and let Mim ply her with another sip of marshmallow-frothed cocoa. For a lump of days, she'd moved back and forth from sleep to a surfeit of delicious food to more treats and gifts and attention than she'd ever imagined possible.

Everyone was being so nice. Lots of people from town had called or sent gifts. They were all horrified about her being kidnapped, especially by Mayor Wellacott. Everybody kept saying how worried they'd been about her and how glad they were to have her home safe.

The family was making a huge fuss. Stephanie had bought her a set of rollerblades and Victoria had promised a major shopping spree at the mall and Hugh had lent her his cassette Walkman and a bunch of tapes with his favourite train-wreck music. Mommy and Mim had taken turns sitting with her until she stopped shivering with fear and started believing that Mayor Maniac and the crazy guy in the house up the hill were really and forever dead.

Slowly, she'd been able to tell her mom about the terrible tricks and the sessions. Mom had listened without a pinch of scolding or disapproval. She'd assured Abigail that none of it was her fault. Mayor Wellacott had been crazy. He'd set the whole thing up to get back at a cousin who didn't even exist. He'd paid off Chef Villet to keep an eye on her and report when she went out alone so the mayor could grab her and lock her in what was left of the old theatre building at the edge of town.

If only she'd known she was that close to home when she got out through the crack in the wall. But the theatre had been torn down before she even moved to Dove's Landing, so she'd never been to the place. She'd had no idea what or where the cement building was when she managed to escape from the cellar.

She started shivering again and pushed the awful memories aside. There were so many good things to think about. Better to concentrate on them.

The best treat of all was Daddy. Abigail spent hours just holding his great big comforting hand. Snuggling against his massive, muscly chest. Felt like forever since she'd last seen him, and he was trying really hard to make up for lost time. Whenever he came to the cabin, he brought her another present: a silver heart, a charm bracelet, hair ornaments. After he showed them to her, he put them all in her pink jewellery box next to the ballerina where they'd be safe until she was ready to wear them.

'So how's my Abby Gail doing this morning? Better?'

He was framed in the doorway. Took up most of the space. He held a small white box wrapped in lavender ribbon. Abigail grinned and felt a swell of love. 'Much better.'

Mim winked at her. 'I'll leave you two alone. See you later, sweetheart.'

Her father strode over and sat beside her on the bed. Had to duck to keep from hitting his head on the frame of the lacy canopy. Abigail noticed he was moving his arm better. So she decided not to worry any more about what was the true story behind his injury. Everyone had told her it was an accident, but when Poppa stopped by once to say hello, he'd mentioned something about a gunshot. One thing about Poppa, he always told the unembellished truth.

Daddy took her hand and set the white box in her palm. She opened it and found a jewelled teddy-bear pin.

'Thanks, it's beautiful.'

'Beautiful like you, darling. I'll put it in the jewel box, okay?' He ambled over to the dresser and flipped open the box. The ballerina popped up and danced to the tune of 'Stardust'. '. . . And I am once again with you . . .'

He returned and sat beside her again. She noticed the serious edge to his expression. 'Glad you're coming along, sweetheart. Be nice getting back to normal. Best thing for everyone.'

She felt the sting of tears. Turning away a second, she swallowed them back. She'd known it was coming.

'You're leaving?'

'Wish I didn't have to. But you know how it is. Time to get back to business. I'm way behind already.'

'Can't I come with you? I wouldn't be any trouble.'

He hitched his massive shoulders. 'I'd like that, but you know it wouldn't work. Old tumbleweed like me's no anchor for a child. You've got school, friends, your family here. But this summer, it's two weeks wherever you say. Deal?'

She drew a rough breath. 'Okay.'

He gave her his traditional round of daddy kisses: forehead, nose, chin, right cheek, left cheek.

'See you real soon,' he said and left the room. She heard the front door slam and moments later the Lincoln's engine roared to life.

Abigail drifted off to sleep again. When she awoke, Mom was sitting on the chair next to the bed. There were two new vases on the sill full of Mim's special 'Sunny Abigail' dahlias from the greenhouse and a fresh pile of get well cards for her to open.

'You okay, sweetie?' Nora said.

'You know he left?'

'Yes. I'm sorry.'

Abigail sighed. Things were so complicated. She was sad about her daddy leaving, but not surprised and not nearly as disappointed as she'd expected to be.

If he'd taken her with him, she would have missed Mom and Stephanie and Mim. She would have hated to leave Miss Schiffman so close to the end of the year. And the sixth-grade kids here had some hayseed tendencies, but they weren't all that bad.

There had been a zillion calls and cards and visits from her classmates since she got home. One of the visitors was this tall, skinny girl, Lenore, who was funny and a wise-cracker and reminded Abigail a little bit of Jeanine. Maybe she'd invite Lenore over for dinner some time. Soon as Charlie hired a new chef. Mom told her Villet had turned the colour of a purple onion when the police showed up to arrest him. Too bad she hadn't been around to see that. Must have been a riot.

'Abby? You okay?'

Mom was staring at her, eyes full of sad questions.

'It's going to be all right, Mom,' Abigail said with a muddled mix of sorrow and resolve. 'I really think it will.'

53

Stephanie stopped by after school to gossip and deliver Abigail's schoolwork. Nora left the girls giggling and chatting and walked towards the studio.

Spring had finally taken firm hold. The air was scented with lilac and new-mown grass. Clumps of daffodils and tulips dotted the greening lawn. There was the persistent clatter of farm equipment.

Nora scanned the inn's tranquil grounds and felt a charge of contentment. Abigail was safe. The hideous nightmare was behind them.

Victoria's shrink, Dr Grove, had made several casual visits and pronounced the little girl resilient and on the path to renewal. There might be psychic bruises, he said, but Abigail would not be marred permanently.

'The important thing is that she's talking about what happened,' he'd told Nora. 'Getting it out.'

And Nora had listened to the little girl as Dr Grove had advised, with a minimum of comment or reaction. She'd managed to hide her rage and revulsion at the hideous torments Justin Wellacott had inflicted on the child. That maniac was gone. They had to try to bury his brutish legacy with him.

She shook her head. Everything was so uncertain, all so unpredictable. Nora knew the only way to deal with the capricious fates and stay sane was to focus on the good things.

And she had an abundance of those. The work she loved. This place, the warm caring people in her life. Above all, she had her daughter, safe and on the way back to normal.

At the same instant, tears blurred Nora's vision and a broad smile tugged at the corners of her mouth. Abigail had said it perfectly. It was going to be all right.

She spotted a distant figure walking towards her from the inn. From the shape and the gait, she knew it was Charlie. Bless him, that man had an uncanny way of sensing when she was in dire need of a hug.

54 The Rutland Raiders had posted their strongest record in team history: twelve wins, one by-a-hair loss. The feat had earned the kids championship trophies and a coveted berth in the regionals. A string of rainouts had pushed the final contest to this chill, bleak late autumn afternoon.

In the bleachers Quinn sat wrapped in a wool poncho, trying to thaw her frozen fingers on the coffee thermos. Funny how she'd thought all the problems would be solved if only Bren managed to make the team. But every game had been an emotional trial. And things had grown even tenser with the penant frenzy and the local world series and on and on.

Except for a two-week stint at baseball camp, Bren had spent nearly every waking minute all summer at his backyard batting tee, practising. For his trouble, he'd gotten so good the coach now counted on him for a base hit – minimum. So when he took a rare break from his batting drills, he used his free time to worry.

Tie score, two out, bottom of the ninth, and poor Bren was next in the batting order. He shuffled over from the on-deck circle. Even at this distance, Quinn could see the slick of terror in the kid's eyes.

Now he was hunched at the plate, head crated in a batting helmet so unwieldy, he looked ready to topple.

'Come on, slugger! You can do it.'

Kid still looked like spare parts and library paste. Slapped together for the short haul.

'Go, Bren-don!'

The pitcher, a suspiciously tall kid, reared back and hurled the first pitch. Bren tensed like a spring. Waited.

Now!

The force of his swing sent him swivelling in a full circle, but the ball landed with a jeering thud in the catcher's perched mitt.

'Damn,' Quinn muttered. 'Bet that pitcher's a ringer.' She was tempted to march over and demand proof of age. Kid looked thirteen, fourteen, at least. Wasn't that a moustache shadow over his lip?

Come on, Quinn. Get a grip.

'You can do it, Brendon!' Her voice was sandpaper from an excess of screamed encouragements. But the boy just had to come out of this feeling like a winner. He'd worked so hard, and the damned team meant the world to him.

The geriatric-looking kid on the mound tossed a cream-puff pitch. Bren swooped to meet it, but all he managed was to nip a corner of the ball with a splinter of the bat. Sent the thing backward in a pitiful hop.

Strike two.

Quinn's brain was taking some wild hops of its own. Maybe she could cast a hex on the pitcher. Maybe a well-timed shriek would be enough to throw the overgrown jerk off his game.

Get a hold of yourself, Quinn. Lunacy will not give Brendon any meaningful advantage.

Then she thought of something that might.

'Hey, Brendon! Remember the magic phrase, kiddo. Works every time.' She thought of how Levitsky had invoked the phrase to keep her from losing it when Wella-cott was coming at her with that blade. Maybe those words were magic.

Positioning the bat, Bren tipped his head and nodded. So he'd heard her.

'Remember, Bren. You can do it, kid!' She thought of the incantation: '*Cogito Ergo Sum. I think, therefore I god-damned am.*'

The moment played in agonising slow motion. The pitcher arched back and let loose. As the ball approached, Bren worked in edgy preparation.

Go!

Quinn couldn't bear to look. But she heard the crack and Bren's exultant cry.

'Yes!'

Opening her eyes, she watched the ball sail in a gorgeous arc past the upturned gloves in the outfield. Her heart soared and flew on the comet's tail. Exerting enormous control, she kept her reaction to a manic whisper.

'And the crowd is going wild,' she rasped. 'And the frenzied fans are rising to their feet.'

She stood, caught the little bandit's eye, and made a victory sign. He allowed a stingy grin as he swaggered back towards the bench. Picture of nine-year-old nonchalance. Well, he was welcome to his mask of cool for now. But tonight, there would be whooping joy in Mudville and an extra special dinner for two at the Sirloin Saloon.

Quinn sat, drained. At the bench, Bren was about to do the same when he suddenly bolted upright and took off like a missile across the field.

What the hell?

And then she saw him. Lanky, curly-locked, lamb eyes so large you could read their dangerous gleam from the parking lot. Quinn's mouth parched and her heart hammered as she made her extremely easy-going way out of the bleachers to meet them.

Come on now, Quinn. It's only Levitsky.

He was coming towards her with a hand on Bren's shoulder and an impish grin that went stiff and awkward as they faced off a few feet from each other at the edge of the field.

'Hey, Gallagher,' he said. 'Bren wrote to tell me the regional championship game was today. Thought I'd drop by to see how it was going.'

'From Virginia?'

'Of course not.' He dipped his eyes. 'I was in Chicago.'

The coach was motioning for all the runts to assemble and shake hands with the losing team. Bren took off to join them.

'That was nice of you to come, Levitsky. I know it means a lot to Brendon.'

'I'm glad. He's a great kid.'

They walked along the edge of the field in silence. A mean

breeze was blowing, but suddenly Quinn didn't feel all that cold. Drawing a breath, she mustered her courage.

'I was planning to take Bren to the Sirloin Saloon for a celebration dinner tonight. Want to join us?'

'If you're sure I'm not intruding.'

She shrugged. 'You have to eat, Levitsky.'

He caught her eye. His was smiling. 'It's nice seeing you, Gallagher. Been a long time. You look wonderful.'

She felt the creeping flush. 'To be honest, I never expected to see you again, Levitsky. I figured you were fed up enough to forget my name.'

'Well, you are exasperating, Gallagher. Headstrong, impulsive. The truth is, when I think of you going head to head with Weir in that house alone, I'd like to wring your reckless neck.'

She liked the concern in his big baby browns. Guy had great eyes. Plenty of interesting stuff behind them too. 'Why thanks, Levitsky. I didn't know you cared.'

'Yes you did.'

She cleared her throat. 'Hey, Brendon! You ready to go to dinner?'

The kid was winding up with the coach. 'Five minutes,' he called.

'Let's wait in the car, okay, Levitsky? It's freezing out here.' Quinn looped an arm through the agent's elbow and steered him towards the jeep.

'So, did you get that wrist slap you expected for sticking involvement in the Weir case?' Quinn asked.

'Actually, not even that. Everyone understood my wanting to see that guy put away. Did you get the execution you expected?'

'Actually, no. I think everyone was kind of glad to be able to close the book on Eldon Weir.'

'I saw the post mortem. That explosion certainly did the job. They only managed to find a few tiny bone and tooth fragments. Not much to go on. Nothing at all identifiable.'

'The important thing is Weir's gone, Levitsky. Shipped priority overnight to hell. Who cares about the packaging or the receipt.'

He frowned. 'I guess. Only . . .'

'What, Levitsky? Don't tell me you're worried that Weir's death was just another one of his illusions. Even he wasn't that good.'

'It would've been nice to have everything neat and conclusive, that's all. With a creature like that, you want to be sure.' He forced a smile. 'Let's forget Eldon Weir, shall we?'

'Suits me.'

They slipped into the jeep and Quinn turned up the heater. Bren tore across the field and hopped in the back seat. 'So Bernie. You see my homer? Guess what? I got to keep the game ball. Can we get going, Quinn? I'm starved. Was that an amazing game, or what?'

Leaning over the seat, he flipped on the radio. Something manic by the Pointer sisters was playing. Perfect.

Quinn resisted the urge to try to calm the kid. She had a feeling that would quite take some time. Runt was fizzing over with joy and accomplishment. Nice.

Beside her, Levitsky now looked genuinely happy as well. Guy had an excellent smile. Smelled wonderful. All that, and he could cook too. If things worked out, Marilyn Holland would probably declare a national holiday. Quinn sighed and started up the car.

Life was good.

The song ended. Time for headline news. Usual stuff, so Quinn barely listened. She caught something about trouble in Afghanistan, a dip in the stock market, drive-by shootings in New York. Everything nice and normal.

'. . . And this just in. Police in Keene, New Hampshire are asking for public help in cracking a baffling local case. Jessica Stone, daughter of the town's deputy sheriff, disappeared three days ago on her way home from school. An intensive search has failed to turn up a trace of the child, who was last seen wearing black pants, a red sweater, and a blue ski jacket. The missing girl is described as slim with long blonde hair and blue eyes. Jessica Stone is eleven years old.'